SCORCHED

"Dynamite characters, a taut plot, and plenty of sizzle to balance the suspense."   —*RT Book Reviews* (4½ stars)

"An intense and mesmerizing read."
                                        —*Night Owl Reviews* (Top Pick)

"A sizzling novel of suspense . . . the perfect addition to the Tracers series."   —*Joyfully Reviewed*

TWISTED

"Thrilling, chilling, taut suspense [and] . . . a steamy and stirring love story."   —*USA Today*

"Don't plan on turning the lights out until you've turned the last page."   —*RT Book Reviews* (Top Pick)

"Griffin excels at detailing the mystery and the chase, and forensic science junkies will love the in-depth look at intricate technology."   —*Publishers Weekly*

"Mesmerizing. . . . Another fantastic roller-coaster ride."
                                                —*Night Owl Reviews*

"Fascinating and compelling . . . kept me guessing until the very end."   — *Fresh Fiction*

"A masterpiece of romantic suspense."   —*Joyfully Reviewed*

"Pitch-perfect plotting, taut suspense, compelling characters."   —*New York Times* bestselling author Allison Brennan

UNTRACEABLE
Winner of the 2010 Daphne du Maurier Award for Best Romantic Suspense

"Evolves like a thunderstorm on an onimous cloud of evil. . . . Intense, wildly unpredictable, and sizzling with sensuality."   —*Winter Haven News Chief*

"Taut drama and constant action. . . . The suspense is high and the pace quick."   —*Publishers Weekly* (starred review)

WHISPER OF WARNING
2010 RITA Winner for Best Romantic Suspense

"Irresistible characters and a plot thick with danger . . . sexy and suspenseful."   —*Romance Junkies*

"A perfectly woven and tense mystery with a . . . compelling love story."   —*RT Book Reviews*

THREAD OF FEAR

"Catapults you from bone-chilling to heartwarming to too hot to handle."   —*Winter Haven News Chief*

"A tantalizing suspense-filled thriller. Enjoy, but lock your doors."   —*Romance Reviews Today*

Also by Laura Griffin

LAURA GRIFFIN

exposed

A TRACERS NOVEL

POCKET BOOKS

New York   London   Toronto   Sydney   New Delhi

Pocket Books
A Division of Simon & Schuster, Inc.
1230 Avenue of the Americas
New York, NY 10020

This book is a work of fiction. Names, characters, places, and incidents either are products of the author's imagination or are used fictitiously. Any resemblance to actual events or locales or persons, living or dead, is entirely coincidental.

First Pocket Books paperback edition July 2013

POCKET and colophon are registered trademarks of Simon & Schuster, Inc.

For information about special discounts for bulk purchases, please contact Simon & Schuster Special Sales at 1-866-506-1949 or business@simonandschuster.com.

The Simon & Schuster Speakers Bureau can bring authors to your live event. For more information or to book an event contact the Simon & Schuster Speakers Bureau at 1-866-248-3049 or visit our website at www.simonspeakers.com.

Manufactured in the United States of America

10 9 8 7 6 5 4 3 2 1

ISBN 978-1-4516-8933-4
ISBN 978-1-4516-8936-5 (ebook)

For Jen

ACKNOWLEDGMENTS

I would like to express my appreciation to the many people who help bring my stories to readers. Thanks to Louise Burke at Pocket Books for her ongoing support, as well as the rest of the amazing Pocket team, including Lisa Litwack, Ellen Chan, Jean Anne Rose, Lisa Keim, Parisa Zolfaghari, and my editor, Abby Zidle. Thank you also to my agent, Kevan Lyon.

I'm especially grateful to the people in the fields of forensic science and law enforcement who answered so many of my questions, including Luke Causey, Derek Pacifico, Erik Vasys, and Tom Adair. As always, any mistakes here are mine.

Also, my heartfelt thanks to the readers who make it a joy to write every story. And to my family, for making it all worth it.

CHAPTER 1

Maddie Callahan's newest clients seemed to have everything—youth, looks, money—which was precisely why she doubted their marriage would work. But she kept her opinions to herself as she snapped what she hoped was the final shot of the day.

"That should do it for the church backdrop. So, we're all set?"

"What about the footbridge?" The bride-to-be smiled up at her fiancé. "I can post it on the blog with our engagement story."

"Whatever you want, babe."

Maddie stifled an eye roll and turned to check out the park. It wasn't overly crowded—just a few people walking dogs—but their light was fading.

"I know it's getting late." Hannah held her hands together like a prayer and looked at Maddie. "But could we get something real quick?"

"We can if we hurry," Maddie said, collapsing her tripod and looping her camera strap around her neck. She waited for a break in traffic and led Hannah and Devon across Main Street to the park, where she deposited her equipment beside the lily pond. She glanced around, cataloging the details of the composition. The wooden footbridge formed a low arc over the water. Sunlight glistened off the pond's surface, creating a shimmery, storybook effect that Maddie had taken advantage of before. As one of the few natural backdrops in this congested college town, the park was a good place for wedding photos—or, as in this case, engagement shots. Normally, Maddie liked using it, but this appointment had run way over schedule, and she was anxious to get back to the lab. She opted to skip the tripod and keep this quick.

Maddie composed the shot as Hannah posed her future husband behind her. With matching white dress shirts, faded jeans, and cowboy boots, the couple's look today was what Maggie thought of as Texas preppy. Hannah settled their clasped hands on the side of the bridge, putting her two-carat diamond on prominent display.

"How's this?" she asked.

"Perfect." Maddie snapped the picture. "I think I got it. Just a few more and . . . that's it. You're done."

Both pairs of shoulders relaxed. Devon looked at his watch, clearly relieved to be finished with what he probably thought was a marathon photo shoot. He had no idea what awaited him on his wedding day.

Hannah turned and smiled up at him. "Do I have lipstick on my teeth, sweets?"

He grinned down at her. "No. Do I?"

Maddie lifted her camera one last time as he reached down to brush a lock of hair from his fiancée's face.

Click.

And *that* was the money shot. Maddie knew it the instant she took it. The ring wasn't in the picture, but she hoped they'd order a print anyway. Maybe they'd put it in a frame on their mantel, where they could glance at it occasionally and be reminded of the genuine fondness they'd had for each other before the years set in.

And, really, what more could anyone ask of an engagement picture?

Her mission accomplished, Maddie collected her equipment.

"How soon can we see something?" Hannah asked as she joined her on the grass.

"Oh, I'm guessing—" Maggie checked the time. Damn, it was already 5:40. "I should have these posted to the site tomorrow, plenty of time to pick one for Sunday's paper."

The bride-to-be looked crestfallen. "You mean, not by tonight?"

Maddie took a deep breath. She counted to three mentally. Yes, her day job paid the bills, but freelance work was the icing on her cake. And that business relied heavily on referrals.

"I'll do my best," she said brightly, even though it meant turning her whole evening upside-down. And that was assuming she wouldn't get called out for some emergency. "I can probably get you something by midnight. If I do, I'll e-mail you the password for the gallery."

"Thank you! I *really* appreciate it. Everyone's dying to see how these turn out."

Maddie wasn't sure who "everyone" was, but she managed to keep a cheerful expression on her face as they exchanged good-byes. Then she hitched her tripod onto her shoulder and trekked across the park.

Her stomach growled as she headed for the garage where she'd parked. She cast a longing look at the sandwich shop on the corner. Food would have to wait. She needed to get back to the lab and send out half a dozen files before she could possibly call it a day.

She ducked into the shade of the parking garage, avoiding the stairwell in favor of the ramp. The blustery February wind had died down, and the air was thick with car exhaust. Maddie hugged the concrete wall so she wouldn't get clipped by a driver rounding the corner. She reached the third level and spotted her little white Prius tucked beside a pickup. She dug her phone from her purse and checked for messages. Her boss, her sister, her boss, her boss.

Shoes scuffed behind her. The skin at the back of her neck prickled. Maddie paused and pretended to be reading something on her phone as she listened.

Silence.

Her pulse picked up. She resumed her pace.

More footsteps.

She whirled around. No one. She clutched the phone in her hand and darted her gaze up and down the rows of cars. She searched for anyone lurking, any ominous shadows, but she was alone.

Almost.

Anxiety gnawed at her as she surveyed her surroundings. It was light out. The streets below hummed with traffic. Still, she tightened her grip on the tripod. She tucked the phone into her purse and felt for her pepper spray.

In the corner of her eye, movement. She pivoted toward it and registered two things at once: *man* and *ski mask*. Fear shot through her. Maddie swung the tripod around like a baseball bat as the man barreled into her, slamming her against the pickup. The tripod was jerked from her grip and clattered to the ground. Hands clamped around her neck. Maddie punched and bucked as fingers dug into her skin. She tried to scream. No air. Gray eyes glared at her through the holes in the mask.

She smashed the heel of her hand into his nose and felt bone crunch. He staggered back. Maddie jerked sideways. He lunged for her, grabbing the collar of her jacket. She twisted out of it and bolted for the stairwell.

"Help!" she shrieked, yanking open the door. She leaped down the stairs, rounded the landing, leaped down more. Her butt hit concrete, but she groped for the railing and hauled herself up. Hinges squeaked above her. Her pulse skittered. Footsteps thundered over her head.

"Someone *help!*"

But they were alone in the soundproof shaft. Another landing, a door. She shoved it open and dashed through. She searched desperately for people but saw only rows and rows of cars. Another door. Light-headed with terror, she pushed it open and stumbled into an alley. On her right, a passageway lined with Dumpsters. On her left, a gray car parked at the mouth of the alley. Someone was inside.

Maddie rushed for the car. It lurched forward. She halted, stunned, as it charged toward her like a rhino. Maddie sprinted away. Behind her, a door banged open. The engine roared behind her as she raced down the alley. The noise was at her heels, almost on top of her. Panic zinged through her like an electric current as her arms and legs pumped. The car bore down on her. At the last possible second, she dove sideways behind a Dumpster and felt a great *whoosh* of air as the car shot past. The squeal of brakes echoed through the alley.

Maddie darted through the space between the back bumper and the Dumpster. She raced for the street. Despair clogged her throat as she realized the distance she'd covered. Where was the ski mask guy? The people and the traffic noise seemed impossibly far away. She raced toward the mouth of the alley as fast as her burning legs could carry her.

The man jumped from a doorway. They crashed to the ground in a heap of arms and legs and flying elbows. Her skin scraped against the pavement as she kicked free of him and scrambled to her feet. He grabbed the strap of her camera, and her body jerked violently. She landed on her side as a fist pummeled her, and pain exploded behind her eyes. She managed to roll to her knees as another blow hit her shoulder. She fell forward but caught herself on her palms and kicked backward, desperate not to end up on the ground under him.

She struggled for her feet, but her vision blurred, and the strap was like a noose around her neck. The vinegary taste of fear filled her mouth. He heaved his weight into her, smashing her against the wall. The strap tightened again. Maddie gripped it with her hands. She tried to buck him off, but he was strong and wiry and determined to get her into a headlock.

He clamped his arm around her throat. She turned her head to the side and bit *hard* through the fabric of his T-shirt. The grip loosened for a moment, and she twisted free of the strap, the arms, the fingers clawing at her. Adrenaline burst through her veins as she realized this might be her only chance.

She rolled to her feet and rocketed down the alley, toward the noise and cars and people that meant safety. *Faster, faster, faster!* Every cell in her body throbbed with the knowledge that he was behind her. Her heart hammered. Her muscles strained. *Faster!* For the first time, she thought of a gun and imagined a bullet tearing through skin and bone. She surged forward, shrieking hoarsely and racing for the mouth of the alley.

Behind her, a car door slammed. Tires squealed over the asphalt. She glanced back as the gray car shot down the alley, moving away from her. Taillights glowed. Another screech of tires as the car whipped around the corner.

Maddie stopped and slumped against the side of the building. Her breath came in ragged gasps. Her lungs burned, and it felt as though her heart was being squeezed like a lemon. Something warm trickled down her face. She touched a hand to her cheek, and her fingers came away red.

Tears stung her eyes as she looked down at herself. Her purse was gone. Her camera was gone. Her phone was gone. *She* wasn't gone, at least. She was here—in one shaking, terrified, Jell-O-y piece. But her knees felt so weak she didn't know if they would hold her up. She closed her eyes and tried to think.

She couldn't stay in the alley. But she couldn't go

back into that garage—maybe never again. She looked out at the street, at the steady flow of cars and people. Her gaze landed on the neon sign in the window of the sandwich shop. It glowed red in the gray of dusk, beckoning her to safety with its simple message: OPEN.

Maddie pushed away from the wall. On quivering legs, she stumbled toward the sign.

———————

The two men were cops, she could tell at a glance. Maddie watched them from her place beside the patrol car, where she'd been sequestered for the past half hour, answering questions from a rookie detective who'd probably been in diapers when she got her first speeding ticket. Maddie knew almost everyone in the San Marcos police department, but it figured the first responder to her 911 call would be someone she'd never laid eyes on before, someone who didn't have the slightest interest in doing her a favor by moving things along. Added to the scraped chin, the swelling jaw, the lost purse, and the stolen Nikon, it was just another part of the crapfest that had become her day.

And if her instincts proved right, the party wasn't over yet.

Maggie watched as the two mystery men walked up to the patrol cars parked in front of the sandwich shop. Definitely cops. But they were more than that, clearly. She pegged them for feds based on their dark suits, and that guess was confirmed when one of them flashed a badge and exchanged words with the patrol officers milling on the sidewalk. Jeff Grimlich—a cop she *did* know—had just emerged from the shop with a steaming cup of coffee. He said something brief and gave a nod in Maddie's direction, sending them her way.

Maddie checked her watch. Whatever these two wanted, it wouldn't likely be quick. She looked them over. The one leading the charge appeared to be her age, in his mid-thirties. His shaved head and his solid, stocky build would have made him look like a bouncer, had it not been for the suit and the determined scowl that said *cop*.

Maddie shifted her gaze to his friend. Taller, probably six-one. Broad-shouldered, muscular, lean at the waist. He had sandy-brown hair that was cropped short on the sides and longer on top. The word *military* popped into her head. It wasn't just the haircut and the build but also the supremely confident way he carried himself. He was watching her, too, but in contrast to his partner's expression, this guy looked utterly relaxed.

"Are you *sure* you don't want to get this looked at?"

She turned her attention to the EMT handing her an ice pack. Maddie pressed the pack to the side of her face, where a bruise was forming.

"I'm good."

"Because it's entirely possible you could have a concussion."

"Thanks, but I'm fine." And a trip to the emergency room was the last thing she needed tonight. She had an aversion to hospitals.

"Well." The woman flipped shut the lid to her first-aid kit. "Suit yourself. I can't *make* you take common-sense precautions."

"Madeline Callahan?"

She turned, startled. She hadn't expected such a deep voice from someone so young. He stared down at her, hands resting at his hips, suit jacket pushed back to reveal a semiautomatic pistol and—as she'd suspected—an FBI shield. She lifted her gaze to his smooth, clean-shaven face. If she was right about the military thing, he must have graduated from the Academy about a week ago.

"I'm Special Agent Brian Beckman with the FBI. This is Special Agent Sam Dulles." He nodded at the bald guy. "We'd like to ask you a few questions, ma'am."

Dulles leaned back against the patrol car parked perpendicular to the one where Maddie stood. Clearly, he intended to hang back and observe. Maybe this was a training exercise.

"Ma'am?"

She looked back at the young one. Beckman. He was watching her intently with those hazel eyes.

"Could you take us through what transpired here, please?"

Transpired. Typical cop-speak. Maddie folded her arms over her chest and leaned against the side of the car. "It was a mugging."

His eyebrows tipped up. "Could you be more specific?"

"Someone attacked me in the parking garage. Stole my purse, along with my brand-new camera."

"Your camera?"

"I'm a photographer. I was doing a photo shoot down at the park—a couple getting married."

Both men were regarding her with frank interest

now, and she had the feeling she was missing something.

Beckman eased closer. "We'd like you to walk us through the entire incident, ma'am. Step by step."

Irritated by the ma'am-ing, she shot a look at Dulles. "Since when does the FBI have jurisdiction in a mugging?"

No answer.

"Maddie?"

She turned to see Jeff walking toward her, hand outstretched. Her brown leather purse dangled from his fingers.

"Oh, my God! Where was it?" She beamed a smile at him and snatched up the bag.

"Scanlon found it under a truck near your car. Phone's in there, too. You just had a call come in."

"Thank you! You have no idea how much trouble this saves me." Maddie already had the phone out, and her heart lurched when she saw the text from her boss. It was just as she'd feared. She was needed at a crime scene, ASAP. He'd sent her a message coded 911 and a street address.

Maddie stashed the ice pack in her purse and shoved the phone into the pocket of her jeans. Now, she *really* needed to leave.

"Ms. Callahan?"

She glanced up. The young agent was watching her expectantly. So was his partner.

"Listen, you see Officer Scanlon over there? The one with the notepad? I guarantee he'll be turning in a full report before he clocks out tonight. You can get the details from him."

"We need them from you," Dulles said, speaking up for the first time. He was still leaning against the side of the car, looking disapproving.

"Is there a specific *reason* the FBI is involved here? I told you, it was a mugging."

"Looks to me like an assault, too," Beckman said evenly.

"Okay, fine. But I really need to be somewhere, like, an hour ago, so unless you can explain how this is relevant—"

"We're investigating a federal case."

"A federal case involving . . . ?" She waited as they exchanged looks.

"There was a theft across the street from here about five-thirty." Dulles nodded toward the park. "Given the timing, we think it could be connected to your incident."

Maddie glanced across the street, where a bank faced out onto the park. A bank robbery certainly would explain the feds, but why weren't there any police cars?

"Take us through what happened," Beckman said, all trace of politeness gone.

And so Maddie did.

———

Brian watched as Madeline Callahan gave a concise but thorough account of the events following her photo shoot. The woman had an eye for detail—that much was clear. She also had an attitude. He wasn't sure where it came from. Most people tended to perk up and take notice when FBI agents arrived on the scene, but this woman seemed mostly annoyed.

Brian watched her, intrigued. She wore faded jeans that hugged her hips, brown leather boots, and a black T-shirt that stretched tight over her breasts. Her arms were folded as if she were cold, and she probably was, given that the temperature had dropped into the forties since dusk. Her curly brown hair was pulled back in a ponytail, but strands had escaped, and she kept tucking them back behind her ears. A nervous habit, maybe? But she didn't seem nervous, and Brian had interviewed more than enough witnesses to know. His attention drifted to those full lips that seemed to taunt him as she talked. He watched her mouth and knew he was going to be fantasizing about it for a good long time.

In an effort to stay focused, he shifted his gaze to the side of her jaw, which was swollen and rapidly turning purple. Her assailant had gotten in a solid punch, and Brian's gut tightened as he imagined some fat, hairy fist connecting with her face.

She was staring at him now, and he realized she'd finished her story.

"So, your camera was directed north," Sam stated, saving him from making an ass of himself.

"That's right."

Brian cleared his throat. "Ma'am, what are the odds you might have inadvertently photographed someone standing in front of that bank at five-thirty?"

She paused for a moment. "I'd say good. But I'd also say the odds of us ever knowing for sure are nil. So, as much as I'd love to help you guys, I think we're all pretty much shit out of luck today." She checked her watch, and a look of anxiety flashed across her face. "And now I *really* have to go."

"Do you need a ride home?" Brian asked her.

She looked surprised by the offer. Then wary. "Thanks, but I've got my car." She cast a glance over her shoulder at the parking garage, and the anxiety seemed to double.

"Would you like an escort?" he asked.

"An escort?"

"To your vehicle."

"Oh. No. Really, I'm fine." She hitched her purse onto her shoulder. "So, if there's nothing else you need . . . ?"

"If there is, we'll call you," Brian said.

Her gaze narrowed. "I didn't give you my number."

He smiled slightly. "We can get it."

They watched her walk across the street, and Brian marveled at her confidence as she returned, alone, to the scene of her attack. After dark, no less. Granted, there were cops milling around, but still.

"What do you think?" Sam asked.

Brian glanced at his partner. "Seems pretty street-smart for a wedding photographer."

"In a hurry to leave, too."

"Maybe she's got a date."

Sam shot him a look.

"What?"

"Shit, Beckman. Don't you ever stop?"

"I didn't say anything."

"You were thinking it."

"You believe she saw them?" he asked, changing the subject.

"I think the timing's too perfect to be a coincidence," Sam said grimly. "A photographer gets mugged right after a kidnapping goes down? By a two-man team, and they don't even get her purse?" Sam rubbed his hand over his bald head and blew out a sigh, reminding Brian what a truly crappy day they'd had. And it wasn't nearly over yet. They still had to get back to the office in San Antonio and help the task force piece together what happened to Jolene Murphy, the star witness in their upcoming case.

The star witness who had gone missing only minutes after leaving her office, which just happened to be across the street from Maddie Callahan's photo shoot.

Sam was right. The timing, the location, the ruthlessness with which they'd gone after that camera but overlooked other valuables—taken all together, it was too much of a stretch. Maddie Callahan had been targeted.

Brian watched the garage now as a Prius pulled out. He recognized Maddie behind the wheel. She turned onto Main Street and sped away.

He pictured the bruise on her face, and his gut tightened again. This case involved some extremely dangerous people, and he didn't like the idea of them knowing Maddie Callahan existed, much less targeting her.

He looked at Sam. "Maybe she didn't see anything," he said hopefully.

"Maybe not. But a woman doesn't just disappear in broad daylight. Someone sure as hell saw something."

"You know, Jolene Murphy could have taken off,"

Brian said. "Maybe we're not dealing with a kidnapping at all but a spooked witness."

Sam sneered. "Trust me, they grabbed her. They want to know what she revealed, and then they want her out of the way. And if we don't find her soon, you can be damn sure we'll be dealing with a murder."

CHAPTER 2

Maddie's headlights sliced through the darkness as she turned onto Cottonwood Road. The bumpy strip of asphalt stretched past a series of mobile homes before making a dip over a low-water bridge. As she rounded a bend, the sight of the small clapboard house lit up like a beacon made her stomach knot.

A homicide. Even if she hadn't been tipped off by her boss's text message, she would have known by the sheer number of vehicles: three from the Clarke County Sheriff's Department, a Delphi Center crime-scene unit, and a white ME's van.

Maddie rolled past everyone and parked beside some mesquite trees lining the road. She popped her trunk and swept her Maglite over the contents. Everything looked to be in order. Her backup camera was nestled in its nylon bag. Her go-kit was neatly packed with spare batteries, extra memory cards, a light meter, and an array of other equipment she might need. She hitched the bag onto her shoulder, looped her camera around her neck, and took a deep breath.

A homicide. Regardless of what had happened

earlier, she needed to bring her A game. She only had one chance to get this right.

Maddie adjusted the camera settings for low light and walked to the spot where a gravel path met the road. She snapped four photographs, at twelve o'clock, three, six, and nine. She approached the house and paused several times for mid-range pictures.

Shoot your way in, shoot your way out. The words of her forensic photography instructor echoed through her head as she stepped into the halo of light spilling from the porch. At the base of the wooden stairs was a cardboard box, overturned and sitting on the dirt. Maddie had a hunch she knew why it was there, but she took a photo of it anyway. Always better to have extra shots than to miss something important.

"Maddie. Where ya been?" Wood creaked as a hefty sheriff's deputy stepped out to greet her. Craig Rodgers lifted the yellow crime-scene tape stretched across the porch and motioned her to come through. "I was starting to get worried."

"Sorry. Got held up. You save me a shoe print?" She nodded at the box.

"Didn't want anyone mucking it up."

"Thanks. Where're all your guys?"

"One's inside. I sent two of them out back to search the yard. Figured we'd keep traffic in here to a minimum."

She was relieved to hear it. Another CSI adage she'd found to be true: The victim died once, but the crime scene could be murdered a thousand times.

Maddie ducked under the tape and spotted the brown clipboard on a plastic lawn chair. After scrawling her information in the crime-scene log, she donned a pair of paper booties and latex gloves from the boxes some-one had left beside the chair. She squeezed past Craig's barrel-shaped chest, and he caught her arm.

"Hey, what happened to your face?"

"Long story," she said, and turned to snap a photo of the door frame. She'd come back later to document the gouge marks in the wood thoroughly. On the plank floor were tiny blood drops that had already been designated with evidence markers. Careful not to trample anything, she stepped over the threshold.

The house was cramped and messy and reeked of cigarette smoke. With a quick glance, she noted a debris-strewn kitchen, a breakfast table heaped with fast-food cups, and a living room dominated by a worn yellow recliner.

She glanced across the room at Brooke Porter. The slender brunette was crouched beside a media cabinet, visualizing latent prints with what cops referred to as her "fairy dust."

"I'm surprised the sheriff called both of us," Maddie said.

"Well, you know. Election year and all that." Brooke glanced up from her work. "Shit, Mad, what happened to you?"

"I got mugged."

"Seriously?"

"Seriously."

"He get your purse?"

"My Nikon." She ignored Brooke's pained expression and darted a look at Craig. "So, what do we have?"

His face was a mix of protectiveness and annoyance, and Maddie ignored that, too.

"Isabella Simmons, nineteen."

Maddie's heart squeezed.

"Neighbor called it in," he said. "She went out to walk her dog and noticed the door standing open. Came over to check it out, found her in the bedroom." He jerked his head toward the back of the house. "Looks like a burglary gone bad. Her wallet's missing from her purse back there. Jewelry box is dumped out. TV gone."

Looks like. Maddie noted the tone of his voice. She took a shot of the hallway and then followed him past a bathroom to the bedroom.

"Watch the blood," he said, pointing at evidence markers on the floor. Maddie passed them without stopping. Before the night was over, she'd photograph all of it, but the ME's guys had beaten her here, and she guessed they were getting impatient.

Isabella Simmons lay sprawled on the floor beside a queen-size bed. She wore jeans, one black sandal, and a tight white blouse that had flecks of something dark on it—maybe blood. One of her arms was flung up above her head, fingers outstretched, as if she were hailing a cab. A curtain of long blond hair covered her face, partially obscuring her wide-eyed gaze. A trickle of blood had dried beneath her nostril, and she had red marks on her neck.

"You didn't move her?" She glanced at the ME's assistants, who were crouched beside a bag of gear. One was reading a thermometer, while the other made notes on a clipboard.

"Waiting for you," the closer one said, and she detected the irritation in his voice.

Maddie lifted her camera and went to work photographing the victim. By some unspoken understanding, all four men in the room stepped toward the door to give her space to maneuver.

Well, as much space as possible. The bedroom was small to begin with, and the walls were lined with overflowing laundry baskets, mismatched chairs, and milk crates brimming with shoes. A wooden jewelry box was dumped out on the floor. Within reach of the victim's hand was a small lamp. Maddie dug a metal ruler from her kit, placed it beside the lamp to provide scale, and snapped some pictures. She did the same for a black sandal peeking out from under the bed.

"You got enough light?" Craig asked from the doorway.

"I'm fine."

With practiced detachment, she photographed the body from every angle, taking care to keep her expression blank. The Clarke County Sheriff's Department didn't see a lot of homicides, maybe a handful a year. But the ME's guys were well versed in death, and Maddie felt their gazes on her, gauging her reaction as she worked the scene. Was she up to the job? Was she going to puke? She knelt beside the bed and took a final shot of the victim's outstretched hand.

Nineteen years old. A lump rose in her throat, but she swallowed it down. Her thoughts went to Isabella's parents, and she felt a swell of sympathy for them. They probably hadn't even been notified yet, and here Maddie was documenting the event that was going to tear through their lives like a tornado.

"She's got something on her fingers," she said as she stood up.

"We noticed."

She glanced up at the deputy beside Craig. Big. Buzz cut. He hardly looked old enough to drink, and he clearly felt threatened by her presence, as if she were trying to tell him how to do his job.

And she was. She and Brooke were here specifically because Clarke County didn't have the budget to keep CSIs on staff. Some of their deputies had had a few training courses and were capable of handling burglaries, car thefts, anything routine. But for something as important as a homicide—especially during an election year—the sheriff called in the experts at the Delphi Center crime lab, where Maddie and Brooke worked full-time.

"Where's Sheriff Bracewell?" Maddie asked Craig.

"Abilene."

She arched her eyebrows.

"His mother-in-law's funeral," he expanded. "He hit the road as soon as I called him."

"Can we bag her hands now?" one of the ME's assistants asked.

Maddie nodded and proceeded with the rest of the room. She spent some time near the door, where a drop of blood had landed on the wooden floor. She photographed the neatly made bed, the makeup brushes spread out over the dresser, the red lipstick—top off— that had fallen to the floor. Maddie glanced at Isabella's face and noted her unnaturally vivid lips.

She swept her flashlight over the walls, the baseboards,

the ceiling—a spot often overlooked by fleeing suspects. She glanced at the undisturbed bed again and at the victim's jeans, which were zipped and buttoned. No obvious signs of sexual assault. Maddie's gaze went to the lipstick, and she composed a narrative: Isabella is home, putting on makeup, maybe getting ready for an evening out. No car out front, so maybe the burglar assumes no one is home. He pries open the door, surprises the victim, strangles her, grabs her valuables, and flees the scene.

Maddie studied the bed again. She turned to Craig. "I need to use the UV light."

"Fine by me."

Craig and Buzz Cut stepped out of the room, and she flipped off all the lights. She took the handheld alternative light source from her bag and donned a pair of orange-tinted eye shields. She shone the ALS on the bedspread and the floor but saw no bright spots that would indicate bodily fluids.

"Anything?"

"Nope."

She glanced at the ME's assistants as they spread out the body bag. She looked at Isabella. She heard the chilling sound of the zipper.

"Wait." Maddie crouched beside the body with the light.

"What?"

"Look at her arm."

She pointed to the bruises, four distinct ovals in a line. Maddie carefully lifted the shirt. Isabella had marks on her abdomen, too, and a large bruise above her eye, which was now staring sightlessly up at the ceiling as she waited to be loaded into the body bag.

"These are old," Maddie said.

"How old?"

"Days, weeks. The ME can determine with better accuracy when he does the autopsy," she said. Clarke County wasn't large enough to have its own ME's office, either, so they used the one in neighboring Travis County.

After carefully photographing the marks, Maddie stood up. "That's it."

She followed the two men back to the living room and watched them carry the stretcher out the back door.

"Find anything?" Craig asked.

"Subcutaneous bruises," she said. "They can show up under ultraviolet light days, sometimes even weeks, after the fact. She have a boyfriend that you know about?"

"We'll find out." He glanced at the younger deputy. "The neighbor still out there?"

"I'm on it."

He disappeared, and they turned their attention to Brooke, who was now dusting the front door frame for prints. Maddie crouched nearby. She examined a wood splinter on the floor atop a droplet of blood. She set up her mini tripod and took half a dozen pictures with the camera facing straight down. She moved on to another splinter a few inches away.

Brooke glanced at her. "When you finish with that, can you do this door? I want to get it off the hinges and take it to the lab."

"For the tool marks examiner?"

"That, and there's a shoe print. Lot of good detail."

Maddie glanced at the front of the door, where there was, indeed, a clear print in the shape of a man's shoe. It looked as though the killer had jimmied the lock and then kicked open the door.

Maddie stood up. "You find her phone?"

"Still searching," Craig said.

"I'd be interested to know who she's been calling or texting tonight and what her plans were."

Craig watched her steadily. "You don't like this for a burglary."

"Do you?"

"Nope." His gaze scanned the messy living room. "This scene is off."

Maddie crouched down and took another picture of the splinter. "This is your case, right here."

He knelt beside her. "A wood chip?"

"Damn, you're right." Brooke stepped over to look at it.

"Right about what?" Craig frowned at the floor.

"The blood trail's leaving the house. See?" Brooke crouched down and pointed at it. "You can tell by the shape—like a comet."

"The blood didn't drip *on* the wood splinter," Maddie said. "The splintered wood landed on dripped blood."

She watched his face as her words sank in.

"The door was busted open after the murder. Damn, I think you're right."

"I don't think this is a burglary at all," Maddie told him. "I think she let him in. I think she knew her killer."

Brian turned onto Maddie Callahan's street just as a familiar white Prius swung into a drive. He parked in front of the house, and she eyed him warily as he climbed out of his Bureau sedan.

"Working late?" he asked, joining her on the driveway.

"What makes you say that?"

Uh-oh. Defensive. And he hadn't even asked a real question yet.

"Just a guess." He nodded at the mud on her boots. "Outdoor crime scene?"

"Something like that."

For a long moment, they stared at each other, and he tried his damnedest not to look at her mouth.

"Where's Dulles?" She glanced at his car. "Don't you guys travel in pairs?"

"He's back at the office, wrapping things up. How come you didn't tell me you were a CSI?"

"How come you didn't tell me you were investigating the theft of a person? They have a term for that. I think it's called kidnapping."

Brian rested his hands on his hips and gazed down at her. She had him there, but he wasn't ready to concede the point.

He looked up and down her street. She lived in a quiet, middle-class neighborhood in a relatively safe part of San Marcos. He shifted his attention to her house. The grass had been cut maybe a week ago, but the hedges badly needed trimming. Her porch light could have used a brighter bulb, but at least she had a security system, according to the sign in the flower bed.

She was watching him, still waiting for an answer.

"I can't disclose details—"

"—of an ongoing investigation. Yada, yada, yada." She tipped her head to the side and looked at him.

A car sped by, and Brian followed it with his gaze. He looked back at her. More curls had come loose from her ponytail, and it was obvious she'd had a long night. But she seemed wide awake, probably running on caffeine and adrenaline, same as he was.

"Listen, Ms. Callahan—"

"It's Maddie."

Exactly the response he'd wanted. "Is there somewhere we can talk, Maddie? I've got some questions I need to go over with you. About this evening."

She watched him for a moment, and he wondered if she thought he'd come here to hit on her. Maybe he should have brought Sam along as a decoy.

"How good are you at ignoring details?" she asked.

"Not very."

"Hmm. Well, at least, try not to put in your report that I'm a chronic slob." She started across the yard. "It's been a hectic week."

She led him up the steps to a narrow wooden porch that looked freshly painted but lacked the decorative touches that many women liked to scatter around.

She ushered him inside and deposited her purse on a small table already stacked with mail. He glanced at the keypad beside the door as she switched on a light and walked into her kitchen.

"You don't activate your alarm during the day?"

"I don't activate it at all." She pulled open the refrigerator and took out a jug of orange juice. "Drink?"

"No, thanks." He stood in the arched doorway

between the kitchen and the living room and looked around. Most of her furniture was beige and nondescript, but one wall of the dining area had been painted vibrant red and covered with framed eight-by-ten photographs. Brian edged closer.

"Wow. You take these?" He glanced up as she came to stand in the archway.

"Yep."

He scanned the shots, which showed soaring cliffs, snowcapped mountains, and water crashing against rocks. Another series showed llamas and birds.

"Is this South America?"

"Tierra del Fuego. I lived there for a year."

"What took you down there?"

She shrugged. "I needed to get away. It was the farthest place I could think of."

He glanced up at her. Then he turned to a tall shelf where she kept a collection of photography books: Annie Leibovitz, Ansel Adams, a bunch more that didn't ring a bell. On one of the shelves was a framed photograph of a smiling little girl at the top of a yellow slide.

"That's Emma, my daughter."

He looked up and instantly knew what she was going to say next.

"She died when she was two."

Brian's chest tightened. He studied the picture again. The little girl had thick blond curls, sparkling brown eyes, and a wide smile.

"She looks like you."

"You think?" She stepped closer and gazed at the photo. "People always say that, but I see Mitch. My ex."

He saw a shadow of something in her eyes, a sadness that would probably never go away. He didn't know what to say.

She stepped back into the kitchen and poured a glass of juice. "You were asking about the alarm," she said over her shoulder. "It's from the previous owners. I've been meaning to have it hooked up since I moved in, but . . ." She shrugged. "It's on my to-do list."

"And you moved in . . . ?"

"Three years ago." She gulped down the juice and plunked the glass on the counter beside a pile of dishes. "Sorry it's a mess in here. I've hardly been home in days."

"Are you hungry?"

She looked at him.

"We could go get a sandwich or something. I noticed there's a diner a few blocks over."

"Thanks, but my appetite's gone for the night. Occupational hazard." She placed the empty glass in the sink. "So, you thought of more questions, huh? Fire away."

He watched her. Everything she'd said sounded cooperative, but there was an edge to her voice, and he couldn't shake the feeling that he'd gotten off on the wrong foot with her.

Maybe it was just that she'd had a shit day. Or maybe she didn't like investigators showing up at her house at midnight and asking lots of questions.

Or maybe she just didn't like him.

But he doubted that was it. Truth be told, women liked him. He took a lot of crap about it from the guys at work, but it was a fact. Part of it was probably the badge—some women had a thing for authority. Part of it was probably his looks, which had always gotten him second glances. Part of it was probably that he liked women and made a point of treating them with respect.

But this particular woman seemed immune to all that. She obviously didn't have a badge fetish.

"Seriously, ask away," she said. "I'm officially off the clock for the night."

"First, I need to know how you heard about the kidnapping."

"That's easy. Grapevine."

"Could you be more specific? We've gone to a lot of trouble to keep the media away."

She crossed her feet at the ankles. "I haven't seen a newscast, so maybe you succeeded. But I spent the evening surrounded by cops, and it's common knowledge you guys misplaced a witness in front of the bank today." She paused. "Who is he, some hedge fund manager?"

Brian reached into his jacket and pulled out a color photo. It was a graduation picture, the kind people tucked into printed announcements and mailed to relatives.

"Her name's Jolene Murphy."

Maddie's brow furrowed as she took the picture. "God, how old is she?"

"Twenty-three. That was taken a year ago. She works at CenTex Bank here in town. She was about to become a key witness in a federal investigation."

Maddie looked up at him, and her feisty expression had been replaced by genuine concern. "And you think she was kidnapped?"

"We don't know for sure. But she didn't show up for a meeting with us today, and this suspect we're investigating has been known to intimidate witnesses." *Intimidate*. There was a euphemism. "The stakes here are high."

She met his gaze. "There's something you're not telling me, isn't there?"

There was a shitload of stuff he wasn't telling her.

"Do you think you might have seen this woman today?" he asked. "Even a glimpse?"

"I wish I could help you, but I really don't recognize her." She handed the picture back. "And I have an eye for faces. Do you have a picture of the people who took her?"

"I don't even have IDs."

"But you think it might be the man who mugged me—him and the driver?"

"Could be connected, yeah. We're probably looking for a crew of four, maybe five people, and you ran into two of them."

She watched him, and the gravity of the situation was clearly sinking in.

"You might still be able to help us," he told her. "I read the paperwork. Officer Scanlon was thorough, like you said." He smiled faintly, hoping to lighten the mood. No dice. "He reported that you swung your tripod at the man who attacked you. Any chance you connected?"

"I sure hope so. Otherwise, that's six years of softball down the tubes."

Score. It was the first break he'd caught all day.

"Where is it now?" he asked.

"What?"

"The tripod. If I send it to the lab, they might be able to get prints or touch DNA."

She just looked at him.

"You're familiar with touch DNA? It's from sweat, skin cells?"

She was a CSI, for Christ's sake. Why did she look at him like he was speaking Chinese?

"So . . . can I get it from you?"

"Actually, no," she said.

"No?"

"It's already at the lab."

"What lab?"

"The Delphi Center."

Brian stared at her. She'd checked his evidence into a private crime lab. Sam was going to flip a lid. The tripod had been his idea.

"Maddie—"

"What's the problem? It's already being processed."

"The FBI forensic lab is the best in the world."

"Ours is better. And besides, I'm friends with a DNA tracer there, and she offered to put a rush on it for me." She tipped her head to the side. "I doubt you have that kind of in at Quantico. Being new and all."

He gritted his teeth. This was just what he didn't need. He finally had a chance at *physical* evidence against Goran Mladovic's hired guns, and his witness had rushed it to some private lab, where he'd probably never get his hands on it again.

"You're not the only one who wants them identified, you know."

Brian caught the determination in her voice. He

looked at her bruised jaw again and felt a renewed surge of resentment toward the man who had hit her.

"Don't worry," she told him. "If Delphi gets anything, you'll be the first to know."

She glanced at the clock on the wall. His cue to leave.

And why the hell not? He'd done enough damage for one day. In the last six hours, he'd managed to lose track of a key witness and possibly the only physical evidence they had that might identify Mladovic's strongmen in time to help her.

"I guess that's it, then. For now."

She led him through her living room to the front door, and his gaze landed on the dormant keypad.

"Lock up after me."

"Yes, sir."

Sarcasm. He looked at her. "You keep any guns in the house?"

"A pistol. Why?"

"Do you know how to use it?"

"Of course."

He glanced outside, then back at her. She looked worried now, and he felt bad about that, but he needed her to take this seriously.

"Be careful," he told her. "These people we're dealing with, they don't fool around."

CHAPTER 3

Maddie dreamed about Emma. She woke up with a damp pillow and a vast, aching hole in her chest.

The dreams came in three types. The first year, they were mostly about the accident. Later, she would dream of Emma sleeping, either curled against her in bed or passed out in her arms in the rocking chair, her little cheeks flushed from nursing. The third dream was of Emma in motion—running, swinging, scampering down the hill at the park, or climbing up the slide.

Maddie loved the third dream, but she hated it, too. For a brief instant—that first fleeting moment of consciousness—she'd think the accident was the imagined part and Emma was still alive and happy and growing. But it only lasted a heartbeat, and then her daughter would vanish like a mirage.

Maddie stared at the numbers on the clock. She rubbed her sternum. It was no use trying to sleep again, so she tossed the covers away and decided to start her day.

Arriving early at the lab meant prime parking,

but it also meant she had to bring her own caffeine, because the Delphi Center's coffee shop didn't open until seven-thirty. She hiked up the building's wide marble steps and was surprised to see Kelsey Quinn seated at the base of one of the Doric columns that flanked the entrance. In contrast to the jeans and work boots the forensic anthropologist typically wore when she was going out on a dig, today she wore slacks and a crisp white lab coat.

"You're here early." Maddie stopped beside her.

"Waiting on bones."

"New or old?"

"Don't know yet. Old, I'm guessing. Some cavers discovered a skull and a long bone over in Wayne County. The sheriff wanted me to have a look." Kelsey gazed out over the dew-covered grounds. "Pretty morning, isn't it? You should get your camera."

Maddie turned to look at the sloping meadow surrounded by tall pecan trees and gnarled oaks. The sun had just edged above the treetops, and the entire landscape was touched with gold. It would have been a picturesque scene, had it not been for the carrion birds circling nearby.

Buzzards gave Maddie the creeps. She didn't like their bald heads, or their beady eyes, or their huge wingspans. Their constant presence served as a reminder that her workplace sat in the middle of a body farm.

"What happened to your chin?" Kelsey asked.

She looked at her. "Is it that obvious?"

"I have a trained eye."

Maddie sighed. Problem was, everyone around here had a trained eye, which meant that despite spending twenty minutes on her makeup this morning, she was going to be fielding questions all day long.

"I got mugged last night. Maybe I should send out a memo." She nodded at the coffee cup, hoping to change the subject. "Did you get that here? I thought they weren't open yet."

Kelsey smiled. "Throw yourself on their mercy, and they'll sneak you a cup."

Maddie used her security badge to swipe her way into the building and made a detour to the coffee shop, where she managed to score an extra-large latte and a blueberry muffin. She rode up the elevator to the photo lab, which shared a floor with Trace and QD.

She and Kelsey weren't the only ones in early. Through a wall of glass, Maddie saw Brooke and one of the trace evidence examiners already at work. The lab seemed to attract people who didn't mind putting in extra hours. There was a connection between the people here, a shared sense of purpose, even though their specialties were all over the map. The Delphi Center covered practically all areas of forensic science—from DNA to dung beetles—and the list was growing.

Roland Delgado glanced up as Maddie entered the room. "Hey, babe."

"Hey."

As part of the Trace Unit, Roland specialized in any evidence that was difficult to see with the naked eye. He had Isabella Simmons's front door up on sawhorses and was examining it through tinted goggles. With his gray coveralls and black combat boots, he looked like an airplane mechanic.

"What do you think of our door?" Maddie asked.

He shoved the goggles up on his forehead and saun-tered over. "I think you're going to love me," he said, making a grab for her muffin.

"Hey! That's my breakfast."

"Thanks for sharing." He popped a chunk into his mouth. "And you brought coffee, too." He grinned at her, and she hesitated only a moment before handing over her cup. He took a swig and gave it back. "You owe me. I've been here since six working miracles on this thing."

"It's true. You're going to be impressed," Brooke said, looking up from a worktable. She had pages of black film spread out in front of her, and Maddie guessed she was preparing to do an electrostatic lift of something, probably their shoe print.

"Okay." Maddie shrugged out of her jacket and tossed it onto a nearby chair. "I'm ready to be impressed. Show me what you got."

Roland gave her a sly smile, which she pretended not to notice. He flirted with everyone. He was good at it, too, and had managed to "date" many of the single, and probably some of the nonsingle, women at the lab. But Maddie never took him seriously. Besides being five years younger—a definite strike against him—he was also a coworker. Maddie's professional world was small, and she'd made a firm decision years ago to keep her private life private.

She pictured Brian Beckman walking up her drive-way, all broad shoulders and cocky attitude. He was sharp, motivated, and brimming with that natural brand of confidence she couldn't help but admire. And admire it she would. From afar. She knew better than to let herself get involved with a strapping young FBI agent who made house calls in the middle of the night.

"First off, good job on those photos," Roland said now. "That's going to be important. Too often, people rush things, and it comes back to bite us in the ass." He returned to the door and pointed at the shoe print left in reddish brown dust on the out-facing side of Isabella's door. "This case goes to trial, the door's going to be key."

"Did you find any fingerprints?" Maddie asked hopefully.

Brooke scoffed. "That's the problem. We found tons—on the door, the coffee table, the million or so fast-food cups in the kitchen. The whole place is covered with prints that don't belong to the victim."

"The neighbor woman told Craig she had a busy social life," Maddie said. "Lot of cars coming and going. Landlord confirms that. He lives down the road, said he's had noise complaints on and off since she rented the house."

"So fingerprints, even if we get a hit in the database, may not help us that much in terms of establishing who killed her," Brooke said. "But look what Roland found."

Roland directed Maddie to the table beside him, where he had a microscope set up. She peered into it and saw what looked under magnification like light blue rope.

"Carpet fiber?"

"Close. It's from the rug in the victim's bathroom."

Maddie remembered photographing the pale blue bath mat. She'd also photographed the sink, the tub, the toilet, and the medicine cabinet, which someone had rummaged through. Prescription drugs were a popular target for burglars.

"Now look at this."

Roland handed her a magnifying glass and directed her attention back to the door, where at the side of the dusty shoe print, she saw a wisp of lint, barely larger than an eyelash.

"It's a match?" She looked up at him, feeling that surge of adrenaline that accompanied a good find.

"You bet."

"Which puts the 'burglar' *inside* the house before he ever kicked in the door."

"Which means the scene was staged, like we thought," Maddie said.

"Here's the scenario I'm thinking," Brooke said, tucking a lock of dark hair into her ponytail. Like Maddie, she wore it up all the time so it wouldn't get in her way. "Some guy, maybe an ex-boyfriend, comes over as she's getting ready to go out."

"According to the texts on her phone, she had plans with friends last night," Maddie said. Craig had discovered the victim's phone amid the mess in the kitchen.

"Right, so here comes Romeo. He's got anger-management issues, which we can guess from Isabella's old bruises. He gets into an argument with her, starts pushing her around, bloodies her nose, and ends up killing her there in the bedroom. Then he freaks because his prints are everywhere—he's been there so many times he wouldn't even know where to start wiping the place down. He decides to stage the scene so it looks like the work of some random stranger, goes out to his car, grabs a crowbar—"

"We know it's a crowbar?" Maddie looked at Roland.

"We need to confirm with our tool marks guy," he said, "but that's my take after looking at the gouges. He jimmies the door and gives it a good kick, leaving splinters everywhere, then grabs some of her valuables and takes off."

Maddie looked at the almost invisible fiber stuck to the door. "Are we sure we didn't pick that up somewhere? Maybe on the way here, in the van?"

"Nope. You got it on film, back at the house." Roland squeezed her shoulder. "Nice work. This chump's lawyer's gonna have some 'splaining to do."

"*If* we ID the chump. And *if* we get him to trial." Maddie was a pessimist. She'd seen too many slam-dunk cases get botched over a technicality.

"Craig will get him," Brooke said. "He spent his entire night interviewing Isabella's coworkers from the bar where she works. One of those women is bound to know if she'd been seeing someone, especially if he was pushing her around. Maybe he's been stalking her or hanging around outside her workplace."

Maddie's phone chimed. She checked the screen and muttered a curse.

"Problem?"

She looked at Brooke. "It's the bride-to-be from yesterday. She wants to know where her engagement pictures are."

"Did you tell her they're gone, along with the fifteen-hundred-dollar Nikon you just bought?"

"Not yet. She's probably going to want me to comp the portrait sitting."

"After you got mugged? What a bitch."

"Which means I'm going to have to go back to that damn park for the third time this week—" Maddie froze. She looked down at her phone as the call went to voice mail. "Oh, my God."

Maybe he's been stalking her or hanging around outside her workplace.

"What?" Brooke asked.

"I just thought of something."

Brooke arched her eyebrows.

"Not this case. The other." Maddie grabbed her jacket and headed for the door.

"Where are you going?"

"Sorry, gotta run. I might have a lead."

———————

Brian had just taken a booth at the Smokehouse when Sam walked through the door.

With Maddie at his side.

She wore jeans and boots again, along with a loose white sweater that draped over her breasts. She had a purple scarf around her neck, and her cheeks were pink—from cold or excitement, Brian couldn't tell.

Sam spotted him, and they made a beeline for Brian's table.

"Look who I found," Sam said, scooting into the booth. Maddie slid in beside Sam and unwound her scarf.

"Hi." She smiled across the table, and Brian's heart gave a kick.

"Hi. You went by our office?"

"Yeah, and it's a lot harder to get a visitor's pass than

I expected. They wouldn't even let me past the guard-house."

"Next time, call ahead," Sam said. "We'll get you right in." He looked at Brian. "She's got something on Mladovic."

Brian watched with interest as she unzipped her bag and pulled out a laptop computer. "I got a call from my client this morning, and it made me think of something."

"Who, the bride?" Brian asked.

"That's right." She powered up the computer and keyed in a password. "You know, I had another photo session earlier this week at the park. Right in front of the bank, where Jolene Murphy works. And I got to thinking—"

"Can I get y'all some drinks?"

They all turned as a smiling waitress stepped up to their table.

"You ordered yet?" Sam asked.

"Just did."

Sam asked for his usual brisket sandwich, and Mad-die distractedly ordered a salad. When the waitress left, Maddie shifted the screen to face the booth.

"Check it out. Ninety-two images of CenTex Bank, exactly forty-eight hours before Jolene Murphy disap-peared."

Brian leaned forward on his elbows to scan the row of photographs.

"Look at this." She clicked on one of the images, and a family of four filled the screen. All of them wore jeans and matching plaid shirts. The backdrop of the photo was a grassy corner of the park, and Brian recognized the building behind it.

"Can you zoom in on the bank?" he asked.

She was a step ahead of him, already cropping and enlarging an image of the bank's front door.

"Hey, that's her," Sam said, leaning forward.

"That's what I thought, too, based on the picture you showed me." She looked at Brian.

"What time was this taken?"

A few more clicks, and she pulled up a file.

"According to the metadata . . . looks like this image was taken Monday at five thirty-four P.M."

"Jolene usually gets off at five-thirty," Sam said. "She was supposed to meet us at Starbucks right after work yesterday."

"Go back to the camera roll," Brian said. "You have any more shots of the bank?"

"Not the bank," Maddie said, "but the area around it. Let me find it . . . wait . . . sorry, that's blurry . . ." She kept scrolling, racing through dozens and dozens of photos. He caught one of some grass, a shoe, a whole series that were completely black. "Damn, where'd it go?" she muttered.

"Don't you ever erase anything?" Brian asked.

"Never." She glanced up at him. "Force of habit. I never delete a picture."

"Even if it's junk?"

"I don't delete anything," she said. "That creates a gap in the photo record. Not that it usually matters with portraits, but for forensic work, it can be important. If some defense attorney sees a gap in the record, it can blow a case wide open. Which means even if I leave the lens cap on or take a picture of my feet, the photo stays.

The jury understands a bad picture. What they don't like is missing evidence."

"Wait, back up," Sam said. "I saw something."

"You're right, that's it." She clicked on an image. "This is the one I wanted to show you. See the street corner here? Look at that car."

Brian squinted at the family portrait. In the background, over the head of the grinning kid, was the wrought-iron fence that surrounded the park. And beyond *that* was a gray sedan. Inside it were two passengers, visible from behind, and one of them was holding something up to his face.

Brian looked at her. "Any way to zero in on that?"

"I already did," she said. "This is exactly what I wanted to show you guys, but I wanted you to see it in context first." She clicked out of the camera roll and opened up a new file. "Check this out. I enhanced this with software. Look."

The new image was much sharper. It clearly showed a gray sedan with two people seated in front. The car was parked on the street perpendicular to the bank entrance, facing the door where Jolene would emerge when she left her job as a teller. One of the men was holding binoculars.

"They cased the scene," Sam said.

"Looks like it to me. I think it's the same car from yesterday, the one that tried to run me down." Maddie glanced at Brian, and he could see the pride glinting in her eyes. This was useful evidence, and she knew it.

Sam looked at her. "You have any more shots like this? Maybe something that shows a license plate?"

"I do, but the light's bad, and it's completely in shadow. But look at this." She opened yet another file, which showed a cropped and digitally enhanced image. In this picture, the car's side mirror reflected the passenger's face. "Part of his face is obscured by the brim of his hat, but still. At least, it's something. I mean, we can tell he's Caucasian, right?"

Brian exchanged looks with Sam. They'd already known their suspects' ethnicity. Mladovic was Serbian, and so were his hired guns. What they needed was a name, an address, a location.

"Any chance you got a vehicle tag somewhere?" Brian asked. "Maybe when they were pulling away?"

The waitress appeared with a tray of food and frowned down at the table. "Uh—"

"Sorry." Maddie slid the computer aside to make room for two big platters, plus her salad.

"Yeah, or maybe when they were parking," Sam said, digging into his sandwich.

"Believe me, I looked. I've been in the photo lab all morning poring over these."

"We should try the bank." Brian looked at Sam. "They've got security cams on every corner of the building."

"We already went through all that. No footage of her abduction, just her leaving work and heading for the parking lot."

"Yeah, but we didn't see the film for Monday. Maybe this gray car—what is it, a Buick? Maybe this Buick passed by, and we can get something."

"Not a bad idea," Maddie said, and he detected

surprise in her voice, as if she'd thought he was too much of a rookie to come up with a lead.

"It's a good thought," Sam echoed. "And you know what? I think I'll get this to go. I'll head back, see what I can get on the surveillance tapes." He flagged the waitress and asked for a to-go box, then looked at Maddie. "You mind making us a copy of those pictures?"

She scooted out of the booth and fished a brown envelope from her purse. "I burned you a disc."

"Maddie, you're a gem."

"Well. I just hope it's useful."

Brian looked at her, then at Sam. "You need me to come?"

"Nah, you two finish your lunch."

After Sam took off, she slid back into the booth, looking slightly flushed. She shut down her computer and zipped it into the bag.

"It's a good lead," Brian said. He went to work on his barbecued ribs as she picked at her salad.

"I hope it helps." Her brow furrowed. "I can't stop thinking about Jolene Murphy. What do you think the chances are of finding her?"

Brian watched her carefully. She meant finding her *alive*, and he put those chances at slim. "We'll find her," he said firmly, but Maddie looked unconvinced. "How's that tripod coming?"

"It's coming." She poked at lettuce, avoiding his gaze.

"Think we'll hear something today?"

She scoffed. "Get real."

"I thought you had an in."

"I do." She eyed his plate and looked up at him. "She's fast, but it's still going to take a few days. Which is better than Quantico, I'm guessing." She paused to watch him as he licked barbecue sauce off his thumbs. "What's your typical lead time on DNA evidence?"

Brian wiped his hands on a napkin. "Depends." He dropped a rib onto her plate. "Eat something."

"I am."

He gave her a baleful look, and she picked up the rib.

"Typically, a few weeks, maybe a month," he told her, which was stretching it. That was *if* they had a comparison sample provided by a suspect. Blind DNA tests were much lower-priority and could take months.

"Well, we can do better than that. My friend Mia will probably get us something in the next few days."

"It still might not be fast enough," he said, watching her. She nibbled the rib clean, and he added another one to her plate. "Anyway, knowing who took her doesn't solve our problems, because we still need to figure out where she is."

Brian tried to read her expression as she stirred her iced tea. He wondered if she knew what had most likely happened to Jolene Murphy by now.

"Maddie."

She glanced up at him. He held her gaze, and he saw it. She knew. She wasn't kidding herself about the victim.

"We'll track them down one way or another," he said. "This is a major case involving half a dozen agencies."

"An alphabet soup," she said, and there was that cynicism again. He was sure of it now—she didn't like cops, for some reason.

"We'll track them down. You can count on it."

She looked at him, and he felt that pull again, the one he'd felt when he first met her. He'd felt it again at her house last night, and now she was sitting right across from him, tempting him in that soft white sweater and watching him with those bottomless brown eyes.

He should ask her out. He asked women out all the time, and most of them said yes. But she had her guard up, and he knew she'd find some reason to turn him down. His gaze dropped to her mouth. There was barbecue sauce on the corner of it, and she caught him staring.

"What?" She dabbed her lip with a napkin.

He should ask anyway. Otherwise, he was an idiot, and he deserved what he got, which was guaranteed to be nothing. But he kept quiet.

"So, who is this guy, anyway?" She pushed her plate aside. "The one you're investigating?"

"Trust me, you don't want to know."

She leaned closer and looked him in the eye. "Yes, I do, or I wouldn't have asked."

Brian debated what to tell her. Part of him wanted to tell her zip. But she was involved in the investigation now, and she at least deserved to know something.

"We're looking at him for a long list of offenses— drugs, racketeering, murder," he said. "He's very dangerous, and so are the people working for him."

"Who is he, some mob boss?"

"Dr. Goran Mladovic, also known as the Doctor."

She looked startled. "He's an M.D.?"

"Yeah, but don't let that fool you. He's lethal when he wants to be. When someone crosses him, he's outright sadistic."

The little worry line was back between her brows. "If you know all this about him, why don't you arrest him?"

"What we know and what we can prove are two different things. It boils down to evidence. And we appreciate your help with that."

"I hope it pans out."

They stared at each other for a long moment, and he saw a flicker of something in her eyes. An awareness.

"Listen, Maddie—"

Her phone chimed. She dug it out of her purse and read the screen. "Damn, I have to go." She looked up at him. "Injury accident up on Route 12."

Opportunity blown. She grabbed her bag, and Brian stood up as she scooted out of the booth.

"Let me know how it goes with the bank cams, okay? I'm very interested in Jolene Murphy's investigation." She pulled the scarf around her neck. "Even if you don't find anything, I still want to know."

"Sure."

"I mean it." She pinned him with a look. "Don't keep me out of the loop—I hate that."

"I won't," he promised. "I'll call you either way."

———

Jolene had to pee. Again.

She lifted her head and took a longing look at the toilet four feet away.

She closed her eyes and bit down on the gag tied around her face. The bandanna was dry as sawdust, just like her mouth. She didn't understand it. How could her body produce pee and tears and snot, when she'd never felt so dehydrated in her life?

Tears burned her eyes, and she squeezed them back. They didn't help. They only made it worse. She looked down at what remained of her hand. It was purple and swollen, hardly recognizable as human, and she'd been trying not to stare at it. If she'd seen something like it on the Discovery Channel, she would have thought it was some kind of exotic coral.

A door slammed. Jolene's heart jumped into her throat. She glanced at the crack beneath the door as the familiar male voice reached her. She listened, trying to tell if he was on the phone again, or if someone else was with him.

Please, no more. The tears were back, making hot tracks down her cheeks. She scooted farther under the sink and pulled herself into a ball. Her heart pounded wildly.

She listened.

He was on the phone, speaking Russian, or Serbian, or some other language she didn't know. He sounded like Katya's father did whenever he got really mad.

The door swung open. She blinked at the brightness. She glanced at his hand—no hammer. The relief was so strong she felt light-headed.

"Let's go," he said gruffly. He crouched beside her, and she smelled the stink of onions on his breath. Her stomach growled, desperate for food, even something as repulsive as whatever he'd been eating.

Metal clinked as he unlocked the cuff attached to the drainpipe.

Where are we going? she wanted to ask, but she

couldn't ask anything. She couldn't say a word, and her desperate kicks and moans over the endless hours had gone unanswered.

He pushed a sweatshirt at her and hauled her to her feet. The hallway was bright and empty. She blinked at it and then turned to face him. Vlad. His name was Vlad. If she ever got this gag off, she was going to find a way to use his name and maybe make a connection. She was going to plead for her life.

She looked at the bandage on the bridge of his nose and the gray eyes, flat and cold.

"Go," he grunted. He grabbed her arm and shoved her toward the light.

CHAPTER 4

By the time Maddie left the building, the sun had dipped below the trees and there was no way she was making it to a seven P.M. yoga class. She tossed the tail of her scarf over her shoulder and started down the stairs.

And spotted Brian getting out of his car. Her stomach fluttered as she watched him walk up the path with that confident gait that was undeniably appealing. She couldn't help it. She found him attractive. There—she could admit it. Not that she'd ever admit it to him.

He stopped in front of her and smiled slightly. "Hey."

"What brings you here?"

"Came to see if this place lives up to all that bragging you've been doing." He glanced around. "You guys are really out in the boonies. Took me forty minutes to get here."

"Yeah, well. Most people don't want a body farm in their backyard." Their gazes locked, and for a moment, they just looked at each other. "I feel a request coming. Let me guess. The bank cams were a dead end?"

"Any chance we can pull up those pictures again, see if we can get more on that license plate?"

"I did everything I could in the photo lab this morning. I wish I had more tricks up my sleeve, but . . ." She glanced over her shoulder at the sixth floor, where all the windows glowed. "There might be something else we can try. No guarantees."

"Lead the way."

He fell in beside her as she hiked back up the stairs to the building's front entrance.

"You always work this late?" he asked.

"Pretty standard." She didn't ask about his hours because she already knew.

"I want that plate," he said. "I've had it stuck in my mind since you showed me that picture. The fact that you got it on film, but we can't read it . . ." He shook his head. "Could trace back to a dummy address, but still."

"No stone unturned. I get it." And she respected it. Cops—even feds—didn't make great money, considering the hours they put in. The ones Maddie knew did it because they were committed to the job.

She felt his gaze on her as she dug out her employee ID badge from her purse. She glanced up but couldn't read the look on his face.

"What?"

"Thanks for doing this," he said in a low voice.

"Of course." She looked down. He was here for work, obviously. But sometimes when he looked at her, she suspected his thoughts weren't work-related.

She swiped her way into the building. The receptionist had left for the night, so the security guard signed Brian in, looking first at his face and then at his

ID, while Maddie subtly checked him out. He'd ditched his suit jacket, so now his FBI shield and holster were readily visible. He'd rolled up his sleeves, too, and she noticed his tan forearms. Even with the long hours, it looked as though he managed to spend some time outside.

The guard handed him a visitor's pass, and Maddie led the way to the elevators.

"We'll try Cyber Crimes." She jabbed the call button. "They test-drive a lot of new software, so they might have access to something I don't." They stepped into the elevator, and the doors whisked shut. An uncomfortable silence ensued. She looked over at him.

"Which floor?"

"Oh." She reached for the button. "Sorry."

Her cheeks flushed as they rode up. It wasn't that he made her nervous, because he didn't. But he had a definite . . . presence. Part of it was his sheer size. He was so tall and broad-shouldered, with that military-straight posture. Part of it was those intense hazel eyes. She snuck a glance at him beside her. He was very nice to look at. But he was also young, possibly even younger than Roland.

"Cyber Crimes is on our top floor, right by DNA," she said. "They work on identity theft, credit-card fraud, child predators, pretty much anything related to the Internet. Recently they've been getting into online criminal profiling."

Okay, now she was babbling. But he politely pretended not to notice as they stepped off the elevator and she led him down the corridor to the glass door marked CYBER CRIMES UNIT. He pulled it open, and she spotted

Ben Lawson sitting at his computer. He looked up as they walked in.

"Good, we caught you," Maddie said.

She made quick introductions as Ben stood. It was a clear case of alpha and beta. Besides their height, Brian seemed to have little in common with Delphi's top cyber-sleuth, who sported shaggy hair, a goatee, and a faded Billabong T-shirt.

"What can I do for you?" Ben looked at Maddie.

"We're here about a photograph—and you know what? I need to run down and get you a disc."

"Don't bother." He dropped into a chair and swiveled to face his computer. "I've got access to your desktop."

"You do?"

"What's your password?"

She peered over his shoulder at the screen. She had no doubt Ben could get past her ridiculously easy password, but she nudged him aside and keyed it in herself.

He grinned. "Your dog? Come on, Mad. I would have expected a little more."

"It's my cat. From *seventh grade*. How would anyone figure that out?" She reached across him and used the mouse to click open the file. "It's this one."

"We're trying to get a read on that license plate," Brian said, easing closer to Maddie so he could get a better look. "Any way to enhance it?"

Ben sat back and stared at the photo for a moment. Then switched into a new screen and opened a software program Maddie had never heard of.

"FillFlash?" she asked.

"It's something we're testing out. It's got some

bugs, but it does a pretty good job lightening up an image."

With a few clicks, the shadowy license plate became brighter. But the digits were still fuzzy. Ben cropped the image, creating a close-up of only the plate. Then he pulled down a new menu and used a few more clicks to sharpen the picture.

Brian whistled.

"Wow," Maddie said. "I should have come to you first."

Ben smiled smugly, and Brian took his phone out.

"Who are you calling?" Maddie asked.

"Sam. I need him to—" He stopped talking as Ben navigated into a new program and entered the license plate into a database. Within seconds, he pulled up a name, address, and driver's license photo.

Maddie's shoulders tensed as she stared at the face on the screen.

"Vladimir Volansky," Ben said. "Now, there's a name you don't hear every day."

"That's him," Maddie said. "That's the guy who attacked me."

Brian gave her a sharp look. "I thought he had a ski mask on."

"I recognize those eyes."

Brian seemed skeptical, and Maddie looked at the picture again. Bile welled up in her throat as she studied those icy gray eyes. It was him—she felt sure of it—and she couldn't believe he lived in San Marcos. Actually, she *could*, because that's where the crime had happened, but the prospect of her attacker living so close made her queasy.

"Could be a fake address," Brian said.

"We can check that out, too."

Ben pulled up a search engine and copy-and-pasted the address. Moments later, they were staring at a street-level view of an apartment complex.

"Looks real to me," Ben said.

Maddie's pulse picked up as she turned to Brian. "Do you think she's there?"

"Only one way to find out."

———————

Brian didn't talk as they drove through San Marcos, and Maddie suspected he regretted bringing her along.

"I can help you ID him," she said, breaking the silence. "And I'll stay out of the way."

He glanced at her, clearly unhappy. He hadn't wanted her to come, but Sam had insisted that it would be good to have an eyewitness along in case the apartment was occupied by more than one person.

"And it never hurts to have a photographer on hand," she said. "I brought my camera."

"You won't need it, because you're staying in the car."

His phone buzzed, and he grabbed it from the cupholder. "Beckman." He glanced at Maddie. "No . . . Yeah . . . Okay, got it."

He veered into the left-hand lane and turned at the next intersection.

"Change of plan. Sam's rounding up SWAT."

"He's bringing a *SWAT* team?"

"This guy's got some weapons charges under his

belt," he said. "Plus a possible hostage. We'd rather be safe than sorry."

He swung into a gas station.

"What are we doing here?"

"This is the meet point," he informed her. "The target lives around the block."

"Do I have time to get some water? There's no line at the counter. It should just take a sec."

"Sure."

"You want anything?"

"I'm good."

She dashed into the store and bought two bottles of water and a pair of Snickers bars. When she slid back into the car, Brian was on the phone.

"—and then let me know." He looked at her. "Okay, see you in a few."

He clicked off, and Maddie could tell he was in a better mood.

"He managed to scrounge up two teams. They're fifteen minutes out. He's also bringing one of our female agents in case we have a traumatized victim on the scene."

Maddie interpreted that to mean the female agent was a rape counselor.

"She can hang out with you while the guys hit the door."

"Make sure I don't get in the way?"

He didn't answer but gazed out the window at the passing cars. Maddie didn't see a gray sedan, and she'd been on the lookout the entire way over.

"How's the bruise?"

She glanced at him and rubbed her jaw. "A little sore."

"Still looks swollen."

Maddie didn't want to talk about her injury. She offered him a candy bar, but he shook his head. She twisted the cap off her water.

"I'm glad Ben was around to help us with this address," she said.

"There's a good chance it's phony."

She looked at him and noticed the tight set of his mouth. "You think she's dead, don't you?"

"That's the most likely scenario."

Maddie glanced out the window and felt a pang of sympathy for Jolene's parents.

"I'll tell you one thing. This guy's going down."

She glanced over, and Brian had a fierce look about him she'd never seen before. "You sound like you're on a mission."

He didn't say anything. Maddie waited.

"Whatever happened, it's on me. I was her contact. Me and Sam."

"You recruited her to be a witness?"

"She came to us, said she had information." He rested his hand on the wheel and stared straight ahead. "You know, I should've seen it. When we met with her, she was nervous—sweaty palms, shaking hands, the whole thing. I figured she was on something."

"So you'd already interviewed her?" She shifted in her seat to face him.

"She said she knew Mladovic, that she had information about illegal business activities. We established that she was legit, but then she clammed up, said she didn't know whether she could go through with it. She told us she wanted a few days to think."

A carload of teenagers pulled up to the gas pump behind them. Maddie watched them pile out and tromp into the store.

"We got tunnel vision," Brian said. "We were so caught up with how she could help us, we weren't focused on protecting her."

"They might have gotten to her anyway, you know."

But she could tell by the grim look on his face that what she said didn't matter. He felt responsible for Jolene's fate.

He turned to look at her. She wanted to say something, but nothing came to mind, so she just sat there, holding his gaze.

He shoved open the door and got out. She felt the trunk pop open. After a few moments, he slammed it shut and slid back behind the wheel.

"Put this on. That sweater's distracting." He handed her a navy-blue Windbreaker with FBI printed on the back.

"Distracting?"

"I don't want him to notice you."

"How's he going to notice me? I'm going to be in the car, like you said."

"Yeah, well, I get the sense you don't always follow directions."

She wanted to argue, but that would only prove his point. She unwound the scarf from her neck and shrugged into the jacket. He reached into the backseat and dropped an FBI baseball cap in her lap. She shot him a peevish look.

"You should conceal your face."

She nestled it on her head and pulled her ponytail through the back. "I look ridiculous."

"You look hot."

"Uh, *no*, I look like some kind of FBI groupie."

The corner of his mouth curved up, and she turned to gaze out the window. *You look hot.* Where the hell had that come from? Her heart started to thud as she felt him watching her.

His phone beeped, and she was relieved for a change of subject as he read the screen.

"Text from Sam. First van's ten minutes out. Second one's not far behind."

She downed some more water as he put the phone away.

"So." She cleared her throat. "Tell me about Sam."

He looked startled. "What about him?"

"How long have you been working together?"

"Two years."

"Is he married?"

"Divorced."

"Hmm. And he's from where, Baltimore?"

His gaze narrowed. "How'd you know that?"

"My grandmother lived there. I remember the accent."

He watched her, and she could tell she'd thrown him for a loop by asking about his partner. If he had any ideas about hitting on her, she wanted to nip them in the bud and save them both the embarrassment.

Maddie glanced out the window again as a man exited the store and stopped on the sidewalk to light a cigarette. She looked at his hands, his face, his body. He glanced up, and she made a small, strangled sound.

"What?" Brian looked at her.

"That's him," she whispered, easing low in the seat.

"With the bandage on his nose? Are you sure?"

"Positive." She remembered the FBI cap on her head and turned away so he couldn't see it. Her heart was pounding now as she recalled his eyes, his weight, his fingers digging into her neck. Right before she'd smacked him in the face and managed to run.

"He's leaving." Brian started the car.

"What are you doing?"

"Tailing him."

"Don't let him see us."

"Call Sam." He handed her the phone as he backed out of the space. "Just hit redial."

As Maddie made the call, Brian reached over and pulled the cap off her head. He tossed it to the floor and turned out of the parking lot as Sam answered.

"Sam, it's Maddie."

Silence.

"I'm with Brian, and we're in pursuit of a black SUV." *In pursuit.* Now she sounded like a cop. "We think Volansky is inside. We just saw him come out of a convenience store."

"You get a license plate?"

"It's too far away. He's three cars ahead of us."

"Tell him we're heading west on Eighth Street," Brian ordered. "Scratch that, he's turning south. Tell him he's going south on—what's that street called?"

"He's turning south on Sycamore," Maddie said. "That's *away* from the apartment."

Brian veered into the right-hand lane. He made the turn, and the black SUV shot forward.

"We're burned." He pounded the wheel. *"Damn it."*

Brian stomped on the gas, and Maddie was thrust back against the seat. She transferred the phone to the other hand so she could fasten her seat belt.

"Maddie? You there?" Sam asked.

"I think he spotted us."

Brian raced through a yellow light. The SUV's brake lights flashed, and it whipped around a corner. Tires squealed as Brian followed.

"East on Fifth." Brian darted a look at her. "Tell him."

"We're heading east on Fifth Street. Where are you guys?"

Muffled sounds on the other end as Sam talked to someone.

"Hold on." Brian flung out his arm and pressed her against the seat as he swung around a corner.

"Where are you going?" she squeaked.

"To cut him off."

Her head whipped forward as he slammed on the brakes and rounded another corner. Then he stomped on the gas again, and they sped down a street. Brake lights glowed in front of them. He swerved into the opposite lane to avoid a pickup. Headlights blinded them. Horns blared. He accelerated past the truck and swerved back, just in time to miss a head-on collision.

Maddie's heart skipped a beat. She clutched the phone in her hand and held her breath as he raced through another yellow light. He slowed at the next intersection and careened around the corner in time to see the black SUV shoot through a red light.

"Shit!" Brian pounded the wheel again.

"Maddie? What's going on?" Sam demanded.

"We're—" She glanced around frantically. "We're near the campus. Approaching Hudson Boulevard."

"You're headed east?"

"Uh—yeah. Now we're turning on Hudson. South on Hudson."

Brian's arm reached out again, and she batted it away. "Drive!"

He swerved around some slow-moving cars and sped through an intersection, but the light ahead was red.

"Watch out!" she yelped, but he was already on the brake. They skidded to a halt only inches away from a crosswalk. A stream of college kids filed past, headed for the bar district, completely oblivious to the hot pursuit going on around them.

Maddie caught her breath. She looked at Brian. His knuckles on the steering wheel were white as he waited for the pedestrians. He darted a look in the rearview and muttered a curse, then thrust the car into reverse.

"Brian!"

He shot backward up the street, all the way to the previous intersection, as Maddie craned her neck around to see the people they were no doubt about to mow over. He shifted gears. Tires shrieked as he shot down a side street. Another hairpin turn, and Maddie closed her eyes.

"West on Pecan. Tell Sam."

Maddie relayed their location.

"We're five minutes from there," Sam said. "I'm

sending the other team to Hudson. Maybe we can intercept him."

"There!" she shouted as they sailed past an alley.

Brian screeched to a halt. He shifted into reverse again and zoomed backward until they were even with the alley. The black SUV was parked in the middle, driver's-side door hanging open. A shadowy figure raced away and disappeared around a corner.

Brian yanked the Glock from his holster and shoved open the door. "Tell Sam where I am!"

"But—"

"And stay here!"

———

Brian heard the man's shoes slapping against the pavement as he rounded the corner.

"FBI! Freeze!"

He bolted ahead. Brian raced after him. The guy was small and wiry but surprisingly fast, and he had a decent lead. Brian turned on the gas and started gaining ground.

The man glanced over his shoulder, then darted right, down another alley.

Brian surged after him. Any doubt that this was Volansky was long gone.

The next alley was really just a driveway behind a building, looked like maybe a movie theater. Volansky ducked behind a Dumpster, and Brian gripped his gun, ready to take him down. But then a door popped open, and a teenager in a red shirt and black pants—probably some theater employee—stepped out. Volansky shoved him aside and darted through the door.

"Son of a bitch." Brian ran to the door and yanked it open.

"Hey, you can't—"

He raced inside and found himself at the end of a long hallway. Moviegoers milled around with buckets of popcorn. Brian's stress level skyrocketed as he thought of the potential for disaster.

A flash of movement. A yelp. The man barreled through a crowd of people. Brian lunged after him, squeezing his way past shocked onlookers. An alarm wailed as Volansky plowed through an emergency exit. Brian dodged around a knot of teenagers, plucking a phone from the hand of some girl as he went. He ran through the doorway and looked left, right. No sign of anyone. He glanced at the pink rhinestone phone in his hand, disconnected the call, and dialed Sam.

A noise to his right. Something hitting pavement. Brian bolted for it. A blur of black as Volansky darted around the building. Brian turned on the speed. He rounded the corner and—

Ping.

He leaped behind a Dumpster.

Ping.

Another bullet hit metal. Shit, two rounds. Close range. His heart jackhammered in his chest. Where the hell was he? Brian leaned his head back, peering through the narrow gap between the Dumpster and the concrete wall, but saw no sign of him. His pulse raced. He hadn't been shot at in years, and he felt the familiar clutch in his chest, the panic pumping through his veins. He took a deep breath and tried to shake it off. He had to focus.

The phone in his hand made a noise, and Brian pressed it to his ear. Voice mail. *Shit.*

"It's Beckman. I'm at the movie theater south of campus. This guy's armed, and I need immediate backup."

A clatter of footsteps, a grunt. He was running away.

Brian shoved the phone into his pocket and crouched low as he rounded the Dumpster. He scanned the area. No one. With his back to the wall, gun up, he hustled to the corner of the building and peered around.

Parking lot. *Fuck.* Hundreds and hundreds of cars and innocent people flowing between them. Brian ran for the lot, mind racing with a long list of bad outcomes to this. Volansky was going to grab a car, that was certain. Would he just take it, or would he put a bullet in someone when he did? Brian took the phone out again and dialed 911, then barked directions at the operator while sprinting for the sea of cars. He reached the first row and dropped to his knees so he could peer under the vehicles. No one hiding or duck-walking around that he could see.

A distant scream, shrill and terrified.

Brian jumped to his feet, searching for the source.

Another scream. He took off toward the commotion. He ran for all he was worth, heart thundering. *Don't shoot, don't shoot, don't shoot.*

Across the lot, a red hatchback rocketed backward out of a space. He heard the squeal of brakes and then the growl of the engine as the car sped away.

CHAPTER 5

Maddie knelt on the sidewalk beside the shoe print. She took a deep breath, held it, then let it out partially and snapped the picture.

Blurry again.

Her hands were shaking all over the place, and she desperately wished for her tripod. She glanced around for something to use as a substitute and spotted the police cruiser zooming toward her. It came to a screeching stop nearby, and Brian jumped out of the passenger side.

"I told you to stay in the car."

Relief washed over her at the sight of him. But she didn't respond, because she didn't want him to see how rattled she was. She put her knee up and rested the camera on it, with the lens angled slightly down.

"Maddie?"

"I need to get a few photos."

"We've got techs for that."

Click.

She checked the screen. At last, a decent shot. She pocketed her metal scale and stood up to look at him.

In the street light, she saw that his face was slick with sweat, but he wasn't even breathing heavily, and here she was shaking so badly she could hardly hold a camera. He'd called her after the carjacking, but the few minutes between hearing those distant gunshots and getting that phone call had been terrifying as she envisioned Special Agent Brian Beckman bleeding out on some street corner.

She looped the strap around her neck. "I needed to document fleeting evidence. Stuff that fades or blows away—strands of hair, dust . . ." She nodded at the sidewalk in front of her. "Wet shoe prints on concrete."

Brian's phone buzzed, and Maddie pulled it from the pocket of the borrowed jacket. She handed it to him and strode back to the SUV, where she could busy herself with more photos of the running board.

Someone had *shot at him* just minutes ago, and he looked completely unfazed. His voice sounded perfectly normal as he stood behind her, talking on his phone. Any doubt that he'd once been in the military was erased.

Maddie crouched beside the black Explorer and clicked a few more pictures of the blood smear on the running board. These particular shots could wait for the FBI crime-scene techs, but extra pictures wouldn't hurt. She studied the blood, knowing it could very well belong to Jolene Murphy. This might have been the primary vehicle used in her abduction. It made sense. The Explorer had tinted windows, unlike the sedan.

The SUV shifted as the police officer ducked inside and reached for the keys.

"Hey!" Maddie shot to her feet. "Hands off. This is a crime scene."

He frowned. "Who are you?"

Who the hell are you? she wanted to ask. This was another rookie she didn't know, but at the moment, that was good.

"I'm the forensic photographer." She nodded at Brian. "We're waiting for the rest of our evidence response team. Until they arrive, no one touches anything. Are we clear?"

She didn't wait for a reply but resumed taking her photographs as the officer stalked off. Footsteps scraped behind her, and she stood up. Brian was watching her, a look of concern on his face.

"You seem upset," he said quietly.

Upset didn't cover it. Maddie took a deep breath and gazed up at him. "What happened at the apartment?"

"They didn't find her. Looks like some people might have been in there recently, but it's empty now."

She bit her lip and looked away. They'd been so close.

"SWAT took off, and our evidence team just showed up to have a look around," he said. "Sam's over there supervising things."

"Where are the shell casings?"

He looked blank.

"From the movie theater," she said.

"Our evidence guys are processing the scene. Why?"

"I'd like them."

"The casings?" He sounded surprised.

"We can run them through our ballistics lab."

"So can we."

"Probably tomorrow."

He rested his hands on his hips and gazed down at her.

"Don't even pretend you can turn anything around that fast," she said. "You have to send them to Quantico, and then it will probably take weeks."

"We need them for the case record."

"You can have them back as soon as we're finished. You can even run them again yourself, but in the meantime, you might have a lead."

She watched him consider what she was offering, and she knew he felt tempted. Her time frame blew his out of the water. Problem was, investigators were notoriously controlling when it came to evidence, and she already had the tripod he'd wanted.

"Give me one of them, at least," she said. "For twenty-four hours."

She could see him starting to cave as his phone buzzed. He exchanged a few cryptic words with someone—probably Sam—and hung up.

He gazed down at her and sighed. "One casing, but I'm going to need it back."

"Fine."

"And I have to drive you home now. Sam needs me at the crime scene."

Her stomach clenched. "The apartment's a crime scene?"

"By the looks of things, yeah."

———

Goran Mladovic eyed the FBI vehicle parked outside his house with annoyance. Not that he minded being under investigation. He'd been dealing with that for years, and Matt Cabrera's task force didn't know its ass from its elbow. It was the agents themselves he found insulting. Cabrera had sent two rookies—including a woman to conduct surveillance on him only hours after he'd made a major play.

Goran's phone vibrated in his pocket, and he read an incoming message from an untraceable e-mail account.

Delivery complete.

He went to his bar and poured two fingers of vodka. Tonight he should celebrate. Only February, and it was already shaping up to be his best year yet, and the problem that had cropped up last spring was about to get solved, permanently. Soon he would be back in business and well on his way to making seven figures this quarter alone.

Goran tipped back his Stoli. Not bad for an inner-city kid who'd grown up on powdered milk and Beanee Weenees.

For the first time in a very long while, he thought of his parents, who still lived in a tiny Chicago apartment that smelled like boiled cabbage. It was an unpleasant place, where Goran had spent an unpleasant childhood. Having a mother and a father with Russian-sounding accents during the Cold War had not been easy. His parents knew English, but his father would lapse into Serbian during his drinking binges, and Goran would end up on the back steps of their four-story building, nursing his bruises and listening to his parents scream at each other through windows opened to relieve the sweltering summer heat. During those miserable afternoons, Goran dreamed of one thing: an air-conditioning unit so that his family could keep the windows shut and prevent the entire building from knowing the extent of their dysfunction.

Goran walked through the hallway now and adjusted the thermostat to sixty-two. Never mind that it was forty-six degrees outside, and he could have opened a window. No one opened windows in his house. Ever. The temperature didn't fluctuate unless he wanted it to. No one besides himself, not even his wife, was authorized to touch the thermostat.

He took his drink and settled into his favorite chair to watch the basketball game. The Devils looked strong, possibly even strong enough to win the whole thing. Another reason to celebrate.

Goran had landed a scholarship to Duke, where his natural intelligence and his striking blue eyes had made both the grades and the women come easy. He'd been denied admittance to Harvard Medical School, but his acceptance at UTMB had turned out to be a stroke of luck that would result in more wealth than he ever could have imagined. What the Texas med school lacked in Ivy League prestige, it made up for in location. *Geography is destiny.* He'd read that somewhere once, and it turned out to be true, as the pinko kid from Chicago started practicing medicine in the Lone Star State.

By the time Goran had finished his residency, he was married, in debt, and supremely motivated to get to the earning phase of his career. Rather than waste his time on a narrow specialty, he'd gone straight into general practice, which was sufficiently flexible to suit his ambitions. By twenty-eight, he was already implementing his master plan to achieve his two principal objectives:

money and power. It wouldn't take him long to realize that they were one and the same.

Goran had set up a clinic in an upper-middle-class suburb of San Antonio and immediately started seeing the sort of traffic he was looking for: housewives with tennis elbow, husbands with erectile dysfunction, everyone with tension headaches and lower back pain. He'd kept his calendar booked, even when it wasn't, and made sure anyone who called, no matter how desperate, waited at least a week for an appointment. Slowly but surely, he had developed a reputation for being expensive but free with his prescription pad. It wasn't long before the myth became reality and then exceeded it, and he was making money hand over fist by providing in-house scripts for a long list of patients who waited days and often weeks for a fifteen-minute office visit.

But then the feds had started nosing around, and the game was up. Temporarily.

Growing up poor had taught him to be resourceful, though, and it didn't take him long to circumvent not only the state medical board but also the federal investigators who had begun sniffing around his practice. With the help of a marginally intelligent attorney, Goran had restructured his business and managed not to lose a single patient. In fact, he'd gained hundreds.

He took out his phone now and composed an e-mail. He would handle things personally this time, and there would be no mistakes. He hadn't gotten where he was by being afraid to get his hands dirty.

CHAPTER 6

The address listed on Volansky's driver's license was about what Brian expected, with a few unpleasant surprises. He stepped through the front door of the apartment unit for the second time that night and traded his shoes for paper booties.

"I talked to the landlord," he told Sam, who was standing beside a sliding glass door and watching a crime-scene tech dust for prints. It was one of the few places to dust, as the unit was nearly empty.

"Where'd you find him?" Sam asked.

"Called the number posted at the front office. Turns out he lives on the premises."

Sam lifted an eyebrow.

"Don't get excited. He doesn't know much. Or so he claims. Says the tenant in this unit wasn't around a lot. Says he leased the place fifteen months ago and paid a year's worth of rent in cash—"

"Cash?"

"Yep. And he was back the first week of January to pay this year's."

"You ask to see the lease application?"

"He thumbed through the files, says he must have 'misplaced' it. My guess is he pocketed some money not to get one in the first place."

"Don't nobody know nothin' about nothin'," Sam said.

"And he was jumpy as hell, which tells me he at least has some idea his tenant's got something going on here."

Brian glanced around, more carefully this time. The only furniture in the apartment consisted of a sofa, a plastic patio chair, and a big-screen TV in the corner of the living area. The bedroom didn't have a bed, and the fridge was completely empty. Brian had checked.

"You get a look at what this guy bought at the gas station earlier?" Sam asked him.

"A six-pack of beer. Why?"

"Anything else?"

"Probably cigarettes. He lit up as soon as he exited the store."

"We need the brand." Sam nodded at the small patio on the other side of the door. "There are some butts out there, all Marlboro Reds. We need to find out if they belong to Vlad or one of his buddies. Maybe we'll even get lucky and find one that belongs to Mladovic."

Highly doubtful, but it wouldn't hurt to try. Brian pulled out his phone and scrolled through three separate messages he'd just received from Maddie, all with photographs attached.

"Maddie got a picture of the SUV's interior," Brian said. "Looks like a six-pack of Bud on the seat, but I don't see a carton of smokes. Maybe he only bought a pack."

"Brian? Sam? You guys need to look at this."

He turned to see Elizabeth LeBlanc standing in the foyer. The agent was even newer to the job than Brian, but they'd brought her along in the unlikely event that they found Jolene Murphy alive.

Brian braced himself as he followed her down the short hallway leading to the bathroom. It smelled like a litter box. A crime-scene tech was crouched beside the bathtub.

"Check out these marks," Elizabeth said.

Brian studied the side of the tub. "What's that from, a hammer?"

"Probably a hammer, maybe a mallet," the CSI said. She turned and pointed to the drainpipe under the sink. "We've also got some scratches here on the pipe. I can't say for sure, but they could be from handcuffs."

"Any idea how old those bloodstains are?" Sam asked.

"Could be days, maybe even weeks. It's hard to pin down."

Brian exchanged looks with Sam. They'd already guessed that Jolene had been held captive here. The question was when. A fast-food receipt they'd recovered from a trash bin was dated two days ago. Brian glanced around.

"What are those marks on the wall?" He tugged Elizabeth aside and crouched down. "See there?"

"Probably from her feet," Elizabeth said. "Looks to me like she was on the floor here, kicking the wall."

"And no one heard anything," Sam said disgustedly.

"Neighboring unit's unoccupied," Brian told him. "Maybe a coincidence, maybe not."

Sam checked a message on his phone and muttered a curse.

"What is it?"

"Jolene's father wants an update."

The family had been hounding them around the clock, and Brian didn't blame them. But Jolene's dad had bought a police scanner and was listening intently to any and all activity that might have something to do with his daughter's disappearance. His frequent phone calls were a distraction.

"I told him I'd stop by tonight." Sam checked his watch. "Now I'm wishing I hadn't."

"Hey, you guys mind taking it into the hall?" The CSI looked annoyed. "I need to finish in here."

"I'm happy to stick around if you need to go," Elizabeth said as they migrated into the living room.

"That'd be good."

"Want me to come?" Brian asked, even though he dreaded the idea. He'd spent half an hour yesterday with Jolene's distraught mother, and it had been miserable.

"I got it." Sam peeled off his gloves. "You should go home and pour yourself a stiff drink. Or better yet, buy a lotto ticket. It's dumb luck you didn't get pumped full of lead tonight."

"He *shot* at you?" Elizabeth looked stunned.

"I'm fine."

"Yeah, sure, maybe after about a fifth of bourbon." Sam jerked his head toward the door. "Go on, get outta here. You've had a shitty day."

Brian walked out to his car and stood for a moment looking back at the apartment building. Cold air whipped through his shirt as he stared at unit 18B.

How long had Jolene been kept there? What exactly had been done to her? And why hadn't neighbors heard anything suspicious and picked up the phone?

A lot of questions, with answers that were guaranteed to infuriate him. Brian slid behind the wheel. He'd been up nearly twenty hours, and—mentally—he was tapped. Physically was another story. He still had that buzz of adrenaline that told him sleep anytime soon would be impossible.

He started the car and glanced at the clock. Eleven-twenty. He thought of Jolene being tortured in that apartment. He thought of his best friend in Afghanistan, who'd been killed right in front of him by a roadside bomb. He thought about fate and luck and all the fucked-up things people did to one another for no good reason at all.

Brian pulled out of the lot, and his bleak mood started to close in on him. He thought about his empty apartment in San Antonio and the bottle of Jack in his cabinet.

It wouldn't help. But he knew something that would.

Maddie wasn't sure what she was doing here. One minute, she'd been curled up on her sofa in pj's, flipping channels and eating Cheetos in a vain attempt to forget the day. The next minute, she'd been zipping up her jeans and caving in to what was sure to be an extremely stupid impulse.

Brian pulled open the door and held it for her as she

ducked under his arm. She stepped into the warm, dim restaurant and was greeted by the tantalizing scent of fresh pizza.

"Pretty crowded for this time of night," she said.

"They're open twenty-four seven." He ushered her to the counter, and she tipped her head back to gaze at the menu board posted above.

Maddie sighed. This outing was testing her will-power on every front. When her phone had chimed and the caller ID had said US GOV, she'd immediately known it was him. She should have felt alarmed or at least annoyed that he'd accessed her private cell number and decided to call at eleven-thirty, but instead, she'd felt vaguely flattered.

Which should have been her first clue that this was a mistake.

"What do you like? Sausage? Pepperoni?" he asked.

"I'm open-minded when it comes to pizza."

Only when it comes to pizza? But she kept the question to herself, because it would sound flirty, and that was definitely something she needed to avoid. This was not a date. Not. A. Date. This was a couple of tired colleagues grabbing a meal after work.

"How about Canadian bacon and pineapple?" she asked, just to test her hypothesis.

He surprised her by shrugging. "Sounds good to me."

"Or wait—on second thought, how about pepperoni and mushroom?"

"Whatever you want. I haven't eaten since lunch. I could pretty much eat a shoe right now."

They placed the order, and the cashier slid their beers across the counter as Brian reached for his wallet.

"I got it." She plunked her purse on the counter.

"No, let me."

"Really, let me. This isn't a date."

There, she'd said the *D* word. She'd meant it quite seriously, but the corner of his mouth curved up.

"All right, then, you get the food, I'll get the beers."

Maddie picked up a plastic number that looked like an evidence marker and found a table in the corner under a neon beer sign. She sank into a chair and shrugged out of her jacket, proud of herself for having cleared the air. Now they could hang out without awkwardness.

She took a sip of her cold beer, which she had to admit tasted better than the diet soda she'd been drinking back at home. She rested the bottle on the table and glanced around. The booths had brighter lights, and some of the customers there had textbooks open. It was a college hangout.

"I like this place," she said. "How'd you find out about it, living in San Antonio?"

"Sam heard about it. We were working a case here in town, keeping pretty crazy hours. It's one of the few places that serves food late. You've never been here?"

"Nope."

His gaze met hers across the table. He was giving her that look again, the one that made her skin tingle.

"So." She cleared her throat. "Thanks for giving me that shell casing. I'll get it into ballistics tomorrow —"

"Hey, I've got an idea. How about we don't talk about work tonight? I could use a break." He tipped back his beer.

"That's fine. I was just—" *Babbling*. She was definitely babbling. It was something she did when she was nervous, and the fact that this nondate was making her that way underscored the fact that she needed to get out more. With men instead of girlfriends.

She reached for some small talk. "So, how long were you in the military?"

He looked amused. "Been talking to Sam, I take it?"

"I just assumed. You seemed pretty . . . undaunted by the whole shooting incident."

"I went through college on ROTC. Did four years with the Army after graduation."

"You served in Iraq?"

"Afghanistan. After my second tour, I decided not to reup."

"How come?"

"Lot of reasons." Something in his tone told her he wasn't going to share all of them. "I couldn't see making a career out of it, for one thing. I was more interested in solving problems closer to home."

"And where is home, exactly?"

He smiled. "This is quite the interview. You ever work as a journalist?"

"I'm just curious."

He took a sip of his beer and rested it on the table. "Grew up in Florida."

"You're kidding." She tilted her head to the side, trying to see it. "I never would have guessed that."

"Inland," he said. "On a farm, actually."

Now, *that* she could see. "Citrus?"

"Dairy." He smiled. "Believe it or not, we grow

things in Florida besides oranges. What about you? Where's home?"

"Well, this is, now. I've been here eight years. Originally, I'm from Dallas."

He lifted an eyebrow.

"You don't like Dallas?"

"Nah, it's fine. It's just . . ." He shook his head. "I had a girlfriend from there once, and she was very—" He stopped and seemed to be groping for a word. Maddie waited, enjoying the suspense.

"She was very . . . ?"

"High-maintenance. Perfect hair, perfect clothes, perfect body."

She laughed. "Gee, that must have been torture for you."

"Believe me, it got old. Anytime we went anywhere, it took her, like, ten hours to get ready. Used to drive me crazy."

"Well." She felt herself relaxing now that the conversational ball was rolling. "Some of my best friends are from Dallas. Not everyone's like that."

"Obviously."

She narrowed her gaze at him. It was another one of those offhand comments that seemed loaded with meaning, especially when delivered with that glint in his eyes.

She needed to tackle this issue head-on. Why was she being such a wuss about it? This wasn't her normal MO with men—usually, she was assertive.

"How'd it go earlier?" he asked. "The injury accident?"

"You said you didn't want to talk about work."

"I meant mine. We can talk about yours all you want."

"It was fine." She turned her bottle on the table.

"Fine?"

She glanced up. "Actually, it was horrible, if you want to know the truth. Motorcycle versus pickup truck."

He winced.

"Two fatalities," she said. "And why anyone would be stupid enough to own one of those crotch rockets and go zipping around on a curvy two-lane road—" She stopped and looked at him. "Oh, my God. You have one, don't you?"

"Guilty."

"I thought you were smart! *Please* tell me you wear a helmet."

He reached for his beer. "I almost always wear a helmet."

"Brian!" She slapped the table. "Do you have any idea what the fatality rate is for motorcycle riders? And that's *with* proper headgear. I should bring you to the ME's office sometime. If you saw what I saw—"

"I'm sure it's bad."

She shook her head and twisted her beer bottle. *Bad* didn't begin to describe it.

"Have you ever been on a bike?"

She looked at him. "No."

"I rest my case."

"What case? You didn't make a case for anything."

"I'll take you on my bike sometime and show you what I mean." He sipped his beer, and Maddie watched, speechless. She imagined herself shooting down the highway on the back of his motorcycle, hair streaming behind her, arms wrapped around him, thighs clinging to him for dear life. Just the thought of it made her insides tighten.

He *was* flirting with her. She'd thought she'd been imagining it before, but now she was certain.

The waitress slid a giant pizza in front of them, and whatever sensible thing she'd been about to say was lost as the smell of garlic and pepperoni wafted up to her. Brian wasted no time digging in.

"I just want to be clear," she said, hating how uptight she sounded. But she genuinely *liked* this guy, and she didn't want to mislead him. "This isn't a date."

"You said that already."

She eyed him suspiciously as she picked up a slice of pizza and tore a strand of cheese.

"It's good," he said.

She took a bite, careful not to singe the roof of her mouth and ruin the whole meal. The sauce was spicy, and the crust was just the right balance between doughy and crisp. She was coming back here again for sure— just maybe not with him.

After another bite, he put his slice down and looked at her. "What if it was?"

"What?" She dabbed some grease from her mouth.

"Us, on a date. I've been wanting to ask you out, although I probably should have started with something nicer than a pizza joint."

She took a sip of beer to fortify herself. She looked directly at him. "Brian, how old are you?"

"Twenty-eight."

She closed her eyes. "Oh, my God." He was younger than Roland. She looked at him again, and he seemed completely relaxed. "Don't you want to know how old *I* am?"

"Thirty-four."

She arched her eyebrows.

"I saw your DOB on the police report," he said. "So what?"

"So, don't you see the problem?"

"What problem?"

She looked at him, dismayed. "Do you have any idea what people say about—" She stopped talking, because the slight smile on his face told her he knew exactly what people said. He swigged his beer, eyeing her over it, and she felt her cheeks warm.

He plunked the bottle down and leaned forward on his elbows. "Look, I can tell you're uncomfortable. So, fine, this isn't a date. It's a pizza. Let's talk about something else."

"Like what?"

"Like, I don't know. Tierra del Fuego. I've never been there. Tell me what it's like."

———

Maddie managed to talk for the rest of the meal as he sat attentively and chimed in with occasional comments and questions. He was a great listener. It was a skill so few people had, and she appreciated it. By the time he'd wolfed down the last morsel of pepperoni, the restaurant crowd had thinned.

He pushed his plate away and rested his arms on the

table. He leaned in conspiratorially, and Maddie found herself leaning closer, too.

"Maddie, can I ask you something?"

"What?"

"Why do you keep looking at my hands?"

She glanced at the long, thick fingers that were curled around his beer bottle. She hadn't realized he'd noticed.

"Habit, I guess."

His eyebrows lifted.

"I pay attention to how people touch stuff."

"Why?"

"People have unique styles of handling things," she said. "For instance, that you hold your beer by the top, where the neck tapers in, when you're taking a sip. If I needed to get prints, that's where I'd go first."

He was looking at her a little warily now, and she smiled. Most people would probably be shocked to know the sort of details CSIs picked up on.

"Also, you eat your pizza taco-style. You fold it in half."

He rubbed his chin, where a way-past-five-o'clock shadow darkened his jaw. "Damn, I never thought about it. I'll have to watch my hands around you. No cleaning my ears or subtly adjusting things in my pocket."

"Yeah, that's not too subtle. And men do it all the time, thinking they're being discreet." She caught a glimpse of his watch and gasped. "Oh, my God, it's after one!" She jumped up from her chair. "We have to work tomorrow. And you still have to drive back."

"It's no big deal." He left some bills on the table and

followed her from the restaurant. "I'm used to long hours."

They stepped into the brisk night air, and Maddie's breath formed a cloud in front of her face. She shivered and fisted her hands in the pockets of her coat. He'd left his suit jacket in the back of his car, but he seemed unbothered by the weather as he walked alongside her. For some reason, she felt comfortable around him, but she resisted the urge to huddle close to him for warmth.

"How long's your drive?" she asked.

"Half an hour. I live on the north side of the city." They reached the car, and he opened her door. "Easy access to San Marcos, Austin, most of the municipalities covered by our field office."

His tone was businesslike, but the look in his eyes was not as he watched her slide in. She leaned her head against the seat as he walked around and got behind the wheel.

The drive back was quiet, and Maddie's thoughts drifted as he glided through deserted intersections to the neighborhood where she lived. It was less than a mile away from the gas station where she'd seen Volansky, in the flesh, only a few hours ago.

"You should think about getting that alarm activated."

She gave him a sideways look. Had his thoughts been on the same path as hers?

"It probably wouldn't cost much, and your homeowner's insurance might knock a few bucks off your rate."

"I'll think about it," she said. It was something she'd been meaning to do for years, but she'd never gotten around to it. Now she felt foolish for putting it off.

She glanced at him behind the wheel of the car, completely relaxed. She remembered the tension in his face as he'd sped through yellow lights and careened around corners in pursuit of a fleeing criminal.

She remembered the sound of those gunshots, and suddenly her stomach tensed. One instant. That's all it took. She, more than anyone, knew how something young and vibrant and beautiful could be destroyed in the blink of an eye.

Maddie looked away. She watched the trees pass by. She watched the tidy little lawns and the manicured flowerbeds and the houses that were locked up securely for the night. A wave of loneliness washed over her.

She could ask him in. He would stay. He would peel her clothes off and warm her bed and make the world feel good again for a few hours.

And no matter how good it was, she'd wake up utterly alone—maybe not in body but in spirit—and she'd have a fresh new batch of regrets. Or worse, she'd have no regrets at all. She'd feel nothing. Just the dull blankness that had been a fixture of her life since Emma died.

She glanced at Brian's strong profile in the seat beside her. She didn't want to do that. She liked him too much to let him see that side of her. It wasn't something she felt proud of.

He swung into her driveway. Before she could think of a tactful protest, he was out of the car and coming around to her door.

"Thanks for dinner," she said brightly as he walked her up the sidewalk.

"You bought it."

She stopped at the base of the steps and turned to look at him. "Well, thanks for the beer, then. And the invitation. I—"

He kissed her. Maddie's breath caught as his mouth pressed against hers and his hand cupped the side of her face. In her shock, she simply stood there and registered every detail of the moment—the chill of the air, the warmth of his fingers against her cheek, the firmness of his lips. Her hand slid around his waist, and she registered the solid heat of him through the fabric of his shirt.

He eased back, and she blinked up at him as he gently stroked his thumb over her jaw.

"I'll call you about that brass." His voice was low and warm.

"What . . ."

"The shell casing." He dropped his hand, and she felt a rush of cool air against her skin.

"Oh." *That brass.* "All right."

"Good night, Maddie." He turned toward his car, and she caught the smile on his face as he walked away.

CHAPTER 7

Scott Black hated testifying. He didn't like ties, or suits, or endless hours wasted on benches outside courtrooms. He didn't like attorneys, period, and he especially hated criminal defense lawyers.

With one exception.

"Your Honor, may I approach the witness?"

"You may."

Rae Loveland rounded the defense table and strode toward him with a gleam in her eye. Her high heels clacked against the floor, and she halted in front of him.

"Mr. Black, do you recognize this document?"

"I do."

"Could you describe it for the jury, please?" She handed him a thin stack of papers and returned to the lectern.

"It's a report from our ballistics lab. An analysis of a firearm."

"Thank you." She tucked a strand of that long dark hair behind her ear. "And can you read the part at the top where it describes the firearm being analyzed in this case?"

"A Beretta nine-millimeter."

"A nine-mil, like the one allegedly collected from my client at the time of his arrest."

"Objection, Your Honor." The county prosecutor got to his feet. "These facts are already in evidence. We showed the videotape of the arrest, and the defendant clearly had the gun stuffed in his pants."

"Sustained."

Rae didn't miss a beat. She'd known her opponent would object, but she was planting seeds of doubt wherever possible.

"Mr. Black, can you tell us what you did with this firearm after it arrived at your ballistics lab for analysis?"

Your ballistics lab. Scott sensed the wording was deliberate, but he couldn't see her game plan yet.

"I fired it into the tank to create a reference bullet."

She looked at the jury. "You just 'fired it into the tank'? Did the gun arrive at the Delphi Center already loaded?"

"It arrived empty. We don't accept loaded firearms."

"So, could you walk us through exactly what you did, step by step, please?"

Scott nodded, Mr. Cooperative. "I put on gloves. I removed the empty firearm from the foam-lined case that was used to transport it. I loaded a magazine into the weapon. I put on safety glasses, and I fired two rounds into the tank."

"To create a reference bullet." She looked at him. "What is that, exactly?"

"It's a sample bullet for comparison with another bullet possibly fired by the same gun." Scott made eye contact with the jury as he got to the technical part. "The inside of a handgun's barrel is rifled, which imparts spin to stabilize the bullet's flight when it leaves the gun. No two firearms make the same marks on fired bullets. The marks are unique to each weapon."

"And what did you do with your reference bullet?"

"I viewed the striation pattern—the unique marks—under the microscope and created a picture that I added to a database of known firearms to see if it matched anything already on record."

"And did it?"

"We didn't get any hits."

She lifted her eyebrows. "None at all?"

"No."

She turned to face the display screen beside the jury box. "I'd like to direct your attention to the photograph shown here. It's a picture made in the laboratory showing the bullet that was removed from the crime scene. Do you recognize it?"

"Yes." Scott glanced at the photo of the mangled scrap of metal caked with dried blood.

"Did you compare this bullet with the reference bullet you created to see if it contained the same striation marks?"

"Yes."

"And what was your conclusion? Did the marks match?"

"I wasn't able to see the striation pattern."

"You're saying it didn't match?"

"I'm saying the bullet was too damaged and misshapen to get usable marks."

"I see. So you failed to discover these unique

identifiers on the crime-scene bullet." She turned to face him with a curious look in her pretty blue eyes. "Is that unusual?"

"Fairly unusual, yeah. But when a bullet travels through a cop's shoulder and a wooden door and gets embedded in a cinder-block wall, that lowers our chances of getting anything."

Her eyes sparked. She definitely wasn't happy to have the jury reminded that her scumbag client was accused of shooting an off-duty police officer who'd tried to stop a convenience-store robbery.

Scott had worked a lot of holdups, but this one was especially callous. The assailant—who'd been wearing a rubber Halloween mask—had shot the cop at point-blank range and calmly picked up his brass before collecting ninety-six dollars in cash and walking out the door as the man lay bleeding on the linoleum.

"Your Honor, permission to approach the witness again?"

The judge gave permission, and she strode up to the stand, looking primed for battle.

"Mr. Black, I'd like to direct your attention to your report again." She picked up the paperwork and flipped the pages. "Could you read your notes at the bottom of page three there?"

He cleared his throat. "Possible blood spatter, trace amount, grip." He looked at the jury. "I noticed a smear of blood on the pistol grip."

She returned to the lectern as Scott's phone vibrated in his pocket. He ignored it, and the call went to voice mail.

"You said 'trace amount.' I take it that means small?"

"Yes."

"And you were the first person to notice this? Even after the gun had been examined by a police detective? He didn't see this smear?"

"Objection, Your Honor."

"You'll have to ask him," Scott said, earning a stern look from the judge.

"Sustained."

"And what did you do after you noticed this trace of blood on the pistol grip?"

"I'd already finished my tests, so I sent it to DNA so they could analyze the blood, see if it came from the victim." Scott was pushing it with that last part, but the judge let it go, and he suspected they'd already firmly established that the blood on the pistol grip belonged to the cop, who'd been on medical leave for eight months.

Rac turned to the jury box. "So you sent the gun from your ballistics lab to the DNA lab so they could analyze this tiny trace of blood, the *sole* direct evidence connecting my client to the victim, is that correct?"

The prosecutor jumped to his feet. "*Objection*, Your Honor."

"Sustained." The judge gave her a warning look. "Watch it, Ms. Loveland."

"Yes, Your Honor." She turned back to Scott. "Is there any chance the tiny amount of blood you discovered could have been picked up at the ballistics lab? While the gun was in *your* possession, not my client's?"

"No."

"It's not possible? The reports show that the gun and the bullet were in your lab on the same day."

"It's not possible."

"How can you be sure?"

He looked at the jury again. "Because we're very careful with our procedures to prevent the possibility of contamination. We don't mix up the evidence like that. We wash our hands between each step in the analysis. We wear gloves when we handle everything."

"You wash your hands between every step?" she asked.

"That's right."

"You *always* wear gloves?"

"When we're handling evidence, yes."

She looked down at her notes, and he could tell she was winding up for a curveball.

"Mr. Black, do you recall what you were doing on the morning of April twelfth of last year?"

Here it came. "No, I don't recall."

"Do you recall conducting a tour of the ballistics lab with staffers from the Wayne County Sheriff's Department, as well as an assistant from the DA's office?"

Scott's gaze narrowed. "I remember that, yes."

"Do you recall meeting my assistant here, Mr. Koenig? Mr. Koenig, could you stand up, please?"

"Your Honor, I object. What is the relevance of this to the matter at hand?"

"Your Honor, if you will indulge me a moment, I'm confident the relevance will become clear."

"You may proceed."

The guy stood up, and Scott recognized him as the rookie attorney who had come through the lab that day with a law-enforcement tour. Evidently, he'd already gone over to the dark side.

"I recognize him, yes."

"And do you recall giving a demonstration that morning, Mr. Black, in which you fired three separate weapons into the tank you mentioned previously?"

"I do."

She consulted her notes. "You handled a Glock nineteen, a Beretta nine-millimeter, and a Smith and Wesson thirty-eight that morning, is that correct?"

"I'll have to take your word for it." Scott braced himself as the curveball flew right at his head.

"And do you recall whether or not you were wearing gloves?"

"No."

"No, you weren't wearing any gloves, or no, you don't recall?"

"No, I wasn't wearing any."

"No gloves?" She turned to the jury. "But didn't you just tell us that you *always* wear gloves in the lab? That it's an important procedure you follow to prevent contamination?"

Scott glanced at the jury. He looked at Rae. She was still making eye contact with the jurors, driving the point home.

She turned to look at him, and he caught the glint of triumph in her eyes. "Mr. Black? Would you care to change your testimony?"

"No."

She addressed the judge. "In that case, Your Honor, I have no further questions for this witness."

The judge looked at the prosecutor, who was staring glumly in Scott's direction. "Would you care to redirect?"

"No, Your Honor."

The prosecutor knew when to cut his losses. Scott gritted his teeth as Rae collected her papers, and the judge dismissed everyone for the midday break.

Scott left the courtroom and entered the throng of courthouse staffers rushing out to lunch.

"Hey, wait up."

He headed for the drinking fountain.

"Scott."

He turned around. Rae fought the flow of people like a salmon swimming upstream. She stopped in front of him and straightened the hem of her jacket.

"You need something?"

"I just wanted to say thank you. For your time today." She squared her shoulders. "And I hope you understand that wasn't personal in there."

"Hey, no worries, Rae. Whatever you need to do to get your man off."

Her cheeks flushed, and he could tell she didn't appreciate the innuendo, especially coming from him.

"My client is entitled to—"

"Your client's a dirtbag, and this is the second time I've been called to testify against him in three years."

She crossed her arms over her chest and glared up at him. "You know, Scott, you really . . ." She shook her head.

"I really what?"

She huffed out a breath as his phone vibrated again. "Forget it."

"I will." He took the phone from his pocket as she turned on her heel and walked away.

"Scott, it's Maddie."

He watched Rae disappear into the courtroom and

felt a twinge of disappointment because she never finished her sentence.

"Are you there?"

"Yeah, what's up?" He headed for the exit, sidestepping the line of people stacked up at the metal detector.

"I was hoping you could do me a favor," Maddie said.

Scott stepped into the sunlight and scanned the meters for his pickup.

"Do you think you have time?"

"Not really. What's the favor?" he asked, even though it didn't matter. He'd do it anyway, because he liked her. Of all the CSIs he knew, Maddie was the least prone to dumb-ass mistakes, such as using a pen to pick up a firearm by the barrel, thereby preserving fingerprints on the weapon but potentially fucking up other evidence.

"I've got a shell casing from a crime scene," she said, "and I told a friend of mine I'd see if I could get it analyzed. It's kind of a rush job."

"Who's the friend?" Scott spotted his truck and saw the ticket tucked under the wiper blade.

"An FBI agent I know. His name's Brian Beckman."

"Never heard of him."

"I bet he never heard of you, either."

Scott dug the keys from his pocket. Maddie had an attitude, and he'd always liked that about her. "This the guy from the lab last night?"

"How'd you know that?"

"Saw you talking to someone on the steps."

"Yeah, that's him. He's part of a task force investigating a young woman's kidnapping."

Scott should have figured it was something like

that. Maddie had a soft spot for anything that involved women or kids.

"So, will you do it?"

"Drop it by the lab, and I'll take a look."

"I already did. Thank you *so* much. I owe you one. So does my friend."

He stuffed the ticket into his pocket. "Yeah, well, *you* are welcome. Tell the fed next time, he can use his own lab."

———

Maddie finished her response to the last urgent e-mail in her in-box and pressed send. She glanced at her watch. Five o'clock, and these photos had been promised yesterday. The investigator who'd been pinging her all afternoon obviously wasn't happy she was running behind, but that was too bad. He could take a number.

"Who's the hot cop?"

She glanced up as Brooke sauntered into the room and dumped her coat onto a chair. "Excuse me?"

"In the lobby. Some delectable-looking lawman is out there asking for you." She smiled. "Is he business or pleasure?"

Maddie's phone rang, and she picked up. "Photography."

"There's a Special Agent Brian Beckman here to see you," the receptionist said.

"I'll be right there." Maddie jumped up from her chair and glanced at her watch again. She knew why Brian was here, and he was going to be disappointed.

"Well?" Brooke was still smiling.

"Business," Maddie said, and headed out the door.

She found him in the lobby and felt an unwelcome surge of attraction. He was leaning casually against the counter and making conversation with the receptionist, who—until today—had been known for hitting the door every evening at five sharp. Brian was once again in dark slacks and a button-down with the cuffs rolled back. At the sound of her footsteps, he glanced over, and the warm look in his eyes made her nerves flutter.

"I got your e-mail," he said by way of greeting.

"Did you read all of it? Mia can't meet with us until tomorrow. She's got a class this evening."

"This shouldn't take long."

Maddie stopped beside the counter and gazed up at him. He had the determined expression of someone accustomed to seeing an obstacle and barreling right through it.

She glanced at the receptionist, who was watching attentively. "Has Dr. Voss left for the day?"

"I don't believe so."

She looked at Brian. "Follow me."

They reached the elevator bank right as the doors dinged open and the Delphi Center's top DNA specialist stepped out.

"Uh-oh," Maddie said. "You're leaving."

"I've got a class at six." She flicked a glance at Brian, clearly sensing the ambush. "And I'm running late."

"Mia, this is Brian Beckman with the FBI. He's investigating my case."

"Sorry to bother you, Dr. Voss, but we need a quick update on your DNA findings from that tripod," Brian said. "It's important."

Mia checked her watch. She shot Maddie a look that clearly said, *You owe me, big time.*

"Have a seat in the conference room." She nodded toward the room behind them. "I'll run up and get my file."

Brian walked into the meeting room and wasted no time making himself at home in one of the faux-leather chairs around the conference table. Maddie stood by the door.

"You don't hear the word *no* a lot, do you?"

"I'm sorry?" He pretended not to understand, and she shook her head.

Brian watched her steadily, and she took a seat across from him in the hopes that putting a table between them would keep her from thinking about last night's kiss. Unfortunately, it didn't. It was still front and center in her mind, where it had been all day.

She folded her arms and looked away, annoyed with herself for being uncomfortable. It was only a kiss, for God's sake. Not even a long one. It had lasted, what, a few seconds? Warmth spread through her at the memory, and she forced herself not to look at him, but she could feel his gaze on her.

"Your friend seemed surprised when you introduced me," he said.

"I imagine she's wondering why the FBI's involved in my mugging."

"You didn't tell her?"

"You told me discretion was important to the case. I've been keeping my mouth shut."

"Good for you."

Mia came into the room and dropped a file onto the

table. She pulled up a chair but didn't even bother to take off her scarf, and Maddie knew they were making her very late.

"Where do you teach?" Brian asked.

"The university." She flipped open the file without looking at him. "It's a CLE class—continuing legal education."

"So, your students are lawyers?"

"Not a group that likes to be kept waiting." She flipped the page of a typed report. "Okay, I swabbed the leg of your tripod where you noticed the blood droplet."

Brian looked at Maddie. "You drew blood? Nice job."

"I got a profile, which I ran through CODIS," Mia continued. "No hits in the Offender Index, but—" She turned the page around and slid it in front of Maddie. "We got a forensic hit." She glanced at Brian. "That means the DNA from the tripod matches an unidentified profile previously recovered from a crime scene."

Maddie skimmed the report, which contained mostly jargon. She noticed the phone number listed beside the contact law-enforcement agency.

"Area code 213. Where's that?"

Brian leaned forward. "Los Angeles. What kind of case?"

"A homicide." Mia flipped through the rest of the paperwork. "I contacted LAPD—they're the agency listed with the record—and they patched me through to a Detective Vega. He was very tight-lipped." She glanced at Brian. "Which isn't the usual reaction I get. Typically, investigators are pretty glad to get a new lead. Especially in an open case."

"You get the name of the victim?" he asked, and Maddie noticed the intensity of his expression.

"Yes, and that's about *all* I got," Mia said. "The name is Gillian Dawson. I also got her date of birth and the date the case was opened. That's it." She stood up and nodded at Maddie. "That file's yours. I've got a copy on my computer."

Brian stood, too. "Thanks for making time for us."

"No problem." She shot Maddie a look that conveyed about a dozen unspoken questions. "We'll catch up tomorrow."

When she was gone, Maddie stared down at the file, shaking her head. "Twenty-one years old."

Brian came around and took the vacated chair beside her. "Mind?" he asked, sliding the papers closer. As Maddie watched him read, her stomach filled with dread. A heavy silence settled over the room. His phone buzzed, and he pulled it from his pocket.

"Beckman." He looked at Maddie. "I caught her . . . yeah. Okay, on my way."

He clicked off, and she knew what he was going to say.

"Hey, you mind if I—"

"Yes." She flipped the file shut.

"I'll make a copy for you."

"First, I want some questions answered."

"Yeah, I do, too. And I need to get this info to the task force so we can develop this lead."

She pulled the folder closer. "The man who attacked me is now linked to a kidnapping *and* a homicide. Who the hell is this?"

"I told you. He's a strongman for—"

"For that doctor, I know. But who the hell is *he*? And don't give me some vague crap about racketeering. What is this about, Brian? Why are these girls being targeted?"

He looked at her, his expression guarded.

"I didn't ask to be in the middle of this," she said, "but now I am, and I want some answers."

"I understand. And I'll explain everything. At least, what we know about it. But it can't happen right now."

She held his gaze stubbornly.

"Listen, tomorrow's Saturday. I can probably get away for a few hours. We can talk then."

She watched him, hating how helpless she felt. She'd never before dreaded going home to her own house, but that's how she felt right now. She felt scared. And the one person who could probably put her fears to rest was racing out the door, probably to jump in front of another bullet.

"Maddie, I promise."

The words made her trust him. She had no idea why, but they did. She slid the file toward him.

"Keep me informed. I don't like being kept out of the loop."

He gave her a rueful look and stood up. "Yeah, I noticed."

Maddie pulled into her driveway, and for the first time since she'd purchased her quaint two-bedroom bungalow, she wished for an attached garage. As it was, the 1930s-era home had only a small detached shed, which was technically large enough to house a Prius but was instead filled with rusted patio furniture, chipped flower pots, and the red Toro lawn mower she'd learned to use when she first moved in.

Maddie checked her mirrors and scanned the empty street before getting out of the car and hiking up her front steps. Years of visiting crime scenes had forever robbed her of the urge to decorate her porch with wreaths or flower boxes or any other items that would proclaim to the world that the person who owned the lone car in the driveway was a single woman.

So instead of a wreath and a welcome mat, she was greeted by a coupon for Chinese takeout and a failed-delivery notice. The package she'd missed was the secondhand Nikon she'd ordered from an online auction site. Maddie stepped into the house and added the camera's present whereabouts to her list of worries, along with the hefty credit-card bill that was coming her way.

She locked the front door and leaned back against it, closing her eyes. At last she was home. She needed a chance to unwind, and she fervently hoped she wouldn't get a call-out tonight. But it was Friday. The odds were against her.

Maddie kicked off her shoes and indulged her inner slob by stripping off her clothes and leaving them where they fell as she walked to the bathroom. She turned the water to molten hot and climbed under the spray to rinse away the day's stress. After a few blissful minutes of simply standing, she washed her hair and scrubbed her face.

Better. She took a deep breath and faced herself in the mirror. Her bruise had turned an ugly shade of brown, but the swelling had gone down. She twisted her hair into a knot and examined the injury. Her emotions had been on a roller coaster since the attack, but the one coursing through her veins at this particular moment was anger.

Maddie slipped into a tank top and her softest pair of yoga pants, an outfit bought with good intentions but which lately had served as loungewear. Continuing the nonhealth kick, she poured herself a vodka cranberry, scooped up her laptop, and settled herself on the sofa.

A pile of client e-mails awaited her, and she quickly clicked through them. The most recent was from Hannah, whom Maddie had squeezed in for another portrait sitting yesterday afternoon. Evidently, Hannah and Devon *loved, loved, loved!!! the new engagement pics!!*

Maddie sipped her drink. She let the compliment sink in. Then she left the world of weddings and smiley faces and typed the words *Gillian Dawson* into the search engine.

USC Student Found Slain in Apartment.

Maddie skimmed through the *Los Angeles Times* article, scrolling down to a color photograph of a striking blonde. She clicked on the picture, enlarging it. Photographs spoke their own language, and Maddie tried to interpret this one. It was a studio shot, probably taken in her senior year of high school. Gillian, a sophomore, had been in a sorority, and Maddie visualized this picture being displayed on a screen in some sorority-house living room, where a bunch of girls in pajamas were munching popcorn. *Ladies, this is Gillian Kendall Dawson of Pacific Palisades. Her mother's a legacy. What do we think?*

Maddie studied the girl's face. According to the article, she'd been bludgeoned to death. She looked at Gillian's sparkling eyes and perfect teeth. A downside of Maddie's profession was that with very little imagination—none at all, really—she could conjure up a vivid image of what this pretty young woman had looked like in death. Over the past four years, Maddie had stepped into houses and trailers and apartments and calmly photographed scenes that would reduce grown men to tears—even long-time cops. She had photographed scores of victims, methodically recording their suffering for others to see. It was what she did. It was her job.

She was the eyes of the jury.

Maddie's current job was unimaginable to the woman she had once been. Not too many years ago, she'd been a portrait photographer, a part-time one, at that. It was a vocation she'd enjoyed, one perfectly acceptable for a doctor's wife who had a child at home and played tennis two mornings a week. When her friends from that era had heard about her career change, they'd been appalled.

"Crime-scene photography? But isn't that . . ." *Revolting? Voyeuristic?* ". . . difficult for you?" was the phrase they usually landed on.

Considering Emma, they meant.

And maybe it should have been difficult. But for Maddie, it wasn't. All she'd known when she'd made the change was that she couldn't go on snapping Christmas-card pictures and children with puppies and babies posed in pumpkins. So she'd packed her camera and gone to South America, a place filled with people and customs so alien to her she may as well have been on another planet.

Which suited her fine.

When she returned to the States after eleven months, she knew only two things for certain. One, that walking out on her marriage was *not*, as her mother had warned her, a catastrophic mistake. And two, her camera had saved her life.

And it continued to save it now, every day, every time she looped the strap around her neck and trekked off to a crime scene with a strong sense of purpose.

Maddie pictured the last crime scene she'd photographed—the black SUV with the door hanging open. She pictured Brian towering over her, his broad shoulders blocking out the street lights, his face slick with sweat because he'd just narrowly missed becoming a crime scene himself.

She pictured the intense look in his eyes. He had that fire inside him. She recognized it, the absolute certainty that he could do anything. Part of her even believed it.

She pictured the look in his eyes later, when he'd bent his head down to kiss her. He'd felt so warm and vital and alive, and she'd wanted to drink him in, even though she knew it would have been a mistake. She knew better than to cave in to temptation like that, and she was proud of herself for resisting it.

Maddie sipped her drink. The cool tartness washed over her tongue, and she congratulated herself on being a grown-up.

A sharp rap at the door, and she jumped. She set down her glass. She looked at the window, and her heart began to thud. Temptation was knocking again.

CHAPTER 8

"Hi."

"Hi." She put her hand on her hip and gazed up at him.

"Can I come in?" Brian asked, as casually as possible, because her expression told him she wasn't happy to see him.

She pulled the door open without comment, and he did his dead-level best not to look down her shirt as he stepped inside. He caught the scent of shampoo and knew she'd just gotten out of the shower.

Yeah, he was an ace detective. The smell of her hair was a big clue, along with the fact that it was damp and pulled back in a messy knot. Instead of the sweater-jeans-boots combo she'd had on earlier, she now wore some sort of stretchy black top and matching pants, and he was *not* going to stare at her, but holy Christ, she was stacked.

"I thought you had to work?" she said.

Work. That was why he was here. He forced himself to focus on those big brown eyes that were gazing up at him with wary curiosity again.

He cleared his throat. "Everyone was breaking for dinner, so I decided to swing by with that info."

She just looked at him.

"I probably won't have time tomorrow," he added, because she still looked as if she needed convincing. She didn't want him here. That much was clear. Maybe she thought he was going to hit on her again, and although the thought had definitely crossed his mind, he'd come here for work.

"Would you like a drink?" she asked grudgingly.

"Sure. What do you have?"

"I'm having a Cape Cod." She turned and walked into her kitchen, and he followed, making a heroic effort not to stare. It was tough. Women with curves really did it for him, and Maddie had the hourglass thing happening in a major way.

"So you want one?"

"Sure. Just the juice, though."

She put some ice cubes in a glass and filled it two-thirds with cranberry juice. "You sure you don't want it with a kick?"

"Yeah."

She added a slice of lime and handed it to him, and he watched her over the brim as he took a sip. He set the glass on the counter, and for a moment, they stared at each other.

"Are you really working tonight?" she asked.

"I really am. Why?"

She shrugged. "It's Friday. It's after eight. I figured maybe you had stuff to do."

"You mean, like a girlfriend? Nope." The look on

her face made him smile. "Just in case you were wondering."

"I wasn't."

"Sure you were."

That got a faint smile out of her as she walked past him, shaking her head. She probably thought he was being cocky. He thought of it as being persistent. He liked her, and he planned to keep on putting it out there until she loosened up and let her guard down around him.

She sank into an armchair, looking a little flustered as she sipped her drink, and he took a seat on the couch.

"I haven't had time for much besides work lately," he told her. "I'm guessing you know what that's like."

She nodded.

"I'm surprised you have time for the moonlighting gig. Don't they keep you pretty busy at the Delphi Center?"

"They do. It comes in waves, though. Don't ask me why." She set her drink on the table and seemed a little more relaxed to be talking about her job. "Sometimes I get called out two, three nights a week. Other times, things are quiet. And when I'm not on the call-out schedule, I'm free to book whatever events I want."

"Make a little extra money?"

"Never hurts."

He wondered if that was the real reason she did it, or if she liked keeping her free time booked so she wouldn't have to fill it with a social life.

"Do you like it?"

"The moonlighting?" She paused. "It's okay. My

forensic work is much more challenging. It's what I care about." She glanced at her computer. "I've been reading about Gillian Dawson."

"So have I."

"Do you think she's connected to Jolene Murphy somehow?" She had that worry line between her brows again.

Brian rested his drink on the table. "Here's what we know," he said, making eye contact. He wanted her full attention, because up to now, he got the feeling she hadn't been taking him all that seriously as an agent, as if he was too green to really know anything. That was going to stop.

"Last year, we were called in on a kidnapping," he said.

"'We' being the FBI?"

"The San Antonio field office. The victim's name was Heidi Beckles."

Her expression darkened. "I remember the case. She was a student at UT, right?"

"A senior," he confirmed. "She went out with some girlfriends one night. They dropped her off at her apartment building. She was supposed to meet her boyfriend at his house later, but she never showed up. He reported her missing, and when police got involved, they found a neighbor who'd seen her getting into a white SUV."

"Was she struggling?"

"Evidently, she was, but the neighbor didn't think much about it at the time. Said he thought she was just horsing around with friends. It quickly became clear that this was a kidnapping."

Maddie sighed. Like him, she'd probably seen plenty

of cases in which someone witnessed something suspicious but failed to get involved until it was too late.

"Turned out this girl's father headed up a tech company that had recently gone public," he said. "He'd just made a boatload of money, and there were stories about it in the news. So right away, everyone was expecting a ransom demand. Her parents waited by the phone, but nothing ever came."

"I remember reading that."

"Then you probably read the rest, too. Exactly a month after the abduction, Heidi was found in a ditch off Interstate 35, south of San Antonio. She'd been bound and gagged. She'd been tortured, too." He paused, remembering the hammer marks in that bathroom where Jolene Murphy had been kept. "One of her hands was crushed, and her fingernails had been pulled out."

She drew back. That hadn't been in the paper. "If she'd been dead that long, how could they—"

"She'd been kept alive," he said. "Probably for at least three weeks."

Maddie closed her eyes.

"That last part's confidential," he added. "Certain details are being kept out of the press."

She nodded. "How is this connected to the doctor you're investigating?"

"That's where Jolene Murphy comes in," he said. "When she first came to us, it was through our tip line. She dropped Mladovic's name, said she had information about illegal activities. The agent heading up the task force tossed this to Sam and me. It wasn't until she showed up that she started talking about Heidi Beckles.

Turns out, both Heidi and Jolene were friends with Mladovic's daughter, Katya."

"He has a daughter? Did you interview her?"

He shook his head. "She OD'd more than a year ago. It was listed as a suicide, but of course, after we talked to Jolene, we went and looked at the case. The ME insists he got the manner of death right, but Sam and I both think there's room for doubt, especially with Jolene missing."

"You think he killed his own child? And now her friends?"

"Honestly? We don't know what the hell to think of some of this. This case has gone sideways on us. It started out as tax fraud, then got into drug trafficking. Now we're looking at possible murder for hire."

"His own *daughter*?" She looked incredulous.

"We don't know that he killed her. We don't know that he killed any of them. We just know his daughter is dead. One of her friends is dead. And now another friend of hers has been kidnapped."

"What about Gillian in Los Angeles?"

Brian blew out a breath, frustrated. "That's another big question mark. She's around the same age as the others, but the crime happened fourteen hundred miles away."

"Did she ever live here?"

"Grew up in California," he said. "We spent the evening on the phone with the investigator out there. They've got her phone records, her e-mails. No connection to Heidi, or Katya Mladovic, or Jolene. She's never even been to Texas, as far as we can tell."

"Maybe it was an unrelated murder. Maybe the guy who works for Mladovic hires out to other people, too."

Brian nodded. "It's possible. Volansky definitely has some shady connections. He's been arrested half a dozen times—drugs, weapons, assault—but so far, he's managed to beat the charges."

Maddie gazed across the room looking pensive and also . . . sad, he realized. She shifted her gaze to him.

"I'm surprised you're telling me this."

"You said you wanted to know. I'm telling you what I know."

She leaned forward and rested her elbows on her knees. "Yes, but why?"

Because I want you to take me seriously, to understand that I'm on this investigation, and I have just as much right to be here as Sam or anyone else. But he didn't tell her that. He told her the other reason.

"I want you to be careful," he said. "These people are dangerous."

"Obviously." She sat up straighter. "But why would they care about me? I'm not in Katya's circle of friends. I don't have information about her father. The only thing I *had* was on my camera, and they already took that."

"The only thing *you* think you had. Who knows what they think?" Brian glanced at his watch and stood up. "I have to get back."

She looked up at him. "But—what are you telling me?"

"I'm telling you to be careful."

A typical weekend job would be a car accident, but the call that dragged Maddie out of bed in the wee hours this Saturday morning was a fire.

She squished across the saturated lawn, rubbing her hands together for warmth as she searched for her favorite Clarke County firefighter in the glare of the portable klieg lights. She spotted him stripping out of his coat beside the ladder truck. Perfect.

"Hi, Nick."

He turned around and immediately looked sorry to see her. "I know what you want, Maddie, and the answer's no."

"Please? I'll be quick, I promise."

Nick sighed heavily and rested his hands on his hips. His face was covered in soot, making the whites of his eyes stand out, and she noticed—not for the first time—that beneath all the grime, he was an attractive man. Of course, like most men his age, he had a wife at home and a baby on the way.

"You guys are like flies, you know that?"

She smiled. "That's why you love us. We buzz around making your job easier."

"Hey!" he shouted across the yard at someone. "Get these barricades outta here so I can move the truck for Maddie."

A young man leaped into action and got busy moving barricades. She beamed Nick a smile.

"Thanks. I just need about five minutes. Right by that oak tree over there should be the perfect spot."

"Stand on the curb," he said sternly. "And what kind

of soles you got on those boots? Last thing we need's an injury."

"Don't worry about me. I came prepared." She lifted her foot to show him the heavy rubber tread on her shoe, and then she stepped back so he could move the truck. He skillfully positioned the rig on the southwest corner of the lot where Clarke County Fire Rescue had spent the past two hours putting out a house fire.

Maddie gripped the cold metal rails and climbed the ladder, taking care not to slip and take a three-story header onto the lawn. When she reached the top, she braced her body against the rungs and composed her shots.

Now that the flames were gone, the crime scene consisted of the charred shell of what had once been a ranch-style home in a suburban pocket of Clarke County. When she'd first arrived on the scene, Maddie had surveyed the emergency vehicles, looking for Kelsey Quinn's Suburban, and she'd been glad not to see it. The forensic anthropologist's presence at a fire typically meant someone had died.

But the family who lived at this address wasn't here tonight, and Maddie felt a sense of relief as she snapped pictures of what had once been their home. The house was destroyed, yes, but at least they still had one another.

Maddie's eyes stung from the smoke, and she dabbed the corners with the back of her hand. As a rule, working conditions at fire scenes sucked. The locations were hot, wet, and littered with safety hazards. Steam or smoke obscured some of the shots she needed. To add to the challenge, many scenes were dark, because either the blaze knocked out electrical systems, or the fire-fighters shut them down when they arrived. Every time Maddie worked a fire scene, she felt she was earning her paycheck.

She clicked a few more photos. Although the kitchen and the garage had been reduced to a blackened skeleton, the living room and the bedrooms were still somewhat intact. Maybe a few sentimental items could be salvaged, but everything inside would reek of smoke. She took a few different angles of the yard, noting the red plastic wagon and the Big Wheel.

After finishing the bird's-eye-view pictures, she scanned the area. Despite the hour, dozens of neighbors in bathrobes and warmup suits still milled around, watching the action. The kids in the vicinity wore jackets hastily buttoned over pajamas. A man in a blue skullcap stood off to the side, talking on his phone. He reached out and snagged a kid by the collar, right as the boy was about to climb onto the running board of the fire truck. The kid's mom grabbed him by the arm and pulled him away.

Maddie scanned the other side of the street, looking at faces and subtly snapping pictures. Based on what she'd heard, this wasn't an incendiary fire, but it never hurt to check people out. Arsonists were known to hang around afterward and enjoy the spectacle they'd created.

Finally, she climbed down from the ladder and joined a cluster of firefighters beside the truck.

"Think we're ready for you inside," the fire chief said, motioning her toward the front sidewalk.

Maddie picked her way over the soggy lawn, stopping twice for mid-range shots. Then she followed him through the front door, which had been hacked open with an ax. When she'd arrived, the house itself had still been burning, and only now was it cooling down enough to walk through.

Maddie glanced around and then adjusted her shutter speed. The klieg lights cast long, eerie shadows over the remains of what had once been a living room. She surveyed the area, making a mental list of all the angles she needed to get. The roof was still mostly intact, and she would need to lie on her back amid the debris to get a shot of the burn pattern on the ceiling.

"Third time this month," the chief said from across the room. "Think we got ourselves a firebug."

Maddie turned and framed up the singed sofa. "Third time?" *Click.*

"The hardware store, the house on Belmont," he said. "Now this."

"I thought the hardware store was looking like insurance fraud?"

"We did, too. But now I'm thinking we got a serial torcher. Come get a shot of this."

He led her across the room to a burned-out hallway. On the Sheetrock, Maddie saw the telltale black V pattern that often pointed straight to the place where the fire originated. The door to a closet stood open, revealing a hot-water heater.

"You don't think it was a faulty heater?" she asked.

He knelt down. "You'd think that, wouldn't you, based on this point of origin? But that's the thing." He looked up at her. "All three cases, we've got a fire that starts right near what seems like a logical point of origin for an accidental fire. But in all three cases, it doesn't add up." He pointed to the sodden carpet. "Dollars to doughnuts, we'll find traces of an accelerant on this carpet."

Maddie crouched beside him and took a few pictures of the carpet, the closet, the Sheetrock.

"Our lab could tell you," she said. "Want me to cut a sample?"

He nodded gravely, and she wondered which made him unhappier, a serial arsonist operating in his county or the bill he was going to get from the Delphi Center for the lab work.

"I'll go get my kit," she said, and left him with his morose thoughts.

Maddie tromped across the lawn to her car and popped the cargo door. She rummaged through her gear until she found her utility knife and several small unused paint cans that could transport carpet samples. Accelerants had to be stored in airtight containers so the chemicals wouldn't evaporate.

She glanced at the neighbors nearby. Some of the older ones had trickled back to bed, but the younger ones were still out in full force. A knot of dads stood talking, while the women tried to keep their kids from venturing too close. Maddie noticed the skullcap guy again. He was looking straight at her.

"Hey, Maddie. What's the word in there?"

She glanced over her shoulder to see Sheriff Bracewell crossing the street. His cruiser was parked behind an orange barricade.

"Inconclusive," she said as he stopped beside her.

He peered down at her from beneath the brim of

his hat and gave her a look that said, *Don't bullshit a bullshitter.* And fair enough—she wasn't exactly talking to the news media. He'd get the info soon enough, anyway, and his deputies were already on the scene, interviewing witnesses.

"The fire chief thinks maybe arson," she said.

His gaze went to the house. "Again? What's he got, multiple points of origin?"

"Just one, I think."

Bracewell frowned. "He find pour trails?"

"Not that I've seen, but I'm about to cut some carpet samples to test for accelerants."

He cursed under his breath as she loaded the pint-size cans into her bag.

"The murder on Cottonwood. Now this." He shook his head. "Not even March, and my budget's shot to hell. Every man I got's putting in for overtime." He glanced at her as she hitched the bag onto her shoulder. "Need me to carry that?"

"Thanks, I got it."

"Why don't you lead the way in? You can show me where it started."

"Actually, you should go on ahead." She glanced at the crowd again, searching for the skullcap guy. "I need to stay out here and get a few more shots."

CHAPTER 9

"This is it? I was expecting a hog."

Brian smiled at her as she slid into his pickup. "Maybe next time," he said, passing her a steaming cup of coffee.

"Oh, my God, you didn't . . ."

"There're some sugar packets in the cupholder."

"This is perfect." She clutched the coffee in her hands and took a big sip as he pulled away from the curb in front of her house.

"Late night, I take it?"

She smiled and dug the sunglasses out of her purse. "Is that your way of telling me I look like hell? Because I'm well aware, thanks."

"That's not what I meant. You sounded tired on the phone."

"I was out till four at an arson scene. By the time I scrubbed the stench off my skin and fell into bed, it was getting light out." She looked him over as he pulled out of her neighborhood. He wore jeans and a pair of sneakers that were obviously well broken in. "Where are we going, anyway?"

"You'll see."

"I wore my Nikes, like you said, but if you're planning to get me out on a hiking trail, think again. I'm not a hiker. On three hours of sleep, I'm barely a walker."

"I think you can handle this."

Maddie wasn't so sure. His cagey attitude didn't put her at ease. Ditto his weekend attire. In a T-shirt, faded Levi's, and a baseball cap, he seemed even younger than his twenty-eight years, and the two-day stubble darkening his jaw added a whole new layer of sex appeal to his usual badass-agent look. Her gaze went to his big, capable hands on the steering wheel, and she had to turn her eyes away.

Why had she picked up the call this morning? She definitely knew better, but when she'd seen the words US GOV on her caller ID, she'd grabbed the phone like an eager teenager.

She took another swig of coffee in an effort to distract herself. "What about you?" she asked. "Did you have to work late?"

"Not too bad. Got home around midnight." He swung onto the frontage road, and she wondered again where they were headed.

"Midnight on a Friday." She shook her head. "Does anyone on your team ever get any R and R?"

"We've been pretty buried. Lately, batting practice once a week is about it for me."

"Batting practice?" She glanced around, alarmed. Sure enough, she spotted the sign for Grand Slam up ahead on the right.

"Thought we'd squeeze in a few hits, maybe get some breakfast."

"We?"

"Don't worry, I'm a member here. I called and reserved a cage."

"That's not what I'm worried about. It's been a decade or so since I swung a bat, and—" She gaped at him as he pulled into the parking lot. "Oh, my Lord, you're serious?"

"As a heart attack." He slipped into a space and cut the engine. "They have softball, too. Or we can do combination."

"Feel free to do whatever you like. I'll watch." She collected her coffee and hopped out of the truck.

He smiled smugly as he reached into the back of his pickup and grabbed a wooden bat. No mitt, so she hoped he wasn't actually planning to *pitch* the balls. Or have her pitch. He led her to the front, where a steady stream of dads and sons was flowing into the place. Brian bypassed the line at the front counter and led her through a video arcade to a pair of glass doors. Her eyes didn't even have time to adjust before they were outside again in the crisp winter air.

"Perfect day," he said cheerfully. "Sunny. No wind." He took his wallet out and used a plastic passcard to swipe his way into the area with the batting cages. "They have pitching machines. I assume you want to do softball?"

Maddie eyed the row of young boys in batting helmets. She looked at Brian. "I can hit a baseball."

"You sure?" The corner of his lip twitched.

She grabbed a wooden bat from the rack mounted by the gate and tested the weight in her hands. She looked at him, and he was watching her with amusement.

"What? That thing's too long for me."

"Hey, whatever you want." He led her down the row to an empty cage with a pitching machine that was already loaded with balls. "Ladies first."

"I knew you were going to say that." She downed a sip of coffee and nestled the cup on the ground beside the gate. Brian was already up at the pitching machine making adjustments.

"We'll start slow," he said.

"Gee, thanks."

She did some quick arm stretches and prayed she wouldn't pull a muscle or something equally embarrassing. She really could not remember the last time she'd hit anything with a bat. It had probably been college, and Brian clearly did this on a regular basis. She braced for humiliation.

Maddie positioned herself beside the plate and lifted the bat. Her pulse picked up, and she took a deep breath. "Ready."

He made a final adjustment to the machine and came to stand behind her.

"Out of the way," she warned.

"I'm okay."

The ball sailed out. She swung and, to her astonishment, connected. The ball hit the netting above her head and bounced down to the ground beside her foot.

"Not bad." He scooped up the ball. "Try widening your stance."

She ignored him and focused on the next pitch. Which she completely whiffed.

"Spread your feet apart." He walked up behind her and adjusted her hips, which was a complete distraction.

She missed the next pitch, too, and turned to glare at him.

"Do you mind?"

He backed away, smiling. "Not at all."

She turned just as another pitch came at her. She let it go and calmly got into position. She bent her knees, took a deep breath, steadied her nerves. *Concentrate.*

It felt good to hold a bat in her hands. Natural, even. The ball flew out, and she reacted on pure instinct.

Thwack.

He whistled. "Nice one."

She turned to him with a grin. "It was, wasn't it?"

"You play in high school?"

She scoffed.

"I'm serious. Heads-up."

Another ball came out, and she hit a grounder. "Middle school," she said. "The Plano Pythons."

"Thought you grew up in Dallas."

"It's a suburb." She swung again and missed. "Oops. Too early."

She waited for her pitch, heard another satisfying *thwack.*

"Okay, your turn." She turned and smiled at him.

"You've got four more pitches." He reached out and caught the ball bare-handed. "Damn." He shook out his fingers and jogged over to switch off the machine.

"You're up," she insisted. "I need a coffee break."

He made some adjustments and reloaded balls.

"How fast does it go?"

"About sixty," he said. "That's what it says, anyway. I think it's more like fifty."

He picked up his bat from where it was leaning

against the gate, and Maddie watched him get into position. The muscles of his shoulders strained against his T-shirt as he choked up on the bat. He looked calm but intent as he waited for the pitch.

Thwack.

It was beautiful. *He* was beautiful. She smiled as she removed her sunglasses and tucked them into the neck of her T-shirt.

"Okay, why are you so good at this?" she asked.

He smacked another ball without missing a beat. "Our office fields a team every spring. We play against other LEAs in the area."

LEAs—that would be cop-speak for law-enforcement agencies.

"And you practice here because . . . ?"

"The place near my house holds clinics on the weekends," he said. "It's usually packed."

Another pitch. Another perfect swing. He was poetry, and she couldn't help but admire him. Just watching him gave her a warm giddiness she hadn't felt in a very long time.

"What?" He slid her a suspicious look.

He knew damn well what, but she didn't stop smiling. "Nothing."

She reached down for her coffee and took a sip as he continued hitting. This was *so* not a good idea, but she was doing it anyway. She was enjoying a carefree Saturday morning with—what had Brooke called him?—a delectable-looking lawman. And as an added bonus, he also happened to be a natural athlete. Of course he was. She doubted his talents were limited to the field—he probably excelled at all physical activities. She sighed contentedly and leaned against the gate.

For a moment, she let herself entertain the fantasy of going to bed with Brian Beckman. She imagined those muscular arms wrapped around her. She imagined clutching his body against her. She imagined his low voice whispering in her ear as he urged her on. And then she wondered what he'd say to her afterward. Would he look serious, or would he give her one of his sexy half grins? Her heart started to thud as she thought of all the things she could do to put a satisfied smile on his face.

She watched him hit a few more balls, savoring the breeze in her hair and the sun on her cheeks. It was a beautiful morning, and although she knew she looked terrible, she *felt* good, better than she should on a mere three hours of sleep.

As often happened, guilt intruded on her sunny mood. As little sleep as she'd had last night, she imagined Jolene Murphy's parents had had even less.

"So," she said, as he sent yet another ball soaring into the netting. "I've been thinking about Gillian Dawson."

He glanced back at her, his eyes serious. "You really want to talk about the case right now?" He turned and smacked another ball. Even distracted, he was spot-on.

"Isn't that why you brought me here?"

"No." He didn't look at her, and she didn't know what to say. Obviously, this wasn't a business meeting, but it wasn't a date, either. There was nothing date-like about hitting baseballs at nine in the morning.

He swung and missed, then darted a look in her direction.

"Did I break your concentration?" she asked sweetly.

He turned toward the machine. "What about Gillian Dawson?"

"I've been thinking about the case," she said as he hit a ball. "You want to hear my ideas?"

He sighed.

"What? I'm not allowed to have ideas?"

He hit a grounder.

"We've got an interagency task force devoted to this thing," he told her. "No offense, but they're not exactly looking for more input."

"The alphabet soup."

"What's your beef with law enforcement, anyway?" He glanced over his shoulder at her.

"I don't have a beef."

"Right."

"I don't. I just know that law-enforcement agencies are made up of humans. And as such, they're prone to *human* error. Even when people have good intentions, sometimes things get missed."

He hit a fly ball, and she ducked for cover.

"Sorry."

She scooted farther away. "Don't you think it's possible a civilian might have an idea every now and then?"

"Okay, what's your idea?"

"I've been thinking about the connection between Gillian and Katya."

He turned to look at her. "What connection?"

"Look out."

"That's it." He glanced at the machine, which was empty now, then back at her. "What connection?"

"That's the thing. I think there *has* to be a connection, even if we don't know what it is yet."

He watched her, neither agreeing nor disagreeing. She could tell he didn't like her involvement in the case, and she wasn't surprised. Most of the cops she knew were territorial.

"Don't you think?"

"We looked for a connection, but we've found zip," he said. "Gillian lived and died in California. Katya and her friends had never even been to that state, except for Jolene, who went to Disneyland when she was a kid. Gillian never went to Texas, as far as we can tell."

"What about cause of death?"

"Still no connection. Gillian was bludgeoned in her home. Heidi was kidnapped, tortured, and strangled."

"Okay, but what about Katya? You said she OD'd."

"Yeah?" He pulled his hat off and wiped his forehead on his shoulder.

"Do you know what she OD'd on?"

"Oxycodone. It was prescribed by her dad, something her mom was taking for back pain."

Maddie cringed. She couldn't imagine Katya's mother knowing that her own pills had been the cause of her daughter's death.

"And like I said, Gillian was bludgeoned. I don't see the connection."

"Except that DNA found at the scene of her murder happens to belong to one of Mladovic's henchmen."

"Right, but that doesn't connect Gillian to Katya or the other girls."

Maddie sighed, frustrated. "Did you check the ME's report to see if Gillian had drugs in her system?"

"She didn't."

"Any chance she had painkillers in her possession when she died?"

Brian watched her, all playfulness gone. She was on to something, she could read it in his eyes. But he seemed intent on keeping her out of the loop on this.

"Well?"

"Well, nothing. She didn't have any prescriptions—not according to her medicine cabinet and not according to her parents."

"Girls' parents aren't always the most well informed about what drugs their daughters are taking."

"What's your hang-up with this drug angle?"

She shrugged. "You brought it up."

"No, I didn't."

"You said Mladovic was being investigated for drug trafficking, among other things. He's a doctor. His daughter died of a drug overdose. Seems pretty obvious drugs are an element in these cases."

Brian muttered something and looked away.

"What?"

"You're not even supposed to know all that. I don't like you involved in this. Mladovic's dangerous."

"Well, too late."

He flashed a look at her.

"And you didn't make me involved. I was involved the moment one of his goons tried to choke the life out of me in that parking garage."

He repositioned the cap on his head. "It ever occur to you to let the police handle anything? Most women would hang back and wait for a detective to call *them*. Or maybe try to forget about it."

"I'm not most women. And like I said, people miss things. Even seasoned investigators." *Which you are not.* But she didn't say that, because she didn't think he'd appreciate the criticism.

He watched her for a long moment. She bent down and retrieved a couple of baseballs from the dirt.

"You're up again." She walked over to the pitching machine and started reloading balls. When she turned around, he had his phone pressed to his ear. Maddie hadn't heard a ring tone, so she guessed it had been set to vibrate.

His expression looked serious as he ended the call. She joined him beside the gate.

"You have to go, don't you?"

"That was Sam," he said, tucking his phone into his pocket. "And yeah, I need to go in." He rested his hands on his hips and gazed down at her, and she resisted the urge to reach up and brush her fingertips over his stubble. She should feel relieved that he had to go, but instead, she felt disappointed.

She enjoyed being with him. It had been so long since she'd really enjoyed a man, she'd forgotten how it felt. His gaze held hers, and she knew she was on slippery ground here.

"Sorry you didn't get much of a turn." He sounded genuinely sorry.

"Hey, I understand. Duty calls."

"We'll do a rain check on breakfast."

"Don't worry about it." She forced a smile. "I'm not much of a breakfast person."

Brian made a quick detour by the vending machine before joining Sam in a meeting room. He was on the phone and glanced up as Brian sank into a chair and twisted the top off a Gatorade.

"Okay, keep us posted." Sam hung up the conference-room phone and looked at him. "How's Maddie?"

"What makes you think I was with Maddie?"

"Because you look frustrated." Sam smiled and leaned back in his chair. "What, she shut you down again?"

Brian swigged his drink. One of the disadvantages to working with Sam was that he didn't miss much—meaning he was fully aware that Brian had developed a fixation on a certain Delphi Center CSI. He plunked down his bottle. Maybe *fixation* wasn't the right word, but it was definitely bothering him that she seemed dead set on ignoring his attempts to get to know her outside of work.

"She's fine," he said now, because dodging the question would only pique Sam's curiosity. He scooted his chair in. "So tell me what we got. You come up with a link?"

"Elizabeth's still working on it," Sam said. "She was here half the night looking for anything to connect this girl in California to Jolene Murphy. So far, nothing." Sam thumbed through the file in front of him. "But we did get some lab results back."

"That was fast."

"They put a rush on it. The blood in Volansky's bathroom comes back to Jolene."

Brian didn't say anything. He would have been surprised if it hadn't.

"And we sent a tool marks expert over to look at those marks on the side of the tub," Sam said. "He agreed they're from a hammer."

Brian felt sick thinking about it. "So they cuffed her under the sink so they could torture her in there."

"That's what it looks like. Thing I don't get is why."

"Because Mladovic is a sadistic shithead?"

"It's got to be more than that," Sam tapped his pen on the table. "I think he was trying to get information out of her."

"Or maybe punish her for sharing information with us," Brian said, feeling guiltier than ever. Why hadn't he fought for surveillance of this witness?

"Maybe," Sam said. "But she hadn't shared much of anything. Not yet."

"But what was she *planning* to tell us? It had to have been something important for him to risk a murder rap in order to shut her up."

They stared at each other.

"I keep coming back to the daughter," Sam said. "Maybe it had to do with Katya."

"Katya's dead."

"Maybe Jolene knew something about that. Take a look at what else we got." Sam fished a paper from the file and slid it across the table.

"What's this?" Brian studied the page. It was a copy of a color photograph showing a brown prescription bottle on what looked like a bedside table.

"Investigator who handled Katya's case e-mailed that over. That's the bottle of pills she supposedly OD'd on."

"Supposedly?"

"Her prints are on it. ME's still saying suicide. Says there were no marks on the body or any indication someone forced her to take the pills."

"Lot of ways to force someone to do something," Brian said.

"And listen to this. The pharmacy listed on that bottle? They claim they have no record of this prescription."

Brian studied the picture more closely, trying to read the address, but the photo only showed the name of the pharmacy and the first few digits of a phone number.

He looked at Sam. "Where is this place?"

"It's right by Mladovic's house, but apparently, his wife used a pharmacy in her grocery store. The obvious question is, where'd this bottle come from that has her name on it?"

"And why didn't the police notice this a year ago?" Brian shook his head with disgust. "Where's this bottle?"

"Who the hell knows? Nobody kept it. When the ME ruled the death a suicide, the cops basically washed their hands of it. Their file on this thing is a joke. We're lucky to have the photos, but that's about it in terms of physical evidence. 'Less someone plans to exhume the body and take another look."

Brian stared down at the photo as questions flooded into his head. "We're talking about a phony prescription with Mladovic's name on it." He looked at Sam.

"Could be."

"Which makes me think either he orchestrated his daughter's death or someone else did. Or maybe it really was a suicide, and the bottle was Katya's idea, to

get her dad in trouble. He'd already been in all kinds
of shit for his prescription-writing practices. She had
to know that. Maybe she set this up as a dying 'fuck
you' to her father."

"Maybe." Sam was being evasive, and Brian knew he
had another theory of what happened.

"At the very least, Mladovic had to know something
was wrong. He knows he didn't write that script,"
Brian said. "And his wife's bound to know she didn't
fill it at that pharmacy. Any normal parent would raise
a big red flag and demand a murder investigation."

"This guy's not your normal parent," Sam said. "Not
by a long stretch."

Brian stared at the picture and wondered for the
thousandth time how the hell Katya and her friends
had become tangled up in Mladovic's mess.

"So there's a very real possibility he murdered his
daughter and staged it as a suicide."

Sam nodded. "Either that—or he knows who did."

———

Goran watched his wife step out of the shower as he
zipped his pants. Maybe it was the excitement left over
from last night, but he actually found himself taking a
second look.

Sylvia was tall and blond and had had the requi-
site plastic surgery for a woman in her late forties. She
had a degree in political science and had begun their
marriage on what she perceived to be equal footing.
He liked that about her. Sylvia had opinions, and she
fought back—which was also to his liking—but she

knew the limits, and in twenty-four years of marriage, she'd never crossed them.

Except once.

After Katya's death, she'd become hysterical and threatened to go to the police with everything. Goran had promised that if she did, he would kill her.

And he didn't break his promises.

Sylvia wrapped herself in a towel. Goran scooped his Mercedes keys from the dresser and headed for the garage. His wife could wait until tonight—one of the few benefits of marriage. Goran checked his trunk to make sure his clubs had been loaded properly and slid behind the wheel. He raised the garage door and backed out of the drive, taking note of the gray Taurus parked conspicuously in front of his neighbor's house.

They were going to follow him around today, hoping to glean some sort of useful information, but as usual, they'd come up with nothing. Goran was careful. He'd learned how and when to slip through their surveillance, and these days, he did it only when absolutely necessary. Last night, for example.

Last night had been good but not perfect. Through skill and patience, he'd extracted most of what he wanted.

But not all.

If he didn't get the rest next time, he'd sworn that next visit would be his last.

Most people did. It was a fact. Because of this, he trusted no one—not his attorney, not his accountant, not his business associates, and definitely not his wife.

Goran didn't trust people; he controlled them. It was a much more reliable way to manage things.

The one thing Goran *did* trust was his product.

No matter what, no matter who, it could be relied upon to get the job done. People thought they were better than science, above chemistry. Rich people, especially, thought they could game the system. But that was because they were either too dim or too deluded to understand the nature of the beast.

Goran understood it well, from both a scientific standpoint and a personal one, which was why he never touched the stuff.

Once it had you in its clutches, it didn't let go. It would sink its teeth in and bleed you of every dollar and every drop of pride. People—no matter what their socioeconomic status—would do anything for it. They might do it in an expensive hotel room or in the back of a Lexus, but ultimately, they would do anything he wanted and pay anything he asked, because they needed what he had.

Supply and demand.

Simple as that.

Jolene was freezing.

She'd been trapped inside the tiny room for hours, with only a sweatshirt and a pile of newspapers. The wind whistled under the door, and whenever there was a big gust, she heard the walls groan and bow inward.

Jolene's hand throbbed. All her fingers were swollen and misshapen, and her thumb poked out at an impossible angle. Two of her nails were gone. Her cuticles were black and crusted with blood. Ever since the drugs had worn off, she'd kept her hand uncovered, hoping the icy air might numb the pain, but it hadn't. Her hand felt like fire.

They'd left her right hand alone. As she'd spent the last hour comparing it with the ruined one, she'd realized the reason. Contrast. They were taunting her, making her focus on the power they had over her. They were reminding her that things could still get worse, that there could be more to come.

Jolene closed her eyes and tried not to think. If she thought too much, she'd cry again. If she let her mind focus on what had happened and what was probably going to happen, she'd lose it. And they got off on that. They got off on her terror.

Her teeth chattered, and she pulled her knees in closer and thought of a song her mother used to sing.

Bye baby bunting. Daddy's gone a-hunting. To get a little rabbit skin to wrap his baby bunting in.

She shivered harder. Her eyes filled as she pictured her mom and dad. She'd made so many mistakes she was ashamed to tell them about. Over and over, she'd messed up. She'd lied. She'd done things behind their backs. But if she ever saw them again, she was going to come clean. She'd tell them everything.

God, she was sorry. She wanted to take it all back, starting with the very first lie.

Jolene's teeth chattered. She pictured her mom and could practically hear her yelling across the soccer field. *Fight for it, Jolene! You go, girl! Show 'em what you got!* The words were comforting in some absurd way, and she managed to force back the tears. She took a deep breath and rubbed the snot from her nose with her good hand.

A phone.

She needed a phone.

She had to get a message out, or they were going to kill her here in this freezing, isolated place.

How did she know that?

She sat up and leaned against the hard metal wall. She'd woken up here groggy and confused, with no memory whatsoever of the trip. They'd drugged her. So how did she know this place where they'd brought her was isolated?

The birds.

They were ones like she remembered from summer camp. She used to lie in her bunk in the mornings, listening to their calls, and so somehow she knew she was out in the country. The stinky apartment was a world away, and this building or warehouse or whatever it was was in the boondocks.

There, she'd figured something out. She leaned her head back against the wall, faintly encouraged by the fact that her mind could function after everything that had happened.

She needed to escape. Or get her hands on a phone. They'd probably kill her if she tried to do either.

But they were going to kill her anyway. She knew it deep down in her bones. They would rape her and torture her and question her some more, and then they'd kill her—just like they had killed Heidi.

She felt a wave of nausea and tucked her head between her knees. *Please, no more questions.* She didn't want to talk about her friends or where they lived or how to get in touch with them. She'd managed to make stuff up, but sooner or later, they'd find out she was lying, and they'd be back for the truth, even though she didn't know it. They were desperate. Had to be. Why else would they keep asking the same questions, over and over?

She bit her lip. It felt dry and cracked. Never in her life had she been so thirsty.

Think.

The bald one—Anatoli—had her phone. He'd taken it from her purse after they'd stuffed her into the SUV. She'd been too shocked even to grasp what was happening.

He'd removed the battery and put it in his pocket.

Was it still there?

And what about *his* phone? He kept it on him—he had to. He was on it all the time, talking to people in that fast, guttural language she didn't understand.

Noise outside the door. Jolene's head jerked up. She stared at the band of light and held her breath.

In the distance, the sound of an engine. Moment by moment, the noise grew louder. She squeezed her eyes shut. Her heart started to race. She hugged her knees to her chest and prayed.

CHAPTER 10

The sound of Maddie's heels echoed down the underground corridor as she walked to the ballistics lab. She waved at Scott through the glass, and he stepped over to open the door.

"Sorry I'm late."

"We got started without you." He looked her up and down as she tossed her coat onto a chair. "Where you been?"

"Court," she said, explaining the fitted gray skirt and high heels—not her usual work attire. She spotted Brian on the other side of the room, standing at a counter and peering into a microscope. She looked at Scott. "So you got something?"

"Go see for yourself."

Brian's gaze met hers as she crossed the laboratory, and she gave him a brief nod before stepping up to the microscope and looking through the lens. On the stage was a spent shell casing.

"This is the one I gave you?" she asked.

"Yep."

Then she looked at his nearby computer monitor,

which displayed an image of a shell with identical markings. According to the notation, the photo showed the shell magnified to ten times its actual size. She studied the image. Whoever had taken the picture knew what he was doing and had used axial lighting to illuminate the casing's details adequately. Maddie wasn't a ballistics expert, but she'd done enough macrophotography of shell casings to know they had a match.

"Where'd this come from?" she asked Scott.

"Los Angeles. It was recovered from the scene of a nightclub shooting."

"When?"

"May eighth of last year," Brian put in.

Her eyes widened. "The weekend Gillian Dawson was killed."

"Who's Gillian Dawson?" Scott wanted to know.

"A college student at USC who was murdered last spring." Maddie looked at Brian. "This shooting, do you know if it was a homicide or—"

"No fatalities," Scott said. "I already talked to the lead investigator. Sounds like a dispute over a stripper who was getting off work. Couple of shots exchanged in the parking lot. Both parties took off."

"I'm going to need that detective's contact info," Brian told him.

"I've got some questions first." Scott looked at Maddie, clearly not happy to be taking orders from a fed. "Where'd you get this brass you brought me?"

She leaned back against the counter. "You hear about the shooting Thursday night over at the movie theater?"

"Some cop dodged a bullet." He looked at Brian.

"*You're* the cop? I didn't hear the FBI was involved."

"We're trying to keep a low profile. It's a sensitive investigation." Brian looked at Maddie. "This adds another link between Gillian's murder and Volansky, but it's still circumstantial. We don't have proof he's the one who fired the gun."

"You need a weapon to match it to," Scott said. "Can you guys get a search warrant?"

"Even if they could, no one knows where he is." Maddie's phone chimed from her coat pocket across the room. She walked over to check it and recognized the number of a prosecutor who'd been hounding her all day for a batch of crime-scene pictures.

"I've got to run upstairs to see about something." She looked at Brian. "You okay to see yourself out? I'll call you later to talk about the case."

He gave her a nod, and Maddie hurried up to her office. She sent out the file and then answered a few of the e-mails that had piled up while she'd been in court all afternoon. Then she loaded her computer bag and headed down to the parking lot, where she spotted Brian waiting for her. Butterflies flitted to life in her stomach, even though she'd half expected him.

He was leaning against her car and talking on his phone, and he didn't take his eyes off her as she crossed the asphalt at a brisk clip. When she stopped in front of him, he ended the call.

"What are you doing now?" he asked.

A cold gust whipped against her legs, and she hugged her coat around her. "Going home."

"How 'bout dinner?"

"I've got work tonight."

"So do I."

She gazed up at him, wondering how he could look so totally relaxed while getting the brush-off. Again.

She suspected it had to do with his underlying certainty that sooner or later, she'd give in—that whole confidence thing again.

"I'm behind on paperwork," she said.

"Girl's gotta eat."

He stepped closer and picked up the end of her scarf. He stroked the wool between his thumb and forefinger. A little jolt of heat zinged through her.

His gaze met hers. "Just dinner." His voice was low and warm, and she didn't believe for a minute that all he wanted was dinner. He eased closer. "I promise not to do anything you don't like."

Maddie gazed up at him and resisted the urge to fall into all that solid warmth that was only inches away. She wanted to. Maybe she should let herself. Maybe for once, she should stop worrying about the consequences and simply enjoy something. A fling. Was serious Madeline Callahan even capable of a fling anymore? She honestly didn't know.

He tugged the scarf, and she leaned closer, tipping her head back to look at him. Those hazel eyes were dark now, almost black. She could read the look on his face, and it made her pulse pound.

A phone buzzed, and she jumped back.

He pulled it from his pocket. "Beckman." Pause. "I'm at the Delphi Center. Why?" His annoyed expression morphed into alarm. "*Jolene's* phone—you're sure?"

EXPOSED   151

Maddie tensed. God, they'd found her. She was in a ditch somewhere—

"Highway 84. Where is it?"

It took her a moment to realize the urgent words were directed at her.

"It's—" Her mind whirled. "It's north of here. Why?"

"I'm on my way," he said into the phone. "Text me the coordinates." He clicked off and jerked some keys from his pocket. "That was Sam. Nine-one-one just got a call from Jolene's cell phone."

She stood perfectly still as the words sank in.

"Come on." He moved toward his car. "Get me to this highway."

CHAPTER 11

"Slow down. We're almost there." Maddie gripped the door handle as he took a curve.

"How far?"

She consulted the screen on his phone. Sam had texted some GPS coordinates, and instead of trying to figure out the car's navigation system, she'd simply clicked open a map on his cell phone.

"Looks like about three miles? Maybe four." She glanced around, searching for familiar landmarks. There weren't many around. It was mostly arid ranchland dotted with scrub brush. She recalled an intersection up ahead where she'd once worked a traffic fatality. She remembered a quarry, too, but that had to be at least ten miles west.

"This is an estimate," Brian reminded her. "It doesn't tell us the exact location, just the cell tower."

"Can't they triangulate it or something?"

"The phone went dead. Or someone killed it. Dispatch said they heard 'labored breathing' and then nothing."

Maddie gripped the door handle. Jolene was alive.

Was alive. But what if someone had caught her calling for help?

Or maybe it hadn't been her at all but someone using her phone.

Maddie's heart raced. Her stomach churned. It made her sick to think that Jolene might have survived all this time and they might still be too late.

"'Labored breathing' doesn't sound good," she said tightly.

His gaze remained intent on the narrow highway, where yellow stripes stretched endlessly in front of them. Maddie glanced at the phone in her hand. Sam was on his way, and so was a local sheriff's unit. The FBI was bringing a canine team to help with the search, but in the meantime, it was just her and Brian speeding down a lonely stretch of highway.

"Look around," he ordered. "Tell me if you see anything. Farmhouses, outhouses, deer blinds, anything."

She searched the roadside, but all she saw was a rugged landscape, dimly lit by the crescent moon overhead.

"Mailbox," she said.

He slowed abruptly, and she pointed to a tin mailbox attached to a wooden post. They passed a dirt road that wasn't labeled—probably a private drive—and Maddie craned her neck, looking for any sign of light beyond the trees. Nothing but blackness.

"Think we should go back?" She looked at him.

"How much farther?"

She glanced at the phone. "Maybe a mile? But you said it's an estimate, so—"

"Sign." He jabbed the brakes, and they skidded to a halt. She spotted the weathered wooden sign on her side of the road, but it was too dark to read. Brian threw the car into reverse and backed up so the headlights would illuminate the faded lettering.

"Eversole Tanning and Taxidermy," she recited. From the sign's condition, she guessed the business was long since dead. "There's probably still a building there, at least."

Brian looked around.

"An abandoned business wouldn't be a bad place to hide someone." She glanced at the sign again and the word *taxidermy* gave her a chill.

"Gate's open," he said.

Maddie looked. A rusted metal gate spanning the dirt road was ajar. A chain and padlock dangled from the metal fencepost.

Without a word, he pulled off the road and slid the car between some cedar trees.

"You're parking *here*?"

"Probably don't want to go racing up the road with the lights blazing." He cut the engine but left the keys in. He looked across the car at her, and the lights of the dashboard cast his face in a greenish glow. That intensity was back. He believed this was it.

"Are you going to wait for backup?"

He didn't answer, and she didn't bother to argue. Anyway, she agreed with him. If Jolene was alive, they had no time to waste.

"Where's your pistol?" he asked, glancing down at her purse.

"In my nightstand at home."

He got out and quietly popped the trunk. The car barely shifted when he closed it again.

He returned with a shotgun, and Maddie watched as he rested it on the console with the barrel pointed at the dash.

"It's loaded," he said.

Maddie's pulse spiked as he pulled the Glock from his holster and checked the clip. He looked out the back window at the empty road.

"We may not even be in the right place," he muttered.

"But you think we are."

"Not a lot out here. I think we should check." He plucked her phone from the cupholder. "I'll take your cell. Use mine to call Sam, give him an update."

"Keep it on vibrate." Maddie took the phone from his hand, switched off the ringer, and handed it back. She felt the urge to say something, but when she looked in his eyes, her mind went blank.

"Be careful," he said, pushing open the door.

"Wait!" She grabbed his arm. "Are you sure—"

"Maddie, I'm not sure of anything. But I need to go check this."

She felt a rush of panic. Tears stung her eyes. She pulled him close and quickly kissed him on the mouth. "You be careful, too."

————

Brian made his steps silent as he moved over the terrain. He stayed near the road, but not on it, as he eased deeper into the property. A large shadow loomed ahead, and judging by its right angles, he guessed it was the old tannery.

Or it could be a house. A dog might start barking, and some angry rancher might come out pointing a shotgun at him.

He paused to listen. No dogs. No cars. All was quiet except for the rustle of wind through the trees.

Quiet but not silent.

They were two different things, as he'd learned in Afghanistan during bitter-cold nights on patrol in the Hindu Kush. So many nights, he'd stared into the blackness around the remote outpost. He'd clutched his M-4 with frozen fingers, sensing more than hearing the enemy in the surrounding mountains. It had been quiet then, too—but not silent—and sometimes only the softest sound of a missed footstep or a falling rock tipped him off to the enemy's presence.

He peered into the gloom now. With almost no light to help him, he squinted his eyes and tried to pick up even the slightest movement with his peripheral vision.

Nothing.

Gripping his Glock, he moved closer to the structure. Twenty paces. Thirty. Forty. When his feet went from uneven dirt to smooth concrete, he changed directions and started walking the building's perimeter.

He eased around the first corner. On the building's western face was a metal door, the type that could be raised or lowered on a track. He noted the six-inch gap at the bottom and crouched beside it.

In the dimness, he spotted the muddy tire tracks on the concrete. His fingers itched for his flashlight, but he left it in his pocket. He studied the tracks. The last rain had been eight days ago. A downpour. Someone had been here within the past week.

He stood and glanced around, skimming his gaze over the shadowy bushes nearby.

He retraced his steps. He avoided the gap under the door in case someone was watching from inside. He crept to the other end of the building and eased around the corner. Another door, but this one was raised completely.

Brian eased closer. He stared into the yawning blackness. A peculiar smell reached him, and he went stockstill as he tried to place it.

A sound—so faint he might have imagined it. He lifted his gun. The wind picked up, and he heard a dull thud as the building's metal walls shifted. Then the gust died down, and Brian listened intently.

Shoes on pavement. He crouched low and slipped inside the building.

———

Maddie stared at the gun beside her. She looked out the window. She hadn't heard a noise from any direction, and she was starting to get worried.

The phone rattled in the cupholder, sending her heart rate into overdrive as she snatched it up.

"Yes?"

"Hey, it's Sam. He's not back yet?"

"Not yet."

"We're on our way, probably ten minutes out. How's it looking there?"

"Dark." She glanced around and felt that clutch of panic again. Because of the foliage, her only visibility was out the rear window, and she hadn't even seen a car pass. "There's not much out here. It's pretty deserted."

"Sit tight, okay? And call me if you see anything."

"I will."

Maddie tucked the phone into her pocket and looked at the shotgun, trying to calm down. She'd never been scared of guns. Her father had taken her hunting with him when she was a kid, so she was familiar with how to handle them. But she didn't shoot regularly, and she'd never in her life fired a weapon in self-defense.

She checked the rear window again. A flicker of light on the road.

Her imagination?

No, it was a car. Her pulse skittered as the trees lining the highway brightened in the approaching headlights.

She pulled the gun across her lap. Would the car speed past or slow down?

What if it turned onto the dirt driveway and someone spotted her?

On impulse, she shoved open the door and squeezed out of the car. Batting away branches with one hand and clutching the gun in the other, she used her hip to shut the door. The road brightened as the engine noise drew closer.

Maddie ducked into the bushes. She pushed her way through the leaves and branches until her fingers encountered the barbed-wire fence on the property's perimeter.

The car slowed. Her heart pounded. They weren't speeding past, but stopping. She peered through the bushes and looked for Brian. Why wasn't he back yet?

And was he close enough to hear that they had company?

She tucked the stock under her arm and pulled out the phone to text him one-handed: *Car coming.* As she pressed send, the bushes became whiter and whiter, until they looked covered in snow. Her stomach knotted with dread as she tucked away the phone and the vehicle rolled to a stop a scant ten yards shy of her hiding spot.

Maddie lifted the shotgun. She used the barrel to nudge a branch aside, giving her a clear view of the roadway. The SUV was pulled over now, engine idling.

Waiting for someone?

She cast a frantic look over her shoulder. Had Brian heard the approach? The ten minutes he'd been gone seemed like an hour.

A door squeaked open. Maddie whipped her head back around. The interior light was on now. Two men sat in front. They were big and bulky, and one had a cell phone pressed to his ear.

Maddie held her breath. She watched them. She tried to memorize their faces, their clothes, any distinguishing features she might later give to police. She shifted position for a better view, but then the door slammed shut, and tires squealed as they sped away.

Her breath whooshed out. She glanced over her shoulder. Through the branches, she saw a light flickering . . .

Fire.

Fear zinged through her. She stumbled from her hiding place. Over the treetops, flames licked up into the night sky.

"Brian!" She put down the shotgun and ducked

through the fence, snagging her hair. She yanked it loose and pulled herself through the barbed wire, then darted through a clump of cedar trees. She reached a clearing and saw a warehouse engulfed in flames.

"Brian!"

An explosion knocked her on her butt. Pain shot up her tailbone. She pushed herself up and gazed, stunned, at the flames and smoke billowing into the sky.

Maddie scrambled to her feet and raced for the building, tripping and stumbling as she went.

"Brian!" Her voice was shrill with panic. She halted and looked around desperately. Dear God, was he *inside*?

Smoke stung her eyes as she raced around the building, searching for a way in. It was stupid—she knew that—but she had to try.

Something clamped her arm and whirled her around.

"Are you okay?" Brian demanded.

She stood there, paralyzed with shock. The fire cast his face in an orange glow. He was dirty and sweaty and *bleeding*, but her relief at seeing him was so intense she couldn't breathe.

"I thought you were *in there*!" She threw her arms around him and squeezed.

"Hey. *Hey*."

Tears burned her eyes. Her lungs hurt. She felt dizzy and confused and terrified right down to her toes.

"Maddie."

She couldn't let go. She clung as tightly as she could, scared he was somehow going to vanish into the flames and smoke.

"Maddie, look at me." He took her by the shoulders and eased her away from him. "Are you hurt?"

She shook her head, unable to talk now because of the rock-hard lump in her throat.

"Say something, damn it."

"I'm fine." She stepped back from him, glanced at the fire, and felt a surge of fear all over again. "I thought—" She couldn't even say it. What if it had been real? People always thought the worst couldn't happen, but it *could*. It *did*.

He turned to stare at the fire, and she took a moment to compose herself. Her palms were bleeding. She wiped them on the front of her coat.

"Chemicals."

She blinked at him. "What?"

"Couple of big metal drums. I saw them inside. We shouldn't stand so close—who knows how many might be in there."

He tugged her back toward the road. The clearing was illuminated by the glow of the fire, and she realized that in her mad dash, she'd covered quite a distance.

He stopped suddenly. "Hear that?"

"What?" But even as she said it, she heard.

Sirens. They were getting louder.

"Come on." He grabbed her by the elbow, and they jogged toward the noise. As they reached the road, a gray sedan plowed through the gate, flinging it back against a tree stump. Sam jumped out of the passenger's side.

"Holy shit, Beck, what happened?" He rushed over and looked at Maddie. "She okay?" His gaze went to Brian.

"I'm fine," she said as a trio of police vehicles arrived on the scene—two sheriff's units and what looked like another FBI car.

"He torched the place."

"Who?" Maddie and Sam asked in unison.

"Mladovic."

"You saw him?" Sam asked.

"Not him, one of his guys."

"What about Jolene?" Maddie touched his arm. "Did you see her in there?"

"No."

"But did you see any evidence—"

"No," he repeated, and the sharpness of his tone made her think the exact opposite—that he *had* seen something.

"I smelled gasoline when I first walked up," Brian said. "And something else—whatever chemicals were stored in there. Then the place went up."

"*While* you were inside?" Sam asked.

Maddie felt sick all over again.

"We need to go after him," Brian said. "I didn't see where he was parked, but   "

"*Them,*" Maddie corrected. "There were two men in front. Looked like they were waiting for someone, and then they took off."

"Which way?" Sam demanded.

"East." She looked at her watch. "But that was at least ten minutes ago. By now, they're long gone."

"We need to try. Or we could set up a roadblock."

Sam shook his head. "They're probably in another county by now, but I could put out an APB." He looked at Maddie. "You get a license plate?"

"Just a description." Guilt stabbed at her. She should have tried harder to get a plate. "It was a gray SUV, midsize, chrome running boards."

Sam jogged off toward his car, probably to call it in on the radio. Maddie looked at Brian. The cut above his eye trickled blood, and she once again felt the tight grip of fear that made it difficult to breathe.

He whipped out his phone and started dialing someone.

"Are you really all right?" she asked.

"I'm fine."

"What did you see in there?"

He shook his head once, sharply, confirming that he *had* seen something but he wanted her to drop it.

"Hey, it's Beckman." He looked over his shoulder at the blaze behind him. "I need an evidence response team out on Highway 84, north of Route 12." He paused to listen, and then pressed the phone against his chest. "Hey!" he called across the driveway. "What's the ETA on that fire and rescue squad?"

Sam looked up from his conversation with another agent, who was also on the phone. At least, Maddie assumed she was an agent. The blond woman looked about Brian's age and had on one of those FBI jackets like Maddie had been wearing the other night.

"Fire and rescue's been diverted," Sam shouted. "They're responding to a car fire west of here. Someone's trapped in a vehicle."

A *car* fire? Maddie's stomach knotted as she thought of Jolene.

"*West?*" Brian looked at Maddie. "But you said they went east. You're sure about the direction?"

"I'm sure. Sam, are you talking rescue or recovery?"

"Don't know."

"Let's go," Brian said. "We need to find out."

———————

The sight of Kelsey's white Suburban parked beside the fire rig confirmed Maddie's worst fears. Road flares and cones marked off the accident scene, reducing the highway to one lane near the blackened wreckage.

Brian rolled to a stop behind the line of emergency vehicles, and they trekked over the asphalt to the smoldering car that was nose-first in a ditch. Smoke and fumes burned Maddie's nostrils. She gripped her camera strap and braced herself for the sight.

Kelsey was crouched at the back of the vehicle, and Maddie could feel the heat emanating from it as they drew closer.

"How'd you get here so fast?" Maddie asked.

Kelsey glanced up from her work. She wore the same clothes she'd had on earlier at the Delphi Center—jeans and a cable-knit sweater but she'd traded her lab coat for a green ski vest.

"I was on Twelve driving home when the sheriff called." She glanced at Brian, and her gaze turned suspicious. "Who are you?"

"I'm with the FBI. What can you tell us?"

Kelsey seemed to ignore the question as she stood up and made notes on her clipboard with a gloved hand. After a moment, she glanced up.

"Nothing yet. The burns are too severe from all the gasoline."

Maddie hazarded a look inside the car. A charred skeleton lay curled in the fetal position on the backseat. The stench of burning flesh and gasoline made her take a step back.

"Hey, Maddie!"

She glanced down the road to see Sheriff Bracewell waving her over.

"Come get a picture of this gas can, would you?"

She started to move, but Brian caught her arm. "Hold up. This isn't your crime scene."

Before she could argue, another car pulled up. Sam and the blond agent got out. Probably sensing a territory dispute, Bracewell abandoned the gas can and stalked over to Brian.

"Who are you?" he demanded.

Brian flashed his badge. "Special Agent Brian Beckman, FBI. We've got an evidence response team en route to this location."

The sheriff's gaze narrowed. "On what grounds?"

"Trust me, you don't want this one," Sam said, sauntering over.

"Who the hell are you?"

Forgoing the badge, Sam held out a hand and introduced himself. Then he turned to look at the smoldering vehicle.

"This is a budget buster. Ditto the factory fire down the road there." Sam had dropped the Maryland accent and was channeling Texas good ol' boy. "Lotta man-hours involved. You're best off letting us pay for it."

"What's all this about?" Bracewell demanded, and Maddie held her breath, hoping Sam wasn't clueless enough to give a glib answer. If he tried to pull a sorry-I-can't-comment-on-a-federal-investigation, Bracewell would take it as a declaration of war. His ego far outweighed his budget concerns.

But Sam pulled him aside to talk, and Maddie returned her attention to Kelsey.

"I take it you're the ME?" Brian asked her.

"Forensic anthropologist."

"And this is your autopsy?"

"Afraid so." Kelsey held the clipboard against her chest.

"And you've already determined there was gasoline involved in this fire?"

"Quite a lot, I'd say, judging from the damage." Kelsey nodded at the car. "Looks like the victim was doused."

"How long until we get an ID?"

Kelsey looked him up and down. She walked to the front of the car, which was significantly less damaged than the back. Not touching the hot metal door, she peered through the broken side window, then stood back and shook her head.

"No purse or wallet, front or back," she said. "Too hot to check the glove compartment yet, but someone removed the plates. I don't have a lot to go on here."

"What about the body?"

"I can get you the big four by tomorrow."

"Big four?"

"Race, sex, age, stature," Kelsey said. "Anything more specific is going to require more time."

Maddie listened to the conversation as she edged

closer to the driver's door and looked inside. She adjusted her flash settings and lifted her camera to get a photograph of the dashboard.

"Vehicle identification number," she explained at Brian's questioning look. "No tags, no ID, but at least you can get started on the VIN."

"Good idea." He turned to Kelsey. "And we're definitely going to need more than the big four. We need to know who this is. How soon for a positive ID?"

"Depends. If I have dental records, it's faster. If not, I'll need to extract tooth pulp, maybe even bone marrow." She glanced at Maddie, clearly concerned. "Why? Who do you *think* it is?"

Maddie opened her mouth to respond, but the words seemed to get stuck in her throat.

"A missing woman," Brian said for her. "She's a witness in a federal investigation."

"This the kidnapping I heard about?" Kelsey glanced over, and Maddie nodded. Her friend knew this case related to her personally. "And do you have a DNA sample?" Kelsey asked Brian.

"I can get one."

"Do that," Kelsey told him. "Send it to Delphi, and I'll work as fast as I can."

CHAPTER 12

Maddie stepped out of the concrete building and tipped her head back to look at the sky. The night was cold and cloudy. She took a big gulp of air and let it sit in her lungs to wake her up. She had a thirty-minute drive ahead of her, and she needed to get it over with before her emotions kicked in and sapped what was left of her energy.

It had been a grueling night. After spending more than an hour at the fire scene, Brian had taken her to Delphi to pick up her car. Then she'd followed him back to the FBI office to debrief with the task force and look at mug shots.

"You finish up in there?"

She turned to see the female agent she'd met at the vehicle fire—LeBlanc.

"They showed me a photo array," Maddie said. "I picked out one of them."

The woman strolled over, tucking her hands into the pockets of her jacket. In khaki tactical pants and an FBI golf shirt, she looked more casual than Brian and Sam.

"One's better than none," the woman said. "Did you hear about the VIN you photographed for us?"

"No." Maddie could tell by her tone of voice that it wasn't good news.

"Vehicle traces back to Anatoli Petrovik, a known associate of Goran Mladovic. Same man you picked out from the lineup, the one in the SUV."

Which meant a clear connection between Mladovic's crew and the burn victim. Maddie closed her eyes. She'd known it anyway, but hearing it confirmed just added to her bleak mood.

"It's a mess of a case," the agent said.

Maddie looked at her. "Sorry, I never caught your first name."

"Elizabeth. Or you can call me LeBlanc, like everyone else." She glanced out over the parking lot. "Team's going to grab a drink now over at Blackjack's Pub. You want to join us?"

Maddie watched her, instantly on guard. Was there a hidden agenda here? An invitation to get a beer with everyone implied that she considered Maddie part of the investigation, as opposed to a civilian witness. Brian had seemed intent on keeping her in the latter category—and controlling the information flow. Despite being unsure of her motive, Maddie was flattered to be asked.

But drinks with the team would include Brian, and that probably wasn't smart. It was getting late.

"Thanks," Maddie said, "but I really should get home."

"Hey, you coming to Blackjack's?"

She turned to see Sam pushing through the glass door.

"She's on the fence," Elizabeth said.

"You know, Beckman took off already." He gave Maddie a knowing smile. "Coast is clear. Come on, have a beer with us."

Maddie felt her resolve slipping. She didn't want to go home to her empty house and her empty bed and her thoughts of those charred remains in the back of that car. She hadn't even taken the crime-scene photos this time, and yet the brief glimpse was seared in her memory.

That was what happened when she allowed herself to develop a personal connection to a case. It was going to be a long, sleepless night—despite her exhaustion—and she wasn't ready for it yet.

A beer sounded tempting, the company even more so. After a bad crime scene, cops were the only people she could stand to be around. They'd seen the same horrors she had, and there was an underlying comfort level, because they didn't pry or push or show the slightest hint of lurid curiosity about her job.

"Come on," Sam said again.

Maddie looked down at her wool coat, which had blood smudges on the front. Her blouse was wrinkled, and her hair was falling out of the neat chignon she'd worn to trial that morning.

"You look fine," Elizabeth said, reading her mind.

"I don't even know where I'm going."

"That's easy." Sam smiled. "Follow me."

———

Brian stepped into the crowded bar and scanned the room, fully expecting to be disappointed. But she was there, sitting at a corner table with Sam and Elizabeth and a few others from the task force. When he'd seen the white Prius outside, he'd thought there was no way in hell he could get that lucky.

He eased through the crowd, reaching the table just as they all scooted their chairs back and stood to leave.

"Hey, look who's here," Elizabeth said, prompting a chorus of greetings from everyone but Maddie.

Sam slapped him on the back. "Damn, Beck, you got stitches? This calls for another round."

"Sorry, not for me," Elizabeth said. "I need to get home."

The others echoed the thought and shrugged into coats. It was late. They had to work in the morning.

Brian made his way over to Maddie. She fisted her hand on her hip and glared up at him, and he felt a warm shot of lust.

"Don't leave," he said.

"You didn't tell me you were going to the ER! I could have driven you."

He sent Sam a look as the rest of the group headed for the door. A trio of women claimed the table, and Brian saw the panic flit across Maddie's face as she realized she was about to be left alone with him.

"Second thought, I better call it a night." Sam squeezed Maddie's shoulder. "Thanks for hanging out, Maddie."

"Thanks for inviting me."

She watched him leave, and then she turned to face Brian, clearly pissed off.

"How come you didn't tell me you needed stitches?"

"Let me buy you a drink."

She checked her watch. "It's late."

"One drink, Maddie. Come on, I just got here."

She looked conflicted. She didn't like being talked into things, which, ironically, made him more determined to try. Before she could think up another excuse, he took her hand and led her to the bar.

"What are you drinking? Cape Cod?"

"I'll have a Sprite."

He gave her a look, and she sighed.

"What are you having?"

"Bourbon."

"Fine, I'll have a bourbon and Coke," she said. "Make it a diet."

Brian refrained from criticizing her drink choice as he flagged a bartender. When he turned around again, she was chatting up a middle-aged man a few stools over. She smiled up at him as he offered her an empty stool.

Brian brought the drinks over. "Nice going. I didn't know you could bat your eyelashes like that."

She ignored the comment as he handed over the glass and squeezed into the place beside her. It was crowded, but he didn't mind leaning against the bar and looking down at her. She'd left her coat somewhere, and he was finally able to get a better look at the silky white blouse he'd first noticed back at the ballistics lab.

She took a sip and rested her glass on the counter. "How many?" she asked.

"How many what?"

She rolled her eyes. "Stitches."

"Six. It's no big deal.

She shook her head.

"So what's the word on the case? You guys were talking about it, right?"

"Part of the time. But then we got sidetracked with Daryl's football stories."

Of course they had. The veteran agent's glory days as a tight end for LSU were one of his favorite topics of conversation, especially if there were any women around. Elizabeth was immune to him, but he probably saw Maddie as fresh meat.

"Don't get too impressed," Brian said. "He tends to exaggerate."

"*Really?* Now, isn't that interesting."

"Why?"

"Because he went on and on about what a great agent you are. 'Best rookie they've ever sent us,' I think were his exact words."

"Huh." Brian swilled his drink, feeling guilty now that he'd insulted the guy.

On the other hand, Daryl had about three ex-wives and a reputation for using his badge to seduce women.

"Sam was singing your praises, too. They seemed intent on impressing me." She gazed up at him suspiciously. "So I have a question for you—and I want an honest answer."

He rested his drink beside hers and waited.

"Did you coordinate this?"

"This what?"

"Inviting me here."

He smiled. "Maddie, I've been in the ER for two hours. I didn't even know you were here until five minutes ago."

Which didn't really answer her question. He'd told

Sam he planned to stop by later, so she was right in sensing that this was a setup.

The woman behind him got up, and Brian claimed her vacated stool. He looked at Maddie, but she still didn't seem convinced.

"How long have you been here?" he asked.

"About an hour." She stirred her drink with a little red straw and looked up at him. Her gaze went to his temple, where he'd caught a shard of debris when the warehouse exploded. Something flickered in her eyes. Sadness? Worry? He couldn't tell.

He leaned closer. "You all right?"

She lifted a shoulder.

He looked down and noticed her hand in her lap. Her left wrist was scraped. There was a smudge of dirt on her cuff, and he realized that, unlike him, she hadn't really had a chance to pull herself together yet.

She watched him watching her. "What?"

"It's been a long day."

Her expression turned solemn. "I'm sorry about Jolene."

He looked at her for a long moment. "I'm sorry, too."

"Your friends think you're being too hard on yourself."

He gazed down at his drink, then up at her. He didn't want to talk about the case all night. He especially didn't want to talk about what a great agent he was and how he was being too hard on himself.

Jolene had been *his* witness. He should have protected her. He pictured her burned remains and got a knot of anger in his gut. He no longer wanted to arrest Mladovic—he wanted to make him pay for what he'd done, or ordered done, to those girls. This case was personal now.

Brian looked at Maddie, with her soft hair and her silky blouse and her feminine hands that were all scraped up—probably from tripping around in the dark tonight while he'd been chasing after a suspect.

He remembered her reaction when she'd thought he was trapped in that fire. She'd totally lost it. He'd practically had to peel her off of him.

This woman was a mix of contradictions—tough one minute, vulnerable the next. Sometimes she seemed happy to be with him; other times, she made excuses to leave. Brian didn't get it. He *knew* she was attracted to him, and yet she kept putting up roadblocks.

"You're a puzzle, Maddie."

She eyed him warily and picked up her glass. For a while, they drank in silence, as the energy of the crowded bar swirled around them. Brian shifted on his stool, and their knees brushed, but she pretended not to notice. He watched her trace the condensation on her glass with the tip of her finger. He remembered what she'd said about paying attention to how people touched things. He'd been doing it ever since their conversation.

He tipped back his drink, watching her, and plunked it onto the bar.

"Why'd you get into this, anyway?"

She looked surprised. "You mean my job?"

"Yeah."

He looked at her eyes as she thought about what to say. Maybe it was the booze kicking in, but she seemed pensive now, maybe a little more relaxed. "I don't know, really."

"Yeah, you do."

"I guess . . ." She stirred her ice cubes. "I guess probably for the same reason you did. I think people should be held accountable."

She didn't look at him, but he studied her face.

"This is about your daughter."

Her gaze lifted.

"The person who killed Emma, was he held accountable?"

She shook her head, just once, and the look in her eyes was so raw he almost turned away. But hell, he'd brought it up.

He leaned closer. "I'm sorry," he said, knowing how fucking inadequate that was.

"Thank you." She picked up the skinny red straw and poked at her ice cubes some more. "How did you know about that?"

"Call it a guess."

Seconds ticked by as he watched her.

"It was a hit-and-run." She cleared her throat. "We'd been at the park playing, and I was parallel parked on the street. I'd just buckled Emma into her car seat and was pulling out when someone took a corner too fast and T-boned us." She glanced up at him. "The damage was on Emma's side. We rushed her to the hospital—"

"We?"

"The ambulance. She slipped into a coma. Never woke up."

"Jesus, Maddie."

The bartender stopped by, and Brian ordered another round. She didn't object.

He watched her, waiting to see if she'd keep going.

He didn't want to interrogate her. He just wanted to listen. The look on her face put a familiar ache in his chest. He'd seen death in combat, including one of his closest friends. It wasn't the same as losing a child—he got that—but the loss had changed him.

"I was in a funk for a long time." She turned her glass on the bar. "My marriage fell apart. I didn't give a shit about anything. Some days, I wanted to disappear. Other days, I was so furious with the world I wanted to kill someone." She shook her head. "I couldn't sleep. I was having panic attacks."

"That still happening?"

She glanced up, and he thought maybe he'd embarrassed her. "It's probably been years." She paused. "I've got my life together now, mostly. But it never goes away."

Their drinks came, and she took a big sip.

"And the police?"

She shook her head. "They never found him. Or her. My own child, and I don't even know. Isn't that pathetic?"

Her voice was tight with anger and guilt and probably a dozen other emotions he didn't understand.

She set her drink on the bar and looked up at him again. "Okay, your turn. Why'd you join the FBI?"

The question caught him off guard.

"Come on." She nudged him with her knee. "Why should you get to ask all the questions?"

"Fair enough." He took a sip of his bourbon. "I guess because I wanted a challenge."

"The Army wasn't challenging?"

"I wanted something different."

"And did you get it?"

"Yeah." He looked at her. "It's definitely hard. Although the Academy wasn't."

"Yeah, I've heard it's a real cakewalk."

He leaned his elbow on the bar. "Well, not to sound conceited or anything, but it was. After everything I'd done in the military, there was really nothing to it."

She smiled and patted his hand.

"What?"

"It's nice to know you've got a healthy ego." She grinned at him over the rim of her glass. "Go on. You were saying?"

"The hard part is the job itself. Building a case. Waiting on agencies to do things. Dealing with red tape, bureaucracy, that's never been my thing." He took another swig. "I'm more of a doer. And patience isn't my strong suit."

She lifted an eyebrow, and he felt a warm tug of attraction. Maybe it was the bourbon kicking in, but she didn't seem so sad anymore. She seemed mellower. Looser.

Brian gazed down at her as the crowd ebbed and flowed around them. He looked at that mouth of hers that had been taunting him since the moment he'd seen it. He had the urge to kiss her, but he doubted that would go over too well in a noisy pub. Still, he was tempted. Sitting so close, it was impossible to ignore all the things he liked about her—her chocolate-brown eyes, the smell of her hair, the outline of her bra, barely visible through her thin white shirt. And that skirt. He never would have guessed gray pinstripes could be a turn-on.

She leaned closer. "Cut it out. You're staring."

"Sorry. I was just admiring your shoes."

"My *shoes*?"

"Yeah, you look nice today."

She winced. "I'm a mess."

He reached over and tucked a lock of hair behind her ear. "You look disheveled. In a good way."

Her gaze narrowed, and she obviously didn't believe there was any "good" way to look disheveled. But there was. He imagined her in his bed, with her hair all wild and her mouth swollen and her skin flushed from sex.

But imagining was about as close as he was going to get tonight, because he could tell that any second now, she was going to make an excuse to leave.

She glanced at her watch, right on cue. "And now—" She downed her last sip. "I *really* need to call it a night." She stood up, forcing him to stand, too. He pulled out his wallet, and to his annoyance, she did, too.

"I got it," he said.

"No, it's okay."

But he wouldn't let her pay. After leaving some bills on the bar, he put his hand on the small of her back and steered her to the exit. She was a little wobbly in those heels, and he wondered how many drinks she'd had with Sam. He pushed open the heavy wooden door, and they stepped outside into the chill.

"Brrr." She shivered and moved for the parking lot.

"Wait." He caught her arm. "You okay to drive?"

"Yeah, why?"

"Because you've been in there a while."

She looked out over the cars and sighed. "You're right. I should probably call a cab."

"I could drive you home."

She reached for her purse. "You've been drinking, too."

Yeah, but he outweighed her by about a hundred pounds.

"There's a diner around the corner," he said. "We could hang out and have some coffee, if you want."

She gave him a suspicious look. "How do you know what's around the corner?"

"Because I live here."

"Where?"

He nodded at the brick apartment complex at the end of the block.

"*Here* here?"

He stepped closer and gazed down at her. "Lot of us live around here. It's ten minutes from the office."

She stared up at him, and he could almost see the thoughts tumbling through her head. Hope flared to life inside him.

"I should call a cab," she said.

He settled his hands on her waist and felt her shiver.

"Or—" He pulled her closer. "You could come home with me and sleep it off."

She laughed as she tipped her head back to look at him. "You want me to come home with you to *sleep*?"

"No."

She gazed up at him, looking conflicted now. She wanted to turn him down again. He could tell. But she also wanted to say yes.

He kissed her. Her mouth was hot and soft, like he remembered it. He coaxed her lips apart and tasted the sweet woman-flavor he'd been craving. His hands went into her hair, and he tilted her head back and kissed her as long as he could—as persuasively as he could—until she was draped around him the way she'd been back at that fire scene. He loved her body. He loved all those lush curves and was dying to slide her out of that skirt.

A cold wind whipped up. She blinked up at him, dazed, and he glanced around. They were still beside the door. He pulled her under the overhang of the roof and eased her back against the wall, using his hand to cushion the back of her head so he could kiss her again. This time, she got into it, kissing him back and digging her nails into the back of his neck. She made a low moan that sent a bolt of heat straight to his groin. God, he wanted her. Now. Tonight.

She turned her head. "Brian." She sounded breathless. And uncertain. She braced a hand against his shoulder, and his heart damn near stopped beating.

Please don't say no. His whole life, he'd never pressured a woman for sex, but at this moment, he was ready to beg. He kissed her again, harder, pulling her closer so her breasts were flat against his chest. He slid his hands down her sides, and she felt soft and perfect and *willing*. He kissed her until she nudged his shoulders back and came up for air.

He looked down at her. "Is that a yes?"

She gazed up at him for what seemed like an eternity as he held his breath and waited for that one little word.

"Maddie?"

He gripped her hips and looked at that mouth and felt like he was going to die if he didn't get her home soon, and she must have read the look on his face, because she smiled slightly.

Then she pulled his head down and kissed him.

CHAPTER 13

Maddie followed him up the stairs, her heart thudding harder with every step closer to his apartment. She was going to do this. She was actually *doing* this. The scuffing of their shoes over the concrete steps was a continuous reminder that with every second, she was getting one step closer to *doing this*.

The redbrick building loomed large in front of her, big and imposing with its endless doors. She glanced at Brian. Alcohol had taken the edge off her nerves, but her pulse still pounded as she thought of what was about to happen. She gazed up at his broad shoulders and felt a shudder of anticipation as he reached the top.

Her toe caught on the last step, and she bumped into him.

"Watch out." His arm wrapped around her waist. "You okay?"

"Yeah, I'm just—yeah."

I'm not drunk, she wanted to say, but then again, maybe she was. A little. She was at least tipsy, and as he looked at her, she could tell he was wondering if she was going to change her mind. For a moment, they stood at

the top of the stairs, buffeted by the wind, and she knew
this was it. This was her chance to back out, her chance
to heed the warning bells clanging in her head. But she
wasn't going to heed anything, because he had that look
again, that fierce *want*. In all her life, no one had ever
looked at her that way. She'd been resisting, but she'd
made up her mind now. She was going to trust him. She
was going to let this happen and see if that look of his
lived up to its promise.

And just like that, her feet were moving again, and
there was no turning back. He steered her to the nearest
door—black like all the others—and she registered the
dull brass numbers as he took out his keys. Vaguely, she
thought she should commit the numbers to memory.
What if she wanted to come back? But tonight wasn't
like that. Tonight was a one-off. She would enjoy it
while it lasted, no repeats, no looking back.

He reached around her and pushed open the door.
She stepped over the threshold as a bright light switched
on. She blinked as she glanced around and got a quick
barrage of impressions—black sofa, huge TV, empty
walls—before the door thudded shut.

Maddie turned to look at him. He stood in the glaring light of the foyer, gazing down at her with a determined glint in his eyes. She glanced at his bandage and
had a quick flashback of the abject fear she'd experi-
enced when she'd thought he was trapped in that fire.

He lifted a hand to her face, and she shook off the
feeling, focusing instead on that soul-searing kiss back
in the parking lot. *That* was the memory she wanted.
She closed her eyes and tipped her head back, wanting the moment back, wanting to think about him and

nothing else, not a single other thing, for the next few hours. And then he kissed her.

She lost herself in the sharp taste of whiskey, the feel of his stubble rasping against her chin as he wrapped his arms around her and pulled her close. His hands slid over her hips, and she twined her arms around his neck and burrowed her fingertips into the silky bristles of his hair. This was what she'd wanted, what she'd been craving and denying herself. Now she sank into him, and the ugliness of the day receded. All the despair and all the injustice faded away, and there was only his mouth and his hands and the solid heat of him. There was something good in that, but her brain was too fuzzy to pinpoint it. But she didn't need to. She wanted to shut everything out and just feel.

She rocked her hips against him, and the low moan in his throat gave her a rush of pride. She loved that she turned him on. The fabric at her waist shifted, and suddenly, his warm fingers moved over her rib cage, sliding up, up, up, and settling possessively over her breast. And then it was her turn to moan as his hand pushed the lace aside, and a thumb brushed roughly over her nipple.

"Maddie." His voice was hoarse. He dipped his head down and kissed her, right through the thin silk, and every nerve jumped. He trailed kisses up her neck and settled on her lips again, rubbing her sensitive skin with his thumb as he kissed her mouth.

Then he shifted, turning her in his arms, and she opened her eyes to find herself being propelled down a carpeted hallway. Anticipation tingled inside her. His hands moved to her hips, steering her as he nipped the side of her neck. They stepped into the bedroom, where she was relieved by the dimness. Even in her bourbon-tinged state, she had enough awareness to know she'd enjoy this more in the dark.

He released her and stepped over to the wooden dresser. His back was to her, and she watched his broad shoulders as his hands went to his belt. He turned and looked at her as he pulled off his holster and laid it on the dresser.

She closed the door, plunging them into darkness, except for the light outside still slanting through the blinds. She looked at the bed, and her skin tingled as he stepped closer.

"What?"

"Nothing," she whispered, wrapping her arms around him, determined not to lose her nerve now.

He pulled her to him and kissed her again, and all the doubts faded to black as his strong arms tightened around her. She wanted him, and he wanted her, and right now, that was all she was going to think about. He eased her back, and the wall was cool behind her as his hands slid up her sides again. He went for the tiny buttons, and she smiled at his frustrated noise as he tried to undo them. She brushed his hands away to do it herself. The instant she finished, he slid the fabric off her shoulders, and she felt the cool air on her skin. His hot mouth fastened on her breast as she leaned back against the wall.

She reached up, but the cuffs of her sleeves trapped her arms, and she had to nudge him away so she could undo the buttons at her wrists. When her hands were free, he tossed the shirt away and pressed his weight into her, pinning her in place as he kissed her. His fingers dug into her bra, and she squirmed against him. He tugged her skirt, hiking it up. He pulled her thigh up to rest at his hip, and somewhere in her mind, she realized that leaning back against this wall, pinned by him, was the most erotic sensation she'd felt in her life. His fingers slid up the back of her thigh, and he muttered something, but she didn't hear it. She didn't care—she was too focused on his mouth and his touch and the rock-hard heat of his body.

He eased her leg down and moved his hands around her waist, searching for the zipper.

"Side," she whispered, and closed her eyes as she waited for him to find it. She heard the rasp of the zipper, the *whoosh* of her skirt hitting the floor. She started to kick off her heels, but he put his hand on her thigh.

"Keep those on."

She went still as she watched him watching her in the dimness. His eyes looked black now, and she could see the shadow of stubble over his jaw. He reached out a fingertip and trailed it over her breast and then her navel, then back up again. His gaze made her skin flush and her insides go all warm and liquidy.

She took his hand and led him to the bed. The mattress creaked as she climbed on and turned to face him. She was on her knees, and her head came to the bottom of his chin.

She hooked her finger inside his pants and tugged him close. She started on his buttons, but he moved her hands aside and did it himself. He threw his shirt to the floor and yanked his white T-shirt over his head, and she was treated to her first real look at the body she'd only guessed about before. Even in the dimness, she could see the definition of his muscles and the dark smattering of hair. She trailed her hands down his torso, and he stepped back and quickly shucked his pants. She felt a sharp jolt of attraction before he pulled her in for another kiss. This one was deeper, more forceful than before, and she tried to match the intensity as his arms wrapped around her. There was something fierce now as his hands explored her skin. This wasn't languid familiarity. This wasn't some halfhearted effort prompted by obligation. Her bra loosened and disappeared, and his mouth burned a path down her neck. He *wanted* her. And not just wanted, *demanded*, with his eyes and his hands and his tongue. His fingers slipped between her legs, and it was an electric shock, and her head connected with his chin as she let out a gasp.

"Sorry!" she squeaked, but the word got smothered as he kissed her again and his fingers slid over her.

And then the world was spinning, and the hot, intoxicating feeling wrapped around her. She clung to his shoulders, tilting her head back and letting the heat take over until she felt as if her body would ignite like a match.

"You like that?"

She tightened her arms around his neck.

"Huh?"

She made a little sound in her throat, and then he planted his knee between hers and eased her back on the bed. Her legs wrapped around him, and soon they were locked in a wrestling match, and she opened her eyes as he planted her wrists on either side of her head. A smile curled at the side of his mouth, and she had enough brain cells still working to know that he thought he'd won something here. She bucked under him and shoved him off. His grunt of surprise turned to soft laughter as she straddled him and cuffed his wrists on either side of his shoulders.

She hovered over him, taunting him, leaning close but not close enough, until he shot upright and lunged for her breast. His hands clamped around her waist, and he held her in place as he kissed her.

He'd been wanting to do this—she could tell—and she sat back and let him do exactly what he pleased, as her body burned and she was on the sharp edge of losing it.

She closed her eyes and shifted on top of him, and then he flipped her onto her back again, and she felt the lace sliding down her legs and her high heels—finally—being pulled off. They hit the wall with a *thud-thunk*, and then his full weight was on her, and they were skin to skin. He kissed her mouth, her neck, her breasts, and then stopped to gaze down at her. She rested her hand on his chest and stared up at him with something close to awe. She loved his heart throbbing under her fingers and his weight pressed between her legs. He reached across her, and she heard the nightstand drawer opening and closing as he took out a condom.

She waited, heart pounding. He looked down at her, and she held her breath as he moved her thighs apart and pushed into her.

She clutched him tight, and for an endless moment, they were locked that way, not moving. Then he shifted his weight and pushed up on his palms and started a slow, steady rhythm that made her mind go completely blank. She pulled him closer. She held on. Every inch of her burned, and she felt the relentless force of him pounding into her.

"Brian."

He quickened the pace. She struggled to meet him, to match him, to make it to that soaring peak.

She needed him to hurry. She needed . . . needed . . . *"Brian."*

His muscles bunched under her hands. His weight drove into her. The earth shifted as every muscle in her body tightened and she held him, clinging to his shoulders, as pure, blinding pleasure surged through her. And then surged again. And just as she shuddered and went completely lax, he gave a last powerful thrust and collapsed on top of her.

———

Maddie woke up thirsty. She looked at the ceiling and felt a jolt of panic at not being in her bed. She felt another jolt as she realized she was in Brian's.

He was sprawled beside her on his stomach. Naked. She was naked, too. She looked at his shadowy form beside her—his muscular back, his narrow hips, his long legs now tangled in the sheets. She closed her eyes and let the memories wash over her. She remembered the slide of his hands, the feel of his powerful body. She reached out and brushed her fingers over his forearm, just to confirm that he was real and not some alcohol-induced fantasy. His skin was warm beneath her fingertips, and she lay there silently as the reality of what she'd done seeped in.

She sat up, feeling a little dazed and a lot exposed. How much had she had to drink? She looked around the unfamiliar room. She looked at Brian. What if he never wanted her again? Or even more unsettling, what if he did?

Maddie slipped out of bed. A wave of dizziness crashed over her, and she touched the dresser to steady herself. She looked around, trying to decide what to do. Her car was still back at the bar. She wasn't in any shape to drive home.

She grabbed a shirt off the floor and tiptoed out of the room. The hall light was on, and she switched it off. Her eyes adjusted to the dimness as she padded into the kitchen, where a light glowed over the stove. She stared at the wall of cabinets. Opening them all was beyond her, so she turned on the faucet. She cupped her hand under it and ducked her head down to lap up water like a feral cat. She glanced into the window above the sink.

Oh, God.

Her hair looked like Medusa. Her makeup was smudged. She had a bruise on her neck . . . She leaned closer. Not a bruise, a *hickey*.

"Hey."

She jumped and whirled around. "God, you scared me!"

Brian leaned against the door frame, watching her. She shut off the faucet.

"Looking for something to eat?" His voice was gravelly, and his hair stuck out on one side. He wore black boxer-briefs, and she tried not to stare at his perfect torso.

"I was thirsty."

He looked at her for a moment, then crossed the kitchen and opened a cabinet. He filled a glass with water from the fridge dispenser and handed it to her.

"Thanks." She gulped down the water and watched him over the rim of the glass. What should she say? He stepped closer, and her heart started to pound.

"That's my shirt."

"Sorry."

He parted the fabric, and her breasts tingled. He had that look again. And as much as she wanted to run away from this stupid mistake, she knew she wasn't going anywhere.

He circled her waist with his hands, rubbing his thumbs over her hip bones as he steered her slowly out of the kitchen. Her feet touched carpet, and the backs of her thighs bumped against the wooden table. He took the glass from her hand and reached over to put it on the counter.

She looked back at the table. She looked at him.

"We should go to bed," she said.

He leaned down and pressed his mouth to her ear. "Not yet."

CHAPTER 14

Maddie squinted through the windshield, wishing she could drive blindfolded. Of course, it had to be sunny this morning. Of course, she had to hit traffic. And of course, she had to have a staff meeting in exactly one hour, so there was no way she could slink into a dark room and crawl under the covers to wallow in misery for the next hundred hours—or however long it took to get rid of her screaming headache.

Beer before liquor, never been sicker. Her sister Tracy's saying came back to her, those helpful words of wisdom that she'd dispensed one long-ago weekend when their parents had been out of town and they'd snuck beer into the house and decided to throw a party. For years, Maddie had had no trouble following the advice, but yesterday she'd disregarded not only her sister's drinking slogan but every other rational thought that had entered her mind.

Now she turned onto her street and wished for a time machine so she could erase last night. Or at least skip over this morning. Her head was pounding, her stomach was doing flip-flops, and she couldn't imagine anything more miserable than an endless staff meeting in a brightly lit conference room.

But then a silver BMW glided to a stop in front of her house, and she realized that she could.

"Shit," she muttered, swinging into the driveway. She thrust her car into park and thunked her forehead on the steering wheel, sending a bullet of pain straight through her skull.

Maddie sat up and looked at her clothes. She checked her reflection in the mirror. Even with sunglasses, it was beyond hopeless. She grabbed her coat and purse from the passenger seat and climbed out.

A trim, smiling, sun-bronzed specimen of male humanity strolled up her driveway.

"'Morning." He pulled off his designer shades, and the smile faltered. "What happened to you?"

"Late night."

His gaze dropped to her wrinkled skirt. Maddie tossed her coat over her arm to hide the dirt on her cuffs.

"What do you want, Mitch?"

He pretended to be offended. "Can't a guy stop by for a cup of coffee?"

She strode past him and up the stairs. "I'm late for work."

"This won't take long."

She unlocked the door, and the high-pitched beep greeted her like a pickax. She hurried across the foyer to tap in her alarm code.

"That's new," he said.

She gritted her teeth as she tossed her purse and coat onto the chair. He'd only been over a handful of times, but he'd noticed every detail. She had no doubt he was noticing details right now, too, including the slovenly state of her living room.

"I've got to get in the shower, so—"

"One cup," he said. "Then I'll get out of your way."

One drink. Brian's words flashed through her mind, and her stomach roiled again. She wasn't up for this. She wanted to tell Mitch to get lost, but he was persistent as hell, and she couldn't handle a fight right now.

"Help yourself," she said, and left him standing in the living room.

Maddie avoided her reflection as she stripped off her clothes and jumped into the shower. The hot spray made her dizzy, so she set the water to lukewarm and quickly cleaned up. She toweled off, brushed her hair, and squirted Visine into her eyes—for all the good it would probably do. She pulled on jeans and an over-size sweater that she hoped would conceal all her cuts, scrapes, and hickeys.

When she walked barefoot into the kitchen, Mitch was pouring a cup of coffee. On the counter beside him was a glass of water and some aspirin from the bottle she kept in the cabinet with the vitamins.

"Thanks." She popped the tablets into her mouth, feeling a twinge of guilt for being such a bitch.

He folded his arms over his chest. "Where'd you get the contusion?"

She looked at him.

"On your jaw there."

"I was mugged last week."

His brows tipped up. "Really?"

"Really."

"Guess that explains the burglar alarm."

She took down a cup and poured herself some coffee. He made it strong, just the way she liked it. She took a sip and remembered all the late nights during medical school, when he'd been cramming for exams and she would get up in the middle of the night to rub his shoulders and make him coffee. It was hard to imagine she'd ever been that in love.

He ran a hand through his thick, dark hair. The years had been good to him. A decade into his career, and he still had his looks, his health. And now he had a big fat bank account to go with it all. He was quite the catch.

"So, you heard about Jennings," he said.

"You mean the wedding?"

"Yeah."

"Well, you know what they say. Third time's the charm." Maddie crossed her arms.

"You going?"

"Not as a guest," she said. "I'm doing the photos."

Todd Jennings had always been more Mitch's friend than hers, but he'd really wanted her to do the photos, and she hadn't had the heart to say no.

"I assume you'll be there?" she asked.

"That's why I came by, to give you the heads-up."

"Thanks."

"And to tell you Danielle's pregnant again."

Pain speared through her. Her throat closed, and she took a second to find her voice. "Congratulations."

"Thanks." He smiled sheepishly. "We had the ultrasound. Looks like another boy."

She felt the familiar tightness in her chest. Her pulse spiked, and suddenly, she was back in that room again, with the cold gel on her belly and her husband hovering beside her. She looked at his hand wrapped around her coffee mug and remembered those same fingers laced through hers as they'd looked at the screen and seen those first blurry images of Emma.

He stepped closer. "You okay?"

"Fine." She cleared her throat. "Fine." She poured the coffee down the sink and immediately wished she hadn't. He was watching her now, and the pity in his eyes made her want to slap him.

The doorbell rang.

She looked over her shoulder. She glanced at Mitch.

"Maddie—"

"Just a second." She rushed from the room, realizing too late that she might have made another misstep. A glimpse through the peephole confirmed it.

She closed her eyes. She braced herself. She swung open the door.

"Hi," she said brightly.

Brian looked at her. He looked over her shoulder. She heard footsteps behind her and pulled the door back.

"Come in."

He looked at her again, and she could swear his body actually expanded as he stepped over the threshold. He thrust his hand out, all confidence. "Brian Beckman."

"Mitch Callahan."

Brian shot her a look.

She avoided his gaze in favor of Mitch, and it struck her how different they were—the man she'd married and the man she'd just slept with. Brian had grown up on a farm, gone overseas to fight for his country, and come home to a job that required him to work long hours and dodge bullets—all for less than six figures a year. Mitch was private school all the way, and although he'd once been passionate about saving lives, now he was mostly passionate about his golf game.

And then there was Emma. The fact that he'd gotten over her, that he'd *replaced* her—twice now—burned like a coal in her chest, and if she lived to be a hundred, she'd never forgive him for it.

Both men were looking at her now, and she realized the silence had become awkward.

"Well." Mitch turned to Brian. "Good to meet you, Brian." Then back to Maddie with a smug look that told her he'd correctly read the situation. "I was just leaving."

She pulled the door open wider.

"Thanks for the coffee, Maddie."

"Sure thing."

She watched him walk down the stairs. She shut the door and turned around.

Brian closed his eyes. "Jesus, Maddie."

"What?"

"Please fucking tell me you're not still married."

"I'm not still married." She strode into the kitchen and took down two fresh mugs. "Coffee?"

He leaned against the doorway to the kitchen, and she could feel the anger emanating from him. She'd known this would happen. She'd known it the whole way home, and yet she hadn't had the guts to turn around and make it right.

She poured a cup of coffee and offered it to him.

"No, thanks."

She didn't want it, either, so she set it on the counter and leaned back against the sink.

"I didn't change my name after the divorce," she said. "Too much paperwork." It was an outright lie, and he probably knew it. But she didn't owe him the real explanation. She didn't owe him anything.

He crossed his arms. He looked down at the floor and shook his head.

"What's the problem?"

He looked up. "What's the problem?"

"Yeah." She went on the offensive. "You've obviously got a chip on your shoulder. What is it?"

"I don't know. Maybe something about how I got out of the shower this morning and you'd up and disappeared?"

"I have a meeting."

"You ever think to poke your head in and mention it? So I wouldn't think you'd been *kidnapped?*"

She almost laughed, it sounded so absurd. But then she thought of Jolene. He felt responsible for that. No matter what anyone said, he believed it was his fault, and that feeling of responsibility spilled over to everyone in his orbit, apparently.

Maddie's head throbbed, and she tried to think of something to say to make this right, but she completely drew a blank.

"Listen, Brian . . . I'm sorry about last night." She shoved the mug toward the sink and looked at it instead of him. "I had too much to drink. I know that's no excuse, but that's what happened."

Silence.

She glanced up.

He shook his head and looked away. "That's just—"
He muttered something she didn't hear.

"What?"

"Bullshit, Maddie."

"What's bullshit?" Anger welled up. She knew it
wasn't all about him, but he was standing in her kitchen
pissing her off, so he was going to get the brunt of it.
"It was stupid. I had too much to drink. I know that
doesn't excuse my behavior, but still—"

"Your *behavior*?" He snorted. "Listen to you. Why
don't you just admit what this is about? You finally let
your guard down with me, and you're embarrassed."

Heat flooded her cheeks. Her thoughts flashed to
that damn table, and she had to look away.

"Brian . . . let's be realistic about this, all right?"

She glanced at him, and he had his arms folded over
his chest, glaring at her.

"Last night happened," she said. "I don't want to
make this complicated."

"Well, I do."

She stared at him.

"You're older than me. So what? We live in different
towns. So what? We work crappy hours. So what? I
know it's complicated, but I like you."

She watched him, at a loss for words. "I like you,
too." Her heart squeezed as she forced the words out.
"As a friend."

He didn't move. He didn't even blink, but something in his eyes hardened.

"Anything else is just . . ." She searched for a word.
"Unrealistic."

He shook his head, and she hated the look of disgust on his face.

"I know the age difference means nothing to you, but you're a guy. It's different. People would talk about me. And our professional circles overlap. God, do you realize how many people we both know? The gossip would be a nightmare."

He looked at her, and she could feel his disapproval. He probably thought she was shallow for caring what people said. But she'd been the subject of gossip during her divorce, thanks to Mitch, and she'd resolved never to put herself in that position again. She kept her private life private.

He shook his head again and looked at his feet. The muscle in his jaw twitched, and she knew he was suppressing things he wanted to say.

Across the house, her phone chimed. She rushed through the living room to dig it from her purse.

"Hello?"

"Hey, it's Kelsey. You need to get down here."

She looked at Brian. "Where? The lab?"

"The Bones Unit," Kelsey said. "I've got something to show you."

"I'm on my way."

"And give your fed a call," she added. "He needs to see this, too."

CHAPTER 15

Maddie arrived last, not because of traffic but because she spent ten minutes in the Delphi Center parking lot with her makeup in her lap, trying to disguise the evidence of her hangover. But of course, it didn't work, and the moment she set foot in Kelsey's office, she could tell that she looked every bit as horrible as she felt.

"Bracewell with you?" Kelsey asked, hanging up the phone at her desk.

"I didn't know he was coming." Maddie followed her into the autopsy room, where Brian and Sam stood waiting by the row of stainless-steel sinks.

"He said he wanted to observe." Kelsey handed her a jar of orange oil, and Maddie rubbed some under her nose, but still, the odor of burned flesh and gasoline was impossible to ignore.

Maddie eyed the lump on the stainless-steel table. The blue sheet did little to obscure the stark reality of what lay underneath. A wave of nausea hit her. She had to force her feet to move. Normally, she wasn't squeamish, but nothing about this morning had been normal. This case was personal. She felt connected to Jolene

Murphy, probably because she'd unwittingly witnessed the incident that set this chain of events in motion. She stared at the sheet, and her thoughts inevitably went to the girl's parents.

"Well, I hate to do this," Kelsey said, "but I'm going to have to get started without him. I need to be in Williamson County by ten o'clock. You mind getting him up to speed?"

Maddie glanced at Kelsey and realized she was talking to her. "What?"

"You mind filling Bracewell in? We need to get going."

"I'll fill him in," Sam said from across the room.

Maddie looked at him over the table. She knew what he was doing. His strategy was to make nice with the locals instead of turning everything into a big pissing contest. It was a refreshing change from what she usually saw when a hodgepodge of agencies was forced to work together.

Maddie eased forward. She glanced at Brian. His expression was unreadable. In fact, it was completely blank. He stood leaning against the counter, and only the tense set of his shoulders conveyed his unhappiness at being here.

"I spent yesterday evening determining the four basic identifiers." Kelsey pulled back the fabric, and Maddie took a slight step back. "Race, sex, age, stature. You may recall that the victim was found at the crime scene in the pugilistic position, also known as the fetal position." Kelsey glanced at Brian and Sam. "That's the result of what intense heat does to muscles and connective tissue. When I got the remains back here, I was able to mitigate those effects and examine the bones more closely. The first thing I noticed was the femur." She pointed at the charred leg bone, which still had bits of flesh clinging to it. "It's about fifty-three centimeters, which is indicative of a tall male."

Sam stepped forward. "It's a guy?"

Maddie glanced at Brian. He looked as surprised as she was.

"Are you sure?" she asked Kelsey, even though she knew the answer. Kelsey wouldn't make a mistake of that magnitude.

"My original conclusion was confirmed through further analysis."

Relief washed over her. She looked at Brian, but he wasn't smiling. He was frowning down at the burned bones.

"So who is this?" He looked at Kelsey.

The door swung open, and everyone turned as Sheriff Bracewell stepped into the room.

"Sorry, but we had to start without you," Kelsey said. "Help yourself to some orange oil over there by the sink."

The sheriff took off his hat and set it brim-up on the counter. He ran a hand through his hair and nodded at everyone.

"'Morning." Ignoring the orange oil, Bracewell stepped right up to the table. He was known to have an iron stomach. Nothing fazed him, not even the most grisly traffic fatality.

"I was getting started with my initial findings," Kelsey said. "To begin with, the victim is a male, about six feet, two inches tall."

The sheriff whistled. "How'd we mistake him for a girl?"

"The pugilistic position of the body was a contributing factor, and also the shrinking of tissue. Plus, the victim was naked when he was killed, so we didn't have clothing or jewelry to guide our initial assumptions."

"Killed?" Brian looked up. "You're certain this was a murder?"

"Absolutely. Aside from the evidence of arson at the crime scene, we also have this." With a gloved hand, she rotated the skull and pointed to a dent. "I haven't had a chance to clean the bones yet, so it's hard to see, but an X-ray reveals a circular depressed fracture made with a heavy instrument. Our tool marks examiner can confirm, but my preliminary conclusion is that this fatal blow to the skull was administered by a hammer."

Brian and Sam traded looks. Maybe they were thinking about the hammer that had been used to break Heidi Beckles's fingers.

"It would have to be someone pretty tall, wouldn't it?" Brian asked. "If this guy's six-two?"

"That depends," Kelsey said. "Maybe the victim was on his knees with his hands bound when he took the hit. In a situation like that, someone Maddie's height could have delivered the lethal blow."

"What about hand damage?" Maddie asked, stepping to the side of the table for a closer look. "Any sign this person was hit anywhere else with that hammer?"

"I did a thorough examination," Kelsey said. "There's evidence of a fractured left tibia and fibula, but those injuries occurred in the past—within the last few years, I'd say."

"So, if this isn't Jolene Murphy, what were last night's fires about?" Maddie looked at Sam. "Is this some other random murder committed by Mladovic?"

"How do we know this is Mladovic?" Bracewell asked. "Maybe it's our firebug at it again."

"Firebug?" Sam looked at the sheriff.

"We got an arsonist operating in Clarke County. He's torched three properties, including a house the other night. Maddie even got a picture of him."

"You took his *picture*?" Brian asked.

"He was in a crowd," she said. "I always take pictures of crowds at fire scenes. Arsonists like to watch. Anyway, he's only a suspect at this point. We don't even have an ID on the man, last I heard."

"Neighbors don't know him," Bracewell said, "which tells you something. What was he doing there at two in the morning? I think he's our serial torcher."

"Fine, but I don't think he's responsible for this, do you? Except for the fire element, these crimes seem unrelated." Maddie looked at Sam. "I mean, the VIN on this vehicle traces back to one of Mladovic's guys, right?"

"Anatoli Petrovik," Brian said. "He's one of his strongmen. But maybe this is him."

"Whoever he is, looks like he got himself fired," Sam quipped. "This is what happens when you piss off Mladovic or botch a job."

Brian looked at Kelsey. "We need a positive ID."

"Well, for that, I'll have to have a DNA sample or some dental records. The ones you had for Jolene Murphy obviously won't help us here."

"We don't have DNA. We don't even have IDs on

everyone in the crew. Not yet, at least." Brian looked at Maddie. "You make any more progress on those photographs?"

"Still working on it."

"What photographs?" the sheriff asked.

"I have pictures of some of Mladovic's men casing the bank two days before the kidnapping," she said. "So far, the faces are obscured. We were able to get a license plate, at least, which led us to one of them."

"Maybe this is Vlad, not Anatoli." Sam nodded at the table. "And we *do* have DNA on him, right, Beck? We got the cigarette butt from that SUV we recovered. Plus, we got his prints."

"Prints won't help in this case," Kelsey told him. "The epidermis is far too damaged. To get a definite ID, like I said, you're going to need to get me DNA or dental records. Until then, there's not much more I can do for you."

She pulled the sheet up over the remains, and Maddie breathed a sigh of relief.

"One thing's definite. This isn't Jolene," Sam said. "Which means there's a chance she could be alive."

"Slight," Brian added.

"Yeah, but it's a chance." Maddie looked from Brian to Sam and back to Brian again. "Someone made that call, right? It could have been her, trying to escape. She could still be alive."

"Maybe." Brian looked at Sam. "Whether she is or not, we're going to find her."

The Murphys lived in a pink brick colonial in a golf-course neighborhood on the west side of town. Maddie had never been there, but it reminded her of the subdivision she and Mitch had moved into after he took his first job at the hospital.

The lots were big, the driveways long. Residents were out this evening, jogging and walking dogs. Maddie spotted the Murphys' house with a handful of cars parked out front. She rolled to a stop across the street, where she had a line of sight to the driveway.

At times like these, the kitchen was the hub. People would sit around the table, drinking coffee and whispering platitudes. The occasional logistical question—roses or lilies? what time for the vigil?—would throw everyone into a flurry of action, until things settled down again and it was back to hushed voices.

Maddie had hated it. The relatives. The clergy. The well meaning neighbors. Just a few days into it, and the mere sight of another chicken casserole had made her physically ill. She'd wanted every one of them out of her house, including her own parents. And when the funeral was over and she'd finally gotten her wish, she'd been left with the cloying scent of flowers and a freezer full of dishes that needed to be returned and an empty house and a deafening silence.

Then she'd wanted the people back, because the silence was so much worse than all of it.

She watched the Murphys' house, and it all came back to her, like that first ache before the onset of the flu. She recognized the setup, the players. She recognized the moves. On duty at the Murphy house right now was the A-team, with maybe a B-teamer or two thrown in there. She knew the players because she'd seen them, in all their hideous desperation, on TV the other day.

Soon after the media had gotten wind of Jolene's kidnapping, Jennifer Murphy had taken to the airwaves, hoping that pleas and prayer groups would somehow bring her daughter back. Maddie had watched, riveted. She'd felt every word Jennifer Murphy said like a dart to the chest, and she'd actually been jealous of the woman because she had the thing Maddie had been denied.

Hope.

Please let her come home. If you have Jolene, please let her come home to us.

A slender silver-haired woman walked up the driveway now, tugging a dachshund behind her. Jolene's grandmother. Maddie watched the woman deposit a plastic bag into the trashcan beside the garage, then pull open the back door to step inside.

Maddie's gaze went to the bay window facing the driveway. A trio of people sat at the kitchen table: Jennifer and two others, a man and a woman. Siblings, maybe? Close friends?

Seeing them reminded Maddie of her own family. It reminded her of their persistent efforts to help her, their persistent gestures.

They'd helped, and they hadn't. Truthfully, Maddie hardly remembered what they'd done and said. Everything had been a blur. And she looked at Jennifer Murphy in her kitchen and knew it was a blur right now for her, too.

Maddie swiped the tears from her cheeks. What was she doing here? It made no sense. None at all. It was actually kind of creepy to drive all the way to a stranger's home and spy on the kitchen from across the street. And yet she hadn't been able to stay away.

She started her car again and pulled out, avoiding the gazes of the curious FBI agents who'd been staked out at the end of the block and had no doubt been running her license plate as she sat there, watching the Murphys' house.

She wended her way toward home, but melancholy overtook her as she contemplated her dark living room and her empty bed and the endless hours of unbearable quiet.

She thought of the invitation she'd turned down as she'd left work earlier, and before she'd even realized she'd made a decision, she was pulling a U-turn and heading east, to the seedy part of town that had all the best bars. She found a parking space and a short minute later found Brooke inside, seated near the pool table, where some guys from the lab were in the middle of a game.

"Hey, you made it!" Brooke's face brightened as Maddie pulled out a chair.

"Hi."

"Our waitress just left." Brooke waved her back. "What do you want, a vodka cranberry?"

Maddie ordered straight cranberry and looked at Brooke. "Sorry, I've got to work later. I'm in court tomorrow, and I'm getting behind."

Brooke eyed her as she tipped her beer back, probably annoyed to be reminded of all the paperwork she'd blown off to go out tonight. She set her bottle down.

"I should probably work, too, but . . ." She shrugged. "It'll be there tomorrow."

Maddie wished she could have that attitude. She probably spent an unhealthy amount of time on her job, but it pretty much dominated her life.

Maybe she should get out more. Socialize. She gazed at the pool table, where Ben and Roland looked to be engaged in friendly game, probably with a wager on the table. They always asked her to play, and she always said no. She watched the next few shots and listened to their banter back and forth.

"They've got a hundred bucks riding on this one," Brooke said, resting her bottle on the table. "You want to challenge the winner?"

"Not tonight."

"I might. I'm feeling lucky." Brooke looked at her, and a sly grin spread across her face. "So, how's Brian?"

"How'd you hear about Brian?"

The grin widened as the waitress swung by and dropped off a glass of juice.

"Ben saw you at Blackjack's. In the parking lot."

Maddie closed her eyes. She heard the clink of Brooke's beer bottle against her glass.

"And don't look like that," Brooke said. "I'm happy for you."

"Why?"

"Because you went for it for once. God. I was starting to think you were off men for good."

"*What?*"

She laughed. "Not really. But Roland was. I guess he couldn't imagine any other reason you were immune to his irresistible pheromones."

Maddie took a gulp of her drink and wished it had booze in it. Someone from work had seen her making out with Brian in a bar parking lot. Very classy. But the damage was done, and all she could do now was hope the gossip would blow over and people would think it was a one-time thing. Because it was.

"What else is wrong?"

She looked at Brooke, and the teasing grin was gone.

"You've been crying," Brooke said. "And I know it's not over a man, so what happened?"

Maddie hesitated a moment.

"I went by the Murphys'."

"The who?"

"Jolene Murphy. I went by her parents' house."

"Why?" But the second Brooke said it, understanding seemed to dawn. She leaned closer, looking concerned. "Did you talk to them?"

"No."

She looked at her, waiting for an explanation. Maddie didn't have one. Brooke was always telling her not to let cases get personal. Maddie knew that. And usually, she didn't. Or actually, she *did*, but she usually kept her reaction to herself.

"Maddie—"

"You're wasting your breath, okay? I know. God, all those yellow ribbons. On every tree."

Jealousy reared its head again. Maddie would have tied a yellow ribbon around every blade of grass if it could have brought Emma back.

Brooke squeezed her hand, surprising her. She wasn't the touchy-feely type.

"You want to talk about it?"

"No," Maddie said firmly.

"Okay, then tell me about the FBI agent." She sipped her beer.

Maddie returned her attention to the pool table. She thought about the tide of gossip. After her divorce, she'd worked hard to set herself apart from it all. Not to let it get to her. To be an island.

I know it's complicated, but I like you.

Maybe Mitch was right.

"You know, my ex told me the problem with our marriage was that I didn't need anybody."

Brooke snorted. "The problem with your marriage was you married a dickhead."

Maddie sipped her drink. It was cold and tart and decidedly lacking in anything that was going to help her loosen up.

Brooke and Mitch were both right. Her marriage had been loaded with problems, and one of them *was* the fact that Maddie closed herself off. It was her natural tendency, but it had gotten worse after Emma died. The pain had been unbearable, like a living thing trying to claw its way out of her chest. She'd somehow made it through one endless day at a time. She'd survived the unfathomable, something you couldn't really know until you were in it.

You're tough, Maddie. You're a survivor. Her parents had told her that over and over during the first year. But Maddie saw her life more objectively now—at least, she thought she did—and what she saw disturbed her. She'd survived, yes, but what did that mean, really? Because part of her hadn't survived at all. Part of her was buried in that little white coffin with Emma.

There were moments now when she knew she should be connecting with people, when she *wanted* to connect with people, but she felt blank. She just felt nothing at all.

I know it's complicated, but I like you.

She wanted to believe him, but she was too cynical to believe anything anymore. Sure, she believed he liked the sex. Who wouldn't? They'd been off the charts together which was a surprise in itself. She hadn't realized she was capable of feeling that.

But aside from the sex, he'd seemed so sincere. She couldn't get her mind around it. Those lady-killer looks, that confident swagger. It didn't make sense, and yet . . . was it possible he *was* sincere? Had she somehow lucked into the last sincere, smart, ridiculously handsome bachelor in the state of Texas?

The answer, of course, was no. The mere idea of it terrified her. She didn't do relationships. She had her work, her mission. It was enough for her. She'd been through too much soul-crushing loss in her life to open herself up to fantasies.

Brooke nudged her elbow. "You okay?"

"Fine."

"You're looking kinda *not* fine. You sure you don't want something stronger than that?"

"Yeah, and actually, I should probably get going." She stood up. "I've still got stuff to do tonight."

Brooke grinned. "I sure hope you mean Brian."

"I don't."

"Hey, not my business. I'm just telling you what I hope."

CHAPTER 16

"What's going on with you and Maddie?"

Brian looked across the car at Sam. "What do you mean?"

Sam rolled up to a stoplight and shot him a look. "When was the last time you talked to her?"

"I don't know. Couple days ago."

Sam laughed. "You're kidding."

Brian looked at him.

"That setup was perfect," he said. "I can't believe you didn't close the deal."

Brian looked out the window as a pair of female joggers crossed the street. Out of habit, he studied their faces. They were the right age, but neither bore the slightest resemblance to Jolene Murphy. He glanced at Sam. "What?"

"You did, didn't you? I *knew* it. You closed the deal, but then you fucked it up. What'd she do, give you the boot?"

Brian didn't say anything as Sam zeroed in on what had been eating away at him for days now. The only thing more frustrating than Maddie giving him the

brush-off was her giving him the brush-off immediately after they'd had sex. He thought back to the argument in her kitchen. Even in retrospect, it was about as
fun as a kick in the balls.

"Damn it, Beckman. I can't believe you." The light
turned green, and he punched the gas. "I thought you
had more staying power."

Brian didn't respond. He wasn't talking about this.
He especially wasn't talking about it with Sam, who
couldn't even keep his own marriage together. Cops
were notoriously shitty at relationships, and Brian's coworkers were no exception.

"That's the problem with guys like you. If there's
ever any effort involved, you give up too easily."

Brian kept his mouth shut. He hadn't given up on
anything—*she* had. She'd actually used the word *friends*,
too, as if there was a chance in hell they could be friends
again. It was flat-out impossible. No way could he go
back to being friends with Maddie after he'd had her
laid out on his kitchen table like a damn buffet.

They turned into the office complex, and the guard
waved them through. Sam swung into a parking space,
and they climbed out of the Taurus as Elizabeth LeBlanc
pushed through the door.

"I just got off the phone with Vega."

"Vega?" Sam asked.

"Homicide detective in Los Angeles," Brian reminded him. "What'd he say?"

Elizabeth stopped in front of them and folded her
arms over her chest. "Turns out Gillian Dawson had
just moved into the apartment she was living in at the
time of her murder."

Brian and Sam looked at her, waiting.

"And guess who the previous tenant was, who'd just been evicted for not paying rent? Nicole Sands of San Marcos, Texas."

"You're kidding. How—"

"Twenty-two years old," she said, predicting Brian's question. "And get this—she's five-two and blond, just like Gillian Dawson."

"Holy shit." Sam looked at him. "They killed the wrong girl."

———

Maddie stepped out of the courthouse into a slap of cold air. She hurried down the steps and searched the line of cars parked on the street.

"Damn it," she muttered as she spotted the ticket stuck to her windshield.

"Maddie."

She whirled around, recognizing the deep voice even before she spotted him. "Hi." She felt a burst of happiness—quickly followed by nerves. "What are you doing here?"

Brian stopped in front of her and gazed down, and she felt a punch of emotion so strong she took a step back. God, he was beautiful—tall and muscular, with his hands tucked casually into the pockets of a suit that didn't look expensive but was perfectly tailored to his big frame. She resisted the urge to smooth her hands over his lapels.

"I was going to ask you the same question," he said.

"I had to testify."

"Again?"

"Comes with the job. You?"

"I was at the bank." He glanced back over his shoulder toward the CenTex building, and she could see by the expression on his face that whatever he'd wanted there, he'd been disappointed.

He turned to look at her. "You done? We could grab some lunch."

The expression on his face was completely bland. He could take it or leave it. But maybe there was more to the offer than she was seeing.

"Well?"

"I don't know," she said.

"What don't you know?" Again, carefully blank.

But fine. If he wanted to act as if this wasn't their first social encounter since That Night, she could play along.

"How about Pino's?" She nodded toward the deli across the street. "They have good subs."

"Pino's it is." He fell into step beside her, and she hitched her purse up onto her shoulder. She glanced over and noticed him looking at her shoes.

Her nerves jumped as she remembered them thudding against the wall of his bedroom.

This was a bad idea. She should make it quick. And casual. When she reached the sub shop, she grabbed the door before he could open it for her.

The restaurant was warm like an oven and smelled of fresh-baked bread. Maddie slipped her coat off and draped it over her arm.

"You know that woman?"

She looked at Brian, who was reading the menu board.

"Navy suit," he said. "Two o'clock."

She glanced across the restaurant, and sure enough, a woman in a navy-blue suit was watching her. She quickly looked away.

"That's Rae Loveland, the criminal defense attorney from the trial this morning," Maddie said. "She doesn't like me much."

"Why not?"

"We've gone toe-to-toe a few times in the court room."

"Really?" Brian looked intrigued.

"She's especially unhappy with me today. I probably helped put her client away for shooting a cop."

"Good for you."

They reached the register. Maddie whipped out her wallet, and for once, he didn't object when she paid for her meal. He paid for his, too. Friends out to lunch. *Not a date. Not even a sort of date.*

They found a minuscule table by the window Brian had to shift his legs around, because they were too long for the narrow space. He dug into his food without even looking at her, and she felt relieved.

She unwrapped her sandwich, subtly trying to pick up on his body cues. He seemed relaxed. Unperturbed. Basically, the opposite of how he'd seemed the other day in her kitchen.

Had it really only been two days?

So much had happened. And so much *hadn't* happened. Jolene Murphy hadn't miraculously been found and returned to her family. The case hadn't miraculously been solved—as far as Maddie knew.

She watched Brian eat his sandwich and wondered if he'd tell her if they had any big leads. Probably not.

He glanced up at her. Then he glanced over her shoulder, and his mouth quirked up.

"What?"

"The lawyer. I'm trying to imagine the two of you duking it out."

"I duke it out with lawyers all the time. The more important a photo is to a case, the more effort they make to discredit me at trial."

He met her gaze, but now his expression was unreadable.

"So," she said. "I'm glad I bumped into you."

"Why?"

"Because I thought you were upset with me."

"How come?" He sipped his drink through the straw.

"You didn't call."

"Neither did you."

She searched his face, looking for any hint of resentment. "So we're good, then?"

"We're friends." He rested his drink on the table. "That's what you wanted, right?"

His tone was blasé, but her guard went up.

"You don't think I can do it, do you?" He smiled slightly.

"Do what?"

"Be your friend without hitting on you."

"I don't think that at all. You probably have lots of female friends."

The smile widened. Shame on her. That was a fishing expedition, and he'd seen right through it. His female friends—or lack thereof—were none of her business.

"So, Maddie." He wiped his fingers on a napkin and leaned his elbows on the table. "Now that the sex thing is off the table, can I ask you a question? Friend to friend?"

Her gaze narrowed at the word choice. But his expression was bland.

"Sure. What?"

"Why'd you get divorced?"

She drew back, surprised. She hadn't expected something so personal. She hesitated a moment before answering. "We grew apart."

He didn't react, but she instantly regretted giving him such a canned answer.

"It was Emma, mostly." She looked out the window, at the hustle and bustle of people going to lunch. "After what happened, I don't know, we just . . ." She hesitated. They *had* grown apart, but that was such an inadequate way of describing the chasm that had opened between them.

Plus, if she was being honest here, it wasn't really accurate.

Maddie sighed. She looked him in the eye. He was watching her now, very carefully.

"Everyone tells you people grieve in different ways." He nodded.

"Turns out, Mitch grieves with his penis." She looked out the window again, because all these years later, she still felt the sting of embarrassment. "He had an affair. Several, actually. The one I found out about was a twenty-five-year-old nurse."

"Ouch."

She shrugged. "It's okay. I'm not sure I even blame him, really. I was a bitch to live with."

"That doesn't excuse infidelity."

She sat back now and looked at him.

"What? It doesn't," he said.

"I'm surprised to hear you say that."

He frowned. "Why?"

"I don't know." Maybe because he was a guy—a young one—she'd expected him to be a little looser in the morals department.

It was a dumb assumption.

"Anyway, it was a messy divorce. Not to mention humiliating." She picked up her drink and took a slurp.

"Doesn't sound very amicable."

"It wasn't."

"So why'd you keep his name?"

She put the drink down. How had they gotten into this extremely personal conversation? It probably would have been easier if they talked about sex.

Then again, they were friends now. Friends talked about things. If Brooke or Kelsey had asked her the same question, she wouldn't have thought twice about answering.

"Emma was two." She paused, searching for words that would make sense to someone who'd never been a parent. "She didn't have anyone but us. Her family." And Mitch didn't count anymore. He'd moved on. Maddie felt the familiar burn in her chest.

Brian was watching her intently. "You feel connected to her. By keeping her name."

She nodded, relieved not to have to verbalize it. This

was harder to talk about than she'd thought. She saw something in his eyes . . . something she recognized, but she couldn't put a finger on it. Not pity, really. Empathy. This man had a heart, and that simple realization made her feel a swell of regret over the way they'd left things.

"What was she like?"

"Who, Emma?"

He nodded.

Maddie smiled. She looked out the window at the traffic, but her thoughts went to one of her favorite memories. They'd gone to a nursery to pick out shrubs for the yard. It was spring, and millions of monarch butterflies were migrating through the area. The nursery was swirling with them, and Emma had stood among the lantana, entranced by all the black and orange wings. Maddie's eyes welled up.

"She was . . . a ray of sunshine wrapped in a little girl." She smiled at him. "She could never sit still, ever. Unless she was asleep. And she had this infectious laugh . . ." A tear leaked out, and she swiped it away. "Sorry."

The look of tenderness on his face made her throat ache. But he didn't look uncomfortable. He didn't look sorry he'd asked, and that mattered to her. It mattered a lot.

She looked away and regained her composure. She couldn't believe they were talking about this. Most people never asked about Emma, never even mentioned her name.

Where did he get all this maturity? Maybe it had to do with fighting in a war. He'd seen death up close. He'd seen suffering. For all she knew, he was suffering from some unhealed wounds of his own that he didn't talk about.

He was watching her, and she looked down at her untouched sandwich, suddenly desperate for a change of subject.

"We have a new lead from Vega."

She pounced on the topic. "The detective in California?"

"LAPD." Brian nodded toward her food. "Aren't you going to eat that?"

She picked up the sandwich. "What's the lead?"

"Turns out the victim, Gillian Dawson, had just rented the apartment where she was murdered."

"Okay."

"The previous tenant at that address was Nicole Sands, a twenty-two-year-old from San Marcos. Her physical description is a lot like Gillian's: five-two, blond, blue-eyed."

"No way." Maddie gaped at him.

"Turns out, Nicole was a high school classmate of Katya and Jolene. She went out there for college, dropped out her sophomore year."

"Oh, my God, Brian. Where is she now?"

"We're looking."

"And you think *she* was the intended victim?"

"It's a strong possibility."

"What other possibility is there? We need to find this girl!" She grasped his arm. "Brian, she could be next on the list!"

"Believe me, we're working on it. We've got half a dozen agents out in LA dedicated to the task."

She sat back and watched him, both shocked and

alarmed. *Another* potential victim. Or maybe Volansky had already realized his mistake and found her.

She closed her eyes.

"That's not all," he said.

She looked at him, and something in his expression made her think that his bumping into her today was no accident, that maybe he'd specifically sought her out to tell her something.

But why hadn't he simply called? Maybe he'd assumed she'd try to dodge him—which she would have.

"What is it?" she asked.

"We're working a theory. Sam's not sure about it, but I'm pretty convinced. We think these murders are all about silencing witnesses. Katya, Heidi, Jolene, and now Nicole. He's tracking these girls down. Torturing them for information, in some cases. Then eliminating them."

"But again, *what* information? We're talking about college kids here. What could they possibly have on him that could be damaging enough to risk committing *four* murders?"

"We're working on it," he said, for the *n*th time.

From the floor, a chime. Maddie dragged her purse into her lap and checked her phone. "Damn."

"What is it?"

"The sheriff needs me out in Wayne County." She stuffed the phone back into her purse. "I have to go."

"One more thing. Where's your gun?" The look on his face chilled her.

"At home. Why?"

"Keep it with you."

She looked at him.

"Okay?"

"But I don't even have a permit—"

"You know how to use it?" he asked.

"Well . . . yeah."

"Keep it with you."

He scooted his chair back and stood up. Maddie stood, too. "You're serious?"

He nodded.

"But what—"

"I don't know what. I'll tell you when I do." He took her coat off the chair and handed it to her. "Until then, you need to be careful."

———

Brian watched her dash across the street and pluck the parking ticket from her windshield. She muttered something he would have liked to have heard as she stuffed the citation into her purse and slid behind the wheel.

His phone buzzed.

"Yeah."

"You talk to her?" Sam asked.

"Yeah."

Brian glanced across the park toward the bank, where he'd left his car. The place where all this had started. He surveyed the bank entrance and wished more than anything that he could turn back the clock.

"Well, how'd it go?"

Worse than he'd hoped for. About how he'd expected. He pictured her talking about Emma. The guilt there ran deep. It was painful to listen to. And he knew her guilt over her daughter was what drove her to spend her career working her ass off for perfect strangers.

"It went fine," Brian said. "She agreed to start keeping her gun with her."

And he'd make sure she did it, too.

"Okay, and what about the bank?"

"Another dead end," Brian reported. "But I thought of something else, talking to Maddie. I may try Delphi again. I met the computer guy over there, and he seems pretty sharp. Think I'll take this to him, see if we can get anywhere."

"He does photo enhancement?"

"He does a lot of things. Most of them on computers."

"Well, take it wherever you want, but do it soon. We're racing a clock here, Beckman. And we're running out of time."

CHAPTER 17

Maddie emerged from her Bikram class energy-sapped and soaking wet. Hot yoga was a bitch, and although she'd been doing it for months, she still hadn't quite bought in to the concept of exercising in 105-degree heat.

She stepped into the drizzle and tipped her face up to the moonless sky. The water felt good against her skin, and for a moment she just stood.

"See you at seven, Mad."

She turned to see Kelsey making a run for the parking lot.

"What's at seven?" she called over the rain.

"A skeleton recovery. You said you wanted pictures."

"What if it's wet?"

"Even better." She smiled. "We'll put up the tarp, and my students can get a sample of adverse working conditions."

Maddie waved and hurried for her car. She slid behind the wheel and toweled off, regretting her recent interest in bone photography. Although an early wake-up call was a great reason not to stare at her phone all night. And an even better reason not to give in to temptation should a hot FBI agent come knocking on her door.

Right. As if that was going to happen.

Maddie stuffed her towel into her gym bag and retrieved her phone from her purse. She'd just missed a text from her sheriff deputy friend Craig Rodgers.

An even better reason to resist temptation—she had a call-out. She didn't bother plugging this one into her GPS. It was an intersection she'd been to many times before, one of those spots in the Texas hill country where curvy roads and steep hillsides made for scenic views and fatal collisions. She texted Craig that she was en route, set her trip odometer to zero, and headed for the site.

As she listened to the *swish-swish* of the wiper blades, she mentally inventoried what she had with her. She should be good, provided Craig had already put out road flares. She thought about the rest of her supplies and reviewed standard ops for a motor-vehicle accident.

READ the scene. Reconstruct, eye level, angles, damage. The mantra had been drilled into her by her forensic photography instructor, whose voice always accompanied her on the way to a call.

Reconstruct. She would approach the scene, looking for road hazards or weather conditions that might have contributed to the crash. The obvious factor was rain, but there could be more, and she braced herself for a tedious night. One of the challenges of accident photography was that the conditions that contributed to many accidents also made it tough to get good pictures.

Eye level. Figure out which vehicles were involved,

and get photographs from each driver's eye level. In the case of a sports car, that meant crouching down. With an eighteen-wheeler, she might need a stepladder.

Angles. Shoot all relevant angles, including north, south, east, and west, and also corner photos of the vehicles. Corner shots would include two sides in the same picture, to provide perspective. Then she had to get interior views, which might show anything from seat belts that weren't fastened to cell phones or empty beer cans. Also, she needed the license plates, which were highly reflective and tricky to photograph at night.

Damage. This was a biggie. She had to get debris, tire impressions, skid marks. In the case of a hit-and-run, it was critical to track down any blood or trace evidence. Sometimes an entire case could be built around a few chips of paint or a few shards of glass.

Crash work was challenging, but Maddie never cut corners. Photos were especially important, because the people involved were often shocked or injured. Sometimes their memories were fuzzy. Sometimes they lied.

Maddie curved around a bend. Through the veil of rain, she saw yellow lights whirring in the distance. A tow truck had already made the scene, and she hoped nothing had been moved. As she got closer, she spotted the wreck—a white hatchback nose-first in a ditch. She didn't see an ambulance, so maybe the injured motorist had already been rushed to the hospital. She parked on the shoulder, flipped on her hazard lights, and went to get the gear from the back.

Reconstruct.

She scanned the scene as she zipped into a jacket and gathered her wet-weather gear. Steady rain. Slick turns. This patch of roadway was known for collisions, but she didn't see a second car, only the tow truck. She grabbed her phone from the console and dialed Craig. Voice mail.

"Hey, I'm on the scene. Call me."

She surveyed the patch of road illuminated by her headlight beams. Raindrops shimmered in the light. Where was the tow-truck driver? She looked over her shoulder. What about the first responder?

The back of her neck prickled. *READ the scene.* Maddie was reading everything about this scene, and something felt off.

Doing a slow three-sixty, she tried to penetrate the gloom of the surrounding woods. She glanced at the phone in her hand as she walked back to her car. On impulse, she dialed Brian.

"Beckman."

She could tell by his voice that he was in the middle of something.

"Hey, it's Maddie."

Static. "—hear you."

"It's Maddie. Sorry to bug you, but—"

Crack.

Searing pain. She dropped to her knees.

Crack.

Gravel flew up, stinging her face. She pitched forward and caught herself on the bumper of the hatchback.

Gun. The word slammed through her brain. She hurled herself into the ditch. Pain lanced up her arm as she bumped against the car.

Dear God, I'm hit.

Another sharp *crack*. She looked around frantically. Car. Branches. Mud. She crouched motionless, trying to absorb the unreal reality as icy water swirled around her ankles. Someone was *shooting* at her.

Panic expanded in her chest like a balloon. She darted around the side of the car and cowered beside the engine block, panting. She looked across the road and saw her phone and equipment bag on the gravel, spotlit by her headlights and getting pelted by rain.

Her chest heaved up and down as she looked around wildly. Her ears rang. And then the high, tinny noise changed into a low grumble that could be heard over the drizzle.

Truck.

Her heart jackhammered. Terror gripped her as she crouched in the ditch and searched the highway. No headlights, but the noise was getting closer. Every cell in her body screamed for her to *move*.

She scrambled up the slippery embankment and darted for the cover of some bushes. Thorns pricked her legs through her yoga pants. She looked around desperately. Where was she? Where could she go? She was surrounded by branches and tree trunks, everything yellow in the chaotic swirl of tow-truck lights.

She plowed deeper into the woods. She peered through the trees and spotted her Prius. Was the passenger door unlocked?

A pickup halted beside her car. A large dark figure leaped from the truck bed. He stepped in front of the headlight beams. She caught a glimpse of the gun gripped in his hand just before he leaned into her car and switched off the lights.

Maddie sucked in her breath. Her heart pounded madly as she listened to his shoes crunch over the gravel. When he hurdled the ditch, she turned and plunged into the woods.

How many were there? Was she surrounded? The branches reached out like tentacles, grabbing her clothes, her hair, her feet, as she pushed through the brush. Her arm was on fire. She knew she'd been hit, but she shoved the thought away as she plowed through the thicket. She had to move. She had to hide. She had to—

The ground vanished, and she was on her butt, slipping down a hillside. Something stabbed at her, snagged her hair. She tumbled to the side as the ground grew steeper and steeper, and she felt herself gaining momentum. She bumped over rocks, tree roots. She flailed with her hands out, grasping for vines, branches—anything to slow her—but the force pulling her was getting stronger. She was losing control. Her stomach dropped out as she actually caught air. She hit the ground again and tumbled through the stabbing darkness.

She smacked into something hard. Her chest seized. She couldn't breathe. For an endless moment, she felt numb.

Then a giant wave of pain rolled over her. Her pulse roared in her ears. She gasped for breath. She managed to get a ragged gulp of air into her lungs as a burning sensation pulsed up her arm.

She clenched her teeth and tried to block out the pain as she rolled onto her side. The air smelled wet and loamy. Her face was pressed against something cold. Leaves? She reached her hand out, and another bolt of pain hit her. It took a moment to catch her breath. She extended her fingers and encountered something hard and textured. Bark. She'd crashed into a tree.

Her skull throbbed. The world was jarringly off-kilter, and she realized her head was positioned lower than her body on the steep slope. Another nauseating wave of pain hit her, and she was sure she'd vomit. But she swallowed down the bitter taste.

She closed her eyes, which made the world only slightly dimmer. She was in the woods. It was dark and rainy. She could hide here.

She could also die here.

Terror washed over her as she remembered the gunshots, as she remembered dropping to her knees. He knew she'd been hit, and he was still out there, coming for her.

He's coming, he's coming, he's coming!

She shifted her body and swung her legs around. Gingerly, she touched the wound on her forearm. It burned. She was soaked and muddy, so it was hard to feel for sure, but it had to be bleeding.

She shifted onto her hip, taking the weight off her arm. Leaves clung to her neck. Some had gotten inside her jacket, and she recalled that it was black, like her pants. Good camouflage. Clinging to that single positive thought, she squeezed her eyes shut and tried to think of a plan. Could she make it back up to her car? Should she try? But the shooter was still searching for her. He probably had a flashlight. He definitely had a gun.

Or two. The first sounds had been the distinctive *crack* of rifle fire. But the weapon she'd *seen* had been a handgun.

He wasn't alone.

Her breath hitched as reality hit her. At least two armed men against a woman with no weapon.

She *had* a weapon. She'd listened to Brian's warning and tucked her pistol into her purse on the way out the door tonight. It was up in her car at the top of the hill, but that may as well have been the top of Mount Everest for all the good it did her.

And she was injured. She thought of being hunted down like a wounded animal and felt a fresh spurt of fear. But her fear was quickly displaced by anger. The very real prospect of getting slaughtered out here in the rain and mud filled her with a blinding fury even more intense than the pain in her arm. Who the hell were these people? They had something to do with Jolene Murphy and everything else, but she didn't understand why they were after her, why they were absolutely intent on killing her. Damned if she was going to let them.

Clenching her teeth, she sat up. A flash of lightning revealed her surroundings in stark black-and-white, but only for a moment, and then she was in darkness again. She felt around with her good hand. She was at the base of a tree. Beyond that, she didn't feel any bushes thick enough to conceal her. She grabbed a root and pulled herself away from the tree so she could scoot farther down the hill. Going up was beyond her. She felt battered and woozy. So she scooted down—slowly, on her butt, until her feet encountered a plant. The first one was thorny, but she kept moving along until she felt something thick and sort of soft, maybe some kind of evergreen.

Light flickered. She glanced up and blinked into the

darkness, trying to make out shapes. The yellow glow had disappeared above the tree line. All that was left was an inky sky, barely lighter than the trees.

A strobe of lightning, and she did a quick glance around. She was in a clump of bushes at the base of a ravine. The walls were even steeper than she'd guessed. Maybe that would work in her favor.

But it was raining, had been since before she'd left the yoga studio. And this area was prone to flash floods. With a sinking heart, she realized she needed to make her way to higher ground.

Maddie's arm burned. Her head throbbed, and the mere thought of working her way back up the slope exhausted her. She felt so tired, so completely drained of energy. She wanted to lie down in a bed of leaves and go to sleep.

An all-new fear sparked to life inside her. Maybe she was tired because of blood loss. She couldn't succumb to that. If she went to sleep right now, she was as good as dead.

She forced herself to move up the hill, a little at a time, digging her thin canvas shoes into the mud and pushing with her thighs until she found a ledge. She waited what felt like an eternity for another flash of lightning and then scooted herself into the cover of a bush. It smelled like a cedar, and she hunched under its branches and peered out at the gloom.

Another flicker. Not lightning this time but a flashlight beam at the top of the hill. She held her breath as it sliced through the darkness, sweeping methodically over the hillside. It disappeared into the trees, but her fear remained razor-sharp as she waited for it to come back.

She looked down at her arm, even though she couldn't see it. She felt the sleeve of her jacket, felt the hole in the fabric where the bullet had ripped through. Another wave of nausea hit, and she leaned against the tree.

Would Craig come looking for her? Would Brian? But he didn't know where she was. Maybe neither of them did. Craig had summoned her to this scene, but something seemed wrong about that now, as wrong as the scene itself.

God, she was so tired. None of her thoughts fit together. She couldn't get her mind to work.

A flash of light, closer. Every muscle tensed as she watched it cut through the darkness. She hunched lower. She watched the beam sweeping back and forth. She tried not to move or even breathe. She watched. She waited.

The light moved closer.

CHAPTER 18

Brian swept his flashlight over the rain-soaked landscape, cursing the weather. It had been raining for more than an hour, and with each passing minute, any trail he could have followed was being washed away. He'd seen no footprints, no tire tracks. Only Maddie's car, and Maddie's camera bag, and Maddie's phone abandoned on the side of the road more than half a mile away.

His foot slipped out from under him, and he caught himself on a tree limb before he took a skid down the hillside. This terrain was damn near impossible, and he couldn't imagine her trekking around out here in this downpour. Below him, water churned through the ravine. Brian's gut churned, too, at the prospect that she might have slipped and fallen and possibly drowned in the rushing water. Did she know how to swim? He didn't know. Brian had grown up on a farm, where the ability to swim was taken for granted. But he'd learned the first week of boot camp that not everyone was raised with a creek or a beach or a swimming pool in the backyard. He'd met full-grown men who could run a mile in less than six minutes but were worthless in six feet of water.

Brian aimed his flashlight at the torrent. He shifted it to the hillside, looking for any sign of movement or clothing or the slightest thing out of place in the rugged landscape.

"Maddie!" he bellowed for the hundredth time, knowing it was probably impossible for even Sam to hear him above the drumming rain.

That's why she hadn't answered—the weather. If he told himself that enough times, maybe he'd make it true.

The *crack* of that rifle crashed through his head again, and he felt smothered with fear. He hadn't been able to get the sound out of his brain since the instant he'd heard it over the phone.

"Maddie!"

His flashlight landed on a tangle of branches and a downed tree that stretched across the ravine. He searched for footing and then hiked up and around it, scanning the ground carefully as he went. Leaves, vines, and rain-slicked tree trunks shimmered back at him, but no injured woman. Not a trace of her.

Brian grabbed a sapling and hefted himself to the top of the incline. From the higher vantage point, he shone the flashlight around again. He tried to ignore the growing lump of despair clogging his throat. He'd covered this ground already, twice. But he'd cover it again. And again. He'd cover it a thousand times if he had to, because she was out here, and he was going to find her.

Unless someone else already had.

"Goddamn it, Maddie!"

He swept his light over the trees and caught something white. His heart flip-flopped. Something white and curved that definitely didn't belong among the mud and leaves. A *shoe*. He lunged, nearly losing his balance on the steep embankment as he rushed toward it. The shoe was half buried in leaves, but as he drew closer, he realized the pile of leaves wasn't a pile of leaves at all but a *person* huddled at the base of a cedar.

He dropped to his knees and dragged her out from under the branches. A startled yelp was the most welcome sound he'd ever heard.

"What happened? Are you hurt?"

He cupped her face in his hand and shone the flashlight in her eyes as they fluttered open. Christ, she was freezing cold. And pale. And glassy-eyed. But she was alive.

"Maddie, talk to me! Are you injured?"

She winced, answering his question, and he jerked down the zipper of her jacket. Leaves were everywhere, sticking to her clothes, her neck, her hair. She looked as if she'd taken a tumble all the way down a mountain.

"Arm," she croaked.

She made an animal-like sound as he shifted her body and caught sight of the blood on her arm.

"He . . . shot me."

Brian's vision blurred with anger as he saw the wound below her elbow, just inches away from her vital organs. The dark smears of blood contrasted with her pale skin.

"What happened?" he asked, stripping off his jacket and his shirt. Where was his phone? He tied the shirt around her wound. The bleeding had stopped, but he had

no idea how much blood she'd lost. It was everywhere—
soaking her shirt, her skin, coating the leaves around
her. He choked down his panic as he tied the makeshift
bandage.

"We'll get you out of here, all right?" Where was his
phone? "Just hang on."

She mumbled something as he located his cell phone
in his pocket and quickly dialed Sam.

"I found her. Where are you?"

"North bank, 'bout half a click from the car," Sam
said. "She injured?"

"Yeah, and I'm going to need your help getting her
out of here. We're on the north side, about a hundred
yards up."

A flicker of light pulled his attention to the ridge
above. He recognized the wide beam of the flashlight
cutting through the black.

"Craig!" he yelled. "Down here!"

Maddie squeezed his arm in a death grip. "No."

Her eyes were wide, frightened. The urgent look on
her pale face sent a chill down his spine.

"Not Craig."

He glanced up at the sheriff's deputy, who'd pulled
up to the scene at the same time Brian and Sam had.
He'd told them he'd been responding to a 911 report of
shots fired at this intersection.

Brian unholstered his Glock and watched the flashlight beam that marked the deputy's descent down the
hillside. Brian wasn't sure what was going on, but Maddie was terrified.

"Craig, go back to the car," he commanded. "Call an
ambulance."

"You found her?" he yelled down.

Maddie's fingernails bit into his arm as the flashlight beam bobbed toward them.

"Go call an ambulance," Brian repeated.

The light paused briefly and then moved back up the hillside. The grip on his arm relaxed.

"He's gone now, okay? Tell me what happened."

"Someone shot me." She clutched his shoulder with her good arm and tried to sit up.

"Whoa, wait."

She pushed herself into a sitting position. "It's just my arm. I can sit."

Beyond the trees, he spotted the narrow beam of Sam's Maglite. Brian whistled to get his attention.

Sam hurried over and dropped to a knee beside Maddie.

"You got a first-aid kit?" Brian asked.

"Nope." He handed Maddie a bottle of water and helped her take a sip. "Damn, girl, what'd you do to yourself?"

His tone was light, but Brian saw the tension in his face.

"She took a bullet. Lower right arm."

"How'd you find me?" Maddie asked, and Brian heard the tremor in her voice. He pulled his jacket around her shoulders for warmth.

"We pinged your phone after you called Beckman," Sam said. "Narrowed your location down, then found your car on the side of the road up there."

"How'd you get here so fast?"

Brian looked at Sam. They'd been beating the bushes for more than an hour. If she thought that was fast, then she'd probably been unconscious part of the time.

"Hey, we're good like that." Sam shone the flashlight in her face, probably looking for a head injury. Her cheeks were smudged with dirt, but there wasn't any blood visible.

"We got an ambulance coming," Brian said. "We'll get you to a hospital."

"I hate hospitals. Help me up."

She grabbed Brian's shoulder and tried to push herself up. Sam tried to keep her down, but she was determined, and Brian stood and helped her to her feet.

"It's just my arm. I can walk."

Brian looped an arm around her waist. She slumped against him, and he felt a tidal wave of relief. She was alive. She was cold, scared, and shaken. She had a freaking gunshot wound. But she was alive, and that was the opposite of what he'd been thinking for the past ninety minutes.

In the distance, a siren penetrated the drizzle.

"Hear that?" Brian pulled her against him, careful not to jar her injury. They took a wobbly step up the hillside.

"I hate hospitals," she repeated.

"Yeah, well." Together, they took another step. "You'll just have to get over it."

———

Maddie stared out the window, transfixed by the raindrops sliding over the glass. She still felt tired. Dizzy. And strangely famished, although she couldn't imagine mustering the strength to sit up in a chair, much less cook something to eat.

"Bet you're ready for a hot shower."

She glanced across the car at Brooke, who had been at her side since they'd started on her stitches. Ten in all. As GSWs went, it was barely a scratch. Hadn't even nicked the bone.

And Maddie still couldn't believe the doctors had used the phrase *GSW* to describe what had happened to her.

She felt dizzy again. She looked down at her mud-streaked clothes. Brooke was right. A hot shower was definitely in order.

"We have a tail," Brooke said. "Just FYI."

"Huh?"

"The sedan behind us? They friends of yours?"

Maddie glanced at the mirror to her right and saw a dark sedan with two people in front.

"They're from Brian's office," Maddie said. "He told me they planned to have someone cover me."

He'd told her that in the chaos of the ER, right before he'd rushed off to an urgent meeting with his team to discuss the latest incident that he and Sam seemed certain was related to their case.

Maddie wasn't so sure. Her head pounded just thinking about it.

"What does that mean, exactly, someone 'covering' you?" Brooke asked as she turned onto Maddie's street.

"I don't know." She sighed. "Guess I'm about to find out."

Brooke pulled into the driveway as the agents rolled up to the curb. They remained in their car talking on phones as Maddie and Brooke got out. Maddie's arm was in a sling, so Brooke gathered her photography gear off the backseat.

"Where are your keys?" Brooke asked.

"I've got them."

Luckily, her injury was to her left arm, not her right, which limited her clumsiness as she dragged out her keys and unlocked the door. She entered the pass code to her burglar alarm as the agents came up the sidewalk.

Both men had thinning hair and slender builds. They looked more like accountants than law-enforcement officers. They certainly didn't look like bodyguards. The taller one stepped onto the porch and introduced himself as a special agent from the San Antonio field office. Maddie greeted him politely and just as politely asked to see some ID.

"We've got instructions from Special Agent Dulles to check the house." He tucked his credentials back into his pocket. "It shouldn't take long."

"Check for what, exactly?"

"It's a security precaution," he said, not answering her question.

Maddie had a loaded pistol in her purse, and that was about the only security precaution she was prepared to trust at the moment, but she stepped back to let them in. As they started poking around, Brooke shot her a look.

"Think you got the second string."

"I think you're right."

"You hungry?"

Maddie hesitated. "A little."

"You go shower. I'll throw something together."

Maddie smiled gratefully and headed for her bedroom, where she dumped her stuff on the bed and toed off her shoes. Next her yoga pants, which were hard to wrestle out of one-handed. Her shirt was torn, and she decided it was history, so she cut it off her body with a pair of scissors.

She set her pistol beside the sink and stood before the bathroom mirror, naked except for her sling. Her face and hands and calves were smudged with mud. She had mud in her hair, too, and leaves and even a few twigs. She turned and lifted her ponytail to see the goose egg at the back of her skull from where she'd crashed into the tree. The doctor had said she had a mild concussion, nothing serious. The local anesthetic they'd given her had worn off, so she popped a few Tylenols and washed them down with a gulp of water as the shower heated.

Maddie eyed her sling, which was going to be a pain in the butt over the next few weeks. The wound was a two-inch gash on the inside of her arm beneath her elbow. She didn't really need the sling, because the bone wasn't broken, but the nurse had recommended it as a reminder to be careful about bumping into things.

Maddie unhooked the sling and got a trash bag from a cabinet. After wrapping the bandaged part of her arm in plastic, she secured it with tape and then stepped into the shower.

Fifteen minutes later, she emerged from her bathroom feeling cleaner but no less rattled by the night's events. She pulled on jeans and a fleece sweatshirt. Then she went in search of food and possibly a drink to calm her nerves.

She walked into her kitchen and saw Brooke—who didn't have a domestic bone in her body—standing at the stove and stirring a pot of soup. Tears sprang into Maddie's eyes.

"I made you a Cape Cod." Brooke nodded at a short pink drink on the counter.

"Thank you." She picked it up and took a sip. "Where did the agents go?"

"I think they're camping out in the car. That's the sense I got. They wanted me to tell you they'll be doing periodic checks of the perimeter, so don't be alarmed."

The doorbell rang, and Maddie jumped. She crossed the house and peered through her peephole, expecting to see the accountants again, but it was Brian and Sam. She pulled open the door.

Brian frowned. "Shouldn't you be resting?"

"Nice to see you, too."

"How's the arm?" Sam asked.

Maddie bolted the door behind them. "Sore." She led them into the kitchen, where Brooke was setting a steaming bowl of chicken noodle soup on the table.

"Hey, the first string's back," she said.

"You don't want any?" Maddie asked Brooke, noting the lone place setting.

"Sorry, I need to get home." She glanced at the clock, and Maddie saw to her surprise that it was almost three.

"Thanks for the soup. And the ride."

"Anytime." Brooke grabbed her purse and nodded at Brian and Sam. "Don't keep her up too late."

When she was gone, Maddie sank into her chair, relieved to see Sam already helping himself to a soft drink. She was too tired to play hostess.

"We've had some developments we thought you'd

want to know about." Sam pulled out the chair beside her and sat down.

"First, before you say anything," Maddie said, "there's something I need to know."

"Craig Rodgers," Sam said. "I know what you're going to ask, and he's not in on it."

Maddie's shoulders slumped with relief. "Are you sure?"

"Not a hundred percent, but we think he's clear."

Brian crossed his arms. "We interrogated him at length."

"We?"

"Sam and I. His alibi checks out."

"But what about the phone call?"

"His cell phone was stolen yesterday morning," Sam told her.

"From where?"

"Locker room of his gym," Sam said. "And we checked out his story. He said he reported it to the front desk there right when it happened, and we were able to back that up. So yes, someone sent you that text message from his phone. But we don't think it was him. Frankly, he was pretty distraught when he heard you'd been summoned to that scene by someone pretending to be him."

Maddie wanted to believe them. She wanted to believe Craig, too. She'd known the man for years. But her confidence in everything, in every*one*, had been shaken tonight.

Brian was watching her carefully, probably picking up on her skepticism. "He passed a polygraph."

"You had him take a *lie detector*? Whose idea was that?"

"Mine," Brian said. "He passed with flying colors. Someone called you to that crime scene, but we don't believe it was him."

Maddie took a deep breath. She looked down at her soup but no longer felt the slightest bit hungry.

Craig wasn't in on her attack. And yet someone knew enough about her routine to summon her to a job and ambush her.

"Why don't you get some of that soup in you?" Sam nudged the bowl toward her. "You can listen while we spell some of this out."

Maddie picked up the spoon and forced down a few bites. It was hot and salty and familiar, and she felt better almost instantly. She waited for them to talk.

Brian remained standing, watching her intently. His protectiveness toward her practically oozed from his pores, and although she told herself he was just doing his job, deep down she knew that it was more than that. If he hadn't gone searching for her, if he hadn't found her in the middle of that storm and dragged her out from under that tree, she could have died, either from exposure or from being hunted down like a wounded animal. She shuddered at the memory.

"Okay, I'm listening." She met Sam's gaze. "Tell me what's going on."

"We believe you witnessed something."

She waited.

"Whether you actually did or not, someone *thinks* you did, and that's why you've become a target."

Maddie swallowed. *Target.* She pictured someone watching her through a rifle scope. She pictured a blurry image of herself coming into focus—no different

from a camera lens, really—as someone carefully composed the shot.

"What did I witness? Jolene's kidnapping?"

"At first, that's what we believed," Sam said. "Or,
better put, what we thought someone *else* believed.
That you'd seen or photographed Jolene's abduction.
Now we're not sure."

"Now our focus is on your subsequent attack," Brian
said.

"You mean Volansky?"

"Him, and also the man driving the car. He saw
you in that alley. You saw him, at least a glimpse. And
although you didn't realize it, you probably photographed him the day he staked out Jolene's workplace."

"Who is he?"

"That's the thing," Sam said. "We don't know. He's
an unidentified accomplice of our primary suspect,
Goran Mladovic. We think he's crucial to Mladovic's
operation, or else he wouldn't be going to all this trouble to silence you."

Maddie looked at Brian. "Any ideas?"

"Nothing solid yet."

She tamped down her irritation. "Okay, no more
games. What is this 'operation'? This criminal enterprise? I want to know what I'm up against here." *And
what Jolene's up against.* The more Maddie learned about
it, the more she felt the girl had never stood a chance.

"You've heard of pill mills?" Sam asked.

"I think so. That's, what, a doctor's office where they
overprescribe drugs?"

Sam nodded. "Used to be they were storefronts.
Pain-management clinics, they were called sometimes.

Walk-ins welcome. Cash-only transactions. Armed guards stationed by the door."

"And Mladovic is running one of these?"

"He was," Brian said. "The DEA tried to bring him up on charges about five years ago, but he had a hotshot lawyer. They couldn't make it stick. Best they could get was a slap on the wrist with the medical board."

"He didn't pop up on our radar again until a few years later, when a sixteen-year-old girl was wheeled into a San Antonio ER and died of a drug overdose. She'd just been to a pill party." Sam paused. "Another teenager died at the same event."

"These kids had raided their parents' medicine cabinets and set up a buffet of drugs," Brian said. "It's become a trend in affluent neighborhoods. They don't know what they're taking, and most of the time, they're taking it with alcohol."

Maddie hugged her arms around herself. "Two teens died at the same party? Was anyone arrested?"

"No, but we linked some of the drugs back to Mladovic. He's popular with the country-club crowd, apparently."

"We started looking at him more closely, and we learned that although he's joined a new 'legit' medical practice and cleaned up his act some with regard to writing scripts, he's still raising some red flags. We believe he may have started importing phony drugs from Mexico and selling them straight to the black market."

"So now you're talking smuggling?"

"He's got a long roster of patients and their friends who are more than willing to pay top dollar for whatever they want," Brian said.

Sam leaned closer. "And here's where it gets dangerous."

Maddie scoffed. "It's not dangerous yet? Supplying children with a drug buffet?"

"He crossed one of the major cartels, the Saledos."

"They're brutal. And they have their hand in everything—drugs, human trafficking, firearms," Brian said. "We even linked them to a terrorist organization a few summers ago. The head of this cartel is extremely violent. And he holds a grudge. No way Mladovic crossed him and managed to get away with it. When he found out about it, Saledo would have sought immediate and painful revenge."

Maddie tensed. "Katya Mladovic. You think they murdered her?"

Brian watched her silently.

"He might have been sending a message," Sam said. "'The gloves are off. You work for us now.'"

"If he's so harsh, why didn't he just kill Mladovic?" Maddie asked.

"Why? He'd be losing potential customers for his product," Brian said. "Better to force his compliance, by killing his daughter, and then use him as a distribution center."

"Plus, he's got stateside connections," Sam said. "More and more, the cartels have been looking for ways to circumvent the border. They actually grow some of their product on this side now."

"And we think they might be making some of their knockoff prescriptions here, too."

"You mean literal pill mills?"

"Exactly," Sam said. "Take an abandoned factory or

warehouse. Set up shop. Get the product directly into the hands of users through already established channels, such as a seemingly legitimate doctor who operates on a cash-only basis."

Maddie's gaze turned to Brian. "The tannery where we were the other night."

He nodded.

"I knew something set your radar off in there. What was it?"

"The smell. And there was dust everywhere. I sent my shoes to the lab, and on the soles they found trace amounts of various chemicals."

"Like what?"

"Sodium borate, for one," Brian told her. "That was probably used in the tanning process. But they also found a substance called—are you ready for this?—ammonio methacrylate copolymer. It's used as a coating for pills."

"We found the same trace substances on the trash bag used to dispose of Heidi Beckles," Sam said.

Maddie flinched. She hadn't heard about a trash bag. "You think she was held in that building?"

"Probably Jolene, too," Brian said. "But when she managed to make a cellular call from the warehouse, they realized it was blown as a safe location for anything, so they destroyed it. Burned up all the evidence—or tried to, at least."

Sam's phone buzzed, and he checked the screen. "I have to take this," he said, stepping into the living room.

Maddie looked at Brian. "I still don't understand why you don't just arrest him. At least, tell me you have him under surveillance."

"We do. But again, it comes down to evidence we can put in front of a judge. Right now, it's all conjecture. We don't have anything linking him to that warehouse, for example. It's only a theory."

Sam reappeared. "I've got to go in again. You staying or going?"

"Staying."

Maddie looked at him.

"See you tomorrow, Maddie." Sam nodded at her. "You take care of that arm."

"Wait." Maddie got to her feet and walked him to the door. "What's tomorrow?"

"I pulled the graveyard shift." He smiled and walked out, and Maddie stood by her threshold.

No fewer than three "unmarked" police units were parked in front of her house. The accountants were in one. Sam was getting into another. Which meant the black Taurus in her driveway must belong to Brian.

She closed the door and turned to face him. "You guys are very discreet, you know that?"

He slouched against the doorway to the dining room, watching her carefully. "We're not trying to be."

Maddie looked him over. His sleeves were rolled up, and she realized he'd found a fresh shirt somewhere. He must keep an entire suit stashed at the office for emergencies.

"What did Sam mean earlier?" she asked. "About the graveyard shift?"

"He's on tomorrow night."

"On?"

"Your security detail. Unless, that is, we get something better lined up before then."

"They're going to be here *overnight*?"

"Someone tried to kill you, Maddie." His jaw clenched as he looked at her sling. "They almost succeeded."

Maddie fumed. Part of it was fear. And her frayed nerves. But she didn't like having things dictated to her, and she didn't like evasiveness.

"What do you mean, 'something better'?"

"We're talking to the Marshals service. I'll let you know."

"You mean witness protection, where you uproot your life and go into hiding?"

Brian didn't say anything.

"Forget it," she snapped. "I'm not going."

He watched her silently.

"I've got work to do. I'm not just going to change my identity and move away because you guys can't manage to get your case together and come up with an arrest warrant."

He didn't react, and her temper festered.

"And you can't stay here tonight," she said.

"Why not?"

"Brian." She lifted her uninjured arm in exasperation. "It's after three in the morning. I'm going to bed."

"So go to bed. I'll take the couch."

"Brian . . . get real."

"What?"

"You know damn well *what*."

"You think this is about sex?" He looked insulted. "You do, don't you? You could have been killed tonight. I'll take the goddamn floor if I have to, but you're not staying here alone."

"I'm not alone! I've got two FBI agents out on my curb. I've got my pistol. I've got my alarm system."

"That's right. And you've got me."

I don't want you! She almost yelled it, but he would have known she was lying.

She *did* want him. She wanted his arms around her and his fingers intertwined with hers, as they'd been the entire ambulance ride, when she'd gripped his hand and refused to let go of him. She wanted his body, warm and solid in her bed. She wanted his Glock on her nightstand to make her feel safe. And the fact that she wanted all those things made her furious with herself. She wasn't needy. She was strong and resilient and independent.

But not tonight. Tonight she felt like a quivering bundle of nerves, and if he so much as touched her, she was afraid she'd dissolve into tears. And all that talk about not wanting any complications in her life would fly straight out the window.

Obviously taking her silence for assent, he sank into an armchair and started taking off his shoes.

"Brian, I'm serious. You can't stay here."

He sighed. "You think I'm trying to hit on you, and I'm not. I'm not even thinking about sex."

She tipped her head to the side.

"Okay, that's a lie. *Now* I am. But—"

"Stop. Just stop." She held up her hand. "This isn't a good idea. For you to be here." She watched his gaze drop to her mouth, confirming what she already knew, which was that she couldn't be around him for an extended period of time. "I don't need you here."

Something flashed in his eyes: hurt. But it was quickly

replaced by anger. "Don't push me, Maddie. It's been a shit day."

"You're telling *me* that? I got shot tonight, thank you very much. And I have to be at work in a few hours."

He looked startled. "You're seriously going to work tomorrow?"

"Why wouldn't I?"

"Why the hell *would* you?"

"Because it's my job. I've got evidence to send out. I've got prosecutors breathing down my neck who have trials to prepare for."

"Can't you take a day off?"

"No, as a matter of fact. I've got responsibilities, deadlines. You think you're the only one who has a job that matters?"

"Fine." He tossed his watch onto the table. "Work it is, then. But your car's not back yet, so looks like I'm driving."

———

Scott pulled off the highway and parked his truck on the shoulder. He surveyed the area, glancing behind him at the ridge about a quarter-mile back, which ran parallel to the road. He'd just hiked to the top of it and taken a look around. It was a good place to set up and wait. According to the police report he'd read early that morning, that was exactly what had happened. Someone had staged an accident at the juncture of two rural highways, called Maddie to the scene, and then lain in wait for her.

Anger tightened Scott's gut as he got out of the

truck. He glanced around, noting the orange spray-paint marks denoting the place where her car had been before it was towed away.

Word of Maddie's attack had spread through the law-enforcement community like wildfire. Cops, paramedics, and firefighters—basically, most of the area's first responders—had heard about the incident before they'd finished their morning coffee.

People were bothered by the attack on a visceral level. Scott understood why. Anyone who made a habit of showing up at crime scenes, often at night and alone, to sort through the aftermath of violent events harbored a secret fear of what had happened to Maddie.

The incident went beyond the day-to-day hazards of the job. Most people accepted those dangers before they scribbled their names into a scene log for the first time. Crime scenes were messy. Unpredictable. Often, the people who'd committed the crimes were still around when first responders arrived. They could be high, drunk, crazy—take your pick. And they were known to turn on police like rabid animals.

But what happened to Maddie was different. It was an ambush. And hearing about it rekindled a deep-rooted fear that every first responder had and no one wanted to talk about. Everyone dreaded the prospect of being summoned to a scene to help a victim and then becoming one.

Scott glanced up the roadway but saw no orange paint marks for the other two vehicles, because those vehicles, according to the report, were "unconfirmed." Maddie claimed to have seen a black tow truck and a white hatchback at the scene of her shooting, but when

FBI agents and sheriff's deputies arrived, they'd seen only Maddie's Prius and her abandoned equipment.

Scott glanced around. The air smelled of cedar and rain. The ground was still damp from last night's storm. He hiked up the road about fifty feet, carefully scouring the area to his right. The buzz of tires on asphalt had him turning around, and he wasn't surprised to see an FBI sedan pulling to a stop behind his truck. Beckman got out and slammed the door.

"Looks like you're doing the same thing I am." The agent walked over. Scott noted the crisp dress shirt and tie and was glad he worked for a private lab that didn't require him to wear a noose around his neck unless he had to appear in court.

Beckman stopped beside the orange markers and frowned down at the pavement. He glanced at Scott. "No bullets recovered."

"That's what the report said."

Beckman watched him carefully, probably trying to figure out if there was a theory buried in that statement somewhere. There wasn't. Not yet. But one of the things Scott had always loved about ballistics work was that it was based on the simple laws of science.

"What goes up must come down," Scott said now.

Beckman nodded. They were on the same page. They were on the same page about Maddie, too. Not that Scott was fucking her. He'd never had the privilege. But he cared about what happened to her, and the prospect of her getting ambushed on the job was unacceptable. Scott wouldn't stand for it.

And he could see Beckman wouldn't, either, which

was a big point in the man's favor. Added to his military service, it made Scott inclined to trust him.

They trekked up the roadway now, scanning the shoulder off to the right.

"Shooter was on the ridge," Beckman said. "At least, according to the report. You been up there?"

"No brass, no beer cans, no cigarette butts."

"That would be too easy."

Scott paused at a curve in the road. He studied the stand of oak trees, then turned back to look at the rocky outcropping.

"You got a laser kit?" Beckman asked.

"I'll bring it out tonight, if it comes to that. Anyway, because of the rain, it might not be accurate. I was hoping I might find something hiding in plain sight."

Beckman crossed the ditch with a long stride. He grabbed a tree limb and pulled himself to the top of the embankment, getting an impressive amount of mud on his shoes. Scott followed.

"Maddie reported three shots," Beckman said, reiterating what was in the paperwork. "One sounded like it hit metal, she said. Since her car is clean, we can assume it hit the white hatchback, near where she was standing."

"Makes sense," Scott agreed. "She said the tow truck was a good twenty yards up."

"So we can probably forget recovering that one. It's probably in a junkyard somewhere, along with the car. That leaves two rounds."

"One of the Clarke County deputies says he spent an hour out here with a metal detector right where Maddie says she was shot."

"Never met the man. You trust him?"

Scott shrugged. "He's pretty green."

"You have a metal detector?"

"In the truck. I wanted to eyeball it first." He did a slow turn, noting everything in the two-hundred-seventy-degree arc that he figured for the target area. Maddie had said it was the first shot that hit her, so he figured that was the most carefully aimed. The other rounds might have gone wild if the shooter panicked.

But Scott wasn't counting on a panicked gunman. The attack had been carefully planned and orchestrated. It involved at least two people—a shooter and a driver—and three separate vehicles. And if Craig Rodgers was to be believed, it also involved the theft of a deputy's cell phone.

Scott skimmed his gaze over the dirt, the leaves, the tree trunks. He looked at a tangle of mesquite and studied a nearby oak.

A yellow chip in the brown bark caught his eye.

"Look," Beckman said, noticing the same thing. He walked over and crouched at the base of the tree as Scott reached into one of his zipper pockets.

"You have a knife?"

"Nope." Scott pulled out a mini flashlight and aimed it at the wound in the tree. Embedded deep in the wood was a shiny bit of metal. "I've got a handsaw in the car. Better to remove the whole chunk, then dig it out at the lab. Metal tools could screw up the lands and grooves." He paused. "I bet that's a three-oh-eight. In wood like that, we might even get some rifling marks."

"You're thinking deer rifle."

"Maybe a Remington 700. That's what I'd use, any

way." He looked at Beckman. "We've got a bullet. Now we just need to find the gun."

———————

Brian swapped with Sam to have the late shift at Maddie's. He spent a few minutes getting an update from the agents parked in front of her house before knocking on her door. The peephole went dark, and he heard a few faint beeps as she deactivated her security system and pulled open the door.

She was in the jeans and black sweater she'd worn to work earlier, but her hair was pulled back now, and she'd stuck a pencil in it to hold it in place.

"What happened to your sling?"

"It was in my way." She stepped back to let him in. "I don't have a broken bone, so I don't really need it."

He glanced at her bandage and felt a fresh surge of frustration. Maybe she sensed his mood, because she turned without comment and walked into the kitchen. He followed her, glancing at his shoes to make sure he wasn't tracking mud on the floor. He'd changed into ATAC boots and tactical pants earlier so he could hit the firing range.

"You hungry?" she asked over her shoulder. "Sam brought sandwiches. Meatball subs, I think."

"I could use some food." Brian peered into the white paper sack sitting on the counter, and the scent of Italian seasonings wafted up to him. Still hot. He pulled out a foil-wrapped sandwich.

"We need to change out that peephole," he told her.

"What's wrong with it?"

"It goes dark when you stand behind it. They make ones that don't."

He glanced up, and she looked annoyed.

"How's the arm today?"

"Fine," she obviously lied. "Did you talk to Agent Hicks? He just left here about three minutes ago."

Something in her tone caught his attention. "We connected on the phone. What's wrong with Hicks?"

"Nothing. He tried to ma'am me to death, though." She opened the fridge and pulled out a jug of cranberry juice.

"Beer?" she asked.

"No, thanks."

He took a plate down from the cabinet. He set his sandwich on it, then got out a glass and filled it with water as she watched him.

Yes, he'd learned his way around her kitchen. He'd learned his way around a lot of things this week, and he could tell it made her uneasy.

He'd discovered that she wasn't much of a housekeeper, but she kept her photo equipment meticulously arranged on a wall of shelves in her guest bedroom. The room also was home to a collection of gourmet cookbooks that didn't seem to be getting much use. And Brian had noticed the rocking chair in the corner with the tattered Peter Rabbit sitting on the cushion.

She poured cranberry juice and added a splash of Grey Goose from the bottle she kept in her liquor cabinet. It wasn't fully stocked, just vodka and a bottle of expensive scotch about two-thirds full. Maddie's ex struck him as a scotch man, and Brian wondered if he was in the habit of dropping by.

"You can sit in the living room," Maddie said. "My table's a mess."

"What're you working on?"

"Framing."

She returned to the dining area, where she checked the screen of the laptop that was open at the far end. The center of the table was blanketed with sheets of cardboard in various shades of beige. On the far end of the table was a large paper cutter and a metal T-square.

"It's a service I offer my clients," she explained. "Frame shops charge a fortune. I can undercut them and still make a profit."

Brian set his plate down on one of the chairs that had been shoved back against the wall. He stood in the doorway and chomped into his sandwich.

She glanced at the computer again before pulling a sheet of cardboard from the stack. Taupe was the color, same as the walls in his apartment.

"It's a time-consuming process."

He eyed the ruler and the curls of cardboard littering the table. "Looks tedious."

"It is. But it's a good way to channel nervous energy. Mind if I keep going?"

"Nope."

He ate his sandwich and watched her get to work. She tugged the sleeves of her sweater up, and he noticed the bandage again. He didn't buy for a minute that the injury wasn't hurting her.

"The matting part is the trickiest." She leaned over the table and made a mark with her pencil. "It's really all about measuring."

"Measure twice, cut once."

She gave him a startled look.

"Something my grandmother used to say. She liked to sew." He popped the last bite of meatball into his mouth.

Maddie nestled the cardboard against the paper cutter, then slid the blade down. She turned the cardboard ninety degrees and made another cut. And another. And another. Then she removed the center rectangle and stepped back to survey her work. She laid the mat aside and pulled out a fresh sheet of cardboard.

"Want some help?" he asked.

She lined up the blade. "Your hands are big."

"So?"

"This requires precision."

"I can be precise."

She glanced up at him, and her cheeks went pink. Yes, he was thinking about sex. No surprise there.

"Fine." She stepped back. "Give it a try."

He dusted his hands on his pants and then stepped up to the paper cutter and aligned the cardboard so that the edge was flush against the side. When he slid the blade down, it bit into the cardboard at an angle, making a sloped edge.

She leaned in to study his effort. "Not bad."

She lifted her gaze, and he felt a pang of lust. She had that effect on him. It was the way she smelled, the way she talked. It was the way her sweater draped over her breasts.

It was the way she looked at him, as if she knew that right now, he was picturing her standing in his kitchen wearing only his wrinkled shirt.

He could see what she was thinking, too: *Not*

happening. The expression on her face was crystal-clear. She expected him to put the moves on her, and she was braced to resist.

Brian suddenly felt determined. He wanted to prove something to her. He wanted her to take him seriously. He wanted that even more than another night of them burning up the sheets together, a night that would no doubt be followed by a morning in which she'd slap him with her regrets.

As he looked down into her dark brown eyes, he realized something else. He wanted a relationship with this woman. A real relationship, and he didn't give a damn about any of the crap she seemed to think was an obstacle.

He didn't believe in obstacles. Obstacles could be overcome. He planned to convince her of that fact. He also planned to convince her that he was capable of more than just a hot bout of sex after a few too many drinks.

Maddie cleared her throat, breaking the silence. "You smell like CLP oil."

"How do you know about CLP oil?"

"My dad." She stepped away from him. "He used to use it to clean his guns."

He watched her as she busied herself cutting another mat. "I was at the range this afternoon."

She looked up, and he nodded at the pistol sitting on the shelf beside her photography books.

"When was the last time you had some target practice?" he asked.

"It's been a while." Not meeting his gaze, she selected a print and positioned it carefully on one of the mats she'd cut. "You know, I've been thinking about this witness-protection thing."

"What about it?"

"It seems pointless. I mean, why spend federal resources to protect a witness who didn't really witness anything?"

"We've established that *they* think you witnessed something. That's why they tried to kill you."

"Maybe so, but the point is, I *didn't* witness anything. I can't testify at trial, so why would the government spend money to protect me?"

Brian gritted his teeth. It was the exact point Cabrera had made at a task-force meeting that morning. The prosecutor in charge of the case had made it, too. Maddie Callahan was a problem, yes, but not one the U.S. Marshals wanted any part of.

Which meant she was Brian's problem. He and Sam had managed to convince everyone that they needed to keep a team guarding her, but that was an imperfect setup. Not to mention temporary.

"We're working on a solution," he said.

Maddie taped another photo, and he noticed the tension in her face. She was feeling the stress of this. It was weighing on her. It was weighing on him, too, and spending a second consecutive night not getting any sleep on her sofa wasn't likely to change things.

"Well, could you work faster, maybe? I don't know how much longer I can do this. My department's short-handed. I've been pulled off the call-out rotation. I'm running out of desk work, and my colleagues have been nice so far, but it won't be long before they get sick of covering for me."

"What's the e-mail you're waiting on?"

"What?"

"You're waiting on an e-mail. What is it?"

She slid a look at her computer. "Ben. He said he'd get me something by tonight."

"That new software program?"

"How'd you know about it?"

"Talked to him about it the other day. He thinks he might be able to bring those faces into focus, from the bank stakeout. We might ID our mystery accomplice."

"Which might be the break you guys need to get a warrant for Mladovic," she said. "Or possibly a lead on Jolene."

Brian checked his watch. It was after eleven, and he was having a hard time picturing the Billabong kid spending his Friday in front of the computer. He was probably home by now. Or out with friends.

Or maybe, just maybe, he was about to send Maddie an e-mail that would be the break they'd all been waiting for. And maybe whatever it was would put an end this suckfest of a week and give Brian a chance to make the arrest that had gone from being a goal to being a full-fledged obsession.

Brian glanced at Maddie's computer, where absolutely nothing was happening. If he wanted a break in this case, he was going to have to find it himself.

CHAPTER 19

Scott awoke to a persistent tapping sound. He chalked it up to the woodpecker outside his window, but as the haze of sleep lifted, he realized it wasn't outside his window but at his front door.

He swung his legs out of bed and glanced at the clock: 7:05. He'd meant to run this morning. But realistically, that plan was nixed last night, when he'd given some guy at the pool hall a chance to win his money back—which he hadn't.

Scott pulled on some jeans and crossed his house.

Tap-tap-tap.

It was a woman's knock, which meant either his sister had a bee in her bonnet or an ex-girlfriend had come by to see him.

Scott checked the peephole. Wrong on both counts. He pulled opened the door.

"I was about to give up on you." Rae Loveland tipped her head to the side and crossed her arms. "I figured you were an early riser."

"Why's that?" He raked a hand through his hair.

"I don't know. The Navy background? Aren't sailors

trained to get up early so they can scrub the decks and all that?"

"SEALs work weird hours."

He regretted saying it the second it was out. He knew plenty of guys who used their SEAL status—or in his case, former SEAL status—to impress women, but Scott didn't need to. He hadn't used the ploy in years.

So why the hell was he using it now, at freaking 0700 in front of Rae Loveland?

"Would you like to have breakfast?"

Scott stared at her. Now that the shock was wearing off, he noticed her outfit. Instead of her typical business suit, she wore snug-fitting jeans, a crisp white shirt with the sleeves rolled up, and loafers. *Loafers*.

He glanced down at his own feet. They were bare. So was his chest. And he noticed she was making a big effort not to look below his neck, as if she were completely immune to his half-naked body.

But he knew better.

And this conversation was a little surreal.

"Breakfast," he stated.

"You know—eggs, bacon, orange juice?" She glanced at her watch. "It's got to be quick, though. I need to leave at eight."

"Gimme a sec."

Five minutes later, he was folded into the passenger seat of her Honda Civic as she pulled into the parking lot of the Pancake Pantry. Scott had never been to the restaurant when it wasn't jammed with people, but it looked as if they'd beaten the Saturday-morning hang-over crowd.

An annoyingly chipper hostess showed them to a

booth near the back and handed them sticky menus.

Scott sat down and flagged a passing server. "Two coffees. Black."

"And we're ready to order, if you don't mind," Rae said. "I'm in a bit of a hurry."

They placed their orders, and the waitress rushed off. Scott leaned back against the seat and scanned the crowd.

"How'd you know how I take my coffee?" Rae asked.

"You strike me as the no-nonsense coffee type."

"Hmm. Good guess."

The word *guess* seemed loaded with meaning, and it took him a moment to get it. They'd never had breakfast together.

Christ, please tell him she wasn't going to go there this morning. She was about six years overdue for an apology, but he wasn't up for it right now.

"You're probably wondering why I asked you here." She leaned forward on her elbows, and he caught a glimpse down her shirt. White lace, just a hint of it. Scott wasn't feeling sleepy anymore. And the apology was suddenly seeming very doable.

She watched him expectantly, and he dragged his attention back to what she'd said. "I figure you like the pancakes?"

"I do." She smiled. "But there's something I wanted to talk to you about. I went to Sherwood Oaks to visit a client last night."

"Not alone, I hope."

"If you're referring to my safety, don't worry. I was armed."

Scott gritted his teeth. *Armed.* Yeah, right. He happened to know that Rae Loveland had a concealed-carry permit. He also happened to know that she'd gotten it less than a year ago, which meant she was probably a lousy shot.

"Next time, take someone. You shouldn't be going out there by yourself. And I shouldn't have to tell you that."

"*Anyway,*" she said, clearly annoyed. "I was meeting with a client in an apartment there. It's a single-family dwelling, but a lot of different people seemed to be using it as a crash pad."

"Who's the client?"

"Chico Gutierrez."

"Shit, can't you get any decent clients? That guy's bad news. And that neighborhood is a war zone."

"If by decent you mean wealthy, then *no*, I can't. I'm a public defender. I defend members of the public who can't afford legal counsel."

"Waste of a fancy law degree, you ask me."

"I didn't." She looked really ticked-off now, and he knew he needed to shut up. She obviously hadn't invited him to breakfast so he could pick on her.

"What's Chico's problem? He selling dope again?"

"Actually, no, he's cleaned up his act. But he's got a court date coming up. His wife's in rehab, and he wants custody of his kids."

Scott kept his opinion of that to himself, as she probably didn't want to hear it.

Their coffees arrived. Rae took a sip, then closed her eyes and gave a low moan.

He had a white-hot flashback: Rae Loveland underneath him with that same blissed-out look on her face.

She opened her eyes. "I forgot how good their coffee is here."

Scott shifted in his seat. "So what happened with Chico?"

"Nothing. But someone showed up to talk to his brother, Luis."

He waited. He'd seen Rae in the courtroom enough times to know she had a point coming.

"The man was white, blue eyes, crew cut. He spoke with a heavy accent that sounded Russian."

That caught his attention. The case Maddie was working on involved some extremely unsavory people from eastern Europe.

"You sure it was Russian?" he asked.

"Not at all. I don't speak Russian—that's just what it sounded like."

Two platters arrived. Scott doused his eggs with hot sauce and waited for her to continue.

"They had some sort of business together, and they took it into the other room. But I overheard what they were saying, and it sounded like a gun sale."

That explained why she'd decided to come to him with this. "You witness the transaction?"

"That's a guess, based on snippets of conversation. But I did some poking around. Luis has some weapons charges on his record. He was busted last spring for unlawful possession of a firearm, and before you ask, *no*, I didn't represent him. Someone else caught that case."

"Go back to the European guy. What'd he look like?"

She drizzled syrup over her pancakes and seemed to think about it. "Five-nine, one-fifty, stocky build, scar on his left cheek. Crew cut, like I said, and blue eyes."

"Not bad." Clearly, she picked up on details.

"Anyway, I'm pretty sure the guy sold a gun to Chico's brother. When they were wrapping up their meeting—this was in the other room—I heard him tell Luis something about how he should get that cobra off his hands because he'd recently used it to shoot a fed."

Scott frowned.

"That's what he said. A 'cobra.' I wrote it down as soon as I got in my car. I'm assuming it's some kind of gun, right?"

"Yeah, I'm just wondering why he'd tell his customer that when he was trying to make a deal."

"Who knows? Maybe he wanted to prove how tough he is. Or maybe he didn't want to piss off a Mexican gangbanger by selling him a dirty gun without warning him to offload it. Luis Gutierrez has some scary friends."

"Ha. Friends? What about him? I still can't believe you went to Sherwood Oaks alone. Next time, call me."

She ignored the offer and picked at her pancakes. "Listen, I know you worked on that shooting case. I know you ran the ballistics." She glanced up at him. "Do you know what sort of gun was used?"

Scott dug into his eggs.

"Do you?"

"How do you know so much about this case?"

"Everyone knows about it. It's the topic of conversation at every watercooler at every police station and sheriff's office within a hundred miles of here, not to mention the courthouse. Some guy tried to gun down an FBI agent at a movie theater. And then what happened to Madeline Callahan?" Rae shook her head. "It's very disturbing."

Scott watched her. She seemed genuinely unsettled by everything. "Why didn't you take this to the police?"

"I don't know. You're involved. You ran the ballistics. I figured you could check on this gun first, see if it's even connected to anything before we bother the police with it. I mean, I hear it's a task force, right? Some big team of agents from all over the place?"

"That's the word."

She continued eating her pancakes, and he watched her.

"How'd you make the connection between the Russian and the cop shooting?"

"*Attempted* cop shooting. The agent wasn't injured."

"No, but Maddie was. And the two events are probably connected."

"It was a rumor I heard. That some Russian mafia guys were involved in that thing at the theater, and also what happened to your friend from the Delphi Center. That's what the scuttlebutt is over at the police station."

"You really keep your ear to the ground."

"I have to." She swigged some coffee. "It's my business." She glanced at her watch. "And speaking of, I need to get going."

"Where?" He shoveled eggs into his mouth. If she said she was meeting her boyfriend, he was going to take his sweet time.

"Beeville."

"As in the prison?"

"They have visiting hours from ten to noon. I've got a client meeting."

"Nice. You plan to wear that?"

She looked down at herself. "Why shouldn't I?"

"Put a jacket on over it. You can see through that shirt."

She rolled her eyes. "Are you almost done?"

He glanced down at his breakfast, which he'd managed to put a dent in despite the distraction of Rae sitting across from him and giving him a tip in the case that had occupied his mind all week.

"Let's go." He stood up and pulled some bills from his wallet, but she was already paying the waitress.

"I asked *you*," she said.

He reluctantly put his money away and followed her out to the parking lot.

"I'm going to need an address for this Luis Gutierrez," he said.

She popped her car locks. "What are you going to do?"

"Pay him a visit. See if he's got a pistol to sell."

"Good luck with that. He'll make you for a cop in about two seconds."

He slid into the seat. "I'm not a cop."

"You *look* like a cop."

He smiled slyly. "I'm a master of disguise. I can look like anyone."

"One of your SEAL tricks, huh?"

"That's right."

Brian caught some disapproving stares as he walked into the office Saturday afternoon, and he shouldn't have been surprised. He was looking a little rough. He hadn't been home in almost three days. He was going on twenty-four hours in the same clothes, and he desperately needed a shave. He'd managed to grab a shower that morning, but he'd refrained from borrowing the dainty pink razor sitting on Maddie's tub. He figured she wouldn't want him using the razor she used on her legs to shave his two-day beard, although he wouldn't have minded at all. In fact, the idea was pretty arousing.

But Maddie would have thought it was crossing some sort of boundary. She was in friend mode, which wasn't nearly as fun as sex-in-his-kitchen mode. But Brian was determined to make her see the light.

He tossed his keys onto his desk and stared glumly at the mountain of paperwork in his in-box. Then he booted up his computer and checked his electronic in-box. Fifty-six messages later, he was only halfway through.

He was so behind. This case was getting to him. And really, it wasn't the case so much as Maddie. She had him by the throat. He liked her way more than he should after so short a time. He'd started to crave her company and get antsy when she wasn't around. He couldn't chalk it up to the bodyguard gig. That was part of it, but it was also her. He'd developed a fixation with her body, her skin, her mouth. He couldn't look at any part of her without thinking of sex.

But it wasn't only the sex. He liked her attitude. He liked her backbone. He liked her age. There was something beautiful about a woman who had been in the trenches of life and was still up for a fight.

But what he liked most—more than all the rest of it—was her eyes, because he could read them. She could say what she wanted, trying to convince him she was tough and brave and didn't really need anyone, but her eyes told another story. Whenever she looked at him, he saw that hint of vulnerability that told him he had a chance.

"Hey, I thought you were on PSD this afternoon."

Brian glanced up to see Sam standing beside his cubicle.

"I traded with someone."

Sam lifted an eyebrow at this news. He wasn't the only one who'd noticed Brian shuffling the schedule of Maddie's personal security detail so he could spend nights at her house. He was sure she'd noticed it, too, but she hadn't said anything.

Sam leaned against his cubicle. "So, what's the update on that ballistics report?"

"Which one?" They were waiting on so many reports now, it was hard to keep track.

"The Highway 106 crime scene."

Brian scrolled through e-mails, looking for the one he'd opened on his phone last night.

"It's a three-oh-eight, like he thought."

"Who's running this again?" Sam asked.

"Firearms guy at Delphi. He said he got rifle marks on the slug, but I'm still waiting to hear if there's a match in the database. Okay, here we go." Brian read the message and muttered a curse. "No match on the slug."

"Then we've got a usable bullet but no gun. Which means another dead end."

"Unless we can get a suspect who happens to have a rifle we can match it to."

Sam shook his head. "I hate this case."

Brian leaned back in his chair. "What about Mladovic? How's that warrant coming?"

"We're working on it. Hey, did you talk to LeBlanc? She tell you about that picture?"

"What picture?"

"You should have gotten an e-mail."

Brian skimmed his in-box until he found a message from Elizabeth. The subject line was JOLENE MURPHY. He skimmed the text of the message before opening the attachment. A color photograph came up on the screen.

"Shit, where'd she get this?"

"She convinced Jolene's mom to let her take another look at her bedroom," Sam said. "This was stuffed in a drawer."

The photo showed four girls in bikinis lined up on a beach, smiling for the camera. Brian's shoulders tensed as he recognized the faces: Katya, Jolene, Heidi, Nicole. Four girls—two dead, two missing.

"Unbelievable, isn't it?"

Brian glanced up. "Where was this taken?"

"South Padre Island, according to Jolene's mom. It was August five years ago. A good-bye trip, she said, before everyone left for college."

Brian looked at the faces. "They went down there alone?"

"With the Mladovics. They rented a condo on the beach."

"Fucking A. South Padre." Brian picked up his phone and dialed a number he knew by heart.

"Who you calling?" Sam asked.

"Friend of mine with ICE. I think I know what they were doing down there."

Sam lifted his eyebrows.

"I think they were heading across the border."

————

Ben eyed Maddie with amusement as he exited the Delphi Center's lobby-level coffee shop.

"Thanks for meeting me," she said.

"No problem." He glanced over her shoulder. "What is this, take your dad to work day?"

Maddie ignored the comment and focused instead on what he was eating. "Tell me that's not the last blueberry muffin."

"Actually, it is, and I plan to eat all of it. I logged eighteen miles on my mountain bike this morning." He looked over her shoulder again as he jabbed the button to summon the elevator. "Seriously, who's the suit?"

Maddie sighed. "A special agent with the San Antonio FBI office." She cast a glance at the glass door, where the agent was supposed to meet her in exactly two hours.

"A pet fed? Sweet." Ben followed her onto the elevator. "Always wanted one of those, preferably a female."

The doors whisked shut, and his gaze dropped to her bandaged arm. "How's the injury coming?"

"Better."

"Does it hurt to handle a camera?"

"Not really," she said, "but I'm definitely learning to do things one-handed. So are you making progress on the picture?"

"I was here until midnight working. Never thought I'd become such an expert in photo software."

The doors dinged open again, and they headed down the window-lined hallway toward the Cyber Crimes Unit. Ben used his palm print to gain access, and Maddie followed him into the empty lab, where rainbow-colored screen savers danced across the monitors.

Maddie grabbed a rolling chair from the neighboring cubicle as Ben logged into his system.

"I'm sorry this is taking so much of your time."

"I'm not." His fingers flew over the keyboard. "This case is top of my list right now. Top of everybody's. We're determined to crack this thing, especially since the FBI isn't up to the job."

Maddie bit back a comment. Investigators were so damn competitive with one another, and it got on her nerves. Why couldn't people just acknowledge that they all worked hard and did the best they could? Maybe because it was a male-dominated field.

"Okay, I was able to get a copy of that new photo software I told you about. The one my friend is working on?"

She scooted closer as he opened a file.

"Wow." She studied the photograph as it came up on the screen. The image of the face reflected in the Buick's side mirror was still dim and fuzzy, although it was much better than when she'd last seen it. Maddie still didn't recognize the face.

"It's quite an improvement," she said, trying not to let her disappointment come through in her voice. "With the baseball hat, though, I still don't recognize him."

"Look again. You sure?"

"I'm sure."

Ben sighed, clearly disappointed. "I was afraid of that." He closed out of the picture and started tapping more keys. "That's why I called another buddy. This guy works for BSS."

"What's that?"

"Biometric Security Solutions. They're one of the leading makers of biometric identification software. We use some of their stuff here at the lab. You know our palm-print access system? That's them."

"They do facial recognition?"

Ben clicked onto the company's website. It showed a sleek silver logo and a digitized image of a human skull.

"Facial recognition, palm prints, irises, you name it. They're making a killing at it. They just got hired by one of the biggest casinos in Las Vegas to create a program that identifies people who count cards."

"Hmm. I never thought about uses like that." Maddie studied the website, which included vaguely worded snippets about "discreet security solutions." She figured the "discreet" part meant that the people the system was designed to recognize had no idea they were being analyzed.

"They do more typical stuff, too," Ben said. "My friend sold a big package to Interpol, for example. They're going to use it to help beef up security at border checkpoints. Are you familiar with how it works?"

"Not really."

"It's based on algorithms."

"You've lost me already. I hated math."

"Well, I'll boil it down. Essentially, this company has come up with some new algorithms that extract landmarks from images of faces captured in photographs and surveillance videos."

"Landmarks. Like facial features?" she asked.

"Exactly. The program basically measures the distances between features, such as ears, pupils, nostrils, et cetera. Then it converts the information to a digital 'map' and stores it in a database. For example, Interpol has a database of mug shots. Investigators can then submit queries on images where they *don't* have an ID and see if there's a hit."

"Sounds like a useful tool."

"But it's only as good as the algorithm," he said. "They've been trying to implement this technology for years to help ID criminals at border crossings— or maybe people on the terrorist watch list, stuff like that—but they've had problems with both false IDs and no IDs popping up. My friend's program is supposed to overcome those issues. I sent him the photograph, by the way."

"You did?"

"He's in Germany right now on the implementation team that's supposed to get this thing up and running. Since you mentioned the Serbian mafia connection, I figured it was worth a shot."

Maddie waited for him to tell her the outcome, although she figured she already knew.

"No match, unfortunately."

Maddie sighed. "So even though we know that this man—whoever he is—is a known associate of Mladovic, and although we know Mladovic frequently associates with criminals from eastern Europe, Interpol has no record of this guy's mug shot in their system."

"Not just his mug shot," Ben said. "The database includes mug shots, driver's-license photos, immigration pictures. It's got millions of records."

"But none of our guy."

"Not that we can find. Which indicates one of two problems. Either the authorities in Europe have no record of the guy—"

"In which case, we can probably assume he isn't Serbian," Maddie said.

"Or the problem is the photo itself. Because the photograph is of a reflection and because part of the face is obscured by a baseball cap—"

"Not to mention the crappy lighting."

"That, too," he agreed. "Anyway, for whatever reason, the image may not be providing enough detail for the program to work."

"Not enough landmarks."

"Exactly."

She looked at the computer screen and turned the issue over in her head. She thought about all the photographs she took at weddings and bar mitzvahs and the digital albums she uploaded for her clients. She thought about Hannah posting her engagement pictures to her personal blog.

"What if we try a different approach?" She looked at Brian. "What about social media? You said Interpol has millions of photos in its database, but think about

Facebook. What do they have, like, a billion users?"

Ben leaned back in his chair and stroked his goatee. "Not a bad idea. We could upload the picture."

"And see if any tags pop up," she said, feeling a spark of excitement.

But it quickly faded.

"It's not going to work," she said. "It's only going to suggest tags based on people who are already associated with someone's profile. How do we know Mladovic even has an account? And how do we know he takes pictures of his friends? We're talking about the mastermind of a criminal enterprise. I doubt he has time to screw around on the Internet."

"You'd be surprised," Ben said. "Maybe he spends hours a day looking at porn. Is this guy married?"

"Yeah."

"Then even if he doesn't have an account, I bet his wife does."

"Maybe," Maddie said, thinking about it. Would Mladovic want his wife using social media? Possibly, if her socializing was good PR for his business. "But even if she does have an account, how on earth would we gain access to it? I don't even know her name."

Ben smiled as he clicked onto a search engine and started typing away. "Maddie, Maddie, Maddie . . ." He shook his head. "How long have we been friends?"

"You think you can crack her password? A woman whose name you don't even know?"

"Give me fifteen minutes," he said. "I bet I can tell you what she ate for breakfast."

Brian glanced at the skeptical faces around the conference table. He looked like shit. He knew that. And he wasn't winning any popularity contests by calling an urgent meeting on Saturday afternoon, but he had a break in the case.

The challenge was going to be convincing everyone else of his theory.

"Okay, let's get started," Cabrera said, sinking into a chair at the head of the table. He gave Brian a hard look. "What have you got?"

Brian scooted up to the table and made eye contact with everyone: Sam, Elizabeth, Hicks. Another agent had Maddie duty, and two more from the team were busy covering Mladovic.

"I spent the last forty-five minutes on the phone with Immigration and Customs Enforcement," Brian said. "Turns out, all four girls in this picture"—he held up the photograph of Katya, Jolene, Heidi, and Nicole—"made multiple trips across the border into Mexico the summer before their freshman year of college."

Everyone's attention zeroed in on the picture.

"So what?" Cabrera said. "These girls were friends, and kids go down there all the time."

"Yeah, but I'm focused on *why* they go down there," Brian said.

"Bar hopping, shopping, hitting the beach," Elizabeth said.

"Let's look at the shopping. Lot of kids—and adults, for that matter—go down there looking for drugs. Besides marijuana, I mean. I'm talking about steroids, painkillers, rave drugs, you name it. The pharmacies sell pretty much everything, and you don't need a legitimate prescription."

At the word *prescription*, everyone perked up. The entire investigation had started with the DEA looking into Mladovic's script-writing practices.

"You're saying these girls were smuggling prescription drugs?" Sam asked.

"It fits," Brian said. "Customs is looking for the big guys—people coming over with their tires and fuel tanks packed with coke. Couple of teenagers in bikinis coming back from a day trip? They don't get as much notice."

"But how does this connect to Mladovic?" Elizabeth asked.

"Timing." Brian slid the photo across the table toward her. "Their first trip on record was five years ago, not long after the state board first notified Mladovic that he was under investigation. He was looking for a way to feed his patients' habits without drawing more attention to himself."

"But how would he make any money at that?" she asked. "They're not just giving stuff away down there."

"Maybe he wasn't at first," Brian said. "Maybe initially, it was just a matter of filling a gap in his supply chain."

Sam leaned back in his chair. "And then he realized the potential and decided to start making his own product."

Cabrera tapped his pencil on his legal pad, still looking unconvinced. "You don't just decide to start manufacturing this stuff."

"Right, but we know he did, at some point. We have the trace evidence from the converted tannery. Who owns that land, by the way?" Brian looked at Sam.

"Some rancher, about a hundred and fifty years old. He's got around five thousand acres and a couple of gas wells. I bet he had no clue someone was out there using his warehouse until it burned to the ground."

"Back up," Elizabeth said. "You're saying he gets the idea to start importing phony pharmaceuticals—"

"The drugs are real," Brian corrected. "It's the labels that are phony. Often, they're made to look like name brands."

"Okay, knockoffs, then. Whatever. So you're saying he starts bringing these in and then decides to start manufacturing them himself to supply his list of patients?"

"Sounds like a lucrative enterprise," Sam said. "But where does he get the ingredients? Opium derivatives are controlled substances."

"We need to find out," Brian said. "My guess is he's got an in with some of the pharmaceutical companies he used to purchase from. Maybe someone's funneling him some of the hard-to-obtain materials so he can make his product."

"Problem is, he's poaching on the turf of all the major cartels," Cabrera said. "Which might explain Katya."

Brian looked at his boss and felt a weight lift off his shoulders. Cabrera got it. Brian could see it on his face.

"That's my theory," Brian said. "Saledo got wind of what he was doing and had Mladovic's daughter executed. Only he set it up like a drug overdose to send a message."

Silence settled over the table.

"Back to the girls," Elizabeth said. "How many of these trips did they make?"

Brian flipped open his notepad and checked the notes he'd made while on the phone. "Six trips over a ten-month period, which would have been their freshman year of college. After that, they stopped going—at least, according to what we know. But I think they still played a role in this. I think that's why Mladovic's been systematically tracking them down and having them killed."

"What role? Why?" Elizabeth looked frustrated.

"Think about it," Brian said. "These girls were spread out across four major college campuses. They were tapped into a whole new market."

"You mean—"

"They were his dealers. And now that Katya's dead, he's decided to cut them out."

CHAPTER 20

The champagne was flowing, the dance floor was hopping, and Todd Jennings's wedding guests were doing their best to help him celebrate his third trip to the altar.

Maddie, meanwhile, was doing her best to ignore the FBI agent who had been watching her all night as she made her way around the ballroom of Sierra Vista Country Club.

She turned to see the wedding planner charging toward her, clipboard in hand. He halted in mid-stride to mutter something into a headset. Then his gaze snapped to Maddie.

"T minus ten. You ready?"

"All set," she said.

"You sure?"

"I'm sure."

The man was the best in the business, but he was über-intense and treated each reception like a shuttle launch.

"Okay, don't forget the flower girl. She is simply *adorable*, and we want a shot of her throwing rose petals at the limousine. And the maid of honor. She's a new client, so be sure to get her, too."

"They're on my list." Maddie lifted her clipboard to reassure him. Pain zinged up her arm, and she did her best not to wince. "Really, I've got it under control."

His mouth dropped open. "No!"

It took her a moment to realize he was talking to someone on the phone. He turned on his heel and dashed away to take care of some mini catastrophe.

Maddie's gaze landed on a waiter passing out flutes of champagne. Drinking on the job was taboo—right up there with going through the buffet line to load up on crab cakes—but she felt tempted tonight. In addition to the typical wedding-reception stress, she was juggling the added anxiety of an injured arm and an FBI babysitter.

Not to mention her ex-husband, who had been eyeing her all night from the side of his very pregnant wife.

"How's the gunshot wound?"

Maddie took a deep breath and turned around. "Hello, Mitch."

"I hear you're having a rough week."

Mitch looked dapper as always in his designer suit. His expression held a mix of concern and curiosity as he tipped back his scotch and soda.

Maddie looped her camera around her neck. "How'd you hear about my injury?"

"Bumped into your ER doc over at the Ale House."

The Ale House was a hangout near the hospital where doctors, paramedics, and other medical personnel liked to blow off steam. Evidently, the grapevine was humming once again.

"They get you stitched up okay?"

"Sure did." She pasted a smile on her face as Mitch glanced at her arm. She was wearing an outfit that concealed the bandage—a black silk shirt and matching pencil skirt, her go-to ensemble for weddings.

"Police have any leads?" Mitch asked.

"They're working on it."

He shook his head. "That's the problem with working nights."

Maddie bit back a retort. She was determined not to bicker, even though that condescending tone of his grated on her nerves.

"Well, I guess business is good. I see you've got a new assistant?"

He nodded at the FBI agent who was standing in the corner impersonating a potted plant. The man had a camera around his neck, but the prop might have been more convincing if he'd managed to snap a few pictures during the course of the evening.

"Yep, booming," she said cheerfully, scanning the ballroom for a photo op that needed her attention. She turned back to Mitch, and he was giving her a look she recognized.

"So. Where's Danielle?"

"Another pit stop. You know how it is."

Being pregnant, he meant.

God, would this night ever be over? Maddie searched for an escape. Her gaze landed on Brian, and her heart lurched. What was he doing here? He stood beside the door to the balcony, with his shoulder propped against the wall. His gaze met hers, and she felt a jolt of heat from the top of her head to the tips of her toes.

"So Maddie—"

"Excuse me." She abandoned Mitch and crossed the ballroom. Brian followed her with his gaze. He had that way of standing, that way of *being*, that was utterly relaxed and yet completely alert at the same time. He'd probably made a good soldier, she thought randomly, and then hated the idea. She could see him being calm and clear-headed in battle but fiercely determined at the same time.

She stopped in front of him just as the band completed a song.

"What are you doing here?" she asked over the applause.

"Starting my shift."

"But—" She glanced over her shoulder and saw the agent who'd been assigned to her slipping out of the ballroom. "I thought LeBlanc was on later tonight."

"She had a conflict."

Something in his tone seemed to challenge her, and Maddie searched his face, trying to read whether he was lying. He'd spent the past two evenings on her sofa, watching ESPN into the wee hours of the night, or maybe *through* the night. She wasn't sure he'd ever actually gone to sleep. The few times she'd crept past the living room, he'd been sprawled back on her couch, arm tucked behind his head, transfixed by the television. He hadn't been intrusive. He'd stayed out of her way. But his continued presence was making her edgy. Now that she was caught up on framing projects and housework and e-mails, she didn't know what to do with herself. The idea of curling up on the sofa to watch sports with him seemed far too relationship-y.

"How's your arm tonight?"

"Fine."

His gaze moved down her body and lingered on her black slingbacks. Maddie's skin heated, and she would have bet money he was thinking about sex.

"Where's your gun?" he asked.

Or maybe not. Maybe *she* was the one who couldn't shake the memory of him sliding those shoes off her feet.

"I—" She cleared her throat. "It's in my camera bag. Why?"

"You should keep it with you."

His voice was tinged with disapproval, and she started to get defensive but then changed her mind. He was right. Instead of arguing, she led him to the spot where she'd left the equipment and started gathering things up. Brian collapsed her tripod, and she tucked it under her arm like an umbrella.

"You ready? I'm parked out back, by the kitchen."

"I'm not ready at all." She glanced at her watch. T minus four minutes. And damn it, now she was doing it. "I've got to get set up at the porte cochere." She started toward the door, but he caught her arm.

"The who?"

"The place where the limo's waiting." She darted her gaze to the ballroom entrance as guests started streaming out to line up along the hallway and throw rose petals. "I need a shot of the newlyweds driving away. It's for the end of the wedding album."

Brian glanced at doorway, and Maddie could tell he didn't like the plan. She shook off his arm.

"Come on, let's go."

"Stick close to me," he ordered. "And don't go out-side."

Maddie tamped down her annoyance as she made her way through the guests flocking down the carpeted corridor. As they neared the foyer, she was relieved to see that the bride and groom hadn't made their appear-ance yet, so she still had time to set up the shot. She hurried for the door, but Brian clamped her on the shoulder.

"Hey, I said *inside*."

"Don't be ridiculous. I need them climbing into the limo."

"Use your zoom lens."

Maddie glared at him, but the hard set of his jaw told her it was no use. This was one of those my-way-or-the-highway moments that had been popping up with infuriating frequency over the last few days.

A flash of movement caught her eye, and she spotted the wedding coordinator waving at her from the other end of the corridor. He tapped his watch frantically and held up three fingers. *T minus three! Prepare for liftoff!*

The lights flickered. She glanced up at the chande-lier, and the room was plunged into darkness. A collec-tive gasp went up from the crowd.

Brian cursed.

"What the—"

"Come on." He took her hand and pulled her away from the crowd.

"Where are we going?"

He didn't answer, simply towed her through the darkness as if he knew precisely where he was going. One by one, cell phones flickered on and penetrated the black. Everyone was chattering excitedly, but she was moving too fast to catch the words. Brian stopped and pushed open a door. He maneuvered her into a storage closet, then squeezed in behind her. The door thudded shut.

"What—"

"Quiet."

A bluish glow filled the room as he lifted his phone to his ear. Maddie glanced around and saw that they were wedged in amid stacks of chairs.

"Bruce? It's Beckman. Where are you?" He listened a moment, and the tense lines of his face sent a chill racing down Maddie's spine. "I'll be right there."

The room went dark again.

"Stay here," he ordered.

"Where are you going?"

"To see what's happening. You have your pistol?"

"Wait! What's going on? Who's Bruce?"

"Stay here, even if the lights come back on."

"But—"

"I mean it, Maddie. Don't move."

———

When Brian returned to the closet fifteen minutes later, he found Maddie sitting on a chair, legs crossed, in the pitch dark. She jumped to her feet.

"What happened?"

"Power surge." He grabbed her camera bag off the ground and picked up the tripod.

"*Power surge*. That's it?"

"Yeah."

She dodged past him into the hallway and rushed to the foyer. Guests were milling around, talking. She stopped and stared down at the flower petals strewn across the floor.

"I'm parked in back," he reminded her.

The look she shot him was venomous. She strode past him down the hallway and into the kitchen. He followed. The room was even steamier than it had been earlier, when he'd made his initial walkthrough of the facility. Half a dozen workers were lined up at sinks, washing dishes with big hoses. The employee exit was propped open with a milk crate, and several waiters in tuxedos were having a smoke. Brian snagged Maddie's arm before she reached the door.

"Hold up." He moved her behind him and stepped out to scan the vicinity around the exit. Then he put his hand on her back and guided her to the Taurus parked in the loading bay.

Maddie slid into the car without comment as Brian dumped her equipment in the backseat.

So she was pissed. Okay. He probably should have gone to retrieve her sooner, but he'd wanted to confirm that the power outage was nothing more than a technical glitch. He scanned the surrounding area now as he walked around to the driver's side and got behind the wheel.

Maddie stared straight ahead as he backed out of the loading bay and headed for the service drive that connected with the highway. He darted another glance at her, but she refused to look at him. He took out his phone and called the head of the country club's security to tell him he was leaving the premises.

"Bruce, I take it?" she asked when he hung up.

"Yeah."

Her phone beeped from the backseat, and she hauled her camera bag into her lap to dig through it. She checked the text message and then muttered something and looked out the window.

"What?"

"Nothing," she said through clenched teeth. Brian waited for the dam to burst. It wasn't going to be pretty. Clearly, she was ticked off.

Well, so was he. A lack of sleep, a lack of sex, and—most of all—a lack of progress in the investigation were making him crazy. Despite today's breakthrough, the task force still didn't have an arrest warrant for Mladovic. Brian tried to conceal his frustration as he navigated his way across town.

This case sucked. Providing security for a woman he craved like oxygen sucked. Standing on the sidelines and watching her ex-husband hit on her sucked.

But what sucked more than anything was his deep-rooted fear that he was going to fail again and that Mladovic was going to hurt another innocent person with complete impunity, and this time, it was someone Brian cared about.

And hey, while he was thinking about it, another thing that sucked was that he'd somehow developed a thing for a woman who'd made it abundantly clear she only wanted to be his "friend." He was doing his dead-level best to go along with that scenario, hoping in time she'd see how wrong-headed it was. He was trying to be patient, hoping she'd start taking him seriously instead of treating him like some error in judgment that she'd made after a few too many drinks. But patience had never been his strong suit, and his supply was quickly running out.

Brian pulled into her driveway and parked at the very end, a short distance from the back door. She stalked up the porch steps and had the door unlocked before he could catch up to her. She silenced the beeping alarm with a few jabs of her finger and turned to face him.

"This arrangement isn't working."

He deposited her tripod on the floor beside his overnight bag. "Oh, yeah?"

"Yeah."

He folded his arms over his chest. "Because it's working great for me—just so you know. I've had about five hours of sleep the last three days. And my coworkers are all over me because you're being such a pain in the ass."

"*I'm* being a pain in the ass?"

"Yes."

Her cheeks flushed as she glared at him. "How, exactly?"

"You want a list? Fine." He tossed his keys onto the counter. "You're one of the few living witnesses in a federal investigation, but you refuse to recognize that fact—"

"We've been over this already."

"—which makes things a hell of a lot harder for people providing security for you."

"If you guys would make an *arrest*, I wouldn't need security."

"The day after being *shot* by someone probably working for our chief suspect, you insist on going into work. Meaning some member of the task force—namely, me—has to chauffeur you around."

Her eyes flashed. She didn't like that description.

"Then, after spending another night on your couch, I get up in the morning, and you assure me you're going to spend your Saturday doing laundry. So I go into the office to catch up on all the shit I've been neglecting, and what happens? I get a call from the agent assigned to you, who was supposed to spend the day running down leads on his computer but instead spent it shuttling you to and from your office—"

"I told him he didn't have to come! He insisted. Which is ridiculous. The Delphi Center has better security than most military bases."

Brian edged closer and glared down at her. "Ever hear of taking a vacation day? Or staying home on the weekend? Ever think of trying to make our job easier instead of harder?"

"What about my job?" she countered. "Who do you think's going to pay my bills if I decide to bag work and miss all my deadlines?"

"Then tonight," he said, ignoring her, "three separate agents try to talk you out of going to a freaking *wedding* with four hundred people, where security is guaranteed to be a nightmare. But do you listen? No. And look what happened."

"Nothing happened! They blew a fuse. So what? And then you stuffed me into some closet and made me screw up my job."

"I have a job to do, too, Maddie. And you're making it damn near impossible."

She took a deep breath and fumed up at him. "Why don't you just admit what this is about?"

"What is this about?"

"Jolene Murphy."

He scowled.

"She got grabbed right from under your nose, and now you're paranoid about me." She paused, searching his face. "I'm right, aren't I? You're terrified of dropping the ball again, so you're not being logical." She swept her arm out. "Don't you see what this is?"

"What?"

"Overkill," she declared. "I've got a burglar alarm. I've got a pistol. I've got FBI agents camped out at my house and tagging along every time I go anywhere. They're watching my every move. Yesterday I caught LeBlanc actually looking through my mail! And you think I don't know about the GPS you put on my car? God, you've probably bugged my phones and read my e-mails. It's absolutely absurd. You're being totally paranoid!"

"I'm not being paranoid," he said. "And this isn't about Jolene."

"Then what hell is it with you?"

Brian glowered down at her. Her eyes sparked, and she looked as if she wanted to smack him.

He kissed her. She stiffened, and he felt her fingers digging into his arm. She was going to push him away and probably kick him out, and he felt a pang of fear that he'd gone too far. So he loosened his grip and slid his hand up her body as he kissed her—as gently as he could, considering how much frustration he'd stockpiled over the last few days. Ever since he'd woken up with the smell of her all over his sheets, he'd been dying to get her naked again.

But damn it, she pissed him off.

"Brian." She tried to lean back, but he pulled her closer and kissed her with all the pent-up feelings he'd been keeping in check. Her mouth was hot and—thank God—open for him now as she made a low moan that gave him a burst of hope. He pulled her hips against him so there was no way she couldn't know exactly what he wanted, and he felt another burst of hope when she didn't pull away.

And he was pretty sure those fingernails digging into his neck were a good sign.

God, he wanted her. She felt and tasted even better than he remembered. He tugged her blouse out of her skirt. The fabric was thin and silky, and he slid his hand under it so he could touch her smooth skin, which was a hundred times better. He slid his fingers up, over her rib cage, and cupped the breast that seemed tailor-made for his palm. But just as he was enjoying the heavy, perfect *rightness* of it, her grip loosened, and she pulled away.

She blinked up at him. "I thought we agreed not to do this."

"You agreed." He jerked her back. She made a little yelp and looked down at her arm.

"Shit, did I hurt you?"

"No." She glanced up at him. Then she looked away guiltily, and he knew what she was going to say. "Brian . . . I can't do this."

"Why not?" How could she not want this? After knowing what they were like together?

"Because. I told you. I don't want to start some—
thing together that isn't going anywhere."

He leaned back against the counter and smiled bit-
terly. He wanted to argue with her, but pride kept the
words lodged in his throat.

He folded his arms over his chest and watched her.
She smoothed her blouse and glanced at the clock on
the kitchen wall. She looked uncomfortable. And embarrassed. And he wasn't going to do a damn thing to
rescue her.

"It's late," she said, picking up her camera bag. "I
think we both really need to get some sleep."

———————

Maddie lay in her bed, staring at the ceiling and running the conversation over in her head.

Worst of all was that look on his face when she'd
mentioned Jolene. She shouldn't have said it. The flash
of guilt in his eyes would be with her for a very long
time. Whatever awful things had happened to that girl,
he felt responsible, and the words she'd flung at him had
made him feel even more so. Picturing his face again,
she felt insensitive and downright mean.

She tossed the covers back and crossed her bedroom
to listen at the door. The house was quiet, not even the
soft drone of the television at the other end of the hall.
She groped for the robe hanging from the hook on the
back of her door. Her hand encountered the silky white
one that was a gift from her sister. Too sexy. She pulled
the old yellow terrycloth one off the hook and wrapped
it around her.

The hallway was dark, and the floor felt cool against her feet as she padded across the house. A bluish glow flickered in the living room, but the volume was muted. Was he asleep, finally? She peered around the corner.

And saw an empty couch.

"Hey."

She whirled around and gasped. "God, don't *do* that!"

He opened the refrigerator, creating a beacon of light as he reached in for a drink. He closed the door, and for a moment, the afterimage of him standing there in only his faded jeans flashed through her brain.

"Can't sleep?" His voice was low and gravelly, and she wondered if he'd actually managed to catch a few winks.

"I'm hungry."

"You missed dinner." He leaned against the counter and watched her as she pulled open the fridge and took out a bottle of juice. Not that she wanted any. Now that he was actually awake, she was rethinking the wisdom of having this conversation right now.

She took a glass down from the cabinet and set it on the counter. He watched her. The light on the back porch filtered through the slats of her miniblinds. Even in the dimness, she was supremely conscious of his broad, bare shoulders and his mussed hair and the stubble darkening his jaw.

God, he was sexy. And she couldn't believe he was standing in her kitchen in the middle of the night. More than anything, she couldn't believe that she'd slept with him. The vivid memory of how he'd touched her and kissed her in *his* kitchen seemed to hover in the air between them.

He was here for work. She knew that. But she also knew it was no accident that he'd repeatedly maneuvered for the night shift.

She should get this over with. She should say what she'd come in here to say and then go back to bed. She poured some juice and stood on the other side of the sink from him, back against the counter. It seemed safer than standing within touching distance.

She took a deep breath. "Brian?"

"Hmm?"

"I owe you an apology."

———

He watched her in the dimness, pretty sure he had no interest in hearing this. She'd said what she meant earlier, and nothing she told him right now was going to change a word of it. Unless she planned to take off that robe she was wearing, there wasn't much she could do that was going to be a game changer.

And considering that she'd come in here wearing the butt-ugliest thing she probably had in her entire house, he didn't think the odds were good that she'd suddenly changed her mind about sleeping with him.

"You're talking about Jolene?" He untwisted the cap on the bottle and swigged some water.

"I didn't mean what I said earlier. About you guys failing. That was unfair."

Actually, it wasn't. He *had* failed. And so far, she'd been the only person who had the guts to say it to his face.

She eased closer to him and traced her finger along

the counter. "I know you feel responsible for that, and what I said was pretty crappy, especially after all the efforts you and your team have made to look out for me."

He and his *team*.

She glanced up at him, and her brown eyes looked black and luminous in the darkness. And damn it, he could smell her hair again. Even from a few feet away, he caught the faintly sweet scent.

She eased closer. "So . . . you're not saying anything. Does that mean you don't believe me?"

"No."

She eased around to face him. "Because I really am sorry."

"Apology accepted. Go to bed."

She gazed up at him, and the air was suddenly charged with electricity. Something in her eyes made his heart thud harder. He wanted to grab her again, but the prospect of getting stiff armed twice in one night kept him cemented in place. He glanced down at the deep V of skin he'd been trying to ignore.

She stepped closer. He held his breath. His hands started to itch.

"Brian?"

"Hmm?"

She leaned up and kissed him.

CHAPTER 21

For a moment, he didn't move. And then he pulled her against him, and she could taste all that lust he'd been keeping in check. It was as though he'd unleashed something, and she'd never in her life felt so *wanted* by anyone. It made her feel happy and guilty and intimidated, all at the same time. He made a low groan in his chest as he lifted her up on tiptoes and pulled her tightly against him.

What was she doing? She didn't know. She only knew that standing with him in the darkness of her kitchen and *not* touching him was too impossible.

She slid her fingers into the soft bristles of his hair and tangled her tongue with his. He tasted so good. His stubble rasped against her chin as he changed the angle of the kiss, tipping her head back to gain access to her neck. She rested her head against his shoulder and inhaled the wonderfully male scent of him. How had she managed to keep her distance for so long? His hands fumbled with the belt of her robe, but it was double-knotted, another pathetic attempt to ward off temptation. He was determined, though, and soon she felt the warm slide of his hand around her breast and the roughness of his thumb. His other hand moved over her hip and pulled her closer.

"I've been dying to do this."

She murmured against his mouth.

"What?" he asked.

"I know."

Suddenly, the warmth of his hand disappeared. He scooped her off her feet, and her breath caught as he carried her out of the kitchen.

"Uh . . . where are we going?" Her pulse pounded wildly as she tried to get her mind around the idea of being *carried* through her house. This was another first.

"Bed." It was more of a grunt than a word. He shifted sideways to make it through her door and dropped her unceremoniously on the rumpled sheets. And then he was right there with her, his big, muscular thigh sliding between her legs. "Another thing I've been dying to do—get in here with you."

He loomed over her, and she could see the heat glinting in his eyes, and her heart started to pound even harder. She remembered that look, that body. She remembered the magic of his fingers. But everything was different this time—clearer, more vibrant, more intense, if that was even possible.

He leaned over her, kissing her thoroughly as his hand fumbled again with her belt. She brushed his fingers aside and tugged at the knot, but by the time she got it open, his hands were already sliding up her thighs and under her nightshirt.

"Just a sec." She sat up to shrug out of her robe. He tossed it aside, then quickly lifted the shirt up and over her shoulders. The cool air swept over her skin, and she was extremely conscious of the fact that she was naked—except for the bandage on her arm—while he still had on jeans.

He reached over her to switch on the lamp.

"Hey!" Her arms came down over her breasts.

"Don't." The heat in his eyes sent a shiver of anticipation through her as he gently moved her arms away. She let her shoulders relax and felt another hot shiver as his gaze moved over her body. "Damn, Maddie."

It was a good *damn*. A complimentary *damn*. A "damn-that-ice-cold-beer-tastes-great" *damn*. His gaze met hers, and she felt her skin flush. He gave her a quick kiss on the mouth.

"Stay here, okay? Don't move."

He jumped up and disappeared down the hallway, and of course, she did move. She switched off the lamp, which was just a tad too bright. Then she hurried to turn on the closet light. She left the door ajar, which created a nice glow in the room but kept her from feeling so self-conscious.

"Hey."

She hurried back to the bed as he stepped into the room again. He watched her, gaze narrowed, as he deposited his gun on the dresser. Then he moved closer to the bed and put a strip of condoms on the nightstand.

Okay. So either he'd planned for this, or he just happened to carry that many around with him. Both prospects made her uncomfortable, so she put the thought out of her mind and shifted her attention to the simmering look in his eyes. She got onto her knees and slid her arms around his neck.

She still couldn't really believe he was here, in her bedroom, after she'd spent so much time convincing herself this was a bad idea. It was hard to think that way now, as he slid his hands up her sides and kissed her with so much skill it made her heart race. His taste was addictive. And his smell. And every single thing he was doing to her felt so good. She realized, with a rush of excitement, that as incredible as it had been last time, there had been a veil of alcohol over it all. She ran her hands over his chest, and everything felt infinitely more intense—the coarseness of his hair under her palms, the warm slide of his hands down the back of her thighs, the sharp male taste of his tongue against hers. Everything he was doing thrilled her, and she tried to focus on that instead of the repercussions she was going to have to face in the morning.

I know it's complicated, but I like you.

He was going to go there again, and her heart made a little lurch as she thought about what she'd say, because her drunken-lapse-in-judgment excuse wasn't going to work again.

But then he was easing her back on the bed, and she forgot about everything. He still wore his jeans, and she got the sense that he was enjoying the unfairness of it as she clutched his thigh between hers and moved restlessly.

His eyes glinted down at her. He leaned forward and kissed her, right beneath her ear, and she wondered when exactly he'd figured out that was her sensitive spot. His mouth glided down her neck, down her body, stopping to linger around her belly button. She propped herself up on her elbows and gazed down at

him in the dimness, and her pulse quickened at the look
of pure male admiration on his face. He slid his hands
over her thighs, and she closed her eyes and tipped her
head back. And when he had her squirming and moan-
ing and gripping the sheet in her fists, he kissed his way
back up her body and hovered over her.

"You are so hot," he said thickly.

She pulled him down for a kiss and reached for the
snap of his jeans. Finally, he got rid of them, and this
time, when he sank down on her, she felt the electrify-
ing friction of skin against skin. She was beyond talking.
Beyond waiting. She wanted him now, but he seemed
to be enjoying drawing it out. She combed her fingers
into his hair and kissed him. And then their limbs were
tangled together, and they were in some kind of intense
race to the finish. He reared back, and she stared up
at him, breathless and dizzy. She heard the tear of a
condom wrapper, felt him moving around in the dark.
Then he shifted her beneath him and roughly pushed
inside her. She cried out, clutching him, but he seemed
to know it was a good cry, because he kept going, setting
a fierce pace. She clung to him, gripping him with every
ounce of strength she had. She kissed him frantically,
loving the hardness of his body and the dampness of his
skin and the raw, relentless force of him. She felt filled
to bursting with need and emotion. They were as close
together as two people could possibly be, and the utter
perfection of being *joined* with him was mind-blowing.

"Maddie." His voice was hoarse, and she clutched
him tighter. "Baby—"

"Yes."

Everything fused in a white-hot burst of light, and

then her body seemed to shatter into a million shimmering pieces as he gave a last powerful push.

He collapsed on top of her. She lay there, boneless. Little waves of pleasure rippled through her as the brilliant starburst faded to black. Seconds ticked by. Minutes.

When she opened her eyes again, she was staring at his neck. On impulse, she sank her teeth into it.

"Ouch." He pushed himself up on his palms. "What was that?"

She smiled up at him. "You taste salty."

He muttered something and flopped onto his back.

"What?" She propped herself up on an elbow and gazed down at him.

"Shit." He let his arm fall over his face.

She smiled. Then she rolled onto her back and nestled her head against him. "Well, that's romantic."

Silence settled over them. She'd used the *R* word. Even in her hazy, blissful state, she realized it was a bad choice. She waited to see if he'd say anything.

But he didn't say a word. He lay beside her, stroking her shoulder and staring up at the ceiling, and the steady thud of his heart against her ear was the only sound. She glided her hand over his chest and felt the texture of his hair under fingertips. His skin was still warm and damp from all the exertion. Hers, too, and it felt amazingly satisfying. She'd forgotten.

A few more minutes floated by. She lifted her head to look at him. His eyes were closed. She watched the steady rise and fall of his chest and confirmed that they were done arguing for the night.

CHAPTER 22

Emma was in a greenhouse, surrounded by butter-flies. Her pigtails were tied with yellow bows, and she wore her favorite overalls with the T. rex on the pocket. Orange-and-black monarchs flitted in and out of the sunbeams and alighted on her outstretched arms.

Mommy, look!

Pretty, sweetie. Look at all your butterflies.

Emma smiled up at her, and Maddie's heart convulsed.

They tickle!

That means they like you. Look, here's another one!

Maddie stepped closer, yearning to scoop her up, to gather her in her arms and shower her face with kisses. But she knew if she moved to touch her, everything would vanish. She settled for smiling.

I miss you, sweetie. I miss you so much.

But Emma didn't hear. She was entranced by the butterflies. She lifted a pudgy arm as yet another one landed on her skin.

Maddie drank in the sight of her— her springy curls, her dark lashes, her perfect little upturned nose.

One of her bows was crooked, and she reached out to straighten it. Her fingertips brushed over the curls— just an instant, but it was enough.

No.

Maddie snatched her hand back, but it was too late, she knew it. *No! I'm sorry! I didn't mean it!* Hot tears streamed down her cheeks, but it was no use.

A heartbeat later, Emma was gone.

———

A faint buzzing noise pulled Maddie from sleep. Her head felt heavy, swollen, and she sensed the headache even before she opened her eyes.

Another buzz.

Brian's phone, she realized. She glanced down at his arm slung over her waist. She felt the warmth of his thighs pressed against her bottom as she glanced over her shoulder to confirm that he was still out cold. Immensely relieved, she lifted his arm and slowly eased from the bed. She grabbed her robe from the floor and, still watching him, wrapped it around her shoulders.

She squinted at the meager sunlight that filtered through the shade in the bathroom as she brushed her teeth and splashed water on her face. She shuffled into the kitchen and spied the overnight bag on the floor. The phone was silent now, but she doubted it would remain that way for long.

Maddie reached for the coffee pot, embracing a few more moments of distraction before reality rolled in like a thunderhead. She counted out coffee scoops, doubling her usual amount because she had company, not to mention a punishing headache. She turned on the faucet and filled the carafe.

Another muffled buzz.

She sighed with resignation and flipped on the coffee maker.

"'Morning."

She turned around. "Good morning."

Brian leaned a shoulder against the door frame and crossed his arms over his bare chest. His gaze settled on her.

"You're popular today," she said.

With a quick glance, she took in his jeans and bare feet. He looked solid and sleepy and not nearly as rested as she would have expected, given the way he'd crashed so hard in her bed.

He was watching her intently, and she started to worry. Maybe he *hadn't* crashed hard. Maybe he was a light sleeper and knew exactly what a tumultuous night she'd had.

The buzzing started up again. He crouched down beside his bag, and she tried not to admire the ripple of muscles in his arms and shoulders as he rummaged for his phone. He checked the screen and stood up.

"I have to take this," he said gruffly.

"Sure."

He disappeared into the back of the house, and the coffeemaker beeped at her. She took down a pair of mugs and filled them. She held the cup in her hands as she let the rich aroma perk up her senses, and she considered the best way to handle things.

When he came back in, he was wearing the gray T-shirt he'd had on when she first went to bed last night. He crossed the kitchen and reached over her to open a cabinet.

"I poured you coffee."

"I need water." He set a glass on the counter and paused to look at her. She saw something in his eyes again. Worry? Wariness? Before she could pin it down, he surprised her by cupping his hand against the side of her face and planting a gentle kiss on the top of her head.

The gesture was so tender, so intimate, she was taken aback.

His hand dropped away, and he reached for the faucet. "How's your arm today?"

"Fine."

But she could tell he didn't believe her, as he leaned back against the sink and swilled water.

"A little sore," she admitted.

He drained the glass and set it down. He glanced at her robe but didn't look at all put off by it as his gaze zeroed in on her bandage.

"I've got to go in this morning." He crossed the kitchen and pulled a pizza box from the fridge. "Want some of this?"

"No, thanks."

So far, this was all pretty normal. Maybe it was going to go better than she'd thought. Maybe they could focus on logistics and sidestep the relationship discussion she'd been dreading for days.

"I have to go in this morning, too," she said.

He shot her a disapproving look as he picked up a slice and folded it in half. "It's Sunday."

"You're working Sunday," she pointed out.

He chomped into the pizza, frowning at her as he chewed.

"I'm meeting Ben," she added, hoping to quell his disapproval.

But the worry line between his brows deepened. He finished off the slice in a few more bites and dusted off his hands.

"You're working on the case," he stated.

"It's the facial-recognition software I told you about. We may have a new lead."

He shook his head and looked away.

"What?"

"It ever occur to you to let law enforcement take care of things?"

She crossed her arms. "Letting the police 'take care of things' hasn't worked out that well for me in the past."

"You're becoming obsessed."

"No, I'm not."

"This isn't about Emma."

The words were like a slap. She stared at him. People didn't talk about Emma. Most people wouldn't even say her name in Maddie's presence.

She cleared her throat. "I'm aware of that, obviously. I care about all of my cases. If I can do something to help Jolene Murphy, I will. If I can do something to help anyone."

His jaw tightened. He had something he wanted to get off his chest, and she instinctively knew she didn't want to hear it.

"I may be gone tonight, too," he said.

"Okay."

"I'm on surveillance at Mladovic's. I couldn't get out of it."

"Why should you?"

He watched her, searching her face. "LeBlanc has the late shift. You okay with that?"

She could tell it would do no good to argue, so she simply shrugged. "If you all feel it's necessary—"

"We do. But things are starting to come together. We're hoping to have an arrest warrant soon, maybe as early as today."

Her stomach clenched. "There's been a break?"

"Yes."

"Jolene—"

"Still missing. This is something else." His gaze held hers, and she felt as if he was searching for some reaction. He wasn't going to tell her the rest of it, and she hadn't really expected him to. Ever since the shooting, he'd been stingy with information, as if by not giving her any, he could erase her involvement.

He stepped closer, and her pulse picked up. She was conscious of his height and his solid strength as he gazed down at her.

"These guys are going to fall like dominoes, Maddie. And when that happens, things will settle down. Everything won't be so difficult."

"You mean for you?"

"For us."

Us. She felt the briefest flicker of hope, but then it was replaced by nerves. She couldn't let him keep pushing this.

He rested his hand at the side of her neck. "After this case ends, I want to try to make this work."

Maddie's heart skittered. She wanted to say something, but everything she could think of seemed wrong.

"Brian . . ."

His gaze stayed on hers, and she felt her stomach twisting into knots.

"I'm sorry. I like you very much. I do. But this is impossible."

"Why?"

"Because . . . of a lot of reasons. Our ages, our jobs, our backgrounds. Because of what people would say."

He let his hand drop away, and she felt her familiar frustration rising to the surface. He'd never even tried to see this from her perspective. "What would they say?"

"You're younger than I am. So people would gossip about me and say I'm just with you for sex. They'd say I'm using you for revenge against my philandering ex-husband."

"So?"

"*So?* Brian, I *hate* being gossiped about. It's insulting to both of us."

"Maddie, who cares what anyone says or thinks? We both know the truth."

She stood there uncomfortably. *What* truth? That this wasn't about sex—at least, not completely? That she cared about this man? That in the impossibly short span of a few weeks, she'd managed to fall for him? It was crazy. She was crazy. And it was reckless, too, because there was no future in it, and she needed to make him see that.

"Brian." She took a deep breath and looked him

squarely in the eye. Her heart was racing now, and she could feel the panic creeping in as the conversation got more and more out of control. "I have to tell you, even if the other stuff wasn't an issue, I don't want a relationship. Not with anyone. It isn't about you."

Something flared in his eyes, and she could tell she'd struck a nerve.

He leaned back against the counter. "You travel light now, is that it? No baggage? Now that your daughter's gone, you're just head down"—he cut through the air with his hand—"straight to the finish line."

"Don't be glib."

"I'm being honest."

"So am I," she said.

"No, you're not. You're being a coward."

Fury bubbled up. "I'm trying to have an open conversation and save us both a lot of trouble."

"Fine. Let's be open, then. Isn't this about Emma?"

"No!"

He stared at her with those hazel eyes, and it felt like he could see straight into her soul. He stepped closer and looked down at her.

"Maddie, come on." His gaze softened. "You think I don't see how torn up you are? You think I don't know that you're working yourself to death and that you cry in your sleep and can't stand to look at little kids?"

Maddie's skin went cold. She felt sick. "You have no right to judge me."

"I'm not judging you." His held her gaze and touched her neck again. "Just listen, okay? I know you're scared. I know that."

"I'm not *scared*."

He just watched her, and she realized it was pointless to argue. So she was scared. Fine. But her relationship fear wasn't the only problem here. Why couldn't he see that?

"Brian, look." She stepped away from him. "You're a good man. And you seem traditional. Don't you want a family someday? A wife and kids?"

He didn't react at all, didn't even blink.

"You don't have to answer that, because I *know* you do. It's in your DNA. I don't want those things anymore. And I'm sorry. I care about you, I really do. But that's why I'm telling you this now. I can't give you want you want. I can't give you anything but . . ." She motioned back and forth between them.

"Sex."

"Yes."

"So you're offering me just sex?" He smiled now, but there was no humor in it. He rubbed the back of his neck. "Because don't think I won't take you up on it. I will." He shook his head, and she saw something in his eyes that looked like resignation. "I'm crazy about you, Maddie. I'll take anything you'll give me."

Her throat tightened at his words, at the utterly honest look on his face. His pride was on the line here. And he was standing here basically tossing it away, just for a chance to be with her and not even have a relationship. How had she lowered him to this?

And she felt a sharp pang of guilt, because what he was saying actually sounded tempting.

But it also sounded terrible. If she agreed to it, *she* would be the one who ended up with her heart shredded at the end of everything.

"Brian—"

A rap on the door had them both turning around. Brian's hand was instantly on the pistol she hadn't even noticed tucked beneath his shirt. He nudged the blinds aside.

"It's Sam." He turned to look at her. "I have to go."

She nodded.

"Hicks is on his way. Do *not* leave without him. Don't go anywhere." He stepped closer. "Are we clear?"

She nodded. She was clear on that. It was everything else that had her completely lost.

CHAPTER 23

"You look like shit." Sam smiled at him over the roof of the Taurus. "Long night?"

Brian didn't answer. He slid into the car and rattled off directions he'd been given over the phone a few minutes ago. Brian saw his replacement pulling up, right on time, but his relief was short-lived as he thought about Maddie's plans for the day. Why couldn't she spend her Sunday lazing around, like most people? He knew the underlying reason, but knowing didn't make him feel better.

Sam turned out of the neighborhood and shot him a look. "So who's this guy we're meeting? And let me tell you, this better be good, because I skipped my coffee to haul ass over here."

"Name's Scott Black. He's the firearms expert at the Delphi Center."

"You met him before?"

"Up ahead on the left, after the gas station." He glanced at Sam. "A few times, yeah. From what I've seen, he's good. Maddie vouches for him."

Sam pulled into the Taco Bell parking lot and swung into a space. Brian spotted the pickup.

"Black F-150," he said, getting out.

The man was already crossing the lot. He wore jeans and boots and had a holster tucked under his jacket. Brian made quick introductions.

"I ran across a gun you're looking for," Black said without preamble.

"Where?" Brian asked.

"Pawn shop off I-35."

"You just 'ran across' it?" Sam sounded skeptical.

"This was off a tip. It's an Ed Brown Kobra pistol. A forty-five."

"Nice gun," Brian said.

"Matte finish. Snakeskin metal slide. Paperwork was fudged, so a cop I know seized the weapon. Shop owner'll cooperate if we lean on him some." Black leveled a look at Brian. "Fired a few test rounds. Casings match the one from the movie theater last week."

Sam looked at Black. "You're telling me someone offloaded this gun after shooting it at an FBI agent? What's this guy, brain-dead?"

"Greedy. Seller probably got at least a grand for it. Pawn shop owner was asking three times that."

"Who's the seller?" Brian asked.

"Luis Gutierrez. Minor-league gangster who thinks he's a gun expert." Black looked from Brian to Sam. "I have reason to believe the weapon was once in possession of someone you're investigating. Anatoli Petrovik's prints were on it."

Sam didn't even bother to conceal his amazement now. "Anatoli sold it without wiping it down?"

"Outside of the piece was clean as a whistle. Not even Gutierrez's prints. These were *inside*," Black said. "You know how it is—guys sitting around, shooting the shit, cleaning their weapons. Their prints are on everything, but later they forget and only wipe down the parts they touched recently, like the grip and the trigger. Shop owner ID'd Gutierrez in a photo array, said he was the seller but gave a different name. Because of his record, looks like Gutierrez used a phony ID when he made the sale."

Brian stared at him, trying to get his head around this stroke of luck. The fingerprints could mean a warrant and an arrest that could shift the tide of the entire investigation.

Black reached into his back pocket and pulled out some folded paperwork. "Here's a copy of the report."

"This tipster of yours," Sam said. "Who is it, some crackhead?"

Black smiled. "Not exactly."

"We're going to need names, numbers, everything you got." Sam slapped Brian on the back. "You believe this? We're finally going to arrest one of these assholes."

"There's more," Black said. "Anatoli isn't the only person who handled that gun."

Brian looked up from the paperwork.

"I lifted a stray thumbprint. Just one, but it's good and clean, so I ran it. Comes back to a Dr. Goran Mladovic."

————

Special Agent Chris Hicks sped through the hills, content to let Maddie sit quietly as he chauffeured her to the Delphi Center. She was glad for the silence. Since Brian had walked out her door, all she'd been able to think about were his parting words.

You're a coward.

The accusation stung. She felt hurt. And angry. But she also felt panicked, because he knew her secret. He knew *her*.

Despite everything people had been telling her for years, Brian somehow could see that she *wasn't* brave, or resilient, or strong enough to carry any burden God placed on her shoulders. She wasn't any of those things people said about her. In reality, she was weak and scared, and Brian was the first to have the courage to come out and say it.

For five years, she'd held her grief in a white-knuckled grip, as if clinging to it would somehow bring Emma back. She couldn't loosen her hold. And if she was honest, she didn't want to loosen it. She didn't want to let go of the one thing she'd been cling-ing to like a lifeline, because it would be like letting Emma go, too. The grief was agonizing, but it was also familiar, and she couldn't imagine living without it. She didn't want to.

So Brian was right. She *was* a coward. And it unnerved her to think of what else he might be right about.

Her heart ached as she thought of the look on his face, the vulnerability she'd seen in his eyes when he'd said he was crazy about her. She felt a fresh surge of fear, because those words had been a trap. He *knew* she couldn't continue to see him and keep it only about sex. He knew perfectly well that the more time he spent with her, the more he'd wear her down, until her defenses were gone and she was trapped in an impossible relationship.

It struck her once again how different he was from Mitch. She remembered what he'd said about infidelity. And the crazy thing was, she believed him. He was strong and committed and loyal. He was probably good at long-term relationships, and he deserved to have one with someone who had everything in life ahead of her.

"Ma'am?"

Her bodyguard du jour was looking at her.

"Yes?"

"Are you all right?"

"Fine. Why?"

"You just seem . . ." He cleared his throat. "I don't know, upset about something."

She watched as he trained his gaze on the road, obviously regretting that he'd said something personal. She surveyed his close-cropped hair, his clean-shaven face, the FBI golf shirt and khakis that evidently passed for weekend attire at the Bureau.

"Let me ask you something, Chris, how old are you?"

He gave her a puzzled look. "Why?"

"I'm just wondering."

"Twenty-nine."

She burst out laughing. "You're joking."

"I'll be thirty next month."

He was actually *older* than Brian. Maddie turned and watched the hills race by in a blur.

"Why?" he said again. "What does it matter?"

She looked at him and didn't have an answer. She had no idea. Maybe it *didn't* matter. Maybe none of her reservations mattered. Maybe she was just throwing roadblocks out there because she was scared of what she felt.

I'm crazy about you.

He'd actually said those words, just minutes ago. Why didn't she believe him? Why didn't she just trust that he was being honest, that he meant it?

Maybe she did.

Maybe that was what scared her. She knew he was sincere, and she was terrified she'd screw it up. She actually had fun with him. She smiled with him. She felt passionate with him. It had been so long since she'd felt any of those things, she didn't believe that it was real. And even if it *was* real, she didn't believe she deserved it.

What if she let go of all that and simply *trusted* him not to break her heart?

Maddie's phone chimed inside her purse. She dug it out, and the screen showed a Delphi Center number.

"Hey, it's me," Ben said. "Where are you?"

"Almost there. Why?"

"I need to tell you something important. You should probably pull over."

Dread filled her stomach. "I'm not the one driving. Why? What's happening?"

"I was here all night," Ben said. "I got hold of my friend in Germany, and working together, we managed to get that picture cleaned up. We got it sharp. Lightened. It's a good image, Maddie."

"Okay."

"Then I used your idea and uploaded the photo to the Facebook account of Mladovic's wife."

She held her breath.

"No tags popped up. But then I got to thinking, since Craig Rodgers was the one who summoned you out to that crime scene—"

"Someone using his *phone* summoned me."

"Right, whatever. I loaded the photo into *his* account, thinking maybe *he's* the key."

"And?"

"A tag popped up right away. Jack Bracewell."

Her blood ran cold. "*Sheriff* Bracewell?"

"That's right."

"You're saying Bracewell helped kidnap Jolene? That he works for Mladovic?" Maddie cringed at her own words—they sounded obscene.

"I'm not saying anything. I'm telling you he's the man in this photograph. Now that I have the name, I've run this image against the photo on file with the DMV, and the software likes him for a match. Jack Bracewell is the man in that car. I've also got about half a dozen candids of him on Craig's page. Looks like they like to go deer hunting together."

"Where?"

"What?"

"Where do they go hunting together?" Maddie's pulse quickened as an idea took shape. "I know Bracewell has a lease someplace, that he goes on trips a lot."

"No idea," Ben said. "You can't tell from the shots. It's just a bunch of guys sitting around drinking beer and showing off guns. Looks like some campers and pickups, but I don't see any landmarks."

"Check the metadata. If those pictures were taken with a cell-phone cam, it's probably embedded."

Silence as Ben carried out her request. Maddie held her breath. Her heart felt as if it would beat out of her chest as she thought about what this could mean.

Bracewell. The last time she'd seen him had been at the Delphi Center, in Kelsey's autopsy suite.

She suddenly felt sick. She gripped the dashboard. God, she'd tipped him off. She'd told him about taking pictures of the unidentified men casing the bank. He knew if she managed to enhance the photos, she'd recognize him.

She'd handed him a motive to kill her.

"I'll be damned," Ben muttered.

"What? What is it?"

"You were right. Location's embedded right in the tag. Maddie, this place isn't far from here at all. You want the GPS coordinates?"

"Send them over."

———————

Sam and Brian sped across town to the home of the judge who they desperately hoped was going to sign off on their warrant.

"Any chance he won't go for it?"

Sam drummed his fingers on the steering wheel. "I think our chances are good."

"He tossed the last one." Actually, the judge had balked at it.

"Our probable cause was weak. This guy likes physical evidence. He'll like these fingerprints."

Brian's shoulders tensed as he thought about everything they had riding on this warrant. He just hoped they could nail it before anything else happened to any of their witnesses. Namely, Maddie. His phone buzzed, and he yanked it from his pocket. LAPD. Had to be bad news.

"It's Vega," he told Sam, and answered.

"I thought you'd want to know," the detective said, "we've located that woman you were looking for, Nicole Sands."

"Where is she?" *And is she alive or dead?*

"She's in lockup. Vice squad picked her up this morning in North Hollywood."

Brian looked at Sam. "You arrested her for drugs?"

"Prostitution. Thought you'd be interested, in case your task force still needs to interview her."

"We do." And if they hadn't been in the process of getting a warrant for Goran Mladovic at that very moment, Brian and Sam would have been on the next plane. As it was, they were going to have to wait until tomorrow.

"How long can you hold her?" Brian asked.

"Not long. We're full up right now. This is her first prostitution charge, and she'll probably be out with a slap on the wrist."

"How long?" Sam asked.

"Twenty-four hours," Brian told him. "Maybe we can get LeBlanc out there."

"Not a bad idea. She'll probably have better luck talking to her than we would, anyway. We should run it by Cabrera."

"Listen, we need to send an agent out to interview her," Brian told the LA detective. "What's her mental state look like? Can you tell if she's using?"

"If she's not, she's the only one in that jail who isn't. But like I said, no priors on the prostitution. Judge is going to kick her loose. How soon can you get an agent over here? Want me to call the LA field office?"

Brian's phone beeped with an incoming call, but he ignored it.

"Tell them to rebook her," Sam was saying. "We don't want her name on any of the paperwork."

"No, we need someone from the task force," Brian told Vega. "We'll get someone on a plane, hopefully by this afternoon. In the meantime, we need you to book her as a Jane Doe."

Silence on the other end as Vega probably contemplated the crapload of red tape this would entail.

"She's already booked."

"I know, but we can't let her identity slip out." Brian pictured the smiling teen standing with her friends on the beach. Every other girl in that photo was either dead or missing. "The witnesses in this case are being targeted. We believe the hit on Gillian Dawson was meant for her, and we can't take any more risks. We're going to need you to rebook her."

"I'll see what I can do."

"No one can know she's in custody," Brian said. "Not even her family."

"I haven't told anyone besides you and the sheriff."

"What sheriff?"

"One who's been calling here. Bracewell."

"Jack Bracewell's been calling you?"

"He's been hounding me all week for updates. He said he's on your task force."

"He's not." The world seemed to shift as Brian put the pieces together. Why hadn't he seen it? "Listen, did you tell him about the case? Did you tell him you have Nicole Sands?"

"Yeah, why?"

"That lying son of a bitch," Sam muttered, obviously coming to the same conclusion as Brian.

Bracewell was the missing link they'd been looking for all these months. He'd helped Mladovic stay one step ahead of law enforcement. He'd looked the other way on a pill mill in his county. He'd been in that car, staking out the bank when Maddie snapped her photos.

Shit. The last time he'd seen Bracewell was at the Delphi Center. Brian hung up on Vega and started dialing Maddie.

"Turn around," he told Sam.

"What?"

"You're on your own with this warrant. I need to get to Maddie's."

CHAPTER 24

Maddie answered her phone on the first ring. "Where'd you go? I've been trying to call."

"Where are you?"

"In the car."

"Where's Hicks?"

Something was wrong. She could hear it in his voice.

"He's right here," she said. "Listen, we—"

"Go home. Turn around right now, and go back to your house. I'm about to send another team over there to beef up security."

"Brian—"

"Just do it, all right? Something's come up."

"Brian, would you *listen*? Something's come up here, too. I figured out the other person in that picture. It's Sheriff Bracewell."

Pause. "How did you know that?"

"My friend Ben at the Delphi Center—"

"I thought you were in the car."

"I *am*. I got a phone call about it. Listen, we figured out that Bracewell's working with Mladovic. And I think I know where they're keeping Jolene."

"You have proof she's alive?"

"You have proof she's not?"

No response. She could almost picture him racing across town in his Taurus, about to blow a gasket.

"Maddie, listen to me. Nicole Sands is alive, and Bracewell knows about it. That means they don't need Jolene anymore to reveal her location. They're going to kill her if they haven't already, do you understand?"

Maddie's skin felt cold as the words sank in. She glanced out the window as the hilly landscape rushed past.

"Maddie, are you listening? I need you to go home. I need you to stay out of this."

"Hicks was ordered to do some surveillance of the property. There's a team on the way."

"Goddamn it, would you *listen*? Stay away from Bracewell. Stay away from his property. Let the team handle this."

"That's the plan. But Hicks is the closest agent, and they want him to gather some intel, report in, and await backup."

"Hicks is your security detail! No fucking way. Tell him—"

She didn't hear the rest, because she handed the phone to Hicks. "He wants to talk to you."

The agent listened for a moment. He turned to look at Maddie, and she could hear Brian ranting at him on the other end of the phone, probably threatening him within an inch of his life if he didn't ignore his orders and turn the car around.

"I know. This is from Cabrera." His face reddened as Brian's voice kicked up another notch. Maddie couldn't hear the words, but Hicks seemed to be holding his ground.

"I told you, no. Unless someone's in imminent danger, I've got orders to wait." After a few clipped words, he hung up and handed the phone to Maddie. She could tell he was embarrassed.

Maddie switched back to the other screen, where she was following a map of the area through the GPS coordinates Ben had sent. "There should be a road up here, and you're turning left. Just after this creek."

They crossed a bridge, and he hung a left onto an even narrower road than the one they'd been on. Maddie glanced around. The landscape had become more and more desolate as they'd traveled west, and they hadn't seen a house in miles. The land was arid and dusty, dotted with scrub brush, cacti, and the occasional head of cattle. They crossed a low-water bridge, and she noted a change in the barbed wire fencing.

"We might be getting closer," she said. "You see any more turnoffs?"

"No."

The road dipped lower, and they were hemmed in on two sides by limestone. They drove in silence for a while, and anxiety started to nip at her. It was isolated out here. They had a twenty-minute jump on the backup team, but she still felt worried. What if they couldn't find it? What if they crossed paths with Bracewell or one of Mladovic's men on this road? The terrain was rugged, difficult. Plus, everyone and their grandmother out here drove a pickup. The Taurus was bound to attract attention. Ditto a SWAT van or whatever sort of vehicle they planned to send.

They rounded a bend, and a trio of buzzards flapped up from the roadway where they'd been scavenging an armadillo. Maddie's stomach did a somersault. The area gave her the creeps. If she felt scared just driving around, she could only imagine how Jolene felt, being held captive out here with no one to hear her cries for help.

"There! On your right!" Maddie pointed at the distant turnoff. She consulted her map again.

It was a dirt road, and Hicks pulled over soon after they passed it. Maddie looked for the best place to hide the car, and her gaze landed on a line of scrub brush.

"What do you think?" she asked, glancing around.

"I think this would be better cover in the middle of summer." He maneuvered the car between a few tall junipers and cut the engine. "But we don't have much choice."

Maddie scanned the area. She listened. She didn't hear a single car, not even in the distance. She didn't hear anything except the faint sounds of the engine as it came to a rest.

Hicks looked at her. "Beckman's not too happy with me right now."

"What'd he say?"

He shook his head. "I'm not going to repeat it."

Maddie unzipped her purse and pulled out her pistol. She checked to make sure it was loaded.

"You know how to use that?" he asked.

"Pretty well."

"Just don't point it at an agent. Those will be the guys in Kevlar who show up in about fifteen minutes." He opened the door. "They know you're in the car here, but it still wouldn't be good for you to wave that thing around."

"And where are you going?"

"I noticed some tire tracks. I need to go take a look."

Maddie tucked the gun into the waistband of her jeans and got out of the car. "I'll help."

"You should stay here."

"Just a quick look. I'm a CSI, remember? You'd be foolish not to let me help you."

She stayed near the bushes as they hiked up the road a few yards. She spotted the tracks at the turnoff and crouched down. Hicks knelt beside her.

"Looks like a pickup truck."

"A dualie," she corrected. "And two other vehicles, either pickups or SUVs."

"What's a dualie?"

"One of those extra-large pickups, double tires on the back. See?" She pointed out the distinctive tread marks in the dirt.

She took a few photos with her phone and stood up. "Bracewell has a dualie. But his aren't the freshest tracks here. Someone else drove through this gate in the meantime."

She stepped over to another set of tire marks that was overlaid with the double-wide tracks. She glanced up at Hicks, who was busy texting info into his phone.

"Tell them there have been at least four different vehicles in and out of here in the last two days, since we had that big rain."

Hicks didn't say anything.

"Which is a lot of traffic on a deer lease when it's not even deer season," she added.

The agent's hands froze around his phone. His gaze snapped to hers. "Back in the car. Now." He grabbed her elbow and shoved her ahead of him. "I hear a truck."

————

Brian barely slowed for the curves as he sped down the highway. He wished he had his pickup, which was much better suited to this type of terrain.

"Has he reported in?" Sam demanded over the phone.

"Negative," Brian said. "Last update from LeBlanc, they were on the highway."

Brian scanned the road in front of him now, looking for the exit. But if his GPS was worth shit—which he doubted—he had another five miles to go.

"What about the hostage rescue team?" Sam asked.

"Their ETA's ten minutes. I might even beat them there."

"Okay, I'm pulling into to Mladovic's neighborhood now. It's just him and his wife home, according to the surveillance team. Let's hope he comes in without a fight."

"Let's hope."

The conversation was surreal. For months, Brian had dreamed of being part of the big takedown. Now it was happening without him, and he couldn't care less. Sam could have the collar.

Brian had his sights set on a new enemy: Bracewell. The key to all of this. He'd abused his power. He'd probably helped kill those girls and destroy evidence.

And with every minute that ticked by, Brian became more convinced that he was the gunman who'd put Maddie in his crosshairs.

Brian had some vicious thoughts in his head, but he pushed them aside so he could focus on the most important objective: getting Maddie out of harm's way.

"Okay, we're at the house now. I'm out, Beck."

Brian spotted the turnoff and slammed on the brakes. "Be careful," he told Sam.

"Yeah, you, too."

———

Maddie sat in the car, alone, scanning the area around her. Her anxiety mounted with every minute that crawled by. No word from the team. No Hicks. Nothing but heavy, nerve-wracking silence.

She pictured Jennifer Murphy staring out her kitchen window with a heart that was slowly cracking in two. She pictured her looking at all the yellow ribbons that were meant to be hopeful but by now must seem cruel. If Jennifer were here right now, she'd scour every inch of this land, every hill and every hollow, no matter what dangers were waiting for her.

Maddie yearned to get out of the car. But Hicks had told her to stay. *Commanded* her.

She looked down at the gun clutched in her hand. She had no formal training. No jurisdiction.

She peered through the windshield again. Her palms were wet. Her heart seemed to be beating a hundred times a second.

If Brian found out, he'd be furious. Brian cared about her, maybe even loved her. If anything happened to her, he'd find a way to blame himself.

Cabrera had ordered her to stay put, too.

Maddie gazed out the window and felt her heart drumming inside her body. She wasn't Brian's wife. She wasn't Cabrera's subordinate. But she *was* someone's mother. That label was branded on her heart forever, no matter what.

They don't need Jolene anymore. They're going to kill her if they haven't already.

Maddie got out of the car. She eased the door shut and stood still to listen. She glanced around to get her bearings.

Slowly, she crept deeper into the brush until she encountered the barbed-wire fence surrounding the property. Careful not to snag her hair, she ducked through it. She felt a rush of adrenaline. She'd crossed a line. There was no going back.

Maddie eased through the foliage, staying close to the evergreens for better cover. She darted her gaze around, looking for any sign of a person or a dog or a vehicle.

A wind whipped up and shifted the branches around her. Something silver caught the light about a hundred yards away. She moved closer. She stared at it through the leaves.

The silver flashed again, and she recognized it. It was a glimmer of hope.

CHAPTER 25

Brian's blood went cold when he saw the car.

Empty.

He pulled into the trees and parked, then jumped out with his gun in hand. No sign of Maddie or Hicks. Nothing.

The car was unlocked, and he reached in to pop the trunk. He held his breath as he went to check . . .

No blood, no bodies.

No Kevlar.

He frowned down at the trunk and closed it. Wherever they'd gone, they'd taken the time to suit up.

He cursed under his breath as he moved toward the fence. What the hell was she thinking? He'd known this would happen the second she told him about this deer lease. She was going to go nosing around, and screw anyone who tried to stop her, including him. She was a CSI and a mother, and besides that, she was stubborn as hell. If there was a chance in a billion that Jolene was here alive, then no amount of logic could keep her away.

Frustration and fear tightened his chest.

Brian closed his eyes and listened carefully. The air was still and quiet. He didn't hear a car or a bird or anything. He didn't hear the *whump-whump* of a chopper or the low hum of an armored van. He wasn't sure how he'd beaten everyone here, but it probably had to do with his triple-digit speed on that highway.

Brian pulled out his cell and sent Maddie his second text in the last ten minutes. He stared down at his phone. Still nothing.

He could wait for his team, as planned, or he could go looking for them. He knew what he should do, and he also knew he wasn't going to do it.

Brian waded into the bushes and ducked through the fence.

———

Right away, he spotted tracks in the woods. One set could have been anybody's, including Hicks. Another set looked small and feminine and might belong to Maddie. Brian followed the footprints, hoping none of Mladovic's goons had the slightest bit of military training. It wouldn't take much to pick up this trail out here. Besides leaving footprints—which, thank God, were now pretty well obscured by dead leaves—she'd also left telltale breaks in the tree branches from where she'd pushed through the brush.

Accident? He didn't know. If she'd been forcefully hauled away, she might have been trying to leave a trail for the HR team that was about to swoop in.

On the other hand, maybe she hadn't thought about covering her tracks when she'd moved through the area. Maybe she'd been thinking about something else, such as the aluminum camper Brian saw looming up ahead at the far end of a clearing. A place to stash a hostage? Possibly. It was the first thing that popped into his mind, and Maddie's, too, he'd bet.

A noise to the east had him whirling around. He heard the clang of metal and several male voices. They were muffled, and as Brian moved through the woods, he saw the reason. Beside a dense clump of trees was a dilapidated barn. The structure was gray and weathered and missing about half of the slats. Brian caught the movement of people inside and eased closer for a better look.

He crept through the bushes, wishing for some woodland cammies. An M-4 would be nice, too, but he only had his Glock.

Three men. One he recognized as Anatoli, smoking and leaning against the back of a large pickup. Another sat on a rusted-out oil drum that someone had turned on its side. Brian did a double-take. Vlad?

He'd been so sure it was Volansky's charred remains spread out on that table at the Delphi Center. What was it Sam had said? *Looks like he got himself fired.*

But there was Vlad, in the flesh, swigging beer and yapping away on his cell phone. So who was the corpse? Another one of Mladovic's disposable goons?

A squeak of metal pulled Brian's attention to the far side of the barn, where someone was climbing out of an old green pickup. He stepped out of the shadows . . .

Bracewell.

Brian's chest burned, and his fingers tightened around his pistol grip. Bracewell was on his cell phone,

and he finished up the call and tossed the phone through
the open window of the larger truck. Brian figured the
truck was his, because he couldn't see the good sheriff
riding around the county in the piece-of-shit clunker
he'd just climbed out of. Brian looked more closely and
noticed the old green truck was up on jacks, and the
two front tires were missing.

Bracewell barked some orders, but the men didn't
move.

Brian scanned the barn, looking for any sign of Maddie or Hicks. Nothing.

The low growl of an engine reached him. Brian
stepped behind a tree and watched as a dust-coated
white SUV roared up the road and came to a halt in the
doorway of the barn. All the men snapped to attention
as Mladovic climbed out.

Brian watched in shock. Either the takedown had
gone to shit, or he'd slipped through his surveillance.
The Doctor barked some orders in Serbian, and Vlad
and the others sprang into action, opening the SUV's
cargo doors and dragging out a pair of tires. They rolled
them toward the jacked-up truck.

Bracewell turned and spat tobacco juice on the
ground. "I'm gonna want a piece of that."

Mladovic's face was obscured now, but Brian could
see from the sheriff's reaction that he hadn't gotten the
answer he wanted.

"Yeah, but *this* isn't what we agreed on." Bracewell
got up in the Doctor's grille. "You said two bodies. Not
three. I got a family here. I can't just hop down to Mexico and leave my shit behind for everyone else to clean
up. Fifty K, or you can forget it."

More words were exchanged, and Brian's gaze veered to the truck, where Vlad was putting on a tire that was probably loaded with cash and headed for the border. Mladovic was smuggling money down, which meant he was leaving.

Suddenly, the argument ceased. Even from a distance, Brian recognized all the signs of a fight brewing. Mladovic stepped closer and said something softly. Bracewell jerked out his pistol and fired off a shot. Anatoli dropped like a bag of bricks.

"That's four bodies." He aimed the gun at Mladovic's chest. "We going for five?"

———

Maddie ducked behind a tree and crouched low. She clutched her gun in her hand and gasped for breath. She was nearly hyperventilating.

That had definitely been a gunshot.

She had to get out of here. She had to get *Jolene* out of here. But where was Hicks? She pulled her phone out to text him and stared down at the screen.

Three urgent messages, all from Brian.

And a fourth message from Hicks, but it was blank. Her stomach plummeted.

God, what did that mean? She glanced around desperately, looking for Hicks, looking for landmarks. She spotted a clump of oak trees beside a large white boulder. Not exactly a landmark but close enough. She sent Brian a message, then moved deeper into the brush to wait.

She was shaking, head to toe. Her T-shirt was soaked

through with sweat, and it trickled down her spine. She felt as though a giant fist was squeezing the air from her lungs as she pictured Jolene, motionless on that brown cot.

Please, please, please.

Something grabbed her arm. Maddie gasped and whirled around as Brian's hand clamped around her pistol.

"Careful with that."

"Oh, my God." She slumped against him. But her relief lasted about a nanosecond, because he was towing her deeper into the woods, where he pulled her into a crouch.

"Where's Hicks?" His voice was low, and his face looked intense.

"I don't know. He went to look around. I left the car. Then I saw the camper. Jolene—" The words tumbled out of her in a rush. "Then I heard gunshots."

He gripped her arm. "When? When did you hear gunshots?"

"I—" She thought back. "It was only one, I think. I heard it a minute ago. After you texted me."

He started to stand up, but she pulled him back down. "Brian, she's *here*! In the camper! I saw her—"

"Jolene's here?"

"Yes!"

"And she's alive?"

"Yes." Maddie's throat tightened. "But she looks so weak. Or maybe she's drugged or something. But we have to get her. Bracewell's here now, and you said they're going to kill her. We have to get her out of there."

He pulled her to her feet. "Show me."

"The guard's gone!" Maddie hissed, pulling him through the woods. "Earlier, there was a man stationed there."

They neared the edge of the trees, and Brian jerked her back and pushed her behind him. He eyed the camper.

"She's on a cot against the far wall." Maddie looked up at him with a plea in her eyes. "I saw her through the window. I think they cuffed her to the bed or some- thing."

"I'll handle it. You get back to the car."

She gazed up at him but didn't move.

"Maddie—"

"Don't be stupid. At least let me stand watch while you go in there."

"What are you going to do if someone approaches?"

"I don't know. Shoot him?"

Brian gritted his teeth. He hated that she was here. And he hated that she was going to cover his ass while he attempted this rescue mission. But a man had just been murdered in cold blood. Everything was coming to a head, and his backup was nowhere.

Brian pulled her into a clump of sagebrush and posi- tioned her out of sight of the other buildings.

"Don't move," he ordered.

He decided on the stealth approach and slipped around the back of the camper, where there was a small window. Too small for a man his size, or even Hicks's. He crept around the side. He noticed the gap between the flimsy door and the curved shell of the camper. Gun raised, he flattened himself against the side and eased open the door. He peered inside.

The camper was empty.

Pop!

Brian dropped to his knees.

Pop! Pop!

He lunged for the bushes. Maddie was racing toward him, full speed, eyes blazing with fear.

"Go!" he yelled, grabbing her hand and pulling her out in front of him so he could shield her with his body. They shoved their way through branches, and Brian pushed her ahead, not daring even to attempt a shot until she was out of bullet range.

"Go!" he yelled, then darted a glance behind him.

A bullet buzzed by his ear, and Brian felt a surge of anger. He lifted his gun and fired it at the blur of movement ducking behind a tree.

Hit! A howl came up from the ground.

An engine roared to life. Mladovic's SUV shot back from the barn, then raced forward, a streak of white between tree trunks.

Was Jolene in that vehicle? Was Hicks?

He turned to look for Maddie, and she was crouched behind a giant oak tree.

"Stay here!"

He doubled back to the site of the downed gunman. He spotted Bracewell on the ground, clutching his knee and writhing in pain. Blood seeped through his fingers, and he was making keening noises.

Brian spotted the gun nearby and kicked it away. He pointed his Glock at Bracewell's chest.

"Where's Jolene Murphy?"

The sheriff's eyes flew open. He stared at Brian with pure hatred.

"Where's our agent?"

"Fuck . . . you," he gasped.

Brian yanked the man's bloody hands behind him and slapped on a pair of handcuffs. He caught movement in his peripheral vision as Maddie walked up and stopped beside the sheriff.

She hauled back and kicked him in the knee. Bracewell howled like a stuck pig.

"Where is she?" She aimed her pistol between his legs. "I'll shoot that thing right off."

"Vlad has her," he choked out.

Maddie looked at Brian as a grumble went up near the barn. The old green pickup shot out from the doors and disappeared down the road in a cloud of dust and exhaust.

"Shit."

Maddie dropped to her knees beside the sheriff and dug a set of keys from his pocket. "His truck." She looked at Brian. "Let's go!"

They left him cursing in the dirt and raced for the barn. Bracewell's oversize black pickup was exactly where Brian had last seen it. The other trucks—and the money-stuffed tires—were long gone. A shotgun lay abandoned on the ground, and Brian grabbed it.

"You drive," he ordered, but Maddie was already jumping behind the wheel. Brian hopped in on the passenger side and didn't even have time to pull the door shut as Maddie barreled full-speed through the side of the barn. Splinters and dust flew everywhere, and it was sheer luck they didn't plow straight into a tree.

Brian looked at her. "This thing has a reverse."

"Where'd they go?"

"East."

She glared at him.

"Take a right."

Maddie swerved right and picked up the road as Brian jabbed the window button and rested the barrel of the gun on the door. If they could get close enough, he might be able to take out the driver.

Where the hell was his team? And where was Hicks? Brian's phone vibrated in his pocket.

"Someone's calling me."

Maddie reached over and dug the phone out of his pants as she sped down the dusty road. She tossed the phone into his lap, and Brian tried to keep the shotgun steady as he pressed talk.

"Where the hell are you?" Sam's voice sounded tinny on the other end of the call. "The Doctor slipped his surveillance. He—"

"I'm at Bracewell's. Mladovic is here! Where the fuck's our backup?"

"What?"

"We need *backup*! Where's the team?"

Maddie hit a bump, and the phone flew to the floor. Brian cursed.

"Get closer," he ordered as the white SUV came into view.

Maddie floored it. The closer they got, the harder it was to see through the cloud of dust. As soon as they hit the highway, though, he might have a better shot.

She hit another rut. "Sorry!"

"Get low!"

The SUV veered off the road and skidded to a stop. The door popped open, and Vlad lunged out.

"Stop! He's running!"

Maddie halted, and Brian grabbed his Glock and jumped out. He sprinted after the man. He heard the engine straining and knew Maddie was right behind him, trying to run the man down, or at least scare him into surrendering.

Vlad turned and fired, a wild-ass shot that didn't even come close. Pure outrage gave Brian the burst he needed to tackle him to the ground. He flipped him onto his stomach. *No cuffs.* He dug his knee into the guy's back and smashed his pistol against the side of his head with a satisfying *thunk.*

A flash of green in his peripheral vision. Brian glanced up and saw Mladovic leaning out the window of the old pickup.

Then everything slowed down.

Mladovic swung his arm around. Brian followed with his gaze and reacted. But even as he lifted his Glock and squeezed the trigger, he knew he was a split second too late.

Maddie!

Her windshield exploded. The truck jerked left.

Blood bloomed red on Mladovic's chest.

Kill shot. Brian knew it instantly.

And then his gaze jerked back to Maddie as the pickup smashed into a tree.

A tremendous *slap*.

Maddie couldn't move. Not a muscle. The world was black, and she was pinned by some enormous weight. The air had been knocked from her lungs, and she couldn't breathe. She tried to blink, tried to lift her head. She couldn't make her lungs expand, and everything around her seemed to slide into darkness.

She felt the pull of Emma.

Mommy.

Her little voice, clear as the sky. Her precious baby *smell* entered Maddie's nose and lungs and filled her to bursting.

Mommy.

Maddie's heart lurched. She wanted to reach out and scoop her up and never let her go. But the world was black, and her arms were pinned, and she still couldn't move.

Maddie.

Someone was calling her.

Brian? Jolene?

Jolene. She'd run from the truck. She'd run away—

Maddie!

———

Brian yanked open the door and found her slumped over the deflated airbag.

"Oh, Jesus." Blood was everywhere. "Maddie!"

He pulled her back, saw the gash in her forehead. Blood streamed down her face. Had she been shot? Blood was all over, but he couldn't find the source of it. In some dim corner of his mind, he registered rhythmic thumping noise he remembered from combat.

"Maddie, come on, baby. Oh, God."

He tipped her head back and searched for the entry wound. Her eyes fluttered open, and Brian's legs went weak. He sank down and had to grab the door to stay on his feet.

She muttered something.

"I'm right here. Maddie, can you hear me?" He spied his phone on the floor and reached around her legs to grab it. Sam was gone, but he dialed 911.

"Jo . . ."

"Help's on the way."

She gripped his shirt. He looked down, stunned, at her white-knuckled fist.

"Jolene."

The one word, perfectly clear. Her eyes were clear now, too, which was indescribably weird with all the blood streaming down her face.

"She ran from the truck. I saw her." Maddie pulled herself forward, falling into him.

"We'll find her. Maddie?"

But she was out of the pickup, staggering across the grass. Brian caught her around the waist.

"Whoa, Maddie—"

"She's *hurt*. We have to *find* her."

Her nails in his arm were like talons, and she kept moving forward, pulling him with her. She wiped her arm over her face and looked shocked when it came away smeared with blood. She wrestled out of her jacket and used it to wipe her face as she glanced around desperately.

The *whump-whump* noise grew louder, and Brian turned to see his backup finally making the scene. The chopper swooped low over the property and hovered above the campground, where just minutes ago, everything had gone down without them. Dust kicked up, stinging his eyes.

Maddie's grip on his arm tightened. Then it disappeared, and she rushed forward toward a girl lying curled in a ditch.

———

It wasn't over yet. They were back. Jolene blinked up at the light. She heard noise, shouting. An enormous man stepped in front of her, blocking out the sun, and she pulled herself into a ball.

Please, no more. Please, no. She pulled her knees to her chest and tried to will herself away.

Jolene.

She went still. Not her mother's voice, but . . .

Jolene, can you hear me?

Not a man but a woman now. A *woman*. Hope stirred inside her. Something warm and soft settled over her like a blanket. Jolene started to cry.

It's okay now. We're here to take you home.

CHAPTER 26

Brian understood now why Maddie hated hospitals. The smells. The waiting. The bureaucracy. After three solid hours, he was ready to climb the walls.

"This is my fault."

He glanced at Maddie in the chair beside him. She was pale and worried and had dots of iodine all over her forehead from where the nurses had cleaned her cuts.

"It's not," he said firmly.

If anyone was at fault here, it was Cabrera, who'd ordered his agent to the scene. Within moments of setting foot on the property, Hicks had crossed paths with a guard and been sprayed with a machine gun. If not for his vest, he'd have been killed instantly. Instead, he lay bleeding in the dirt as Mladovic's man rushed to sound the warning.

But Maddie thought everything was her fault, and she'd been a bundle of guilt and nerves for the past three hours.

The ER doors slid open, and Sam strode in. Brian and Maddie stood.

"Any word?" Sam asked.

Maddie shook her head. "Still waiting."

"I got hold of Hicks's fiancée," Sam said. "She's on her way over. And I just heard from LeBlanc," Sam looked at Brian. "She helped execute a search warrant over at Bracewell's. He had a Remington 700 and a box of .308 Winchester ammo in his closet. We sent it to Scott for testing since he did the original slug."

Brian glanced at Maddie to see if she understood.

"You mean . . . ?"

Sam nodded. "The working theory is that he summoned you out to that accident scene and set himself up on the cliff to wait. Turns out one of his cousins owns a towing company. We think that's where he drummed up the rig and the decoy car."

Maddie looked away, and Brian could tell she still hadn't quite gotten her head around it. She'd worked with the man for years. A betrayal like that had to burn.

"Where's Bracewell now?" Sam asked.

"Third floor," Brian said. "There's a pair of agents stationed outside his room, in case he gets any ideas about hobbling out of here." He gave Sam a long look. "And Mladovic is dead. He didn't make it through surgery."

Beside him, Maddie tensed. How did she feel about seeing him take another man's life? He didn't know because for the past three hours, she'd hardly said anything.

"You okay?" Sam asked.

Brian gave a sharp nod. His conscience was clear. But he was still going to have to justify his actions to a review board.

The double doors swung open, and a doctor in bl

scrubs stepped out. Brian tried to read the verdict on the man's face as he walked over.

"Is the agent's family here yet?" he asked.

"They're on their way."

The doctor looked from Brian to Sam, then back to Brian, probably weighing how much to tell when they weren't next-of-kin.

"When they get here," the doctor said, "tell them he's in recovery."

Maddie slumped against him, and Brian put his arm around her.

"We put two pins in his leg and gave him four units of blood. His condition is stabilized. We should know more within the hour."

He disappeared back through the doors. Brian turned to Sam and saw his own relief mirrored on his face.

Sam clamped a hand on his shoulder. "You need to get back, Beck. I'll stay here and wait for the fiancée."

Maddie looked alarmed. "You have to go in?"

"I need to debrief."

"Didn't you already do all that back at the deer lease? You were stuck there for an hour."

"That's just the beginning."

A commotion across the waiting room caught Brian's eye as Jolene's grandparents entered the ER. They fell into a hug with Jolene's mom, and even from across the room, Brian could see the tears of relief streaming down their faces. Jolene was in the back, being checked out by a doctor. She was going to need extensive surgery on her hand and probably years of counseling, but she was alive, which was more than Brian or Sam had dared hope—more than anyone had dared hope.

Except Maddie.

Brian looked at her now, watching the reunion. She looked spent, both emotionally and physically.

"Let me run you home," he said.

Sam shot him a look that told him he needed to get his ass back to the office for paperwork and interviews. But Brian ignored him. He took Maddie's hand and led her through the sliding doors into the crisp winter air.

She stopped to blink up at the sun. "What time is it?"

"Three."

"Seems later than that."

He'd parked illegally and was glad to see he hadn't been towed. He opened the passenger door, and she climbed in without a word.

He glanced at her as he slid behind the wheel. "I'm going to be at least a few hours. Maybe more."

She didn't say anything, just looked out the window as they left the hospital parking lot.

Brian trained his gaze on the road ahead. She'd been through a shock. They both had. Brian had ended a man's life today. Just *boom*, gone.

But that wasn't the moment that had made Brian's heart stop. The sight of Mladovic aiming that gun and that window bursting—*that* image was going to have him waking up in a cold sweat for a long, long time.

He loved her.

It had hit him today like a sucker punch. He loved her, and he had no freaking idea how he was going to get her to love him back. But he had to do it.

He glanced over as she stared out the window with that faraway look on her face. It was a look he'd seen on the faces of soldiers after a firefight.

"Maddie?"

She looked at him.

"You all right?"

"Fine," she said.

The rest of the trip was silent. Brian pulled into her driveway. He started to get out of the car, but she put her hand on his knee.

"It's okay."

He looked at her and felt his heart sinking. He couldn't control her. He couldn't *make* her want him. And knowing he couldn't made him feel more powerless than anything in his life.

"You need to go." She glanced at her curb, where for the first time in days, there wasn't an FBI vehicle. She looked at him and cleared her throat. "When you're finished with everything . . . will you come back?" The look in her eyes was tentative. She was uncomfortable even asking.

He leaned over and kissed her. "I'll come back," he promised. "Soon as I can."

CHAPTER 27

Maddie walked up to the beveled-glass door and surveyed the cheerful pots of marigolds decorating the porch. She spotted the bell, but the door swung back before she could ring it.

"Hi."

"Hi." She smiled at Mitch, who was clearly surprised to see her. Actually, he seemed dumbstruck. She'd never been to his house before.

He glanced over his shoulder. "The baby's sleeping, so we're trying not to let people ring . . ." His voice trailed off as he looked her over. She looked him over, too, taking in his bloodshot eyes and food-stained T-shirt. He looked like a man on paternity leave.

A brown-eyed child peeked out from behind his leg. "Who are you?"

Maddie's breath caught. She opened her mouth to answer, but nothing came out.

"This is a friend of Daddy's. Go finish your show, sport."

Mitch mussed the boy's hair, and he scampered away.

Maddie recovered her voice. "He looks like Emma."

Mitch stepped out onto the porch, closing the door behind him. He smiled and tucked his hands into his pockets. "I think it might be more accurate to say he looks like me." His gaze traveled over her and landed on the yellow bag in her hand.

"I brought you something." She held it up. "Actually, it's for Conner."

Maddie hadn't received a birth announcement, but she'd heard the details from one of their mutual friends.

Mitch gave her a quizzical look now as he took the bag and dug through the tissue paper. He pulled out a polished brown box made of inlaid wood. A look of recognition came to his face.

"Where'd you get this?" He opened the lid, and twangy notes of "You Are My Sunshine" drifted out. "This was mine as a kid."

"Your mom gave it to us." She smiled. "Don't you remember?"

"No."

"God, Mitch." She shook her head. Some things never changed.

He stared down at the box. Then he looked up, and she saw tears welling in his eyes.

"It was in Emma's room," he said. "I remember now."

Maddie cleared her throat. "It's your family heirloom. I thought Conner should have it."

He looked at her, and a timeworn understanding passed between them. He knew the effort it was for her to stand here and not run away. A lump rose in her throat, but she forced it down. This was harder than she'd thought.

"Thank you." He tucked the box back into the bag and set it down at his feet. When he looked at her again, she could see the questions percolating.

And she didn't want to answer them. Once upon a time, they'd been on the same journey. Together. They'd shared everything. But that was over now, and she didn't want it back.

He took a small step forward. She stepped back.

"Give my best to Danielle." She smiled. "And congratulations."

———————

Brian had the hedge clippers out when she pulled into the driveway. Maddie sat for a moment in the car, just watching him as he hacked away at her overgrown holly bushes.

She got out. "I brought lunch."

He glanced at her and wiped his forehead on his bare arm. "I'm starving."

"You're always starving." She walked across the lawn to kiss him and got sweat on the tip of her nose.

"You smell like grass clippings." She said it with a scowl, but she secretly loved it. It was one of the many things she'd learned to love lately, along with the sneakers in her living room and the overnight bag that had become a permanent fixture on the floor of her closet. He never seemed to unpack it, even though weeks ago, she'd started throwing his wash in with hers and putting his clothes away in one of her dresser drawers.

She sat down on the top porch step. He tossed the clippers onto the lawn and sank onto the step beside her.

"No shoes, no shirt, no service."

"Too bad." He kissed her again. "This is the price you pay for getting your hedges trimmed."

She handed him a lemonade. "Yeah, I've noticed you're kind of manic about those. Must be your farming roots."

"Safety." He took a big slurp, and she admired his slick chest as he heaved a sigh. "Don't want burglars coming around."

"Well, in that case, thank you."

He rested the drink on his knee and leaned back against the wooden post. "So where were you all morning?"

"Had some errands to run. I went to see Mitch."

His gaze darkened.

"I took him a baby present."

He leaned forward, and the look of concern on his face made her heart squeeze. He tucked a lock of hair behind her ear. "You all right?"

"Yeah." She let out a sigh. "I am."

He looked at her for a long moment, and she shifted her gaze to the yard. Locusts hummed in the distance, and she watched the dragonflies hover over the lantana.

She didn't say anything. He didn't push. Maybe he'd become accustomed to her silences, or maybe he felt secure enough not to need a lot of reassurance.

For a man who claimed he didn't have much patience, he'd given her oceans of it.

He squeezed her hand. "How about after I finish up the back, we go hit some baseballs?"

She looked at him. "I love you."

His eyebrows shot up, and she felt a twinge of panic,

because he looked so surprised. Her heart began to thump against her ribs.

"I've been meaning to tell you for a while now. I just—" She stopped. Swallowed hard.

She probably shouldn't tell him how she'd tried to say it before but nearly choked on the words. The three simple syllables had paralyzed her.

"I love you," she repeated, and this time, it felt liberating, especially when a smile spread slowly across his face.

He pulled her against his chest and dropped a kiss on her forehead.

"That's all I get?" she asked. "A sweaty kiss?" Her heart was still pounding, but she could hear his pounding, too, and she knew it was okay. She picked up his hand and laced their fingers together.

"I love you, too, you know. Why'd it take you so long to tell me?"

She smiled. "I guess maybe I was scared . . . like you said."

"Scared of what?" He squeezed her. "That I'd show up with my U-Haul? That I'd march you down the aisle?"

"Maybe a little."

He laughed. "You haven't even met my family yet. Or come on vacation with me. You've never even ridden on my bike."

Her heart pounded even harder, because despite the joking tone, she knew he was serious. He was going to take her to meet his family. And take her on his bike. And maybe ask her to marry him someday.

They weren't there yet, but it was out on the

horizon—a shiny possibility. Thinking about it made her happy and sad and hopeful, all at the same time. She looked up at him and felt overcome with love.

"Let's start with your bike," she said, and pulled him down to kiss her.

Enjoy this sneak peek
of Laura Griffin's next gripping novel of suspense

Available from Gallery Books
Spring 2014

Andrea Finch had never been dumped at a barbecue joint, but there was a first time for everything.

She watched her date, who looked out of place sitting at the scarred wooden booth in his charcoal-gray suit. He'd come straight from work, as she had. He'd ditched the tie but still seemed overly formal in a restaurant that had paper-towel rolls on every table and classic country drifting from the jukebox.

"So." Nick Mays took a swig of beer. "How was your day?"

Andrea smiled. He sounded like a tired husband, and they'd only been dating a month.

"Fine," she said. "Yours?"

"Fine."

For the dozenth time since she'd sat down, his gaze

darted over her shoulder. When his blue eyes met hers again, she felt a twinge of regret. He really *was* a nice-looking man. His main problem was his oversize ego. But Andrea was used to men with big egos. She'd been surrounded by them since she'd first entered the police academy, and they'd only multiplied when she earned her detective's badge.

"Listen, Andrea"—he glanced over her shoulder, and she braced for the speech—"these last few weeks, they've really been great."

He opened his mouth to continue just as a waitress stepped up and beamed a smile at him.

"Y'all ready to order?"

Nick looked pained. But to his credit, he nodded in Andrea's direction. "Andie?"

"I'm good, thanks."

He glanced at the waitress. "Me, too."

"So . . . y'all *won't* be having dinner with us?" Her overly made-up eyes shifted to Andrea. She tucked a lock of blond hair behind her ear and looked impatient.

"Just the drinks for now." Nick gave her one of his smiles, which seemed to lessen her annoyance as she hustled off. The smile faded as he turned back to Andrea.

"So I was saying. These past few weeks. It's been a good time, Andie. You're an interesting girl."

She gritted her teeth. If he was going to use frat-boy speak, she was going to make this *way* harder for him. She folded her arms over her chest and cast her gaze around the restaurant, letting his comment dangle awkwardly.

Tonight's crowd was thin, even for a Monday. Maybe the weather was keeping people away. Austin was set to get sleet tonight and her lieutenant had called in extra officers, expecting the roads to be a mess.

"Andrea?"

She looked at him.

"I said, wouldn't you agree with that?"

A skinny young man stepped through the entrance. He wore a black trench coat and clunky boots. His too-big ears reminded Andrea of her brother.

She looked again at Nick. "Agree with what?"

His mouth tightened. "I said, it seems like neither of us is looking for something serious right now. So maybe we should cool things down a little."

She glanced across the room as the kid walked toward the double doors leading to the kitchen. She studied the line of his coat, frowning.

"Andrea."

"What?" Her attention snapped back to Nick.

"Christ, you're not even listening. Have you heard a word I said?"

She glanced at the kitchen, where the clatter of pots and pans had suddenly gone silent.

The back of her neck tingled. She slid from the booth.

"Andie?"

"Just a sec."

She strode across the restaurant, her gaze fixed on the double doors. Her heart thudded inexplicably while her mind catalogued info: six-one, one-fifty, blond, blue. She pictured his flushed cheeks and his lanky body in that big coat.

A waiter whisked past her and pushed through the doors to the kitchen. Andrea followed, stumbling into him when he halted in his tracks.

Three people stood motionless against a counter. Their eyes were round with shock and their mouths hung open.

The kid in the overcoat stood a short distance away, pointing a pistol at them.

His gaze jumped to Andrea and the waiter. "You! Over there!" He jerked his head at the petrified trio.

The waiter made a strangled sound and scuttled out the door they'd just come through.

Andrea didn't move. Her chest tightened as she took in the scene: two waitresses and a cook, all cowering against a counter. Possibly more people in the back. The kid was brandishing a Glock 17. It was pointed straight at the woman in the center—Andrea's waitress. She couldn't have been older than eighteen, and the gunman looked almost as young. Andrea noted his skinny neck, his *freckles*. His cheeks were pink—not from the cold, as she'd first thought, but from emotion.

The look he sent the waitress was like a plea.

"You did this, Haley."

The woman's eyes widened. Her lips moved but no words came out.

"This is *your* fault."

Andrea eased her hand beneath her blazer. The kid's arm swung toward her. "You! Get with them!"

She went still.

"Dillon, what are you—"

"Shut up!" The gun swung back toward the waitress. Haley. The trio was just a few short yards away from that gun. Even with no skill whatsoever, anything he fired at that distance would likely be lethal. And who knew how many bullets he had loaded in that thing.

Andrea's heart drummed inside her chest. The smoky smell of barbecue filled the air. The kitchen was warm and steamy and the walls seemed to be closing in on her as she focused on the gunman.

His back was to a wall lined with coat hooks. She counted four jackets and two ball caps—probably all belonging to the staff. Was anyone else hiding in the back? Had someone called for help?

"*You* did this!" the gunman shouted, and Haley flinched.

Andrea licked her lips. For only the second time in her career, she eased her gun from its holster and prepared to aim it at a person. The weight in her hand felt familiar, almost comforting. But her mouth went dry as her finger slid around the trigger.

Defuse.

She thought of everything she'd ever learned about hostage negotiations. She thought of the waiter who'd fled. She thought of Nick. Help had to be on the way by now. But the closest SWAT team was twenty minutes out and she *knew*, with sickening certainty, that whatever happened here was going to be over in a matter of moments.

"I trusted you, Haley." His voice broke on the last word, and Haley cringed. "I trusted you, but you're a lying *bitch*!"

"Dillon, please—"

"Shut up! Just shut up, okay?"

Ambivalence. She heard it in his voice. She could get control of this.

Andrea lifted her weapon. "Dillon, look at me."

To her relief, his gaze veered in her direction. He was crying now, tears streaming down his freckled cheeks, and again he reminded her of her brother. Andrea's stomach clenched as she lined up her sights on his center body mass.

Establish a command presence.

"Put the gun down, Dillon. Let's talk this through."

He swung his arm ninety degrees, and Andrea was now staring down the barrel of the Glock. All sound disappeared. Her entire world seemed to be sucked by gravity toward that little black hole.

She lifted her gaze to the gunman's face. *Dillon.* His name was Dillon. And he was eighteen, tops.

Her heart beat crazily. Her throat tightened. Hundreds

of times she'd trained to confront an armed assailant. It should have been a no-brainer, pure muscle memory. But she felt paralyzed. Every instinct was screaming for her to *find another way*.

Dillon's gaze slid back to Haley, who seemed to be melting into the Formica counter. The others had inched away from her—a survival instinct that was going to be of little help if this kid let loose with a hail of bullets.

Loud, repetitive commands.

"Dillon, look at me." She tried to make her voice firm, but even she could hear the desperation in it. "Put the gun down, Dillon. We'll talk through this."

His gaze met hers again. He rubbed his nose on the shoulder of his coat. Tears and snot glistened on his face.

"I'll kill you, too," he said softly. "Don't think I won't."

"I believe you. But wouldn't it be easier just to talk?" She paused. "Put the gun down, Dillon."

She could see his arm shaking, and—to her dismay—hers began to shake, too. As if she didn't know how to hold her own weapon. As if she didn't work out three times a week to maintain her upper-body strength.

As if she didn't have it in her to shoot a frightened kid.

He was disintegrating before her eyes. She could see it. His Adam's apple moved up and down as he swallowed hard.

"You can't stop me." His voice was a thread now, almost a whisper. He shifted his stance back toward Haley, and the stark look on her face told Andrea she'd read his body language.

"I'll do it."

Andrea's pulse roared in her ears. The edges of her vision blurred. All she saw was that white hand clutching that big black gun.

She took a breath.

And don't miss the following excerpt from

SCORCHED

The previous book in the Tracers series
Available now from Pocket Books

Gage pulled his pickup truck into the parking lot of O'Malley's Pub, way more than ready to put an end to his crap day.

It had started at 0430 with a training op on San Clemente Island and ended less than an hour ago with a brutal run through the obstacle course on base. Under normal circumstances, he liked training ops—especially ones that involved high-altitude jumps. And the O-course hadn't been a problem for him since BUD/S training.

But these weren't normal circumstances. Gage was coming off a shit week following a shit month at the end of a shit year. His shoulder hurt like hell despite endless rounds of physical therapy, and his head was in the wrong place. Gage couldn't find his zone—hadn't been able to in months.

O'Malley's was quiet for a Friday, which suited him fine. He took a seat at the bar and ordered a beer. After knocking back the first swig, he stared at the bottle and forced himself to confront the nagging possibility that maybe, just maybe, he was losing his edge.

A young blonde approached the counter. As if to confirm Gage's depressing hypothesis, she ignored the empty stools next to him and chose one three seats over. She tucked her purse at her feet and barely gave him a glance before flagging the bartender to order a drink.

Ouch. Not the response he usually got from women in bars—especially this one, which was popular with SEAL groupies.

On the other hand, Gage really couldn't blame her. He'd come here straight from the base, not even bothering to shower after his sixteen-hour ass-kicking.

Gage glanced across the room at Mike Dietz and Derek Vaughn, who had managed to clean up before coming out. They'd left the base not long before Gage, so they must have set the world record for speed showering. Clearly they were looking to get laid tonight, whereas Gage was simply looking to get hammered. It had been that kind of week.

Derek caught his eye and walked over. "Hey, Brewski," he drawled, "you want in on this game?"

"Nah, I'm good."

"Come on, bro." He glanced over his shoulder at the two brunettes who were hanging around the pool table. "Callie's sister's in town. You need to come meet her."

"Really, I'm fine."

"You're killing me."

"Let Dietz talk to her."

"He has to cut out after this. Some family thing." Derek

clamped a hand on his shoulder, and Gage made an effort not to wince. "Seriously, do *not* leave me hanging here, man. You can have Tara. She's older, but probably no less talented than her baby sis." He grinned and slapped Gage on the back. "Come on. It'll snap you out of your shit mood."

Gage glanced at the women and he knew Derek was wrong. Nothing would snap him out of his mood tonight.

"You're not still hung up on Kelsey, are you?"

"Hell no."

"Then what's up?" His brow furrowed. "Having a bad day?"

It was common knowledge that Gage had taken Joe's death two months ago harder than anyone. And it wasn't just because he knew the man's family and had once dated his niece. Even before all that, Gage had had a special bond with him. Joe Quinn had been a demo expert, same as Gage, and he'd taken Gage under his wing during his very first year in the teams.

"I'm fine," Gage said, and his friend gave him a long, hard look.

"Not so sure about that. Those are two hot-looking women. But, hey, your loss. Lemme know if you change your mind."

Derek returned to his game of pool, and Gage nursed his beer while watching the mirror behind the bar. The blonde was still there and she had a drink in front of her now. She stirred it with a slender red straw as she glanced over her shoulder again and again. Gage checked his watch. Ten after nine. Her date was probably ten minutes late. Suddenly she smiled and jumped up from her stool as a man in service khakis entered the bar. He crossed the room in a few strides. The woman threw her arms around his neck and kissed the hell out of him.

Gage felt a stab of envy and looked away. He remembered Kelsey kissing him like that—in this very bar, too—right before he'd drag her home with him to set his world on fire. That's how they'd been together—weeks and months of no contact, then completely unable to keep their hands off each other when they finally got together.

Which wouldn't be happening again anytime soon. Or ever.

Last time Gage had seen Kelsey was at her uncle's funeral. She'd been seated at the front of the church with her boyfriend at her side—some FBI hotshot she'd dated back before she met Gage. Seeing the two of them together had been hard enough, but when they'd stood to leave the church and Gage glimpsed the ring on her finger, it was like a kick in the gut. He'd been blindsided by hurt and anger—which made the entire day of Joe's funeral all the more torturous.

Good times. Gage tipped back his beer. He felt someone behind him and knew who it was when he got a nose full of cheap perfume.

"Hey, sailor."

Callie's sister had a friendly smile, and Gage did his best to return it. It wasn't her fault he was in a foul mood.

"Hey there," he said.

"I'm Tara." She rested her hand on his forearm and eased close, giving him a perfect view down her low-cut shirt. "My sister says you know your way around a pool table. Wanna play with us?"

Gage looked down into her pretty blue eyes. She was young. Built. Eager to please. If he couldn't have Kelsey, he should have someone else. He couldn't wallow in celibate misery his whole life, could he?

Problem was, he'd been down this road and knew

where it went, and waking up tomorrow with some girl in his bed wasn't going to solve his problems, just create a few more.

Gage glanced at the mirror behind the bar as a woman who looked remarkably like Kelsey stepped through the door. He blinked at the reflection.

No way.

But there was no mistaking her. Six feet tall. Long auburn hair. In a bar filled with hot and available women, she stood out in her jeans and no-nonsense T-shirt. She rested a hand on her hip and scanned the room.

Gage drank in the sight of her body, her lips, her skin. She'd gotten some sun recently. He remembered she'd been on a dig when they'd called her about Joe, but that was probably over by now and she was back to her job at the crime lab.

But what did he know? Maybe she'd been on her damn honeymoon.

"Uh, hello? Earth to Gage?"

He snapped his attention back to the woman beside him. Her friendly smile had dimmed.

Then he glanced over her shoulder at Kelsey, who was indeed still standing there, in the flesh, in the middle of O'Malley's Pub. What was she doing here?

Kelsey spotted him and froze. She glanced at the woman beside him, and for an instant the startled look on her face made him feel good. He could tell she wanted to bolt, but instead she walked straight up to the bar and ordered a drink.

"Excuse me, would you?" Gage picked up his beer and walked over to Kelsey. She'd chosen a stool on the corner, which didn't leave him a place to sit, so he rested his bottle on the counter and stood beside her.

"Hi."

"Hi." She avoided his gaze, but smiled at the bartender as he delivered her beer.

"What brings you to town?"

She glanced over her shoulder at the pool table, where Derek and Mike were finishing a game. Gage ignored their curious glances.

At last she looked up at him. "I came to visit my grandmother. We're cleaning out Joe's house."

He'd figured as much. Joe had never married, and Kelsey was the closest thing he had to a kid. He'd helped raise her after her father died in a car wreck when she was young.

So now she was here to help go through his stuff, probably put his house on the market. It made sense. Gage hadn't actually believed she'd flown all the way out from Texas just to see him.

She reached down and picked up her purse from the floor.

"I was hoping I'd run into you," she said casually, unzipping the bag. "We came across something, and my grandmother thought you might want it."

Her grandmother.

Kelsey handed him a white envelope. He hesitated a moment before taking it. Joe's family had wanted him to have this, whatever it was. The very idea humbled him.

Gage opened the envelope and pulled out a photo that he recognized instantly. The picture was from Afghanistan. Half of his team stood on a mountaintop, lined up in full gear. They'd just flown out from Bagram for a six-month tour, most of which had been spent assaulting cave complexes. Just three years after the towers had fallen. They'd been full of energy and optimism, good and ready to kick some terrorist ass.

Gage studied the faces: Derek, Mike, Luke, a few others who'd left the teams. It was a snapshot in time, but he felt a surge of love for these guys who had had his back on so many different occasions. They'd taken bullets for one another. It was impossible to describe what that meant to anyone who hadn't been there.

Gage couldn't look at Joe's face. He ran his thumb over the edge and focused on the rugged Afghan landscape. At times it was hell on earth. Other times it was beautiful.

He glanced up, and Kelsey was watching him with those bottomless brown eyes. He cleared his throat. "Thank you."

"You're welcome."

Gage unbuttoned the front pocket of his BDUs and tucked the envelope inside. He looked at Kelsey and felt a sharp stab of regret. After their breakup, she'd done a damn good job of keeping her distance. He didn't really blame her. The breakup had been his choice, not hers. The last time she'd flown out to visit him, she'd told him she couldn't handle the long distance anymore, the constant stress of his deployments. She'd given him an ultimatum— her or the teams. Torn between Kelsey and the SEALs, he'd done the only thing he could do—he'd chosen the SEALs. But it wasn't the end of him wanting her. And it wasn't the end of his bitterness. Even now—*especially* now, with her sitting there beside him—he still harbored a deep resentment toward Kelsey for making him choose between her and his job. And toward the man who'd come along in his absence and put a ring on her finger.

But along with his bitterness was something else, something he tried not to think about but couldn't ignore with Kelsey sitting so close. Truth was, he missed her. He missed talking to her, hanging out with her. He missed that little line she got on her forehead whenever he ticked her off. Hell, he even missed her freckles.

And, yes, he missed the sex. He itched to touch her right now and had to rest his hand on the bar to keep from running it through her hair.

"Is that why you came looking for me?" He held her gaze for a long moment, not sure what he wanted her to say. He knew what he wanted to say to *her*.

How could you get engaged to someone so soon after we broke up? Was it that easy to move on?

But he didn't ask, because the answer was a resounding *yes*.

"Actually, there was something else, too." She cut a glance at the pool table, and her businesslike voice told him the other reason wasn't nearly as personal as he would have liked.

"Joe had some books and CDs in the office at his house." She looked back at him, searching his face for something. "Apparently he was learning Tagalog. Was he headed to the Philippines?"

Gage didn't say anything. He couldn't talk about the when and where of what they did, and the fact that he couldn't had been an ongoing source of friction between them. Kelsey had always accused him of being too closed off—not just about the job itself, but about how it affected him personally. Maybe so. But Gage had never been big on talking. Like most SEALs he knew, he was a doer, not a talker.

She sighed, obviously frustrated by his silence. "I was just on Basilan Island."

"Why?" He frowned.

"We were excavating a mass grave there."

Gage clenched his teeth at this news. Basilan Island was

home to some extremely dangerous people, and the military ops going on there were totally covert. Gage had been involved in a few, and he'd heard rumors. There was some serious shit happening in the Philippines right now, and he didn't like the idea of Kelsey anywhere near there. He didn't want her in the same hemisphere.

"Has the island become a haven for Al-Qaeda?" she asked, completely point-blank. Gage had often admired her straightforwardness, but it could be annoying, too.

"Was your team on its way there?" she persisted. "Is that why Joe wanted to learn the language?"

"That's classified."

Classified. She hated that word, and Gage couldn't count the number of arguments they'd had over it.

She shook her head and looked away. "I should have known I'd be wasting my time trying to talk to you."

He bristled. "Hey, you came to me, babe. Don't blame me for wasting your precious time. And what does it matter now, anyway?"

"It *matters* because I'm working on something that could be important." She picked up her beer and took a sip. She looked flustered now, and he didn't know whether it was because they were fighting again or because this was a touchy subject. She plunked the bottle down and looked up at him. "I was hoping you might give me a little information so I don't make a fool of myself raising a stink about something that could be nothing."

"I can't talk about operations. You know that. You need information so bad, why don't you ask Blake?"

Kelsey's *fiancé* worked counterterrorism. And Gage could tell by the look on her face that she'd already asked him.

"What, 007 wouldn't talk to you? So you decided to try

me? Maybe you thought I'd bend the rules just to do you a favor?" He leaned closer to her. "Sorry, babe, no can do. You want someone to bend the rules for you, go ask your boyfriend."

She looked away and muttered something.

"What?"

"You know, I predicted you'd be this way."

"That's me. Mr. Predictable."

"You know what's really disappointing, Gage? I'd hoped we could be friends now." She stood up and collected her purse. "After Joe and everything and all the crap that happened, I'd hoped we could at least have that."

She pulled out her wallet and left some bills on the bar. Gage caught sight of her hand.

"Hey." He grabbed her wrist as she turned to leave. "Where's your ring?"

She jerked her hand back and glared up at him. "I left it at home."

Kelsey moved for the door, and Gage's shit luck continued as Callie picked that exact moment to slide onto the vacated stool. "Come on, Gage. We need you to come play."

She rested a hand on his waist and gave him a coy smile. It was a smile that had worked on him before, and he could tell Kelsey knew that as she glanced back and then stalked out the door.